The New Internationals

Also by David Wright Faladé

Fire on the Beach

Away Running

Black Cloud Rising

The New Internationals

A NOVEL

David Wright Faladé

Atlantic Monthly Press
New York

FIRST EDITION

Published simultaneously in Canada
Printed in the United States of America

This book was set in 12-point Adobe Caslon by Alpha Design & Composition of Pittsfield, NH.

First Grove Atlantic hardcover edition: January 2025

Library of Congress Cataloging-in-Publication data is available for this title.

ISBN 978-0-8021-6406-3
eISBN 978-0-8021-6407-0

Atlantic Monthly Press
an imprint of Grove Atlantic
154 West 14th Street
New York, NY 10011

Distributed by Publishers Group West

groveatlantic.com

25 26 27 28   10 9 8 7 6 5 4 3 2 1

For my Monica
(1973–2022)

The New Internationals

CHAPTER ONE

"In plain view," Cecile heard. "People only truly see what you permit them to."

She sat beneath her bedroom window, opened a crack, as she eavesdropped on her father, who spoke low, though not at a whisper.

"If you want them to be invisible, where better than right here in Le Vésinet, surrounded by neighbors who are used to seeing them every day?"

February 1943. A mercenary winter, the cold relentless and indifferent, Cecile's breath pluming. She rose just enough to sneak a peek: her father, in the shadows beside the back door of their cottage, wearing a homburg and his olive mack though it wasn't raining, but over pajamas and with house slippers on. Opposite him, the uncle of the children who, until a few days before, when the Vichy police took their parents, had always lived two houses down the lane.

"Of course, this is what I want," the uncle said. The yellow cloth Star of David, sloppily sewn on, lay askew on the left breast of his vicuña topcoat. "Surely you can do something for them."

Them: Martine Goldschmidt, a year younger than Cecile; her brother Joël, a few years older, already preparing for the *Bac*. The third one, a baby girl, had been at home and was taken along with the parents. Nothing could be done for her.

"It's a lot to ask of my friends," Cecile's father said, hunching his neck into his collar and shifting from one foot to the other, hesitant now. "Listen, things are turning in the war. You should hold out. The Allies are coming."

The uncle dropped to a knee, clutched her father's hand in his own. "But they're just children, Alain. Please!"

Her father jerked free. "My friends have risked so much already!" Cecile recognized his show of sounding exasperated, pretending to feel put-upon. She'd witnessed it often enough toward her. "Finding the person who can come by the appropriate watermark. This one's signature, that one's seal—these things cost." His voice calmed then. "You understand?"

The uncle returned two nights later. He gave her father a roll of bills, some rings, and a bracelet of green gemstones. A few weeks passed and Martine matriculated at Institut du Bon Sauveur, the Catholic school where Cecile's parents had enrolled her the year before, and like Cecile, Martine no longer wore the Star.

The Occupation. Le Vésinet, once a quiet suburb, had turned into a Nazi outpost: German soldiers everywhere, their horrible blood-and-black standard hanging from every flagpole, from every state building, from the rail station. Printed signs appeared in the doors of restaurants and cafés, of butcher shops and bookstores: JÜDISCHES GESCHÄFT. Few could read the writing. Everyone understood. None resisted.

Before the war, no one in Cecile's family had professed their Judaism, though, of course, they knew themselves to be Jews, and no one had worn the Star of David, as pendant or otherwise—not Mamie Lucie or Daddie Georges, not the aunts or uncles or cousins. This changed. The police came for Lucie, Cecile's dear old grandmother—only one suitcase allowed, nothing more. Daddie Georges was already dead; he'd shot himself in his antiques shop on Rue du Faubourg Saint-Honoré, a bullet to the head, understanding what would follow the German arrival. Cecile's father disappeared for several days. Her mother would only say that he'd gone to visit acquaintances in Brittany. Upon his return, she unstitched the yellow Star from their clothes. But only them. The aunts and uncles and cousins continued wearing it.

Still, Cecile's mother rarely left the cottage anymore, and never on Tuesdays, when businesses opened their doors to "Israelites." She refused

Aunt Sylvie's invitations for the weekly games of Belote, those from Cousine Mathilde for afternoon tea, and Cecile wondered: Were one or the other to turn up unexpectedly at their door, in a panic, would her parents cower behind the curtains until she left or let her in?

It was thenabouts that they placed her at Bon Sauveur, yet another layer of cover. The headmistress insisted on a holy confirmation. Cecile wore a white gown and veil stitched from hard-to-come-by fabric and borrowed white gloves that reached past her elbows. Her mother, in the pews of the palled chapel, clutched a bouquet of lilies identical to those that the other mothers carried. The dour priest, the tasteless wafer. Kneeling there, all eyes upon her, Cecile understood the event to be just another negotiation, as though who she was could be thus transacted, her dutiful submission in exchange for the delusion of sanctuary.

Her suspicions were verified as she loitered one night near the town square with her classmate Katya, just before the government curfew and well after the one imposed by her parents. Cecile spied her father at the Café de la Gare, seated with his suspect friend Marcel—a bully-boy Hardy to her father's venal Laurel—and two women who laughed loudly and wore cloche hats and dresses of a sort her father would never permit Cecile to wear. Neither was Marcel's wife or her own mother. One had the Goldschmidts' gemstone bracelet on her wrist.

Katya's parents were Russians who'd fled the revolution, industrialists who split time between Rennes and Paris, so Katya was one of Bon Sauveur's year-round boarders. At every opportunity, she and Cecile would sneak off the school grounds and knock around Le Vésinet. They'd scrounge for still-smokeable butts on the floors of cafés until the barmen ordered them gone, and once Katya snatched a whole cigarette and whatever coins came away with it from the upturned hat of a beggar. He chased them. The girls only escaped when a group of German soldiers ordered the man to halt. They watched from behind a stone wall as the Boches shoved the man about and finally made him drop his pants right there on the street, to prove he wasn't a Jew. Back at school, she and Katya hid in a storage room, smoking and laughing about the scene, stripped to the waist to keep the rank evidence of their wickedness from corrupting their navy Bon Sauveur sweaters. Katya's breasts overflowed the cups of her brassiere, and she rhapsodized about her dream of becoming a film star, the next Lana Turner.

One afternoon, walking arm in arm down Avenue d'Aligre, they came upon three German soldiers leaning on the hood of a parked Citroën as though the car was theirs to perch upon, kepis tilted back on their heads, rifles lying against the curb. Katya cast a flirtatious glance as they passed, and Cecile jerked her sleeve. "Stop that!" she whispered. "They're Boches. They're the enemy."

Katya, mouth pouty, said, "But aren't they boys, too?"

The Germans: sporting crew cuts and dressed in field gray, but also ruddy cheeked and pimply, flaunting the crooked smiles of teenagers on holiday.

One extended his arm, as though to signal that they halt. "Do not be afraid." His French was formal and precise.

"Me?" said Katya. "Of *you*?"

"Then why don't you stop and talk to us, then?" said the second, more easily.

Cecile tugged Katya's sleeve for them to leave, to continue on, but Katya freed herself. She put her hands on her hips.

"It's you who ought to be afraid. You'd think you'd have learned your lesson by now, after Stalingrad."

The two boys snickered, poorly disguising their irritation. The third stepped forward, gazing diffidently between Cecile and his jackboots.

"*Ich spreche kein französisch,*" he said.

She knew no German but understood his cautious smile. It only meant to say "Hello, how are you?" and "If we can work through this inability to speak a common tongue, maybe we could have a *diabolo menthe* together sometime?" He held a black-matte Zippo that had 9TH INF REG'T/"OLD RELIABLES" engraved on its face, in English.

"Katya," Cecile pleaded.

Though they confided everything in each other, she hadn't told her friend that she was a Jew. Still, with Cecile's sudden arrival at Bon Sauveur, with her belated confirmation, how could she have not surmised it?

"Katya," Cecile repeated. "Now."

"I'm about finished!" the other snapped, holding a Gauloises from one of the boys' packs, elbow resting on the table of her jutting hip.

"*Es ist alles in Ordnung,*" the *diabolo menthe* boy said to Cecile, his voice coarse and low, his smile jagged but sweet. "Please," he said in English.

Katya caught up to her at the corner. "I can't believe you just left me like that." She ran her arm through Cecile's, matching Cecile's stride but looking back, tossing her hair in a broad arc. She held the soldier's pack of cigarettes and offered one to Cecile.

Cecile threw her a sharp look.

"Smokes are smokes," Katya said. "What's the harm?"

On her way home from school one day, Cecile spotted Joël Goldschmidt, the boy from two houses down the lane. It wasn't the first time she'd seen him since the night she'd spied on his uncle and her father in their back yard. She'd once chanced upon him in the town center, watching right then left as her father and Marcel furtively spoke with a railway conductor. She and Katya had continued along their route, Katya jabbering on, not noticing.

Neighbors her whole life, Cecile thought now, yet she'd never really known Joël. For no reason she could explain, she followed him—fists bunched in his pants pockets, black beret pulled low over his brow—past La Poste and onto the Allée des Bocages, until he vanished in a jumble of boys on the football field there.

The next morning, on her way to the *tabac* for her father, she felt a hand clutch her shoulder. "Why were you trailing me?"

Joël—lanky and disheveled, sharp angles in the folds of his sweater.

They were on a quiet alley between two streets. "It's Martine" was all she could think to say, "your sister," though she hardly knew the girl any better than she did him.

His face did not release. "Martine?"

"The headmistress is concerned," Cecile said, and this was true. She'd overheard her telling Bon Sauveur's nurse as much. "She still stays to herself and won't speak to anyone."

"And what do you expect me to do about it? Martine is safe."

"But she's your sister."

He didn't reply, just let loose his grip and walked away. Cecile ran after.

"Don't follow me," he told her.

"Why?"

"Just don't."

She continued anyway.

He whirled around and pointed a finger directly into her face. "These aren't schoolgirl games. Ask your father." And he pushed her hard, the heels of his hands striking her breasts.

The eruption of pain sat her down more than did the weight of the blow. When she looked up, he was running off, dodging onto the avenue.

That Saturday she told her father that Joël Goldschmidt needed her to bring him a screwdriver and some pliers for the task asked of him. Her father rested *Le Petit Parisien* in his lap, shifting in his chair and appearing confused. Still, he rose and exited the room. "Don't meddle your nose in these things," he said upon his return, extending the tools toward her. "I'm not asking. I'm ordering you."

"I don't know where to take these," Cecile said.

"To the Jacqueminet's." Back in his chair, he'd returned his attention to the newspaper. "Pass through the back gate and knock on the cellar door."

When she did and Joël opened it, his look of disgust surprised her. She'd managed to convince herself she might see relief in his face, or gladness even, something other than the violence now in his eyes.

"What are you doing here?"

She pushed past. "You left before we'd concluded our business."

The cellar was musty and cold, with a single overhead electric light and an unmade cot in the corner.

"What business?" he said.

"About your sister."

"I told you." He closed the door but remained beside it, resting his hand on the knob, seeming impatient for her to go. "There's no 'business' to be done on that count."

"So, I can assume it's all right for me to leave her to herself."

"It's what I do."

There was a wooden stool beside the row of wine racks. She sat, deliberately prodding at his peevishness. "And what's your business with my father?"

"That, you'll have to take up with him."

Cecile let her face soften. "We've known each other our whole lives. Why do you hate me now?"

"We were never friends," Joël said. "But I don't hate you."

"Then why won't you tell me about my father?"

"Because it's not my place to."

"Then tell me about you. Why did you flee École Saint-Christophe?" The school where her father had arranged for him to be placed.

"I didn't flee," Joël said, the violence again rising to the surface. "What's there for me in learning math and kneeling before a goy god? A war is going on. The charade of Catholic school is well and good for my sister and you. Me, I have other responsibilities."

"And how do you know that I don't have other responsibilities, too?"

"You? You're a stupid little girl who befriends stupid Russian girls." He smirked. "I've seen you together. Don't you know what they do to us, the Russians?"

She returned his glare. "Oh, I know. It's you who doesn't know half of what he thinks he does. You don't know who comes to our house, the secrets that are passed."

His face gave then and he moved away from the door, as though no longer urging her imminent departure. She'd finally struck the right note.

* * *

Joël slept most days. On nights when he wasn't out with her father and Marcel, she snuck from her house and passed them with him, on his cot that was, in fact, just a few planks of wood and a blanket. This, until the night she arrived and knocked and knocked and he didn't open the cellar door. Monsieur Jacqueminet appeared at the kitchen window, in a bathrobe and shooing her away with an irate wave of his hand, his eyes pleading that she be quiet.

"The boy has moved on," he hissed. "Now go!"

She again tricked her father into revealing Joël's whereabouts, and the next time he was forced to relocate, just a few weeks later, he told her the new address before disappearing.

Though they were always alone, just the two of them, they never touched as much as the aching inside her desired. Even when she lay in only a blouse and panties, they often just held one another, sometimes not even that. The first time he did more, he was solemn, angry even, but eager. And he wasn't gentle. Yet, it pleased Cecile to please him, to give him a comfort that he couldn't get from the few people who remained for him.

"I was home, you know," he told her, "the day they took M'man, Papa, and my baby sister." He lay on his side, his back to her, and spoke toward the wall. "Nearby anyway."

Cecile pushed in close, as close as she could, the head of a bent nail digging into her ribcage, and she draped an arm over him.

He didn't pull away. "It was just past lunchtime. We were returning from Uncle's, Martine and I, and we watched from the corner. The men who led my mother from our house, they were French, not German."

Cecile remembered the day. She'd been in literature class; they were reciting monologues from Molière. For Cecile, it was to be Magdelon from *Les Précieuses Ridicules*. She remembered this specifically, because the note instructing her to report to the headmistress's office had saved her the embarrassment of having to stumble through a work that she'd failed to properly memorize. In the office, she found her mother, in her Burberry trench coat though it wasn't raining and the slippers she only wore around the house. She carried a large handbag over her shoulder and took Cecile by the arm, and they left.

Cecile had known nothing at the time of what had provoked the unexpected appearance. Her mother explained nothing. Twice, they circled Bon Sauveur's walled grounds, then she led Cecile down Rue de Seine to the river and back, conspicuously avoiding the town center. And she asked Cecile question after idiotic question, things she might of a five-year-old, eyes flitty, glancing about, but smiling the smile of a milk cow.

"*Oui*, Maman. Math is going better."

"No, no. No need for more notebooks."

What seemed like hours later, Cecile spotted Joël and Martine in a pack of other children in the park. She tried to go to them, to be free of the anxious, ceaseless scurrying, even if it meant playing with neighbors she hadn't much cared for before that moment.

Her mother jerked her arm—"No!"—and they hurried past.

They walked until, with nightfall, fewer and fewer people were out in the streets and there was no place to go. Her father was seated in the front room when they returned, red-faced, *Le Petit Parisien* in his lap, apparently read top to bottom, maybe twice, so late was the hour. Her mother finally let go of the feigned poise and crumpled in a heap. Cecile's father took her up in his arms, a rare gesture of affection, as she revealed the terror of seeing the gray bus pull up in front of their house, then the relief and guilt of watching the police go next door and to the next one down. With this, Cecile had finally understood what had provoked the unending afternoon.

Joël, his back to her now, spoke to the wall. "She turned her eyes away. She wouldn't even look at us."

Cecile could picture it: Madame Goldschmidt, marching between two officers in leather coats from her house to the waiting bus, panic-stricken but proud, trying to maintain some semblance of dignity after spotting her children at the street corner, watching.

"It was to protect you," Cecile said. "So those Vichy bastards wouldn't recognize you and get you and Martine, too."

He broke from her embrace. "Not M'man, you stupid cunt. Your mother, shunning us in the park."

Cecile turned her back to him then. What else to do? She'd not acted to help them either. When had she ever done anything for anyone other than herself?

The Reynals, who for a fee of ration cards had agreed to let Joël move into their basement, lent him a radio, which was contraband for Jews, provided Joël promise to listen only with the volume very low. He and Cecile hunched beneath a blanket, head-to-head near the speaker. They listened to the broadcast execution of twenty-one Communist Resistants accused of shooting a Kriegsmarine officer in the Metro.

Cecile said, "Why not me, too?"

"Why not you too what?"

"To get involved, to help the struggle?" She leaned her body into his. "We could run off to the countryside, you and me together, to the Massif Central. They say there are more partisans there than here. Or we could form our own group, a Jewish brigade."

Though she couldn't see his face, she could feel his smirk. "You do best to stay out of our way, that's how you can help the struggle. Why, you're not even a Jew."

She sat up abruptly, uncovering them.

He appeared to enjoy her dismay and confusion. "Your mother's mother," Joël said, "a good Catholic from Brittany. She gave your father the documents to vouch for your racial 'purity.'"

The trip he'd taken at the start of the Occupation.

Cecile had been told that her mother's father had fallen in love with a dancer from his cabaret, a country girl who'd come to Paris to find fame and who had abandoned Cecile's mother when she was just a baby, the pregnancy unplanned for and unwanted. But that girl, a Gentile, and so Cecile and her mother, not Jews?

"You see, you have no real obligation to 'the struggle,'" said Joël. "You can quit me without guilt. You've done your good deed for the sad Jew boy."

"It's not just you who suffers, you know," Cecile said.

"Oh?" That smirk. "*You've* suffered?"

"It's not just you."

He grabbed one of her breasts, hard. "You think this is a game? Do you know what would happen if the Nazis were to catch you here with me?" He tightened his grip. "The things they would do to you?"

She slapped away his hand. "Why do you have to be cruel, Joël? Why with me?"

"I'm being honest, to wake you from your pathetic slumber."

How much was too much?

"Honest?" she said. "Here's honesty: You lug boxes and run errands. You're no grand spy, no great resistance fighter. You deliver parcels for my father and don't know who benefits or how much for your effort."

"I'm spy enough to know that you and your Jew-hating Russian friend wag your asses at German soldiers like bitches in heat."

"You're not even spy enough to know that I don't see Katya anymore. Haven't in months."

"Your father, the service he renders—he's a true hero. But you? You're a reckless, stupid girl. If you have no role in this fight, if your own father mistrusts you, look no further than your reflection in the mirror for the reason why."

An eye for an eye: Joël had taught her this. "You want to know what kind of hero my father is? He profiteers off the weak like you and your sniveling sister. Do you think he hides you out of selflessness and goodwill? No, your uncle pays him."

"My uncle can afford to. Besides, such things cost money."

"Money to put jewels on his mistress's wrist, to buy booze for his friends at nightclubs."

"What in this life is free?" Joël was standing now. "And what's the cost of you constantly hanging around—the cost for me?"

"It's me who pays." She stood, too. "You lost your precious *M'man*, and now you want a mother to replace her, a mother and a lay, and I've been fool enough to try to oblige you."

The look in Joël's eyes. She thought he might strike her.

Monsieur Reynal thrust his head through the cellar doorway. "Be careful, that noise! Imbeciles. I'm risking my family's lives here. Now shut your traps."

Joël, who had turned to face the door, didn't turn back after the door closed. "You should leave," he said.

She did and didn't return, only glimpsing him from afar thereafter: once, across the town square when she loitered with friends, not Katya but other girls from Bon Sauveur; another time at the rail station, with her father and Marcel, lugging some packaged somethings that were too many for the two men to carry. How narrow his hips, his shoulders—she had not noticed before. The stoop when he walked.

August 1944. General Leclerc's tank division rolled into Paris, and the next day, Charles de Gaulle paraded down the Champs-Elysées, declaring that the city had been outraged, that she'd been broken and sacrificed, but that now she was liberated. The Free French flag hung from windows where before had been blackout curtains—people everywhere, dancing and kissing and crying, celebrating even as combat continued in pockets around the city. Not long after, the uncles and aunts and cousins that remained packed what little they'd managed to hold on to and boarded ships bound for Brazil and Argentina. Or Palestine. Her father's cousin Irène, who Cecile hardly remembered from before the war, left to join the struggle to form a Jewish state so that, Irène proclaimed, there would never be roundups or pogroms again.

Cecile began skipping Bon Sauveur as often as she attended—no one seemed to notice—and with a pad and graphite pencils lifted from the school, she sat on the green metal benches along the banks of the Seine and drew flowering horse chestnut trees, birds on branches, strollers strolling. Nothing helped. It all felt false. More and more she just walked, forgetting the pencils at home and so not sketching, carrying a book but not reading, to Le Pecq, to Montesson, to Chatou, neighboring villages that looked as they always had, only without Nazi flags. One afternoon in Maisons-Laffitte, she wandered through what seemed an El Greco painting: a rubbled bridge, unpassable though still standing; houses, red-tiled roofs on four stucco walls, glassless windows baring charred darkness inside; the skeletons of trees, scorched and stripped of their leaves, branches beseeching the sky.

In the town center, in the lawns beside the chateau, she happened upon a crowd. A mob, really. It swarmed around a man in a suit coat and tie but carrying his trousers over one arm, properly folded at the crease.

A collaborator.

The man moved decidedly but with no clear direction, to the right then to the left, always forward but never arriving. Wiry schoolboys broke from the mass, whipping fists at him then retreating into the pack. One in a beret, stoop-shouldered but broad in the waist, waved a long-barreled revolver in the man's face. The man refused to lower his gaze.

Free French soldiers lined the lawns, helmeted and armed but otherwise indifferent. Here and there, photographers. A newsreel team, their motion picture camera on a tripod. Cecile imagined the sequence of still images, ticking into motion.

The mob grew, pushing Cecile toward the public square in front of the chateau, and there, Cecile saw the woman. A girl rather, not much older than she, coppered blond like Katya, as naked as a scar. A man held each wrist. The one on the right, in workman's coveralls, had a pistol; the one on the left, in a pinstriped suit and bright orange tie, smiled the smile of a jackal, venal and amused, a Gauloises pinched in the slit of his mouth. As the girl had no shoes and the cobblestones were cracked and mismatched, she moved gingerly, stumbling every few steps, one or the other man yanking her arm upward to keep her aloft, her breasts bobbing tempo rubato, the mob roiling, a path clearing.

She wasn't resisting, not one bit. Sure, the man had a pistol, but given his downcast eyes, the embarrassed look, it might as well have been a banana. The other, in pinstripes and the loud tie, bounded forward but paid more attention to the others all around than to her, his smile a black gash, the Gauloises not even lit.

The girl looked over one shoulder then the other. It wasn't shame on her face. When you're naked like this, how can anything else feel more humiliating? It's too late for shame, for regrets or might-have-done-differentlies. You look over one shoulder, over the other, but you're merely looking for a familiar face. Maybe just for another woman in this mob of men and boys. (Boys! Still in short pants and knee socks.) There must be a woman here who might betray a hint of compassion, eyes that understand, that convey something like: Had it been my Maurice that was taken, who knows what I would have done? It was never that the Untersturmführer was so kind—though he was certainly more gentle than this one, than Jackal, with his sweat-slicked grip. It's just that, who else was there to turn to for ration cards for meat?

This one, Jackal, jerking her forward over an unobstructed path—his sanctimonious smile and boastful stride were meant to show what? That he had acted? That he'd actually done something? Where did he imagine she would go were he to loosen his grip? Was he afraid she'd approach one of the few women present and that the woman might offer a shawl with which to cover herself, the scarf from her head? And then what would he do, so satisfied with his performance thus far this afternoon, four years along and all these days after de Gaulle's return? What would he do, with his bravery exposed as mere joining?

(And if the girl's eyes found Cecile's in this mottle of sneers and upturned collars and low-pulled hats, would Cecile turn from her gaze?)

Cecile saw it at the same moment as the girl: the makeshift scaffold, a common bistro chair raised at its center. So predictable. Of course, they would take this, too.

They sat her violently, Jackal and some other, the diffident pistol man now gone. The shears snagged, wrenching her head forward. Jackal yanked it back. The mob roared. The girl stared over their heads.

There was a detonation of air, more movement than sound, and the mob burst open. In the cleared space not three meters from Cecile was the trouserless man, trussed and ablaze, black smoke throbbing skyward, the pale of his face a fist. A leather belt cinched his arms at the elbows, behind his back; another bound his knees; and a third, his ankles. He didn't shriek or groan or even die. He gritted his teeth, writhed, and kicked.

It didn't take long. He stilled, his clothes charred, his head pink and wet. Now and then, a jerk or twitch. The air stank of gasoline. The boy in the beret, jerrican at his feet, leaned over what was left, pretending to light a cigarette with the heat of him.

The photographers rushed forward. The mob closed in. Cecile heard behind her: "*Bien fait pour sa gueule.* He got what he deserved, the dirty fascist."

She didn't turn and leave, or even turn away. She watched herself as from the vantage of the newsreel team, pushing in with the others, drawn to the cameras rather than to the trouserless man, clenched and raw and black. In her mind in that moment was only the composition of the picture—curiosity about how the sepia prints would turn out. The stone façade of the chateau behind; the mass of thrust-forward faces; her newly darned wool skirt. Would the lens capture the pattern of the plaid?

And then she remembered the rest. Her grandmother Lucie, her grandfather Georges. Joël's mother and father and baby sister. Was this justice for them?

For what man and what woman in this mob didn't have a place on the scaffold for something they'd done to assure survival—a rashly made accusation but for indispensable ends: for a laissez-passer to get out of the city or government tickets for coal?

Or for the things not done? For the expedient cover of Bon Sauveur, of white gloves and holy confirmation?

Cecile felt shame—shame—to be part of a people who would do this to one another: Vichy against Jew, Frenchman against Frenchman. Victims all, and victimizers too.

She decided to have no part of it, none. She simply refused.

Then what would she do, who might she become?

A vagabond meandering the countryside or some distant land—the Wandering Jew they so obsessed over. Or maybe she'd belt out Piaf in the Metro for loose change or a cigarette. No matter. Just not this.

CHAPTER TWO

Cecile met Minette on the bus ride from the rail station in Marseilles to the Communist Youth Conference in the countryside, in May 1947. It was the second spring after the war, and things had begun to seem as before, though, of course, they were not and never would be. The cream-over-green bus was half-empty, with only about twenty people on board, mostly young men, mostly French—the only other female, the beautiful black girl who, like Cecile, had a row to herself. Dark curls draped over the girl's shoulders, and she had the long neck of a dancer. But she wore a gingham shirt rolled at the elbows and denim trousers that made Cecile's pleated skirt and cardigan seem embarrassingly bourgeois by comparison.

The girl peered at a *Pif le Chien* comic in her lap, sometimes audibly snickering. Then she noticed Cecile staring. "What!" she snapped. "Did you think that niggers can't read?"

Two boys in the row behind her laughed nervously.

"It's the comic" was all Cecile could find to say, pointing to the stack of them beside the girl on the bus's bench seat. She was going to add that she liked *Pif* too, but the girl spoke first.

"Or maybe you think I should be reading something like this instead?" She removed a thick book from the military rucksack at her feet and dropped it in the passageway between them. It landed with a *thunk*. "You read it."

Cecile picked up the book: *Das Kapital*, all three volumes collected in one edition.

She held it in her lap, sitting stiff-backed and staring straight ahead. The girl returned to her *Pif* and to her snickering.

The bus made a restroom stop and the girl left her seat. Cecile placed the book on it. For the rest of the trip, with her face down, she used the white space on the title page of *Gigi*, the book she'd brought along, to sketch as best she could despite the jolts and lurches of the bus: dinghies on the harbor at Cassis; the Romanesque spire of the church at La Ciotat. When it got too dark to draw, the flushed light of sunset now faded to night, she closed her eyes, though sleep wouldn't come.

The bus was one of several that converged at the camp just after midnight. Cecile's mother often scolded her for being impetuous and headstrong, but she felt nothing like that now, on her own for the first time. She felt self-conscious and small. Holding her suitcase in one hand and worrying the ends of her hair with the other, she tried to meld into the group of conferees trooping toward the dormitory, aiming above all to remain unseen by the girl from the bus.

The other one found her in the crowd, though. The beautiful black girl handed Cecile a few of the *Pifs*, her face unapologetic, yet softer too. "I've finished with these," she said, then she told Cecile her name: Minette.

The dormitory, a hastily constructed block of wooden building, sat on a hillside. Girls stayed in one large room of stacked beds in rows, boys in another. Minette dropped her rucksack and comics onto a bottom bunk and nodded for Cecile to take the one above. Cecile went to the bathroom to change into her nightgown, and when she returned, the overhead lights now extinguished, Minette was already under the sheets. She'd changed into her shift right there in front of the others.

The air breezing through the unshuttered windows smelled of the sea. Minette said, "I'm not ready to sleep."

Cecile settled onto her bunk then leaned over the edge of her mattress. Minette began recounting her life story, the shadow of her head resting in the pillow of her interlocked fingers. Cecile had taken her for *martiniquaise* or *guadeloupéene*; in fact, she was Paris-born and -raised, her mother

French, her father Senegalese. "We let a two-room flat in Ménilmontant," Minette said, as though boasting. But the neighborhood, in eastern Paris, was known to be raucous and rough—so different from Le Vésinet, the suburb where Cecile lived.

"My mother, my Tantie Arlette, and Luc and Irène, my brother and sister," Minette continued. "Papa comes home on weekends."

Cecile whispered downward. "In my house it's just me. Well, my parents too, of course."

Minette said, "As soon as I was old enough, Papa started taking me to Communist League meetings."

"How long ago was that?"

"Three years now. The day after the Free French chased the Fritzes out of the city."

Some girl a few rows over shushed them.

Minette spoke more loudly. "Papa says only the Reds can fulfill the claims of the national slogan." She imitated a husky voice. "Fraternity be damned—these bastards can like me or not. Just make sure my children and I have the liberty and equality we've been promised."

Another shush, and Minette shot back: "Mind your own self!"

"Speak more softly," Cecile warned, giggling.

"I have the liberty to speak or to sleep. It's my right," Minette said, not softly at all. "Fraternity be damned!"

Girls shifted in their bunks but went on sleeping, or pretending to, the shusher now silent. Minette resumed telling her story.

Morning brought its own revelation. Rocky hillsides savage with scrub, Corsican violets, and wild rosemary, the sky a ruthless blue. Puffs of wind, hot breaths from North Africa. Hyères, the village down the slope, as from a dream: Roman-style houses, the Mediterranean just beyond, teal become cobalt become indigo the farther from shore it stretched.

To start the day, the conferees—a few hundred, maybe more—did calisthenics in uniformed rows, singing "L'Internationale." Cecile had trouble keeping up with the jumping jacks and the knee bends and all the stanzas (*Forward, brothers and sisters! / This is the final struggle / With the Internationale / Humanity will rise up!*), taken as she was by the varieties of green all around and the warmth so thick it was like she could cup some in her hands. Most of the others were French, of similar age to Cecile, eighteen-, nineteen-, and twenty-year-olds. Many wore wooden sabots and hand-me-down blue smocks, clearly from rural families. There were also Arab boys and Indochinese, a few Africans too—some, like Minette, apparently of mixed heritage.

The organizers had scheduled the conference to coincide with International Workers' Day, and the first lecture, in the large hall, began after calisthenics and covered the pressing issue in the country, the persisting shortages. Everything was rationed, petrol and soap and paper, milk for butter, flour for bread; long lines stretched out the doors of bakeries and food shops. The speaker, a French boy in denim top to bottom, made the case that it was all part of a ploy by the French Right to establish Gaullism, bringing de Gaulle to power instead of rendering it to the people.

"Did we learn nothing from Germany in '33?" he shouted. "Will we allow fascist thinking to take over our government like the Nazis did back then?"

By the afternoon lecture, both Cecile and Minette were bored and distracted. They penciled mocking retorts on their scratch pads to things said from the lectern. Eventually, the back-and-forth took up where their conversation of the night before had left off. *My father is my idol and my model*, Minette wrote, *unlike those peacocks who cluck of their heroic Resistance when who among them ever actually DID anything?* Her next entry filled nearly the entire page and read like a passage from a novel:

> *After returning from the battlefield during the Great War, Souf Traoré, a valiant Tiralleur Sénégalais, refused to return to Africa. Raised under the colonial yoke and now having risked his life for France, was he not French, too? This was his assertion.*
> *He was given a terrible time for it. He tried to pursue higher studies, but administrators always found excuses to deny him admission—his*

inadequate preparation in the colonial school in Dakar; the subjects he had not taken. He was often harassed by police and was twice detained.

Minette grabbed Cecile's pad in order to carry on writing while Cecile read.

After years of struggle, Souf Traoré was finally able to secure steady work in the coalmines in the North. By this time, he had impregnated a Parisian girl—the love of his life! He split his time between the two, weekdays in the mining camps at Lewarde and weekends with his family in the capital. He made the three-hour commute by train, Friday and Sunday nights.

Cecile was impressed by the story and didn't mind that Minette wasn't curious why she did not write herself. It kept Cecile from having to make things up to conceal the shame she felt about her own father. The Free French government had awarded him a medal for his activities during the Occupation (*activities*, the citation read, vague and noncommittal) and appointed him to a post in Le Vésinet's town hall. He used the position to continue the profiteering he'd done during the war. Given the fuel scarcity, bicycles cost as much as cars had in '39, before the German invasion. Yet every morning he donned a Bleu-Blanc-Rouge sash over his suit coat and pedaled off on a three-speed Singer Porteur, as though gloating. On his return in the evening, he carried on the bicycle's front rack for the whole world to see a half dozen eggs or an extra portion of flour, slices of roast pork, and once a whole chicken. When Cecile asked to attend the youth conference, he'd mocked her. "A week of indoctrination with the vulgar Communards? Bah!" It was her mother who'd come up with the money, pilfering from the weekly allowance allotted for household upkeep and miscellanies.

She leaned toward Minette. "You're right," she said. "Your father is a hero."

"Yes," said Minette, pausing her scribbling. She pointed to Cecile's chest, to her Star of David pendant. "You're a Jew?"

Cecile had bought the necklace in the first weeks after the Liberation and worn it since, visibly, insistently, on the outside of garments. Yet now, with this new friend, she didn't know what to say.

Minette sucked her teeth. "Tsst. It's good. Marx was born a Jew, too."

The third night, they slipped from their bunks, dressed quietly, and snuck out the dormitory window. "They'll be waiting for us," Minette whispered. "The ones I told you about."

Two African boys. Boubacar and Sebastien, she'd called them.

Cecile stooped beneath the window ledge before following Minette out into the night. "You're sure this is a good idea?"

It wasn't that she believed the nasty things her father said about Africans, whom he claimed were loyal but stupid and lusted for French girls—of course not. Still, the few she'd chanced upon, on excursions into Paris, always clustered in groups and laughed boisterously; some casually spat on the sidewalk, indifferent of proper manners; and none seemed to see them, the French, looking past or through them. Cecile hoped that the fluttering apprehension she now felt stemmed from the late hour and the backcountry dark, that it was just natural caution, visceral and involuntary, before wandering beyond the compound with two boys she did not know, and that it wasn't something else, something that, like her stark blue eyes and sudden peevishness, she might have inherited from her father.

She repeated, "You're sure?"

"Why not?" said Minette. "Let's see what happens."

The boys sat on the ground beside a shed on the exercise field, two shadows that rose up with the girls' approach. Without speaking, they turned and set off into the scrub brush and sage, silky shapes against the broader night—one thin, his movement sparks of nervous energy; the other thicker, striding easily through the shrubbery and bramble.

From the outline of their forms, Cecile thought she recognized them from the lecture hall but wasn't sure.

In an open space surrounded by trees, Minette announced, "Here," and all four sat, Cecile beside Minette and facing the boys, Hyères down the hillside, streetlights twinkling. The night was chilly, though Cecile felt warm, her cheeks flushed.

"I've had enough of this crap," Minette said.

"Of our midnight stroll?" the thin one teased. "Already?"

"Of this retreat. The instructors are simpletons, and the others act like campers on holiday. League meetings back home are far more edifying. And inspiring!"

"But aren't we just campers on holiday," the thin one insisted, "only surrounded by like-minded comrades?"

"Maybe you, *mon camarade* Boubacar. For me, this is serious business." The shadow of Minette's form raised up, electric and rigid all at once. "This Marshall Plan that they're proposing reeks of de Gaulle. He wants to rally support for the Americans and use it to quash the Communist Party."

"No one disputes this," the other boy said, his voice a slow rumble—deep, his pronunciation precise. "But the problem remains. The economy is in a shambles, and there's no way to rebuild it without aid."

"What about Soviet aid?" said Minette.

"Soviet *aid*," the second boy said, "is a military invasion. How long before their tanks reach the Pyrenees?"

Minette dismissed him with a suck of her teeth. "Spoken like a true Frenchman."

The insult struck Cecile as unduly harsh, though the African boy—as best as she could tell in the dark—seemed unfazed, merely chuckling in response.

Minette continued: "De Gaulle wants the Communists and the Socialists at each other's throats so that he can swoop in and establish a totalitarian state with himself at its head." The shadow of her form leaned forward conspiratorially. "But there'll be a series of mobilizations in the fall before the elections. We'll show them what we can do."

The thin boy—Boubacar—said, "Mobilizations, mobilizations . . . It's all we hear about. But what exactly do the Communist deputies mean by this?"

"Does the word scare you?" said Minette.

"As a matter of fact, yes. As a colonial subject, at the mercy of the government's whims and liable to be expelled from the country, these sorts of things *do* concern me, whatever party is in power."

Cecile heard Minette's derisive snicker, now familiar to her, a signal that she might say anything, however harsh, which compelled Cecile to jump in: "I'm sure it'll be mass walkouts and marches and the like, actions to make our voices heard."

"But how do walkouts and marching in the streets fill food pantries?" Boubacar said, more toward Minette than Cecile.

"So skeptical," Minette said, only with less venom. "Why are you two even here?"

"Why, to be convinced," said Boubacar, playfully. "So, convince me."

Cecile watched his form move closer to Minette's. Then she heard the second boy's lulling voice: "And what about you?"

"I agree, of course," she said, a little more brusquely than she might have otherwise. "First the Nazis and Vichy, and now the Americans? France is a country of victims, and the future is not with victims, it's with—"

"I meant, where are you from, what do you do?"

"Where am I from?"

"I'm sorry," he said, "I've been rude. We haven't properly met. I'm Sebastien Danxomè." He scooched nearer to her, appeared to offer his hand. "But please, call me Seb."

"*Enchantée.*" She found his hand, and they shook. "Cecile Rosenbaum."

The outline of his form seemed to soften, his shoulders easing. "Yes, Boubi told me."

Boubi, she thought. A nice nickname in place of the unwieldy Boubacar.

But how did Boubi know her name? And who told him? Minette? She scrutinized what she could make of Seb's face, hoping to find some clues about what else he might have been told.

All she could see was shades of darkness against the greater dark.

"I'm from Paris, like Minette," she said. "Well, Le Vésinet really, just outside. But I want to move into the city."

If she could convince her father, of course, which was far from certain. Which was more unlikely than not, in fact.

"For university?" he asked.

She'd earned her *Bac Littéraire* the month before, but no. "A job," she said. "I hope to get hired at the Louvre."

"You're an artist?"

He sounded impressed—needlessly. Her sketching and painting were just hobbies, ones she hadn't even told Minette about.

"No, no," she said. "Although, after I've gained some experience, I want to study art preservation and museography. Provided I get admitted to the program."

A breeze kicked up, rustling the scrub.

Burying her neck into the collar of her jacket, she confessed: "My sketching and painting only enrage Papa. '*Pas serieux,*' he says."

Seb appeared to be probing the dark, as she had before, searching for the features of her face. He said, "Maybe your future husband will be more supportive of your dreams than your father."

It sounded like an attempt at flirtation.

"Ha!" they heard. "We're New Women! We don't need the approval of men to follow our pursuits."

Cecile hadn't realized that Minette was listening. Her and Boubi's forms were close enough to seem to be a single, thick shadow. Cecile heard stirring over there now, a sigh, the sounds of kissing.

Which was a relief. She was tired of rhetoric and declamations. She wanted to know about these boys that they'd snuck off to meet: where they lived; how they lived; what caused them to be here in France where there was so much racism rather than at home in Africa.

"And you?" she asked. "You're at university, then? What's your course of study?"

"If only . . ." The tone of Seb's voice shifted, seeming to pull back. "I *hope* to enroll, I work at it every day. In truth, though, I'm just a laborer"— he said this lower, as though apprehending that Minette might still be eavesdropping—"a handyman. I help at École de la Sainte-Famille, whatever needs doing, mostly groundskeeping and in their storeroom."

Cecile felt so strongly that she could read his face, despite hardly being able to see it, that she imagined their eyes meeting. She spoke low, too, for the same reason as him. "And that's not good enough?" she asked.

"My father sent us here to pursue our studies. So, no, being a worker bee isn't good enough."

"Us? You and Boubi?"

"My sister and me. Jacqueline is finishing her first year at École de Médecine."

"The national medical school! Impressive."

The entrance exam was said to be grueling—five consecutive days of testing, a different subject each day, three hours per sitting. Cecile knew the odds to be long for even the most well-prepared students; only a tiny fraction were admitted, just the very top scorers.

Maybe he sensed skepticism in her pause, because he added: "My sister is brilliant, the smartest person I've ever known."

She hoped he hadn't taken her silence for base racism—she recognized, of course, that an African could be just as intelligent as anyone! To change the subject from her bungling, she asked: "When did you arrive? After the war?"

He calculated: "I'll be twenty-two in December, so . . . fifteen years ago."

"You were just seven!"

"Seven, yes. Jacqueline was nine."

"You were here through the Occupation?"

"Our father put us on a ship in '33. Who could have seen it coming?"

Cecile shuddered to imagine their terrible experiences in that time of animosities and betrayal, two children, and Africans at that, when there had been so few in France. (There were still hardly any now, despite the increasing numbers who'd turned up since the end of the war.) She said, "And you haven't returned, not once? Don't you long for home, don't you miss your mother, doesn't your sister?"

He laughed but without humor. "Jacqueline's the oldest, my elder. In African families, that matters. She does what Father bids done."

"Which is what? Earn a degree?"

"More than that." He paused. "You see, my grandfather was a king—"

"A king?"

"My grandfather and his forefathers, yes—the founders of Dahomey. I'm my father's only son. I *have* to succeed. I've got the name to uphold."

So many questions—so, so many. Like, how had they managed, and where had they lived, a nine- and a seven-year-old princess and prince, alone in a foreign country? And why, with this mandate from his father to complete university and accomplish something, was he just a "worker bee," doing menial work?

She didn't know how to ask. His reserved manner—not coy, just formal—didn't invite prying.

In fact, she found his sense of discretion alluring.

Minette, still one shadow intertwined with Boubi's, called across the dark: "The youth congress they talked about, in Romania next year—we should all travel there together."

Cecile heard Boubi say, "That would be great!"

Minette added: "The old is being purged. We, the young, are the New France. We have to prepare ourselves to help shape it."

Boubi said something to her, too low to hear, and she burst out, "No!" and then laughed. Soon they could be heard kissing again.

"It's late," Seb said. "Maybe we should head back?"

"Sure," said Cecile, though she was certain no one in the dormitory had noted their absence. Who was even awake at that hour?

He rose casually, and she followed suit. They headed toward camp. Minette and Boubi never disentangled.

He stopped a few meters short of the window to the girls' room. The bulb under the eaves of the building revealed more of him than she had yet seen—chiseled cheekbones and jawline; a tight crop of hair; his eyebrows, charcoal strokes over the surrounding dark.

Though he'd urged their return, it was as though he didn't want them to part. He whispered, "So, you and the *métisse*"—he meant Minette— "I'm surprised to see you've become such good friends after her outburst on the bus."

He'd been there!

She hadn't noticed him. She felt mortified now.

"She's more paw-pad than claws," Cecile said. "But I've never met anyone like her."

Which was true. Minette had Katya's daring and dash but was principled, *engagée*. Her brass helped unloose Cecile, made her feel less like a child always asking permission.

"There are no mixed-race people in Le Vésinet," she continued, trying to explain the attraction. "No blacks at all, in fact."

It was a strange connection, even to her own ear. And he looked on, quizzically. "I'm learning a lot from her," she said as a way to finish the half-formed thought.

"And this New Womanhood? Is it a real thing?"

She laughed. "Of course, it is!" she said, and echoing Minette, she added: "Does the idea frighten you?"

"Should it?"

Her response was to push in close, her lips finding his.

It was a strong reply, finally.

She stepped away then, climbed in through the open window before he might say or do anything more.

Seb didn't come to breakfast the next morning. Neither did Boubi, but Minette didn't seem to mind. "There's a rally Saturday," she said, "at the

Champ-de-Mars. It's supposed to be big, with student leaders from the Sorbonne. We should go!"

The Champ-de-Mars was in Paris. "Saturday?" said Cecile. "We'll still be here."

"Not if we leave today."

Cecile dunked a slice of the stiff black bread into her bowl of watery hot chocolate. "Today?"

"The bus takes twenty hours," said Minette. "We would arrive Friday night."

Cecile glanced around the dining hall at the other conferees, all the boys and girls chatting. It was true: the lectures were boring and the debates facile; she didn't want to see one more newsreel about the exploits of the Red Army. But leave today?

"Stop looking for him," Minette scolded. "When he realizes you're gone, how much more mysterious, more sexy, will he find you to be?"

Cecile dunked the plank of meaty bread then bit off a piece and ground and ground it with her teeth, trying to ignore the joyous gabbing and laughter all around, the wafts of rosemary and the sunlit heat.

She pushed away the bowl of flavorless chocolate. "The train is faster. We could be there tonight."

"I don't have money for that," Minette said, her mouth full of half-chewed food.

"The bus, then," said Cecile.

She didn't look around to see if Seb had come in yet.

"*Oui!*" Minette said. "We're New Women, independent and free. This is what New Women do."

CHAPTER THREE

They packed during the morning lecture and set out without telling anyone, walking the three kilometers from camp down the narrow, winding road to Hyères. Minette dressed in denims with the cuffs turned up and a green-checked shirt, her rucksack over a shoulder. For Cecile, it was the khaki trousers she'd brought for calisthenics and Minette's red cotton pullover, every few steps shifting her suitcase from one hand to the other. The pullover didn't hang on her like it did over long, slim Minette, but the way it hugged her curves pleased her all the same. She was what Mamie Lucie, who had introduced her to art, would describe as "Rubenesque" (and what her father fliply called "chubby"), and she recognized herself to merely be cute where Minette was striking. Still, she liked borrowing Minette's look. She thought it suited her, too.

A lorry picked them up outside Hyères after only a few minutes' wait on the roadside. The driver was going as far as Marseille, which they cheered, as it was their destination too. They rode on the empty flatbed in back, each bump in the road jarring, each bend shooting Cecile into Minette or Minette into Cecile. They burst out laughing with each collision.

On a long, smooth stretch, Cecile yelled over the shear of the wind: "Let's take the train. We can cash in my return ticket, buy two with what's left for as far as the money will take us, and hitch a ride, like this, the rest of the way."

"*Oui, fillette!*" Minette said. "Now you're thinking. We'll be there in time for supper."

The lorry dropped them at the Old Port. Fishermen darned nets on the decks of their luggers, rocking on the bay beside the stone wharves that lay buckled and crumbling, decimated from the wartime bombing. Minette asked directions to the rail station then passed her arm through Cecile's, and they strode forward at a clip.

They passed a lot strewn with pulverized stone and blackened wood and rent metal. Only the back wall remained, the glass of its windows blasted out, and a single brick pillar. Somehow, the buildings bookending either side stood largely unharmed. Minette, surging forward and chirping ceaselessly, didn't seem to notice, unfazed by the destruction that remained all around, and Cecile wondered at how she could be.

Minette's life was action without apology. She trained her eye toward the future. Cecile wanted to know the world that had produced a girl such as her.

A broad white-stone stairway led up to the rail station. Inside, the sharp Midi sunlight, refracting through the vaulted glass ceiling, burnished the surfaces of things—the sinewy iron of the newspaper kiosk; the curve and sheen of café tables; the grainy green jackets of the many soldiers all around, some of whom were black.

"*Tirailleurs Sénégalais!*" Minette said. "Like my father!"

She knelt and removed a compact from her rucksack and studied herself, expressionless, turning to one side, then the other—a habitual gesture, almost a ritual one; vain maybe, but artless too. Cecile rarely lingered before her own image longer than the amount of time it took to apply eyeliner or rouge. Mamie Lucie had once chided her that, if she insisted on standing so long before the mirror, one day she would see the devil in it, and Cecile had felt self-conscious since.

"Come on," Minette said, snapping closed the compact. "Let's get tickets."

Cecile gazed at the overhead board above the SNCF booth, inspecting the departure times. After handing her return ticket to the blue-uniformed agent and requesting the exchange, the man scrutinized it and then Minette.

"Let me get this straight," he said. "You want to trade this one to Paris for two to Clermont-Ferrand?"

He was old and splotchy, and his hat didn't fit.

"Yes," said Cecile. "Or as far as what remains of its value will take the both of us."

He gazed from Cecile to Minette. "Lapalisse actually, and six francs to spare. But Lapalisse, *ma fille*, is *not* Paris."

"Hurry up, man!" Minette flashed. "Our train is in a few minutes."

"Young woman," he said, "you behave as vulgarly as a strumpet."

"Ha! Don't you wish?" said Minette. "My preference is for more intact men."

The agent's face flushed, but he said no more. He tore up the ticket in deliberate strokes, took his time writing carbon-copied new ones, and slid the originals across the counter.

Striding toward the train platforms, Minette called back: "Tell me, is that the uniform you wore for Vichy? The cap you donned before banging on the doors of Jewish families?"

The others in line glared, with pinched mouths and hateful eyes.

But Minette laughed.

Cecile laughed then, too—uncomfortably at first, more affect than genuine feeling. Aboard the train, it came more easily, their playful banter saucy, seductive. They were New Women.

Minette slept most of the trip. Unable to herself, Cecile sketched on the blank pages of *Gigi* (of which she had yet to read a single word). In rhythm with the rocking of the train, she began by tracing the outline of a face. Pulling the lines long and brushing in thick strokes, it became Minette: her electric mouth in repose; a spray of hair and the strangely aquiline nose; her cheek pressed against the car window.

Shortly before three, the train arrived at Lapalisse, a village with a chateau on a bluff, overlooking a river. They bought Gruyere sandwiches at the bakery beside the station and asked directions to the roadway that led to Paris. It was only a few kilometers, they were told. Once arrived,

they stood beside the two-lane, treelined Route Nationale 7. Though there
was no traffic—not a single car—Minette predicted: "A couple of pretty
girls on the side of the road? *Tu parles!* We'll get rides quick, be home in
time for dessert."

And she was right. A long-haul truck, the first vehicle to pass, jerked
to a halt beside them. The driver pushed open the passenger door. He sat
heavily on the bench seat, in blue coveralls rolled at the sleeve and spotted
with grease, and though he appeared to be hardly older than Cecile and
Minette, he sported a fat, drooping moustache that made him look like a
history-book illustration of a Gaul.

"Where you going?"

"Paris," said Minette. "Or as near there as you're going."

"I'm going all the way," he said, leering—as much, at least, as the
silly moustache would allow. "I'll take you all the way, if that's what
you want."

Minette ushered Cecile up onto the long bench and climbed in
after. The truck lurched forward, the gears grinding with each shift up
to speed. When he reached the top gear, he let his thigh fall to the side,
where it rested against Cecile's. In the tight space of the cab, there wasn't
room to move her own away.

They rode in silence, Minette looking out the side window, Cecile
out the front, at the stretches of field and cylindrical bales of sun-bleached
hay rolled like giant pastries and neatly stacked along fence lines. The
trucker bypassed Jaligny, only rooftops and its chateau's spires apparent
in the distance.

"You girls live in Paris, then?" he said.

"No," said Minette. "We're going to Paris to visit our father."

"*Your* father?" He looked from one to the other.

"The government is holding him there," Minette said, "until his
execution."

Papa, a collaborator? thought Cecile.

Why not?

"So, you two are sisters?" the driver asked.

"Maman cooks and cleans," Minette said. "Mine does. She's the family servant."

"When Maman was pregnant with me," said Cecile, "my maman, he couldn't help himself."

"How could he?" Minette said. "My maman is so beautiful. So he ravished her."

A rapist? thought Cecile. Papa?

"Jeanne-Marie Celine de Bossigny," Minette said, extending a hand across Cecile.

"And I'm Alphonse," Cecile said.

The driver looked from one to the other then at the road again. He released the wheel with one hand and reached across Cecile to shake with Minette and after with Cecile—a thick palm and a painful grip. Approaching a village, he slowed the massive truck, working the gearshift, his meaty thigh tightening as he forced down the pedal. Then it lay against Cecile's again. The signpost read BESSAY-SUR-ALLIER.

"I have stories to tell, too," he said, "but maybe mine are true."

The gears ground as they crawled through town.

"Two girls alone," he said. "Quite foolish, isn't it, to put yourselves at such risk?"

The quiet village, its shuttered houses and empty streets. His heavy thigh.

"Surely you've read the news stories about Pierrot le Fou and his Front-Wheel-Drive Gang," he said.

Neither girl said anything, both facing forward. Cecile could feel his leer.

"The famous bank robber," he added, for emphasis.

"If you're Pierrot," Minette said, "why are you driving a clunky old truck and not a Citroën 11?" She turned toward him. "And if we're two girls together, then obviously neither of us is alone." And before he could say more or get the truck back up to speed at the village edge, she swung her rucksack across Cecile and struck him in the face and scurried out.

Cecile followed close behind.

Running back toward the village center, Minette called over her shoulder, "*Sale con!*" with the truck lurching to stop, brakes squealing, its passenger door flapping closed then opened then closed, the latch finally catching.

An elderly woman emerging from a shop, in a headscarf and pulling a shopping trolley, stared as Minette and Cecile dashed past.

They waited a half hour inside the rail station, inspecting each person who entered, though there were few, to be sure that "Pierrot" had cleared the area. Then, they returned to the town's edge. It was a rural stretch. Vehicles were rare. Occasionally, a farmer on a horse-drawn wagon clopped by. Each time, Minette and Cecile asked, "*S'il vous plaît*, Monsieur?" pleading and smiling. The man would return the smile but explain that, regrettably, he was only going a few kilometers up the road, not far enough for the ride to be worth it.

A long-haul truck rounded the bend, decelerating abruptly, the driver clearly spotting them. But Minette and Cecile waved him off and fled into the field, running until they heard his engine rev and the truck take off again. The driver blared his horn an angrily long time.

Five o'clock became six became suppertime, daylight dimming, night coming.

The girls made stools of their bags. Cecile had been taught that it was undignified to sit in this way—knees splayed, elbows on thighs—but in their current situation, it felt entirely appropriate. She gazed down the unchanging and empty stretch of macadam and bordering fields. With the breeze, the heads of the leafing trees were a ripple of green.

"Don't fret, *fillette*," said Minette, "a ride'll arrive. We just have to wait for it."

As if there was anything else they could do.

She sensed Minette staring.

"You've never slept with a boy, have you?" Minette said.

"What?"

Cecile's suitcase was taller, so she found herself perched above Minette.

"You're a virgin!" said Minette, smiling slyly. "That's why you didn't want to leave: you wanted the African boy to be your first."

Cecile didn't respond. She rotated toward her friend instead, straddling her suitcase, as though seated atop a tiny pony. "And you?" she said. "I imagine Boubi wasn't your first."

"Mine was four years ago." Minette spun on her rucksack, facing Cecile, too. "I was sixteen."

"Who was he?"

"Just a boy who lived in the building next to ours," she said. "His *lycée* was nearby mine. Papa knew his father from league meetings before the war and asked that the boy walk me to school—the Fritzes being all around, you know, and me looking as I look."

Cecile wondered if she was referring to her race or to her beauty, though either might have drawn the unwanted attention of German soldiers. Both would have, in fact.

"He was sweet, really," Minette said. "Attentive and slow."

"Did you date long?"

"Oh, we never dated. We only did it twice. After the second time, I told him to stop walking me to school and to leave me alone."

"Why?"

"He got attached," Minette said, "immediately." She stuck out her tongue and feigned nausea. "White boys are fine for play, but anything more . . ."

"Minette!" Cecile swatted her arm.

"Seriously? Regular sex with one? Just think of your father—the colorless loose skin, the spindly little legs. Would you want to have to share a bed with *that* forever?"

They both laughed. Though Minette hadn't met Cecile's father, she'd described him to a T.

Cecile wondered what Minette thought about her—about the wan skin that wouldn't hold a tan; about her chestnut hair that, no matter the product used, could not be teased into liveliness. Cecile wanted to believe that, given how close they were becoming, Minette no longer saw her race.

But she feared that Minette found her to be pitiful, too—colorless and bland, the gawking white girl from the bus.

Minette removed her compact and peered into it. "They call me a mongrel and say I'm neither, not black nor white, but I'm both. Me, people like me—*des métisses*, mixed-bloods—we inhabit the in-between. I know things others cannot know."

Though Minette's seat was lower, she seemed to loom over Cecile.

"I can have whomever I want," she said, "but I've always known I would end up with a black man. An African likely, though maybe a *métisse* like me. It's not prejudice. It's just that I deserve someone who knows like I know, who sees things clearly."

Cecile envied Minette—her perspective, her life. Since the war, Le Vésinet had seemed insufficient, small, a toy village filled with papier-mâché houses and plastic trees, tin figurines of people frozen in place as they enter the bakery or stride down the street—gestures of motion without any real movement. She longed for more, for something different, not just the old ways of being but for new views.

Minette grabbed her hands and squeezed for a long instant. "An African boy would be good for your first. A French boy would only dote over you, and you might submit to bourgeois inclinations." She turned on her rucksack seat, in the direction of oncoming traffic—of which there was still none. "Just be sure to be careful. Make him use a condom, or at least pull it out."

"Minette!"

"What would your parents think if you brought a tan little baby home to Le Vésinet?"

Minette laughed. Cecile, too—less at the thought of it than so the subject might die. She'd lied to her friend about her virginity. But Joël was the past, and leaving it behind struck Cecile as good and brave and true.

A tractor hauling hay bales took them to Moulins, the girls riding atop the trailer of dusty crop. Though the distance was only twenty kilometers, the trip took over an hour at a deadening pace. The frigid air, with nightfall, distracted the girls from the everywhere-itching on their necks and backs and arms, up and down their legs. Pitying them, the farmer took them to the city's northern edge, well out of his way. Cecile and Minette thanked him profusely, though Minette, scratching and scratching, looked only grudgingly thankful.

They were still hours from Paris, with no place to sleep nor money to pay for lodgings, not even enough for food to calm their stomachs' grumblings. Cecile proposed that they camp in the neighboring field. They wouldn't be seen in the dark, she reasoned, so they'd be safe should anyone wander by; they could huddle together for warmth; and in the morning, traffic was sure to be heavier.

"Are you crazy!" said Minette.

She began walking up the road, waving and waving at each set of passing headlights, though they were few, eventually stepping out into their paths to be seen. Cecile trailed behind, dispirited, waiting for the other to get tired and reconsider.

Six sets of lights later—after twenty, maybe thirty minutes—a car finally stopped. It was a Renault sedan and bore the cross of Lorraine, the Free French insignia, on the hood and doors. The young-faced captain and his much older driver were headed to the military camp at Fresnes, south of Paris. "Still thirty kilometers or so from your destination, I regret to say," he told them.

"But much closer than here," said Minette, "and *not* that field."

The captain turned repeatedly in his seat during the drive and tried to make conversation, but Cecile and Minette hardly paid any attention, wriggling on the rear bench and scratching at the all-encompassing itching. Cecile gave one-word replies. Minette didn't even pretend to want to. He eventually just faced forward.

The captain had his driver take them all the way to Le Vésinet, dropping them in front of Cecile's door on Allée de la Muette. The white-stone cottage was still, the blue shutters dark. It was past four in the morning.

Cecile wasn't expected for three more days. She quietly led Minette to her bedroom, whispering apologies. "It's utterly bourgeois, but take my bed. A night to yourself in a quiet room, to recover from the long and difficult trip." She pointed out the washbasin in the corner, where Minette could clean off the bits of hay.

Herself, she didn't even attempt to deal with the itching and the grime. She went to the front room, to the sofa there, exhausted, more tired than she could remember having ever felt. Fully clothed, she stretched long then curled into a ball and was certain she had only just shut her eyes when she heard a shriek—faint, and at some distance, as in a dream—but a shriek for sure. She lay there, certain it couldn't have been a dream as she hadn't yet fallen asleep, her logic illogical even to her, with the daylight filtering through the shuttered windows and the rising sound of sobbing.

Cecile sprang up and stumbled toward her bedroom. She found her mother, collapsed in a heap at the foot of her closed door, in a nightgown but no robe.

"It's all right, Maman," she said. "It's all right."

Cecile remembered where she was, how she had come to be here.

"She's a friend," she explained, her father in his pajamas down the hallway.

Her mother held the knob in one hand and with the other covered her eyes. "That bush of black hair all over the pillow, and when she sat up, the strange girl," she said, taking in Cecile now, who knelt beside her. "What is Josephine Baker doing in your bed!"

Minette, Cecile, and her mother laughed about it over breakfast later— in the dining room rather than, as usual, in the kitchen. Her mother, still embarrassed but amused, served coffee and the previous day's ration bread on Mamie Lucie's favorite Tétard platter, which Cecile's father had recovered during the war, after Lucie was taken. Cecile recognized the gesture as one of respect for their guest and so tried to not let the platter's opulence embarrass her.

The weight of the sterling silver dish made it difficult to carry, though her mother pulled it off gracefully. She wore an elegant robe that Cecile recalled from her earliest memory—a sundress really, yellow with lace fringe, her hair tied up in a matching wrap. The three sipped from their bowls and chatted, about the scorched beauty of the Midi, about the girls' adventurous return. Cecile's mother at once giggled and also admonished their recklessness. And when, dropping her eyes, she attempted to again apologize for the earlier scene, Minette burst from her chair, jiggling her rump toward them, doing the Banana Dance around the table.

Cecile and her mother could not stop laughing—a *fou rire*, uncontrollable.

Cecile's mother went to the cupboard, and Minette, indicating Cecile's Star pendant, whispered, "She doesn't wear it?"

"Never did. Papa either. Only me, since de Gaulle freed the city."

Cecile didn't want to be misunderstood.

"I don't believe in God, mind you." She pointed out the window. "But all those bastards who conspired with the Nazis. Or who did nothing while the Nazis did what they did. I wear it now by choice, to spite them."

Minette's knowing smile reassured Cecile that she'd struck the right note, the one she'd been hoping for.

Her mother began collecting the empty plates. Minette offered: "Please, let me help you." But before her mother could accept or demur, Minette popped up from her chair and recommenced her jumping and jiggling dance around the room.

Cecile's mother bent over double, another *fou rire*, clutching the dishware to her belly so as not to drop any.

Cecile, too—her stomach clenching, her eyes tearing.

Her father, having slipped out of the house long before, had missed the whole thing.

CHAPTER FOUR

Cecile's father called her request for permission to move into the city a harebrained idea. "So that you can traipse about with coloreds and filthy Communards and libertine intellectuals? Absolutely not." Her mother appeared saddened by the request, and also a little hurt, but she interceded on Cecile's behalf all the same. The quarrel was fierce, loud enough to follow through Cecile's closed bedroom door, her mother cross in a way she hadn't heard before.

"Alain Rosenbaum, listen to me! In normal times, children go to school, they learn from lesson books and recitations and exercises. But her education was the Occupation. It's her point of reference, the base on which she's had to build everything that's happened since."

"Spare me, please." The ensuing silence was brusque—chairs shifting about, their legs scraping sharply against the wooden floor. "With the meat I managed to put on the table? Enrolling her in that Catholic school? The girl hardly noticed the Occupation. I made certain of it."

"For you and me, it was something suffered and survived. I remember every roundup, to the day, to the hour—your own mother!" There was a pause. "And the Goldschmidts . . . Poor Carole, her baby on her hip." Her mother's voice evened. "But Cecile, how can we know what she saw while she was beyond these walls, what she experienced?"

Her father made some exasperated sound, a phlegmy exhalation of air.

Her mother wouldn't relent, though. "You look and see the same girl who got up each morning and went to class and at day's end sang for us the hymns she'd learned in choir. But how could she be? No, she has to learn to be a woman in her own way, whatever that might mean."

Cecile scooched nearer her bedroom door, thinking her father's retort too low to hear, when it swung open, him filling the space, holding the Tétard platter by the handles.

"It's all that's left of your Mamie Lucie, of Daddie Georges. I'll hawk it to get the money. When that's used up, it's all gone. You succeed, you fail, either way, there's nothing more."

Just as abruptly, he left.

His words stung, as intended. Cecile would give anything to see her beloved grandparents alive, to have things as they'd been before. But they weren't as they had been and never could be again.

Daddie Georges had owned an antiques boutique on the swank Rue du Faubourg Saint-Honoré before the war and been elected president of the Antiquarian Society of Europe. Cecile's father used those connections to secure a position for her at the Louvre—entry-level, in the ticket booth and as a *surveillante de salle*, but it was a start. She let a room at the Hôtel des Beaux-Arts, a *pension* across the street from the famous art academy, in the heart of the Quartier latin. Her new home—the first on her own—was tiny, just a bed, a chest of drawers, and a washbasin in the corner, with a shared toilet down the hall. Still, she felt autonomous, adult—free. The hotel provided sheets, but Cecile used the ones her mother had packed— "To remember us by," she had said. They were soft and smelled of Persil, her mother's preferred detergent, but not at all of her mother.

Seated on a stool before the mirror and using photos from the new *France-Soir* supplement, *Elle*, as a guide, Cecile took scissors and a comb and cut her hair, reasoning that shorter would be easier to manage. It came out more Eton crop than bob, more Joan of Arc than Dita Parlo, but it felt right somehow. In her first few days, she found simple clothes at second-hand stores in the neighborhood—denims, cardigans, plain blouses—to fit this new self.

Her "new" self?

No, her awakened self.

Arriving for her first shift, Cecile noticed *Action* magazine at the kiosk beside the staff entrance to the Louvre and bought it. A few days later *Intransigeant*, newly reappeared since the Occupation, was on the rack, and she got it, too. As much as keeping up with the current debates, she liked the stern look the magazines provoked from her supervisor, Monsieur Petit. A pince-nez-wearing Right Bank type, Petit had been a longtime acquaintance of Daddie Georges, though he kept a cool distance from his staff, relatives of friends or not.

Petit insisted that female employees wear skirts to accompany the dark museum blazers required of staff. As the thrumming queue in the cobblestone Cour Napoléon grew and Petit became more hustling errand boy than tyrannical overseer, she would drape her blazer over the back of her chair, and he either did not notice or no longer cared. He intrigued Cecile, with his gangly build and distracted stare, his imperious air and complete inability to command respect. "A stork with frustrated artistic aspirations," she called him to Minette, sharing a sandwich in the Jardin des Tuileries during Cecile's lunch break her first week. This spurred her friend to improvise a straight-backed, high-kneed gait, prancing around the park bench.

The sheer number of daily visitors surprised Cecile. It felt too normal—*beyond* normal, in fact, as though the previous years had not happened—yet unfamiliar all the same. She'd hear the buzzing languages of tourists from all across Europe, some from even farther away. Groups of GIs speckled the crowds. But mostly, it was fellow Frenchmen. During shifts as a *surveillante de sale*, she would survey their passage through the gallery she'd been assigned. They were often alone and always moved slowly, almost reverentially, from tableau to tableau. There appeared something redemptive in their faces, as though, in scrutinizing the classical works, they were gazing in a mirror, finding a grace they'd forgotten they had once possessed.

Cecile wasn't sure such self-satisfaction was earned. She too vividly recalled what they'd all been through—the whispered pettinesses and furtive persecutions, the betrayals.

The École du Louvre was in a remote part of the museum, the Aile de Flore, and she rarely had occasion to be in that corner of the grounds. Likewise, she rarely encountered any of the students. She'd imagined—naïvely, she now realized—that they might all form one big group, employees and students together, maybe even a few professors. But their very existence seemed more rumor than fact, so rarely did she encounter anyone from the school, and Cecile quit trying to cross paths with them after her first days on the job.

She saw Minette as often as she could, typically a few times each week, for lunch during her shift or a coffee after it, or when league affairs brought Minette to the quarter. Sometimes it was just her, at others her and friends—spirited girls and boys who Cecile tended to like. But Minette's activities remained a bit of a mystery, and Cecile wasn't always invited.

She hadn't moved into the city with the intention of becoming an artist. But with so many free evenings and now living in the "City of Art," she thought that she might be capable of it. She bought a tripod easel and set it up beside her window. With the radio she'd brought from Le Vésinet tuned into the Armed Forces Network—Glenn Miller and Benny Goodman and the Andrews Sisters—she sketched her room from various angles and did color studies. She bought more tubes of paint, and the color studies evolved into abstractions—slashes and streaks of overlay and form. Her "Sonia Delaunay phase," she jokingly thought of it.

Minette had introduced her to the AFN, claiming that it was the only station worth listening to and instructing her how to find it on the dial. How strange, Cecile thought, that someone who shouted her hatred of everything American could love so many American things, jazz and Hollywood and even these Andrews Sisters, with their staccato phrasing and cheery voices:

He puts the boys asleep with boogie every night
And wakes them up the same way in the early bright

Cecile continued with the abstractions for a time, trying to imbue them with meaning, as they must clearly be expressions of what she was feeling deep inside. But they meant very little to her beyond exercises, and besides, she had trouble naming the feelings.

Next, she attempted scenes from her memories: her bedroom at home; the façade of Institut du Bon Sauveur; Sunday table *chez* Mamie Lucie. Lucie and Georges had lived in a great two-storied stone house in Croissy-sur-Seine, one village over from Le Vésinet. Aunt Sylvie and Cousine Mathilde, their husbands and children, sometimes more distant cousins that Cecile barely knew—all would congregate at the long table in the dining hall, never for Shabbat and those rituals, just the typical family Sunday meal, at midday, with proper manners and in formal attire, each course served on the Tétard platters. Mamie Lucie's big voice carried over those of all the others, chiding the parents, indulging the children.

Cecile remembered lingering in the kitchen with the servants, Corinne and Clémence, beforehand while the adults had aperitifs. The girls would seat Cecile at one end of the long butcher block as they chopped vegetables and seared meat, teasing her and telling stories that Cecile laughed along with and that were clearly about her family, though she could never really follow the gist, the savory, wet smoke from the stovetop so thick she could taste it. Mamie Lucie would come find her. She'd direct the girls sharply then offer Cecile a sweet from the pantry.

Sculptures stood here and about on the lawn of the manor, in the parlor one of Picasso's *Harlequin* paintings that the adults oohed over. Lucie had passed her love of art to Cecile. Most precious to her were her Gauguins, of which she owned several. Her favorite, an original *Annah the Javanese*, hung in her bedroom.

"An artist sees what others cannot," she'd instructed, peering up at it. "Look how he idealizes—how he exalts, even—her dark skin. He's made the aboriginal graceful and beautiful."

Upon that first viewing, Cecile had merely seen a naked girl seated uncomfortably atop a blue fauteuil. Embarrassed by Annah's buoyant breasts and by the bold dispassion of the black triangle below, Cecile had almost missed the strange, distracted monkey seated at the girl's feet. After a few visits to see the painting, alone, not with her grandmother, the naked girl with full lips and a flat nose became more. She became textured colors and arcing lines; she became the conversation between shadow and light at play on her face; and in this way, she conjured in Cecile a desire for which she didn't have words. Whether it was the alluring unease evoked by the girl in the picture or a longing to be the person who'd aroused in her this emotion, Cecile could not know, as she hadn't yet at the time understood how to differentiate the two feelings. But thereafter, rather than cavort with her cousins or sneak off to be with the kitchen girls, more and more Cecile would sit on the stone benches in the garden, scratching lines on notepads, making rudimentary sketches.

Then came the war, then the German army. Lucie, between fits of tears, cursed Daddie Georges for his cowardice, blubbering that he'd been old and doddering and a fool for doing such a thing to himself, convinced that all would return to normal once the country accepted the German presence. A few days before they came for her, a band of masked men broke into the manor while Lucie sat alone, dining on the scraps that Cecile's father was able to scrounge up for her. The Picasso and Gauguins already gone, confiscated by the Germans, the bandits stole what remained and vandalized the rest. Lucie had told Cecile's father that one of them, as he was leaving, spat at her feet: "You're one lucky Yid to come away with your life." She'd said she recognized the voice as that of Philippe, the kitchen girl Clémence's husband.

Cecile wondered: How to capture that in a picture?

Minette had given Cecile very specific directions, but the family's flat was still hard to find. The neighborhood was all steep streets and leaning tenements and squat row houses with peeling stucco and gray metal shutters. The clack of wooden wheels laboring over cobbled stone; the sharp rawness of offal; gangs of children running pell-mell around horse-drawn wagons and between bicycle taxis: this was Minette's everyday world. Cecile found it strange and immediate, almost foreign—though not scary, like people said. She'd thought that she would see blacks and North Africans and maybe even some Indochinese, but no, not a one.

Turning up Rue Boyer, she passed a cobbler seated on a stool in his shop—a cubbyhole the size of her closet in Le Vésinet, with a hanging bulb overhead. He wore blue coveralls and a beret, a Gitanes hanging from his lips, and he leaned studiously over a boot that needed resoling. Cecile knew it was wrong, but she wished she had her sketchpad and pencils, or better still, one of those Argus Brick cameras that fit easily inside a purse. She could imagine Minette deriding her: "What? To document the lives of the exotic animals at the zoo?" Still, she wanted some way to capture the scene.

She found the nameless passage that Minette had described, between buildings numbered 28 and 26. It was long and narrow, without sun. Minette had told her that their ground-floor flat had no number but gave directly onto the alleyway, two doors in. Cecile knocked at what she hoped was the right one.

When the man who must have been Minette's father opened the door, his smile greeted her first, followed by a hug that lifted Cecile clear off the ground. "*Bonjour, ma fille!*" he said.

It was the first time Cecile had seen tribal scars—three parallel slashes on each cheek, darker than the dark of his skin. They surprised but didn't unsettle her in the least.

"*Bonjour,*" she replied. "I'm so sorry for intruding on your weekend with family."

He wore brown corduroy pants and a collared red shirt and was thick through the chest. "*Si'il te plaît,*" he pleaded, the scars arcing and shrinking as he spoke. "You're a sister to my daughter, and so you are a daughter to me."

Minette appeared beside him, just as tall, standing nearly shoulder to shoulder, and not at all diminished beside his husky width and booming voice. "*Ouais, fillette!*" she said. "You finally made it."

Aside from their shared height, though, she looked very little like her father, the African features softened—the lips not quite so thick; eyes almond-shaped but green; her wavy hair without the tight kinks.

Monsieur Traoré ushered Cecile inside with a wave of his hand, passing along to Minette the box of petit fours from Fauchon that she'd brought. Reputedly the best in the city, they cost half a week's salary but befitted the honor she felt at having been invited over. Minette disappeared through a door with the box while Cecile followed Monsieur Traoré to the front room—a cramped space with two facing sofas, a coffee table in between, and a stout armchair. And everywhere were books: rows of them on shelves that covered each wall, paperbacks and hardcovers, with individual volumes lying atop the shelved rows and even more stacked on the floor nearby. In Le Vésinet, first editions lined her parents' bookshelves, valuable for their rarity more than their content, and most were unread.

Monsieur Traoré gestured for Cecile to sit. "Minette tells me you're at École du Louvre and will be a famous artist."

"Me? Ha!" She had told Minette no such thing.

But she liked that Minette thought of her in this way. "I merely work at the museum," she said, adding, "though I hope to be admitted to the school one day."

"Stop being modest," said Minette, returning and taking a seat next to her father, on the sofa opposite Cecile. "She's brilliant, Papa. You should see her drawings."

The only ones Minette had seen were the doodles she'd done in *Gigi*, on the return from Hyères.

Monsieur Traoré, leaning over his lap toward her, elbows on knees, asked Cecile: "Tell me, who are your influences?"

"My influences?"

"The artists whose work you admire, the ones after whom you model your own work." His face was completely open. "Your teachers, really, because attempting to imitate others is how we ultimately learn, isn't it?"

Though she thought often about art and about artists, she hadn't considered it in this way. "My grandparents, I suppose," she said. "They weren't artists themselves, but they knew a little about it."

"Knew a little?"

"They were collectors." Admitting this embarrassed her, especially given the modesty of the Traoré home. But Monsieur Traoré seemed genuinely curious to know. "Of antiques, mostly, but they also owned some pieces. Those artists were my first influences."

"The Impressionists, that lot?" Monsieur Traoré asked. "Or even older still?"

"Picasso, a few Légers," said Cecile. "My grandfather was fond of Raoul Dufy."

She purposely omitted the Gauguins, though she wasn't sure why.

"Picassos," said Monsieur Traoré, sounding disappointed. "They're impossibly dear and completely overvalued, if you ask me."

"You think so?" Even though she found Picasso's style inaccessible, she recognized his genius. "You don't find merit in his work?"

"Oh, there's merit in it. For certain, he's done something new. But . . ." He paused in reflection, the arcing scars still.

Minette's silence, listening intently before and patiently waiting now, surprised Cecile. It was so unusual not hearing her voice an opinion.

Monsieur Traoré took up again: "When I first arrived in the city, those avant-gardists were all the rage—Picasso, Braque, their circle. I'll be frank, though: I never understood the allure. They deem African statuettes and masks noble, or more pure maybe, but they call them 'primitive' and miss the point completely. Those things aren't art but everyday objects. Sacred, yes, but in the way that life is sacred, just part of our day-to-day. His colonialist arrogance—ignorance, really—demystifies Picasso for me. The work seems more clever than smart."

For smart, Monsieur Traoré's analysis struck Cecile as brilliant and on point.

Her mind went from Picasso to Gaugin, the man Lucie had worshipped and had taught Cecile to, too. She recalled Annah the Javanese, staring alluringly back at the artist. How old had the model even been?

Cecile realized that she'd been duped into ignoring the fact that the painting was just of a seated child as helpless and exposed as the monkey at her feet.

"I understand that they're gone," Monsieur Traoré said, lowering his eyes. "Your grandparents, I mean. Please accept my deepest sympathies."

Minette lowered hers, too.

"Just know, *ma fille*, that death is only a curtain. The dead are on the other side"—he gestured, the sweep of his hand encompassing more than just the room—"watching."

The idea felt strangely comforting—not melancholy or sinister, the things she usually felt when she recalled Mamie Lucie and Daddie Georges.

A woman entered, barely as tall as the middle row of the bookcase, carrying a green tin tray with Cecile's petit fours laid out on a plate and a teapot in the shape of an elephant, steam rising from its upturned snout. "So, you're an artist," she said, abruptly joining the conversation, two beats behind. "It's good. Inspiring propaganda is a weapon in the struggle."

Minette didn't particularly look like this woman either, no more than she did her father. It wasn't just that the woman's complexion seemed so wan next to Minette's earthen amber. It was that Minette's eyes and mouth had shape and life where this woman's head and face might have been balled dough.

Maybe the aunt, thought Cecile, for how could beautiful Minette have a mother as bland as this?

The woman set the tray down on the coffee table. "Minette tells me you're *engagée*. What do you think of our 'esteemed' de Gaulle, then?" Before Cecile could respond, she raised a petit four–clutching fist. "He may be a hero to some, but I see him for what he truly is." Biting into the tiny cake, she spoke as she chewed. "Cozying up to the Americans? *Mais non, mon cher Général* . . . France will go the way of Hungary!"

She wasn't bland at all—anything but—such big brass coming from this small woman. Monsieur Traoré looked on adoringly, pink cake crumbs flecked across his dark lips.

A boy and girl entered—*café au lait*-colored like Minette, also beautiful—and crossed to a bookshelf, scrutinizing a particular row.

"And how is your homework coming, *mes chéris*?" Madame Traoré asked, distracted from her polemic.

Cecile seized the opportunity, whispering to Minette: "I see where you get your passion."

"Perhaps," Minette said. "But my values?" She tilted her head toward her father.

Madame Traoré left momentarily, returned with a large bowl, and sat it on the arm of the sofa. Monsieur Traoré came alive. "Cassoulet," he said, "what a treat!" He grabbed an unhinged door that was leaning in the corner, laid it over the top of the coffee table, and covered it with a cloth—*Et voila!*—the space transformed into a dining room. Cecile sat beside Minette on one sofa; the brother, Luc, and sister, Irène, on the other. Monsieur Traoré, in the armchair, made the top of the door the head of the table. Madame Traoré, on a kitchen chair at the other end, ladled large portions of the chunky stew onto plates.

Mealtime was frenetic with conversation, Monsieur Traoré challenging his wife and elder daughter, playfully more than at variance with their views, all of them speaking with their mouths full of half-chewed food. Now and again, Monsieur Traoré would toss up his hands theatrically, exasperated at something that had been said. "*Mais non!*" he would object, and turn to Cecile. "I suppose you side with them?"

Cecile would smile politely, demurring.

And how she wished for that Argus Brick (regardless of Minette's pillorying). Or a motion picture camera, to fully feature all the movement and sound: Minette, on her feet, insisting on a point; Monsieur Traoré's sculpted face, listening intently; Luc and Irène poking each other under the table, alternately smiling complicitly or feigning injury.

The raucousness went on long after seconds had been served and eaten, only waning when Luc and Irène looked utterly miserable, sitting deathly still, no longer fidgeting. Madame Traoré, lighting a cigarette, dismissed them from the table—"*Allez, allez!*"—and the children dashed from their chairs and through the door. She began clearing the dishes.

Cecile joined her, as her mother had taught her, grabbing her plate and those of the children.

In the kitchen—just a sink beside a narrow counter, an icebox in one corner and a tall stool in the other—Madame Traoré indicated with a nod where to deposit the dirty dishes. Cecile did, then returned for more in the other room (where Minette remained in fierce debate with her father, neither offering to help—in fact, quite the opposite: not even leaning aside so Cecile could readily reach their plates and cutlery).

"The stew was wonderful," she told Madame Traoré, back in the kitchen, holding the plates as there wasn't room for them on the counter. "Maman never makes homey recipes like this."

Madame Traoré released a rush of breath, almost a scoff: "Pff! In Le Vésinet? Of course she doesn't." Her cigarette bounced with each syllable. "No need to stretch a dozen into twoscore out there."

Cecile wondered if she should feel insulted. She for certain felt guilty, having inadvertently bad-mouthed her mother. Her intention had only been to compliment Madame Traoré.

"I met Souf when I was sixteen," Madame Traoré said, facing the sink, transferring dishes into the sudsy water. "He was nearly thirty and still suffering from the war. Shell shock, you understand. We married after two months. It was the best decision of my life."

"How beautiful," said Cecile, surprised by the disclosure—so personal, completely unexpected—and also a little unsettled. Sixteen? Older maybe than Annah the Javanese, but barely.

Madame Traoré indicated for Cecile to place the dishes in the space she'd cleared. Cecile did and then waited in silence a long moment, wondering if there would be more revelations. When it seemed not, she slipped out the door, into the other room.

Dessert was what was left of the petit fours, accompanied by tea from the tacky teapot. Madame Traoré smoked cigarette after cigarette, staring vacantly out the sheer curtains (though there was nothing to see but the other side of the alleyway), as Monsieur Traoré and Minette continued their back-and-forth. It unnerved Cecile—Madame Traoré's abrupt confession and disengagement now, insipidly smiling as she sipped Earl Grey from one of the mismatched cups.

Cecile became suddenly aware of her own silence, of her deferential smile, of their lacking. She couldn't help but associate them with the other thing she shared with Madame Traoré—their skin, whiteness, the absence of color.

Cecile's growing unease compelled her to jump in, mid-debate: "*Mais non*, Monsieur Traoré! After all the strife these past years, all the hatred and division, maybe the country needs someone, anyone—maybe even de Gaulle—to bring us together."

Both he and Minette stared in response—just silently stared.

Madame Traoré smirked, as though Cecile's comment confirmed something she had beforehand presupposed.

Cecile's life had been difficult. She knew herself to have been maltreated, too, but maybe not maltreated enough by comparison, and she feared that, with her remark, she'd ruined it—this connectedness, the kinship that had developed with Minette's family. Minette's flashing anger—"Don't be an imbecile!"—seemed to confirm it.

But Monsieur Traoré patted Minette's arm, and she stopped.

"At whose expense, *ma fille*?" he said to Cecile, his eyes soft, even as the question implied something sharper. "It's always those on the lowest rung, the poor and people from the colonies, who suffer when the nation aims to come together like this. There has to be a scapegoat, or the country would only have itself to blame for its troubles."

He crossed to Cecile, took her hands in between his thick and callused ones. "It's us, with justice on our side, who will create a new France."

He seemed to include her in the "us" and she felt relief.

"Yes," she said. "But of course."

Madame Traoré rose and left the room.

CHAPTER FIVE

On the ground floor of the *pension* was a restaurant that served inexpensive meals to lodgers. Most were students, a hodgepodge of bourgeois types, uptight and neat, the girls long and lean, the boys clean-shaven. There was also a spattering of boys from the colonies—just boys, no girls. They were courteous, studious, and solitary. Standing in line to enter one evening in early summer, she heard a vaguely familiar voice, grave and throaty and rich: "I like what you've done with your hair."

She turned to find the African boy from the youth conference, Seb. He was nicely dressed, elegant, even if his jacket and pants were a bit worn.

"You don't remember me," he said, his voice less sure now, his face shadowing.

"Of course, I do," she said, and his face opened again. How white his smile! She remembered his face doing this very thing in the nighttime dark in Hyères, when he laughed at something that had been said.

Seeing him in daylight, she noted that he didn't have tribal scars like Monsieur Traoré did, and she wondered why.

She asked, "Do you live here, too?"

"No, but not too far away. At a rooming house by the Panthéon, at the top of Rue de la Montagne Sainte-Geneviève." He quickly added: "I have friends who live here, though."

She perched a hand over her brow, making a playful show of looking about for them.

"They're out," he said. "You're alone? Shall we sit together?"

They took a table by the window. Each ordered pot-au-feu, the daily special.

Cecile asked, "So, you have the day off from work?"

"I quit accepting shifts," he said, "until after the entrance exam."

"The *concours*?" Competitions for admission to the Grandes Écoles, the country's top universities, typically took place in the spring. "Haven't they already been held?"

"It's a special seating, at the beginning of September. Beaux-Arts is still trying to make up for the wartime disruptions."

"Beaux-Arts!" The most renowned art school in the world. Monet studied there. Renoir, too. She was happy for him, and also a little bit jealous.

She asked, "So, you paint or draw or . . ." Another thing in common between them.

"I want to become an architect," he said. "But I never had the chance to finish my *Bac*." He looked embarrassed, dropping his eyes. "The war, you understand."

The Beaux-Arts exam was among the toughest—tougher even than the one his sister had passed, for École de Médecine. Without a high school degree, she wondered how he imagined being able to compete.

"I'm sure you'll do well," she said. "*Quand on veut, on peut.*"

It sounded trite, even to her own ear.

"I attempted the test a year ago," he confessed, "but didn't make it past the first day, general education." He shifted in his seat. "I was preparing during my off hours from work, you see. But this time, I study daily, especially during this final stretch—all day long."

The waiter brought their dishes. The broth smelled richly of beef, but the bowl was all turnips and carrots, a gelatinous sheen floating along the top.

"This is what meat stew looks like when there's no meat," Seb said.

"They even dared to place a bone in mine," said Cecile. She lifted it out with her fork: striated white; no marrow at the core.

They laughed but plunged in. He offered her the breadbasket. She took a piece.

She recalled him telling her about an exacting father, a strict older sister. "I could help you," she said. He was clearly a smart boy. How much trouble could it be? "If you'd like a study partner, I mean."

"It's kind of you to offer. Boubi—my friend you met—studies literature at Paris V and is supposed to talk me through his notes."

He looked discomfited.

"Has he not followed through?"

"Not yet, no. He's so smitten with the *métisse* girl . . ."

"Minette?" Cecile didn't know that she'd been seeing Boubi.

Seb nodded, his face seeming to pinch at the thought of her, and for the first time his smile concealed more than it revealed. "It's hard for him to find time."

"Well, I have plenty of it, after work," she said. "For general education, things like that—it would just be rehashing old material for me, the stuff we learned in *lycée*."

His face opened again. "I'd like that. Thank you."

Both sopped up the last of the broth from their bowls with pieces of bread. When the waiter returned, Seb insisted she have dessert. "You've lost weight since I first saw you and look a little pale."

"Thanks a lot!"

"I didn't say you don't look good. I was just voicing concern for your well-being."

She found herself dropping her eyes.

Each had a slice of tarte tatin, he grabbed the check and paid for both meals, and they agreed to meet again soon.

Cecile called Minette from the telephone box in the lobby to tell her about the encounter.

"Seb, did you say? Do I know him?"

"From Hyères," Cecile pressed. "Boubi's friend."

"Ah, Boubi," Minette said, her voice feathered with affected pity, "the one who won't learn to not crowd me."

How could Minette not remember? Cecile wondered. She removed another coin from her change purse despite the line forming outside the box.

"Seb, huh?" said Minette. "Not so tall, thick through the chest, as dark as the tread of a tire?"

It wasn't a particularly flattering description.

"That's him," Cecile said. "Maybe you could arrange a get-together, the four of us?"

And Minette did—dinner at Boubi's place, for that Friday. He lived just past Bastille in a building without a concierge. Cecile found her way down the long and unlit hallway to the back stairs, then up to the third floor, number 305. She wore denims, with Minette in mind, but a lavender cardigan over a frilly white blouse, with Seb in mind, too.

Minette answered her knock, in a dress Cecile hadn't seen before, sky blue and cinched at the waist. Cecile couldn't remember seeing her in anything other than trousers, in fact. She hugged Cecile. "*Et voila!* All of us arrived."

Boubi was in shirtsleeves and an apron, and he and Cecile kissed cheeks four times. Seb offered his hand, a formal sort of greeting, but he smiled the smile she remembered from the hotel restaurant. He was dressed in corduroys and a dark jacket—sober but stylish.

The char of pan-fried fish filled the one-room flat, the sharp smell of piri piri tickling up a sneeze in the back of Cecile's nose. Fresh fish was impossible to find and horribly overpriced if you did, but Boubi had come up with two small carp and, on a hot plate on his dresser, cooked a traditional dish that he called Tjéboudienne. He told them that his mother often made the recipe and that it reminded him of Dakar.

The four of them sat on stools around the tabletop Boubi had made of his bed. Minette, her lips shining from the palm oil and licking her fingertips, teased: "So you think this meal will rouse up the Senegalese in me? Is this how you court a girl?"

Seb chuckled, and Boubi shot back: "Don't *you* dare laugh. It was you, was it not, who was lying in wait for that one?"

Boubi pointed toward Cecile. Seb's face froze.

Minette goaded Boubi: "Go on."

"Why, he'd spotted her at the hotel a few days before—"

"It was complete happenstance," said Seb, "truly."

"—and he waited out on the street for the opportunity to ambush her in the lobby."

"Aw," Minette said. "Isn't that charming?"

By her tone, it was clear she didn't find it to be, even as Cecile, who blushed, did.

The evening passed in this way—too quickly for Cecile—with teasing and laughter, and with stories about Africa, the boys' home. Boubi's memories were big and boisterous, full of color: the baobab under which his father and uncles gathered to smoke thin reed pipes and palaver; his mother in a pagne dress, carrying on her head a weave basket with vegetables and fruit from the market; the terra-cotta walled compound that housed his elementary school and the chaos of all the children. Seb was more reserved, a sort of melancholy suffusing the few anecdotes he told—a strict, laconic father; a smiling but fragile mother; aunts who instructed traditions. Even Minette reminisced about the place, though she'd never been and only knew of Africa what her father had told her.

For her part, Cecile remained mostly silent. She didn't want to make herself an easy target, as she had at the Traorés', especially being the only white person in the room. Although Cecile had only just met Minette's family, Madame Traoré had harbored clear convictions about who Cecile was and was not: a rich bourgeoise; blandly white; conventionally *française*. But who was she to sit in judgment of Cecile? (Much less of Cecile's mother!) The bombastic windbag spouted political rhetoric, but it no more made her a militant than the elephant teapot made her African, or anything more than merely a wife, serving others.

After dessert (a tin of grocery store cookies that Cecile had brought, having learned her lesson about Fauchon), she and Minette rinsed the dishes at the sink in the corner while the boys shared a cigarette at the room's single window, blowing smoke out into the night. Minette handed her a plate, gesturing toward Seb with a look. "Are you happy, then?"

Cecile dried the dish, trying to conceal her smile. "It's been a terrific evening."

Minette handed her another. "Well, we're not done yet." She called toward the boys. "Boubi, didn't you say you'd received an envelope from home? *Allez*, then, a nightcap at the Danton! Some friends are gathering there."

The Danton, at Place de l'Odéon, was a workingman's café, loud, its zinc bar lined with laborers in blue coveralls, the platter-sized tables around the room bunched with leftist students. The garçons wore the traditional black waistcoat and long white apron and were as peevish as the ones at the Deux Magots, down the boulevard, where famous intellectuals lounged with their wealthy patrons and fawning toadies. Cecile's group crowded around a table with Minette's friends, whom Cecile recognized from a previous rendezvous here: a Ponts et Chaussées student named Jean-François; a girl, Laure; and her boyfriend, Salim.

Boubi held up an envelope, several hundred-franc banknotes visible through the slit-opened crease. "When the postman deigns to finally deliver the mail," he announced, "money arrives from Dakar." He called to a waiter who was rushing past: "A round of *demies*, my treat!"

The garçon brought the glasses of headless and flat one-percent beer. The government had ordered that all grains considered *panifiables*— breadable—be supplied first and foremost to bakers, the unbreadable barley included, leaving very little for brewers. The murky, biting one-percenter was what resulted.

Jean-François, in a red cardigan over a yellow shirt (a nod to his political affiliation), peered into his glass, exasperated. "The Frenchman and his baguette! What price won't he pay to keep one on each table?"

"Pass that here, then," Laure shot back, "if it's not to your liking."

"Should you even be drinking?" Minette said. "Didn't you convert?"

"I've decided on Islam, yes," Jean-François said, "in solidarity with our North African brothers. Conversion, though, is for a later date."

Jean-François held an unlit cigarette—one of his "discards"—between two fingers. He gathered up unfinished butts whenever he found them and collected what tobacco remained, to be rerolled into thin though normal-length sticks after he'd accumulated enough.

Salim rolled himself one from Jean-François's tobacco pouch, which lay in the center of the table. "The Koran *does* have a thing or two to say about the consumption of alcohol," he warned, taking a long drink then lighting the discard with Jean-François's Zippo. "Me, I missed that lesson at the mosque."

"Clearly," said Laure, squeezed beside Cecile, also helping herself to Jean-François's pouch.

The coarse tobacco burnt pungent, like chocolate smoke, filling Cecile's nose and mouth. Though she rarely partook, she was tempted to then.

"Let's go to Le New York," Minette said, placing her mostly full glass on the tabletop and pushing away. "Good music there, I hear—and better beer, for sure."

Le New York Diner, on a side street off the Champs-Elysées, was one of several cafés turned American soda fountain, opened by entrepreneurial Parisians who hoped to profit off the GI presence in the capital. Very hip, very in.

Jean-François spat a dismissive puff of air but joined the others, rising. Cecile took a long swallow of her one-percenter, attempting to finish it out of respect for Boubi's generosity. Then she glanced toward Seb, suddenly self-conscious at her bad manners—gulping down her glass like a bulbous-nosed drunkard, as her mother would say. Unladylike.

Seb was gulping down his own, likewise glancing at her, also embarrassed and apologetic. He dabbed the corner of his mouth with a finger and, in that moment, like her, felt that their eyes had fully engaged, truly meeting.

The group capered down Boulevard Saint-Germain, Minette and Cecile out front, arm in arm, skipping and giggling. This drew the attention

of men passing by. But when Cecile looked back, Seb's attention was fixed
on Salim and whatever he was saying, pretending not to notice—though
he had, in fact. Even when Cecile was aping her showboating friend, Seb
found himself drawn to her, to her sincerity, to an earnestness that she
seemed incapable of disguising, however much she tried.

Once the group crossed the Seine, the array of their skin tones provoked a different sort of stare—disapproving and cold, typical of the stuffy
Right Bank. Cecile and Minette strode forward, bumptious, Cecile affect-
edly pshawing the leer of a man in a bowler hat, out walking his *chouchou*,
Minette's laughter serving as a chorus. At Le New York, too: the place
was packed with GIs who gaped as they entered, disdain as heavy on the
air as the smell of frying grease. The American soldiers, huddling over
tabletops, seemed to be speculating in lurid detail about who among the
group was doing what with whom.

Brassy bebop blared from box speakers in the corners. All the swivel
chairs skirting the long counter were occupied by French boys in plaid
shirts and suspenders, yammering at their girlfriends in knee-length skirts
and flat-soled gym shoes, hair pulled tight into ponytails—the latest fad, à
l'américaine. The group squeezed into one of the few free red-vinyl booths.

Jean-François pointed toward the GIs. "Why are they even still here?"

Boubi said, "Why, to impart the wisdom of American abundance,
of course. Didn't you know?"

The joke fell flat.

"Look at them," said Jean-François. "They don't speak two words of
French and say idiotic things aloud, as though we French don't understand
English."

"That we don't bathe," said Laure. "That we girls wear trousers to
hide our hairy legs."

"Here!" Minette threw one of hers onto the tabletop, revealing a
calf. "For their enjoyment."

Laure played at rubbing it longingly.

"Seriously," Jean-François said. "It's a second occupation, as vile as
the one before."

He said "occupation" louder than the rest of what he'd spoken, though none of the Americans seemed to understand. But Cecile thought: Really? As vile as that? She stiffened in her seat.

Seb, beside her, offered a gentle smile that suggested empathy with her reaction, though she hadn't spoken it aloud.

"Their presence here evens things," Salim said. "This is how the French behave in my home."

Jean-François was silent then, looking into his lap.

Minette said, "Americans! They're the grandsons of outcasts, of prisoners and whores, no different than the Australians, and no better. Gangsters run the government and starving children beg for pennies at the feet of women in furs."

Seb leaned his lips to Cecile's ear—closer than he'd intended. "Wasn't it her idea to come here?"

"It was," she said. "Minette can be mercurial."

Both watched as Boubi nabbed a passing waitress, in a fitted white dress—like the kids at the counter, also à l'américaine. He ordered four bottles of Coca-Cola and seven straws, which was met with boos and hisses from their booth. Cecile and Seb joined in, sharing a conspiratorial smile.

"I have to save money for the rest of the month!" Boubi pleaded. "I have to eat!"

Turning back toward her, Seb whispered, "Night in Tunisia."

Cecile faced him. "But I thought you said you were from Dahomey?"

"The music," he said, pointing to the speakers. "It's the name of the song."

The horns, the vigorous rhythm. It made her think not so much of a souk or the kasbah but of New York, though she'd never been there either—what she imagined Harlem to be.

The neighboring GIs stared as the group passed the four bottles around the table. When one got to Jean-François, he dipped his straw in and turned toward them and raised the bottle in toast. "*Vive la Coca-colonization* of France!" he said, half in French, half in English.

"*Vive la Coca-colonization*," Minette echoed, taking the bottle and finishing the rest. "Now come fuck yourselves with it," she said in French, smiling broadly toward the GIs.

The Americans returned it, forced "You're welcome's" to the presumed "Thank you."

"Night in Tunisia" ended, and someone changed the record—the scraping sound of needle meeting groove. Another began, this one with singing. Cecile didn't recognize it either. The woman's voice was a controlled quaver, sultry all the same. After years of school lessons plus a holiday trip to London before the war, she followed the lyrics easily.

> *The evening breeze*
> *Caressed the trees*
> *Tenderly . . .*

"It's the American Negro Sarah Vaughan," Seb said, placing his lips next to her ear again, consciously this time, skin nearly meeting skin.

Cecile didn't know who Sarah Vaughan was, but her voice made Cecile feel warm. Or was it *his* voice, just as liquid as the singer's?

She leaned in closer. Seb raised his arm, accommodating her beneath it. As in Hyères, outside the dorm room window and just before the kiss, he could smell her musk.

CHAPTER SIX

"Tell me about your home."

Seb heard Cecile more than he could see her, nude on his bed but blanketed by the near dark of the room. Still, he imagined the details of her: those eyes; cheeks like pulsing suns; the mouth that made him think of fruit—mangoes, papaya, flavors that he hadn't tasted in so long he couldn't rightly recall the actual tastes but that he craved all the same.

"Tell me what it's like," she said, and he responded: "My home is the center of the Earth, the mother of everything. The deep greenness and wet heat. Rich colors like you've never seen."

That much he remembered.

Cecile shifted, resting her head on his rising and falling chest.

Seb and his sister lived in adjoining rooms, and the thought of her look, were she to discover Cecile here with him, caused him to drop his voice another register.

"The silence isn't like the silence here, automobile engines and the murmur of too many people living on top of one another. It's the drumbeat rhythm of tall women with babies tied to their backs, standing in threes around a wooden mortar and pounding manioc to pulp with long-stemmed pestles. Their song makes the nearby children dance. Bats as big as loaves of country bread hang like ornaments from branches, waiting for night to fall."

These memories, though—they might be manufactured reminiscence more than actual remembering. What was left, after all, after fifteen years gone?

But he liked that Cecile evoked this in him.

They'd been meeting at the Café Tournon beside the Jardin du Luxembourg evenings after her shift, a midway point between her rooming house and his. They reviewed material that might be on the entrance exam, Cecile illuminating various areas of general education and art history, then afterward—as on the night of Boubi's Tjéboudienne—this.

"Dahomey," she repeated, echoing his pronunciation—though not as softly as he would have liked, despite his warning about his sister next door.

She sat up, pulling the sheet to cover herself, uncovering him. "The name of your home is almost the same as your own."

Even in July, the sharp night air chilled his bared skin to gooseflesh. "They're one and the same," he whispered. "With an *x* is the ancient version. The different spelling makes for a slightly different pronunciation."

"What does it mean?"

"In the belly of Dan," he said, and her silence told him that she didn't follow.

He'd expected she wouldn't be able to. He began the story the way he remembered Zansi—his sister Jacqueline—would when they were children, newly arrived, and she would talk him to sleep.

"In the beginning was the Leopard, ruler of all the beasts of the forest." Zansi had always spoken very formally, as though the subject matter necessitated it, and he did now, too. "He wanted to extend his power over man as well, so one night he mated with a princess from the Tado kingdom. Together, they made Agasu."

"A-ga SOO?"

"Agasu, yes. Part man, part leopard. Agasu married and had three sons, all man. Each left Tado and moved toward the east, one settling to rule in Porto-Novo, another in Allada, the third, named Dacodonu, going north of there. The king of the land he came upon was called Dan."

"Not Dan short for Daniel, I suppose?"

Seb laughed. "No. This was centuries ago, well before the priests brought their saints. Dan's kingdom traded in slaves, selling them to Allada, who would shepherd them down to the coast. Dan granted Dacodonu plots upon which to establish himself and his Leopard-descended people, and when Dacodonu returned and asked for more, Dan gave it to him. Dacodonu came back a third time, asking for more land still, and Dan teased the young prince about his insatiable appetite."

Seb mimicked a chiding voice the way Zansi would back then: "'Even if I bestowed upon you my entire kingdom, you wouldn't be satisfied until you'd built upon my very own stomach.' When Dacodonu led an army against Dan, he didn't exile the defeated king or sell him to the coast. He struck him down, slit him open, and built the royal palace in the belly of Dan."

"Oh . . ." he heard, Cecile's voice troubled.

He imagined her face, which was tender despite her plays at toughness. She could as easily look pained as pleased, and both expressions called out to him. "It's just a legend," he said, apologetically, "the story our elders tell."

She said nothing.

To staunch the silence, he continued: "The descendants of Dacodonu reigned over Dahomey from the palace in Dan's belly for two hundred fifty years, until the French finally conquered Gbéhanzin, my grandfather, and established colonial rule."

"Your grandfather sold slaves, too?" she asked.

Many, many, Seb thought. All the Dahomey kings did, over more than two centuries.

He rolled, turning his back. He didn't want to have to apologize for things for which he didn't feel accountable. He *did* want her to understand, though.

"Here's how my father told us. Yes, our forefathers sold slaves, but there wouldn't have been any to sell if it hadn't been for the *Yovo* markets that demanded them."

It didn't seem any more satisfactory an explanation than when his father had used it, and Seb heard in his own voice the very defensiveness he was trying to avoid.

Seb's memory of his father was impressionistic, more shifting images than a set picture. He vaguely recalled a shadow of dark face and rectitude, in a European business suit and tie, even there in the heavy heat of Dahomey. His father was an intellectual and a journalist. Seb knew that he'd founded an anti-colonialist newspaper, but he didn't know much more than this, not even the name of it.

The rumble of his father's voice, scolding, returned clearly, though: "In everything you do, you must make Dahomey always greater!" He would accept nothing less. Admission to the best universities, that was the outward assignment, explicitly stated. But success at school wasn't enough. Seb and Zansi were expected to prevail, to make France take note. He must become the first African to construct skyscrapers, and she, the first Dahomeyan to cure an incurable disease. "To prove to the *Yovo* that we are not savages," his father had insisted.

And it troubled Seb. For didn't the emphasis on distinguishing one-self in this way not have, in fact, the opposite effect, didn't it confirm the assumptions that such a distinction presumed? To be the first of a group to accomplish something that ones from other groups had already achieved—didn't the belated success merely verify that a lag had previously existed? And wasn't this supposed lag—a consequence of their "savagery," of their lack of civilization—the rationalization for the colonial conquest to begin with and of their continued subordination? This chasing after validation from the *Yovo*—there was something abject in it.

Seb said none of this. But, as though she could see his thoughts, Cecile asked, "*Yovo*?"

"European," he explained. "Or white, I guess."

He felt her stiffen, though she didn't say anything more. Then he felt her warmth pushing into his back, the softness of her breasts.

The next thing he would say, eventually, was that it was late, that they both had obligations in the morning. They would dress and slip down the stairs, and he would walk her through the quiet Quartier latin to her hotel.

He recognized the knock at his door early the next morning: a firm rap-RAP, ending decidedly on the second. Zansi poked her head in before he could respond. "Aren't you ready yet?"

He stood at his closet, buttoning his shirt. "In just a minute."

Zansi's eyes scanned the room, the textbooks strewn about the floor, the untamed piles of papers on the desk. He wondered if the mussed sheets betrayed the secret of his night with Cecile.

He didn't meet his sister's eyes. "I'll be out directly," he insisted.

The door clicked closed.

He'd noted that Zansi was wearing the light cardigan she'd knit herself and a beret—simple but elegant. He pulled on his navy sports coat, the more casual of the three he owned. He knew he should wear a tie, to match her level of formality, but didn't feel like it. He stepped out into the hall.

She started down the staircase. "We can't be late. It's a very important meeting."

He passed her, bounding down two steps at a time. "We won't be."

Outside, the streets were as quiet as sleep, the afternoon heat a blanket. They rounded the Panthéon, the shrine to France's *distingués*—the citizens who had brought honor to the country. Seb surged ahead. He knew she wouldn't want to walk this fast, as it would cause her to arrive at M'Bokolo's apartment in a sweat and looking harried—not the proper appearance for the recently elected first president of the African Students' Union of Francophone Colonies, the ASUFC. And he knew that she knew what he was doing, dashing forward as though he also felt compelled to be on time. He did it anyway.

"You nervous?" he asked, walking backward in order to face her.

"Me?" She was as tall as any man on the street and kept a determinedly dignified pace, allowing herself to fall behind—though not by much. "Hardly," she said.

M'Bokolo responded to Zansi's knock at his third-floor flat on Boulevard Saint-Germain, greeting them with an exaggerated bow. "Ah! Mademoiselle le Docteur Danxomè and her brother, the young regent. Please, come in."

Unlike French women, Zansi didn't kiss anyone in greeting, not even her brother. Offering her hand to shake, she said, "I'm not a doctor yet, and frankly, what's left to rule of our humble colony? The crowds of men lining up for work tickets? The indigenous football clubs that play against the colonial troops?"

Today, even her levity was earnest, more pointed than playful.

M'Bokolo was a doctoral student in chemistry, one of only a few Africans in his program, the son of one of the first European-trained physicians in the Congo, from the capital Brazzaville and not the bush—all facts he was quick to let others know. "But this is precisely the problem that the young regent here will remedy, *n'est-ce pas*, son of Gbéhanzin?" He slapped Seb on the back. "You're the infant shark who, like your grandfather, will chase the French out of all of our seas!"

Seb slipped by and tried to meld in with the twenty or so others gathered in the dining room and adjoining study. There were more present than he'd expected, a nod to the authority that his sister commanded. He spotted Boubi, in a blazer and tie that looked new.

"*Salut*," he said.

They shook.

"*Salut*—" Boubi held on a beat too long, with a mocking smile, "—young regent."

Seb looked over at M'Bokolo. The silly bows and put-on respect—he was all airs and affect. Even after two years in Paris, M'Bokolo couldn't adjust to not having a houseboy to pick up after him.

Where Zansi and Seb lived in a rooming house filled mostly with students and day laborers from the countryside, M'Bokolo lived in an apartment that was of the scion of an African family of means. There was a dining room (though cluttered with piles of unwashed clothes and random objects), separate from the kitchen (sink full of dirty dishes); a proper *salle de bain*, with detached WC (filthy); and two airy bedrooms full of light (the latter for his mother and father, when they visited). At their rooming house, the WC was in the hallway, a shower closet on every other floor, and both he and Zansi kept a gas-fired hotplate in their rooms to warm water for tea or tins of soup, or to grill day-old bread.

Zansi supplemented her meager monthly stipend from the scholarship she'd won with occasional work in the religious bookstore at École de la Sainte-Famille, where she'd sheltered during the war. After Seb failed his previous try at the Beaux-Arts competition—the year before, the first seating after the Occupation—the nuns had agreed to hire him, too. This was their sole source of income. Their father's troubles with the colonial administration kept him from earning enough to send anything, though occasionally a few banknotes would lie in the folds of a letter.

"Let's start," Zansi said, standing at the head of the dining room, removing documents from her leather satchel.

M'Bokolo said, "But Mademoiselle la Presidente, we're still missing Tal Amahdou, Soummomi Kali, Sylvestre Diallo, several others."

"We decided last time," said Zansi, "that if we're going to be a serious political organization and not just a social club, then we must behave as one."

"Indeed," a voice from the group teased, "just like the colonizers, prompt and punctual."

"*Indeed*," she shot back, not in the least bit cowed—and not one whit less serious. "That is, if we intend to attain the goals we've set for ourselves and for our continent."

As members of a dissident political organization, they risked harassment by the authorities, maybe even deportation. All of them understood this. So, Zansi's gravity brought them to order.

Most of the other members of the ASUFC were from Senegal, the Ivory Coast, and Congo. Only a few hailed from Dahomey. Yet, when some members had mumbled concerns about such a hodgepodge of ethnic backgrounds during the initial meeting, Zansi had cited a Dahomeyan proverb in response: "Why bother trying to separate the cold water from the hot?"—suggesting that they were all brothers, weren't they? Her election as president soon followed.

M'Bokolo had glad-handed everyone he could in order to be named secretary and in this way to save face at having lost the presidency to a woman—one of the very few women in the group.

At the previous meeting, they'd settled the question of whether or not to ally themselves with the Communist Party. (No, as Zansi had argued all along; she called their youth wing the Young Bolsheviks and thought its members pranksters and political reactionaries—*pas sérieux*, maybe even dangerous. Seb and Boubi's report about their uninspiring trip to the conference in Hyères had brought the others to her opinion.) The sole point on the agenda at this meeting now was how to counter the recent attack from the Ministry of Education. The minister was pushing for legislation that would force African students to pursue postsecondary education *only* at the inferior and terribly underfunded university in Dakar. The ASUFC understood this to be a ploy to keep them out of the country and thereby squelch the voice of their budding anti-colonialist movement.

As M'Bokolo began a punctilious reading of the minutes, Boubi and Seb sat side by side in folding chairs toward the back of the room. Boubi whispered, "How goes your exam prep?"

"I'm still waiting for some help from you on that score," Seb whispered back.

"Your *Toubab* girl is giving you all the help you need," he said, smiling knowingly. "Or so I've heard anyway."

Toubab, the Wolof word for *Yovo*: his white girl.

Boubi was the only person there who knew about Cecile, and Seb didn't want this public forum to be the way that Zansi found out about the relationship. He threw Boubi a look that he hoped would silence him.

Strangely, though, Seb also felt an echo of warmth in his chest to hear it said aloud: "*his* girl."

Cecile was his first—not his first intimacy, but the first girl he was with who he wanted to see more than once, who he wanted to get to know, and who he wanted to know him, deeply, closely. The ones before Cecile did not care to, even had he attempted to reveal something of himself. They were girls he'd sought out in the alleyways above Pigalle or the bars at Place de Clichy, infrequently though more than a few times. He would hunch his neck in the turned-up collar of his jacket and bury his hands in his pockets and offer his coin to whichever one did not look hurriedly away or betray her revulsion with a leer or bray to the other *cocottes* along the street about the droll sight of "a black" coming on to a French girl.

Being with Cecile made him forget those hateful encounters. Her presence in his life calmed his malaise about his own presence in France. Telling her his stories helped him to better remember them, which helped root him back there, back home, despite the many years away, despite the great distance. He recognized the fact that she was *Yovo*—French, not African, not Dahomeyan—and that Zansi would disapprove, a proxy for their father's disapproval. So, he kept the relationship a secret, basking privately in the light and heat that Cecile cast on his darker places.

Boubi stared at him, awaiting a reply, but even with Boubi, Seb preferred not to disclose too much. He pointed to his friend's new clothes instead. "Nice."

Boubi slid a finger along the length of his tie, to show off the pattern. "One needs finery when attempting to lure fine company."

"The *métisse*?"

"Her, yes, and others too. I'm a man of varied appetites," Boubi said, though it sounded more bluster than substance.

Zansi's voice interrupted them: "Boubacar, you're a belletrist." She was glaring directly at them. "Maybe you could take charge of drafting the letter to the minister."

Both Seb and Boubi sat up straight, eyes on their laps, like schoolboys called out in class.

"*Oui*, Jacqueline," Boubi said. "Of course."

"We'll need it, as I'm sure you just heard, as soon as possible."

"*Oui*, Jacqueline."

Zansi resumed her address to the larger group, and Seb slunk down in his seat, sure that all eyes remained fixed on him. He raised his own when it seemed safe to.

M'Bokolo, the sycophantic stooge, was still attempting to reprimand him with a scowl. Seb looked past him.

CHAPTER SEVEN

Seb walked more casually on the return. He and Zansi took the long way, over to Rue de la Montagne Sainte-Geneviève and up the steep hill, headed toward their neighborhood grocery. Zansi insisted that they share at least one meal daily, even if just breakfast. The meals were never much. How extravagant could they be, with only a hot plate and not even a proper table to serve the food on? But she'd said that, this way, at least they'd be able to keep up with each other's lives, sister and brother, despite their many other obligations.

Though École de Médecine had let out for the summer, Zansi maintained a daily study schedule all the same, and she made sure that Seb did likewise, as the entrance competition was just six weeks away. If he was to succeed—to be the first Dahomeyan accepted to Beaux-Arts, the first West African to penetrate the insular field of French architecture—then he must work as hard as she did. Though never directly stated, it was understood.

Zansi was good at everything and assumed he was, too. This was not bearing out.

The *concours*: his first pass at it, the year before, had taken place too soon after the turmoil of the war. He'd made an excuse of glitches in the system—insufficient advising, confusing logistics—as factors in his poor result. But he knew that, above all, he'd botched the preparation. He'd worked hard, but haphazardly. Given his stunted schooling, just navigating the library stacks had been foreign to him. Though his sister might not appreciate it, Cecile's help this time around was a godsend.

Zansi strolled leisurely alongside Seb, matching his pace, hands clasped behind her back, but her thoughts were clearly still on the meeting. She said, "I hope Boubacar won't procrastinate. Our timing couldn't be worse, with the August closures upcoming."

Seb felt compelled to defend his friend. "He'll get it done. And maybe the timing is perfect. Now that the Socialists have forced the Communists out of the government, maybe they'll see approving a straightforward and just request as an easy way to gain popular support from a constituency that they're losing."

She stopped, staring quizzically at him, and he recognized how naïve he must sound. "Seriously?" she said. "Do you honestly think Auriol and Ramadier respect colonized Africans enough to care whether any will support them? Socialist or no, they're still French, Kannou."

Kannou, short for Kannoukpô. Their aunt Fifonsi had named him this at birth. In Fon, their mother tongue, it meant "The rope is not yet at its end!"—our lineage is not near finished. Their father insisted on the use of their Christian names, but Zansi (named "Born during the night" by Fifonsi) made a point to call him by the traditional one when it was just the two of them, as likewise he did her.

She continued: "The president and PM mistake all of us colonized for Communists anyway. They didn't send Leclerc to Indochina to garner local support and muster up votes."

At the corner, they paused to let a bicycle taxi pass. The back cart was empty, but still the cyclist struggled to get up the steep, steep hill. When he'd cleared them, they strolled ahead.

"I got a letter from Father," Zansi said.

"What does he say?"

"He was wondering at the lack of news. Well, at the lack of news about you." Then she confessed: "I wrote him about the education minister and our possible counteractions, but he reproached me for distracting you from your test prep."

Zansi, on the wrong end of their father's anger for a change? It was usually him.

Even irritated, she was always formal, her voice measured. "He fights colonialism at home, he creates a newspaper for that express purpose, but for us to get involved . . . I guess I expected him to be proud."

"Will you write him back?"

"Maybe you should instead. He complains that he never hears from you."

Seb didn't relish the task. He never knew what to say to their father.

They arrived at the Alimentaire Générale, the neighborhood store that sold a little of everything. Zansi didn't enter but stopped in front of the door and faced him.

"Whatever else Father may have gotten wrong, in one thing he was right. We're here, you and I, for just one thing, to make Dahomey always greater."

He didn't respond. What was there to say? He was working as hard as he could.

"I worry about you is all," she continued. "To succeed on this exam will demand a single-minded focus in the time that remains. I know you like Boubacar, I like him too. I just worry that some of his friends are a bad influence."

Zansi didn't know Cecile personally, as far as he could tell—and certainly she didn't know about Cecile and him. If she did, she would be making his life miserable. By Boubacar's "friends," she meant the so-called Young Bolsheviks—Minette, others Zansi knew mostly by reputation.

He said, "You don't need to worry about me. I don't take my cues from anyone."

She pulled him close, abruptly. "You can accomplish this, Kannou. Not because Father wants it but because you're my brother and I'm your sister, and if I can succeed here, then so can you, whatever the obstacles. You are Danxomè. You are Gbéhanzin."

It was a gesture rarely shared, this warm embrace, and it caught him off guard. The genuine tenderness he felt at moments like this, however infrequent, always stirred him. This was the Zansi he remembered from their childhood—not the scold and the rod, not their father's agent, just Zansi, the only family he'd had since the trip over.

Their father had booked them passage on the packet steamer *Roma*, Cotonou to La Rochelle: in steerage—third-class, down below, behind the hold where they kept the coal for the smokestacks—as two unaccompanied children could not be expected to care for themselves, alone in a second-class cabin. Bunks, four-deep, filled the length of the jointed and creaking bulkhead, houseboys in most, traveling back to France with their Monsieurs and Madames, who had quarters on the upper deck. The houseboys lay wide-eyed in the shadows of their berths, hardly moving, mostly silent though never seeming to sleep, just breathing in then out with the exhale of steam from the engines. Seb—Kannou—remembered lying there engulfed by the wet heat, his neighbors panting and wheezing above and below him, his stomach seizing.

Zansi was only nine and no more knowing than he of where the ship was taking them or of what, once there, would be their fate. Yet she slipped away from the women's section each of the five nights of the voyage and climbed into his bunk. She held him and whispered the tales of their grandfathers, of the kings of Dahomey; she sang the songs that their broken-hearted but obedient mother had sung to them in the weeks leading up to their departure; she did whatever it took to calm his uncontrollable trembling.

> *Too-too, my little goat!*
> *For whom are you crying?*
> *Your mother is gone to market*
> *Who will,*
> *Who will comfort you?*

That was Zansi! His only family, his beloved older sister!

She smiled at him now, still all warmth. Then, just as abruptly the smile dropped. They stepped out of the way of a woman in a headscarf exiting the store, Seb caught the door before it closed, and Zansi entered, him just behind.

"Ah, good afternoon, Mademoiselle Docteur," the grocer said over the jingling bells on the door.

"Monsieur Besse," Zansi said, "how has your day been?"

Circling the counter, he offered a hand, first to Zansi, then to Seb.

"Taxing," he said, his expression turned sour. "It's as though all these testy *maîtresses de maisons* don't remember that, only a few years back, luxuries like flour or canned compote were impossible to get, much less Reinette apples or fresh endives."

"So, it's a day like every other one, then?" Zansi said.

"Alas, yes," said Besse.

Besse was likely only a few years older than Zansi and Seb, at most, but he already had a wife and two sons. A transplant from Gascony, he claimed to be as dislocated as them, his *"amis africains,"* and so he said he felt compelled to keep an eye out for their well-being. He made sure they got the best of whatever fruits or vegetables were available that day and, always, the best value for their money.

"How can I help you today?" he asked.

"We'd like two cans of sardines and three of the endives you mentioned."

Besse's face fell. "But Mademoiselle Docteur, that's not a meal! A meal can never be just meat and vegetables." He waved for them to follow. "Come with me."

His shelves, lined with canned goods, disguised the fact that the store had previously been a wine shop. He led them to the back, where a tight stairwell smelling of musk and wet stone wound downward. It was pitch-black. Seb heard: "My lower levels are still, regretfully, empty. But on this one . . ."

Besse hit a switch. Now illuminated, Seb saw wall-to-wall bottles, nearly every rack full.

Zansi said, "What a selection you've acquired since you last brought me down."

"Mostly just table wines," Besse said, falsely modest. "I've found a supplier from Tarbres, not so far from my hometown, who works for the Rothschilds and has agreed to bring me affordable but quite reputable bottles, when space in his truck permits."

"Clearly, the space has permitted of late."

"Like you Africans, we Gascons are a proud lot who look out for one another."

Besse commenced a tour, removing certain bottles, explaining their provenances and specific qualities. Zansi paid the same close attention she would to a physiology lecture, but Seb hung back, half listening. There was too much to do, too many other, more significant things to ingest and retain. But where Zansi had a mind that was curious about everything and forgot nothing, Seb picked and chose what to focus on and when to feign interest.

Zansi's gifts—her supple mind, her tireless drive—had enabled them to survive in France. How else could they have made it, a seven- and nine-year-old, in a country where they were viewed as objects of curiosity and treated no better than trained monkeys? It was she who had perceived that their father's cousin, a former petty functionary in the colonial administration who'd retired in France and offered to take them in, merely intended to make glorified servants of them. He'd given them pallets in the kitchen to sleep on and only taught them rudimentary arithmetic and letters, and only for an hour each day, after their morning chores brush-scrubbing shirt collars and hand-washing damask table linen, sweeping the floors and polishing the silver.

Three years along, at twelve, she'd led Kannou out of that house. She'd found them room and board as servants with a neighboring French couple. The new servitude would still be servitude, she'd explained to Kannou, but the couple had agreed to allow them to attend school. With their father's intervention—a sharply worded letter—his cousin had let them go.

The nuns at École de la Sainte-Famille, Zansi's school, were drawn to her obvious talent, and when the Germans came, four years later, the sisters had taken her in as a full boarder. The brothers at Kannou's École

Ange-Gabriel hadn't been nearly so bold. They'd put Kannou out. It was Zansi's mentor, Sister Justine, who'd found him an apprenticeship with a village carpenter in Burgundy, away from unscrupulous Vichy officials and Nazis bored with Jew-chasing who might take interest in a rarity like an African boy.

Kannou had refused to go. He'd begged Zansi to sneak him into her tiny room in Sainte-Famille's dormitory. He would sleep under her bed, he would eat whatever she could slip from the dining hall. Exiled from family, expatriated from their home—that was one thing. But if she sent him to the countryside, they would be separated from one another.

Zansi had insisted. Sheltering him in Burgundy was their only recourse.

She'd earned enough doing the French couple's laundry at night to accompany him on the train ride down. Kannou had sat teary and silent the whole way. And the parting had been impossible. He'd holed up in his room, a cubby in the carpenter's attic, for several days after. With increasing hunger, he'd finally come down, and the carpenter and his wife, Monsieur and Madame Des Launiers, had welcomed Kannou to their dining table.

Despite the insularity of life in a village of only a few hundred, Kannou came to feel a certain ease in Burgundy. Until then, he'd shown himself to be capable in most academic subjects but not much better. School, which he attended there half days, seemed particularly tedious and little rewarding. The challenge of crafting a shapeless hunk of wood to suit the requirements of a larger structure, on the other hand, gratified him. When, a few years along, Des Launiers took him out of school altogether to continue his apprenticeship full-time, Kannou, at fifteen, experienced only a tinge of doubt.

He felt wholly invigorated by the order in his life. Up at dawn hauling cords of wood from the shed to the workshop. Building a fire in the hearth. Laying out the appropriate tools for that morning's tasks: crafting shingles for this contract, shaping joints for that one. Before long, Des Launiers began to give him more exacting assignments: replacing the legs of a seventeenth-century chest of drawers; directing a group of day laborers installing a barn door. He went from being "the African boy" to just "the boy" to Seb. Like all artisans, he wore a blue smock and wooden clogs and took his post-work beer standing at the bar, smoking Gauloises and playing cards. (Because of his age, the barman, Jean-Guy, cut his beer with *limonade*.) It was wartime, and there was never enough of anything, but there was always Pernod. Sometimes Romuald, another artisan, would order pastisses for the group. "*Allez*, Jean-Guy. One for Seb, too," he would say, and then he'd call for the balls. "*Alors*, a quick round of pétanques before heading home?" They would move out onto the town square, six or eight of them, some removing frocks, others merely rolling up their sleeves. They'd tease and taunt, tossing the metal balls down the gravel stretch between the green municipal benches.

He and Zansi had written almost daily at first. But with the demands of their respective lives and the difficulties of the Occupation, the letters became more sporadic. When she learned that Des Launiers had pulled him out of school, she wrote in a rage. *What would Father think! Is that why he sent you here, Kannou? To become a roustabout, a common laborer?*

She was right, of course, but what was he to do? Some young people were sent to nearby cities to attend *lycée*, as there wasn't one in the village. Who would sponsor such a trip for him? Not Des Launiers, who needed him in the workshop. And why should Kannou risk it, with Germans everywhere, especially in the cities? The nuns protected Zansi. Who would protect him?

She would, she wrote back. *Our forebear, King Agaja, was exiled among Dahomey's enemies*, her letter had read, *and when he returned, he'd been made stronger. Like him, you have a duty, and it's not making barn doors and fence posts. My duty is to guide you on this journey.*

He bristled at those words: *My duty is to guide you.*

He didn't want to leave. He also knew that he'd submit. Deference to his legacy demanded it. So, Kannou prepared for his departure. It was February 1944.

Des Launiers was furious upon learning the news. He only assigned Kannou to menial tasks thereafter. Kannou became a mere servant again, as upon their arrival in France.

It took until May for Zansi to raise the money for the trip. She arrived on a Saturday afternoon, older than he remembered, virtually a woman. As happy as he was to see her—after nearly four years—he also found himself feeling angry, and scared. Who knew what awaited him in Paris? Hiding in a cellar? And this for some schooling that, in those circumstances, wasn't even likely possible?

Zansi ignored Des Launiers's threats to call the Vichy police and took Kannou back to the rail station. She could only afford third-class tickets, guaranteed passage but unreserved seats in a compartment of wooden, straight-backed benches. A few stops along, the train filled with German troops, en route to the northwest where a major Allied offensive was expected. The Fritzes were boisterous, many sipping from flasks. They jabbered among themselves, some with the French passengers, too, but none seemed to pay the least attention to the two Africans in their car, though Zansi and Kannou were probably the only two any of them had ever seen.

A drunk infantryman leaned toward them, and Kannou tensed. He only asked for a match, though, then offered Kannou a portion of his sandwich. Before Kannou could accept, Zansi led him by the hand into the corridor, and at the next station—just a platform, an elevated cistern, and beyond, miles of rolling hills—she directed him off the train.

"But why?" he protested, watching the last car pull away.

"It wasn't safe."

No village, not even a farmhouse in view. "How will we get to Paris now?"

"We'll walk," she said. "I have a baguette and some preserves."

"The Fritzes were fine! None of them cared two whits about you or me."

"It was not safe," she insisted, and she set off walking, not following the tracks, which he suggested, but the nearby road, which would be more serpentine and, as a result, much longer.

They walked three days, occasionally getting a ride in the back of a truck or on an ox-drawn wagon. When, later, they read the headlines that the Allies had bombed that particular troop transport, killing several hundred on board, he asked her how she'd known ahead of time that they should quit the train. She gazed at him with the same commanding confidence it seemed she'd been born with. She said that she just knew it wasn't safe.

"Some things can't be explained. It's my duty to take care of you until you find the right path. In this, I cannot fail."

Seb looked up from his daze to find both Zansi and Besse staring impatiently at him, one or the other having asked something about the bottle that Besse now extended in his direction.

"Or this one?" Besse repeated. "A nice Bordeaux?"

The label read GRIVEPONT.

"It's just a small table wine, you understand," Besse said, "but I think you'll find it quite good with sardines."

"Unfortunately, we can't afford such luxuries today, Monsieur Besse," Zansi said, removing her ration card. "But please put a bottle aside for us. Until next week, say."

Besse scolded. "I'm not proposing you buy this, Mademoiselle. I'm asking you to serve as my tasters. Tell me what you think, so I know if I can trust this peddler from Tarbres or if he's just another crook."

"In that case, thank you."

They followed Besse up the steep and winding stairwell. He stamped Zansi's ration card with the food items and the date, and Zansi and Seb said goodbye and left. They climbed the rest of Rue de la Montagne Sainte-Geneviève to their hotel. In Zansi's room, she prepared lunch then laid it out on a blanket on her neatly made bed.

Seb uncorked the bottle, poured two glasses, and offered her one. When she reached for it, he pulled it back, mimicking a chiding father: "Just so long as you understand, dear sister. You weren't sent here to learn about wine."

She smiled and snatched it from his hand, none spilling over the rim. "No," she said. "We're here to make Dahomey always greater."

CHAPTER EIGHT

"Here, let me show you," Seb whispered, rising and removing a waxpaper-wrapped package from the trunk at the foot of the bed. "I'll have to flip on the bulb."

If Zansi was up and out in the hallway for whatever reason, she would notice the light and might knock on the door. Still, he wanted Cecile to be able to see this.

"It's an Abomey tapestry." He stretched his arms wide in order to hold it fully open—a series of appliqué figures in rows, sewn over a rectangle of black cloth, bordered in orange. Europeans condescendingly called such work "naïf," but the tapestry was resplendent with symbol and meaning.

Cecile teased out the sounds of the word—"AH-boh-may"—then shifted onto her side beneath the sheets, head resting on the triangle of her arm, taking it in in all its splendor. "Tell me the story it tells."

"Several stories, in fact. Each figure represents one of the twelve kings of Dahomey."

He knew all of them by heart, and for some, the meaning behind the symbols, too. There was Kpengla, represented by a bird with a pebble in its beak; Agonglo, a palmyra palm tree; and two different buffaloes, one dressed in finery and, farther on, another without adornment. (One was Tegbessou, the other Guézo, though he confused which was which.)

Cecile asked, "So these are your grandfather and great-grandfather and great-great . . ."

"My grandfather, for sure," he said, "and his father, too. The earlier ones would have been great-grand-uncles or distant cousins—grandfathers in name only. The ascendancy didn't necessarily pass from father to son."

"But they're all blood, all kin?"

"All, yes."

Had a cool draft not made him suddenly aware of his nakedness, he wouldn't have remembered his penis, hanging limply in front of her. Standing there on display, he marveled at the ease he felt with this girl.

She sat up and let slip the sheet, exposed now too, just as at ease as he was. Seb took in the swell of her breasts, her ribcage curving to hip, the darkness where her thighs met.

She traced the appliqué images with a finger. "Who's the lion?"

"Glélé, my great-grandfather." For this one, he knew the meaning behind the name, as Zansi had often spoken it. He echoed her words: "Once the young lion has grown his teeth, terror spreads among his enemies."

Her finger outlined the stitching of another. "And the lizard?"

"A chameleon. Akaba." He didn't remember more than this.

"And the bird and drum?"

"The first of the Abomey kings: Ganyé Hessou. His name means 'You can't keep a bird from singing. Like a drum, the bird will be heard.'"

"Gone-yay hay-soo," she repeated. "This one is you. You will ace the exam, you *will* be heard."

He turned his face to hide his smile, both sheepish and pleased.

"The last one here is Gbéhanzin," he said, dropping one corner of the tapestry in order to point to the appliqué shark, at the far side. "My father's father, his blood father."

She fumbled over the pronunciation. "Gabee-han-sin?"

"It's easier if you don't pronounce the *g*. BAY-han-zin." Then he pointed to the smaller figure beside the shark. "The two arms, holding up an egg, that's his full name: Gbé, We, Hanzin, B'ayi, Djelé." All the kings' names were abridged, but Seb had memorized this one in its full length. "The universe upholds the egg that the Earth desires."

"Then why the shark?"

"That's his strong name. 'The shark becomes enraged and troubles the coast.' He was the king who repelled the French invasion, before he was eventually overrun."

Seb regretted not knowing any more than this. His father refused to speak about Gbéhanzin.

"And your father's symbol?" Cecile asked, lying back now, raising the sheet to her chin.

"Only kings got strong names. My father was never king, so he wasn't renamed."

"What was—*is*—his name?"

"Sebastien."

"Like you." She looked surprised. "Why a Christian name?"

"He was raised by the Catholic missionaries who trailed the soldiers."

But how to explain the rest, things he hardly understood himself—the things that had led his father to reject his own father's name and everything that Gbéhanzin had stood for?

He began: "You see, Gbéhanzin hid Tata Sokamey, my grandmother, who was his favorite wife—and pregnant—rather than drag her along when the French expelled him to Martinique. She eventually sent my father, as a boy, to the priests—to protect him from enemies and rivals. The priests accepted my father but refused to use his Dahomeyan name."

Cecile didn't miss the irony of it. "Wait. So, your father kept the name that the colonizers gave him over the one his father had chosen, then he passed it on to you?"

Seb signaled that she lower her voice. "Jacqueline," he reminded her.

It was also a way to change the subject.

Light from the street reflected off the pendant in the cleft between her breasts. It struck him. She was never without this Star of David, but he didn't know what the thing actually said about her. What was he to understand from the trinket? She professed faith in nothing, belief in no religion; and of the war, of what her family must have suffered, she rarely spoke at all. When he asked, she deflected the question or remained vague.

He never pressed, out of respect for her sense of discretion. They spent hours alone together, at the Tournon reviewing Cecile's notebooks from *lycée* or in this room talking through the night, but what did he know about this girl who was *his* girl, about the woman he was so smitten with?

He pointed to the fourth symbol in the first row, a caravel. "This one, Agaja—he was the greatest of the kings."

"A-ga-JAH," Cecile mouthed. "In what way was he greatest?"

"Because in everything he did, Agaja made Dahomey always greater." He folded the tapestry, replacing it in its wrapping. "The symbol of the ship means 'The taker of caravels' and signifies how he opened Dahomey up for trade with the Europeans."

He slid in beside her beneath the sheets.

"Agaja, when he was a boy, was a hostage in a neighboring kingdom. As much an exile as a prisoner, really. This was in the 1600s, when Dahomey was still weak. His father had pledged him to the neighboring king in exchange for an end to his army's annual marauding after the winter rains. Agaja learned the ways of the enemy during his separation from home. He returned stronger and won the throne."

Cecile didn't react as he'd expected, lying very still, her face blank. He must not be telling it right.

He assembled the shards of memory, all the details Zansi had told him—Zansi, who cherished Agaja's story more than even that of their own grandfather, Gbéhanzin. She would reiterate its lessons whenever she deemed Seb in need. On the *Roma*, as he'd lain sick and trembling in the stacked berths below deck, she'd chanted the words their mother had chanted to them in the lead-up to their departure: "*Allez*, my little goat! You are Agaja. Separation is a gift that leads to strength." After engineering their escape from the house of their father's exploitative cousin, she'd told him: "Agaja found his way out of Yorubaland, and with the Yoruba king's blessing. Father's cousin saw nothing." And in the letter she'd written him in Burgundy: "Agaja couldn't see the coast over the rooftops of his neighbors. So, the Dahomeyan princess guided his path from Abomey to the sea."

Seb began again: "Ouidah, another kingdom, this one situated between Dahomey and the sea, had dominated the region for years, even more than the Yorubas had. Houffon, the Ouidan king, had formed alliances with the *Yovo*, assuring them that their caravels would find abundant stores of merchandise in his capital that were cheaper than at Accra or Elmina, to the west, along the Gold Coast. In exchange, Houffon got modern flintlock muskets, a stockpile of them, plus whatever else the *Yovo* carried from their colonies—tobacco, I suppose, sugar, that sort of thing."

"*Modern* flintlocks?" Cecile teased.

"For that time, yes." She seemed more engaged now. "Houffon lorded over the kings whose lands surrounded his own. Dahomey was tiny by comparison, just the city of Abomey and the forest immediately around it. But Houffon found Agaja, more than the others, to be a particularly quarrelsome neighbor—starting trouble with lesser kingdoms and the like. To remind Agaja of his place, Houffon sent him a coded message in the form of a caravan of gifts and treasures. There were forty-one baskets of cowry shells, forty-one casks of brandy, forty-one bushels of tobacco leaves, forty-one rolls of India cloth, and forty-one crates of brass pots."

He'd made up the last two, unsure of what exactly had been presented to Agaja, only remembering that Eastern cloth and brass hardware were still highly valued in his homeland.

"Forty-one?" Cecile asked.

"It signifies 'a full amount,' the perfection of royalty." This was the answer Zansi had given when he'd asked the same thing.

"But why forty-one? Why not a round number—one hundred, or fifty, or a thousand?"

"I'm not sure," he confessed, embarrassed that he didn't know. "It's what Jacqueline told me, what our Aunt Fifonsi told her."

He shifted onto his side, and she did too, now facing him.

"Agaja very well understood Houffon's meaning, flaunting his great wealth, and he countered. He couldn't match it in riches, so he did it in symbol. He had the hundred-kilometer route between Abomey and Houffon's capital lined with enemy skulls."

"Oh, my . . ."

"War was the currency Agaja dealt in," Seb explained. "It was the language he understood. He also sent forty-one slave women, brides for Houffon, the forty-first being his own eldest daughter, the beautiful Na Geze. And to celebrate the union, Agaja sent forty-one barrels of palm wine, homegrown from his forests. Houffon accepted the offering as penance for Agaja's impertinence. But to mock the meagerness of the gifts and fete the dominance of Ouidah, he and his chiefs drank their own casks of French brandy, as they publicly demeaned and humiliated Na Geze and the other brides."

Cecile stared at him, the shadows of her face still.

"The next morning, drums raised the alarm that an enemy army was approaching. But Ouidah's generals had been laid low, the brandy unleashing a terrible thunder in their heads." Those had been Zansi's words: "unleashing a terrible thunder." Seb continued, "Houffon himself staggered about, unable to rally his men."

He remembered Zansi, after lights-out, bouncing lightly from one foot to the other in their father's cousin's kitchen, acting out this part of the story and singing the tale. Here in his room, he whisper-sang it into Cecile's ear, chanting the lines in French:

We're digging up, turning over, plowing up our spirit.
Let the men harvest the manioc!

He repeated it, his voice animating, the words cascading:

We're digging up, turning over, plowing up our spirit.
Let the men harvest the manioc!

His history unfolded like a film in his head when he told it aloud to Cecile like this, the images palpable and real. How he was enjoying the telling!

"It was Agaja's shock troops singing their war song—a corps of women warriors called *nyekplo hento*. It means 'razor-women.' They carried these great scimitars and had amassed in the forest overnight while Houffon and his generals drank."

Seb whisper-sang:

Until our mouths choke upon the dirt,
The bloody way will remain bloody.
Ouidans, you will be danxoménu!

Cecile said, "And from this, black people made jazz?"

He laughed but quickly returned to the story: "Ouidah fell into a panic. The *nyekplo hento* swarmed Houffon's palace while the regular troops overran the rest of the city. The razor-women found it abandoned, so they set it ablaze. Next, they descended on the Python Temple. The python was a sacred being, Houffon's fetish. So the temple, this sort of chapel filled floor to thatched roof with them, was the holy center of all Ouidah—their Saint Peter's. The razor-women grabbed up serpents by the tail. 'If you're truly gods,' they taunted"—he mimicked the gesture on the air above the bed—"'then save yourselves!'"

It was as though he could see the fierce warrior women holding the hissing and ess-twisting snakes, then lopping off the heads with their arced swords.

"The *nyekplo hento* built a fire and roasted and ate each python, scores of them."

"Oh, my . . ." Cecile said.

"The Ouidan army was ten times the size of Dahomey's, but when they counterattacked, their flintlocks wouldn't fire. The night before, during the celebrating, Na Geze had slipped into the armory and doused the gunpowder with Agaja's palm wine, which Agaja had known pompous Houffon would shun in favor of the *Yovo*'s liquor."

He paused to catch his breath.

"Houffon's soldiers scattered. Houffon himself fled into the forest, a squad of razor-women on his tail. Agaja now controlled Ouidah, so he controlled the coast."

Seb shifted onto his back. "Me, my role is to be like Agaja. When I return, I am to make Dahomey always greater."

"This Agaja," said Cecile, "if he was so great—"

"He was. Under him, Dahomey became the leading kingdom in all of West Africa."

"Then why did he establish this greatness by selling slaves?"

The sharp tone of her voice surprised him. And the look on her face, what he could see of it in the shadows of his bed: utter dismay. Or was it revulsion?

"You called them 'merchandise,'" she said. "They were people."

Seb sat up, pulled his knees to his chest. "What else could Agaja do? Day after day, *Yovo* caravels cluttered the waters off the coast—the Portuguese and the French, the Dutch and the English. This was the reality of that time. The Ouidahs or the Yorubas would have eventually overrun Abomey, and it would have been Dahomeyans who were carried off. Agaja recognized this and made the Ouidahs *danxoménu*."

"Dahomey what?"

"*Danxoménu*." Another of the rare words he remembered of his language. "It means 'property of Dahomey.' The Ouidahs became subjects."

Cecile rolled onto her back. There was no warmth. They were two bodies in a bed.

"It's late." She slipped her feet to the floor. "I should go."

"I'll walk you," he said.

Out on the street, he raised his collar against the stiff breeze. Paris was quiet, the entire city like a sleeping village. At Odéon, the waiters at the Danton and across the street at the Relais were long gone. Only janitors remained, dressed in white coveralls, mopping the floors and squeegeeing the broad plate-glass windows. Seb watched them as he and Cecile passed by. Down Boulevard Saint-Germain, the Rhumerie Martiniquaise, where their group sometimes went to dance, shone bright, the shadows of late-night revelers spilling out its doors. Seb and Cecile wove their way to Rue Bonaparte and arrived at her building, never speaking.

Facing one another in the unlit vestibule, Cecile said, "It's the women, you know."

"The women?"

"Na Geze," she said. "She caused the defeat of the enemy king."

He tried but could not read her strangely rigid expression—so unlike her. "Of Houffon," he confirmed, "yes."

"And what about the razor-women? Who do you think dreamed up that idea, some man?" She grabbed at him, there, and he squirmed away. "Not with what they were meant to slice off with those weapons."

The concierge peeked through the curtains covering the glass panels of her door, clearly displeased at the noise.

Cecile didn't lower her voice. "In your culture, women are everything. You only remember the kings."

Seb sank his hands into his pockets. "You're angry."

Rather than reply directly, she said, "I'd invite you up, but I know you don't want your sister thinking you haven't spent the night in your room."

He'd wanted to share what he knew of his history, and he'd thought she wanted this, too. "I'm sorry I told you those stories," he said, sad that their wonderful night had come to this.

Then he felt the sadness turning to anger. In books, the *Yovo* traders and missionaries described the Abomey kings as despots and savages who practiced ritual sacrifice and sold their brothers into slavery; they used this to justify colonizing his country. And now, her too judging them?

He refused to be made to feel guilty for who he was, not by a *Yovo* girl. He added, coolly: "I didn't mean to upset you."

"They took my grandmother," she said, "and what had she done to deserve it? And this girl, not long after de Gaulle liberated the city." Cecile smiled weakly. "She'd been Fritz-énu during the war."

Seb smiled too, reflexively, despite the moment. Fritz-énu: a play on words, a combination of his language and hers. Property of the Fritzes. The girl must have been a collaborator.

"She was made into a public spectacle," Cecile said, "paraded around then shaved. But what was she guilty of? Surviving?"

Finally, he understood. For her, his stories weren't about the triumphs of his forefathers. No, she identified with the slaves. This was what the Star of David pendant told about her.

He pulled her to him. "I'm so, so sorry." He felt he could hold all of her, her whole self, in his arms. "To have to listen to things like what I told you—how thoughtless of me."

They held each other a long time.

"You have to go now," she said. "Jacqueline." She headed toward the stairs that led to the residential floors. "So, go."

He watched her disappear up the dark stairwell.

CHAPTER NINE

Early on, Cecile had resented the Louvre's stodgy dress code and would don trousers from time to time despite Monsieur Petit's scowls and carping—maybe even to provoke them. Increasingly, she began to choose skirts to match Seb's more formal look, when they would meet after work. Seb was always in a jacket and a collared shirt, sometimes with a tie, even when they were just meeting for exam prep, and she liked appearing equally nice when beside him.

Mercifully, the hours leading to their rendezvous passed quickly, especially in the ticket booth. She was handed coins and bills and passed back change, all day long the same, and unless Minette stopped by for lunch, the next thing Cecile knew, her shift was over. She'd hustle off, stopping at her hotel en route to the Tournon for her study guides and notes, and also to pick up her mail. Her mother wrote weekly, sometimes more often, usually with a few banknotes included. The money always helped. Cecile made more than many but less than the amount that she could spend, even in a city where so little was available. A spritz of eau de toilette and a quick brush of her hair, and she would be off again.

The end of August neared—only a few short weeks before the entrance competition. (And where had the summer gone!) On this day, Cecile had left work fifteen minutes early, at the first opportunity when Monsieur Petit wasn't paying attention, and she'd not stopped at her hotel. She took their usual table at the back of the Tournon and flagged a passing garçon. "Do you have cream today?" she asked.

Recognizing her as a regular, he said, "For you, Mademoiselle, always."

"A *café crème* then. *Merci*."

"And for your friend? Earl Grey?"

"I'll let him order for himself when he arrives," she said.

The waiter smiled and retreated.

The final push before the test wasn't the reason for her early arrival. The opposite, actually. Her life had become wholly interlaced with Seb's—with his acceptance to Beaux-Arts, yes, but also with more than just this—and she needed to slow down and consider it all, to catch up to her racing emotions and take an accounting of exactly what it was she was doing, especially considering that, soon, the exam would be taken and the hours together preparing for it, over.

Seb was everything that the others—Jean-François, Laure and Salim, even Minette—were not. He opened the door and let others pass first. He sat properly at a table and ate with the appropriate utensils, not devouring the whole meal with only a spoon or drinking water straight from the bottle, merely because to do so was to bellow a symbolic "Fuck you!" to the mores of the larger society. He was poised when he debated yet he questioned everything, the Soviet approach to European reconstruction as much as the US general Marshall's proposed plan, President Auriol's conciliatory Fourth Republic as well as the viability of violence as a response to the nationalists in Indochina. A Zionist group calling itself Irgun Zeva'i Le'ummi carried out bombings throughout Europe, and when Cecile argued that they were freedom fighters and the action justified, Seb countered: "But in Rome? When they struck the King David Hotel in Jerusalem, I got the logic. A hundred civilians killed, yes, but it was an attack on the British in the British Mandate. Horrible, tragic—and arguably necessary. But how does an assault on war-ravaged Italy advance their cause?" And he was right. The two Italian kids who were blown to pieces while leaving the neighboring nightclub could have been them, Seb and her.

Cecile admired his grace, his keen intelligence, but more than this, she adored him. Lying in his bed in the dark, nestled in the crook of his arm, her body become one with his, was a feeling of home unlike any she'd known. She felt safe, serene, yet energized too—inspired, like Sundays *chez* Mamie Lucie.

And she knew that he felt strongly for her, too. His attentiveness; a reassuring hand on the small of her back; the way she caught him gazing at her when she would glance up and he'd not expected her to. This mattered. No need for self-flagellation to demonstrate herself worthy of affection, no begging for approval. This was nothing like being with Joël.

Still, despite this growing feeling, things sometimes took a strange turn, unpredictably, and she couldn't pinpoint the reason why. It was like an invisible door would push up between them at random moments, and she didn't have the key to unlock it. The distance between them, though short for sure, seemed impassable, and it had something to do with the words.

Cecile thought about the strange muddle of sounds to which he'd introduced her: *na daho*, "elder sister"; *nyekplo hento*, "razor-woman"; and the names of his forefathers—Agaja, Guézo, Gbéhanzin . . .

Gbéhanzin: the last king of Dahomey, who had refused to bow to France and had driven back the colonial soldiers bent on his submission. He had to be banished to Martinique to forestall the uprisings that were certain to arise should he be allowed to stay in Africa. Seb's father's father.

Seb wove the words into stories that were colorful and larger than life, his thick voice animated and resonant. But the grandeur he breathed into the words didn't match the underlying truth of those very stories. It was as though he didn't recognize that he spoke of betrayal and horror and masses of captives shackled neck to neck and herded to the coast to be sold. It was as though he didn't see that, whether only a pretext for the colonial conquest or not, the French had been determined to abolish the slave trade, and wasn't there something right and good in that?

The contradictions rattled Cecile. She didn't know how to point them out without seeming to imply a savagery in him that his intelligence and demeanor in every way refuted.

She heard the clack-clack of dispensing coffee grounds behind the bar, the hiss of the machine, and a few seconds later the garçon arrived with her order. The wall clock above the door read 6:10—still a few minutes before he would arrive. Cecile sipped the fluff of aired cream, inhaled the rich mix of tart and sweet.

"The naked girl in Maisons-Laffitte." These were just words now too, strung together in place of the specific images that she struggled to recall anymore. "The trouserless man," his flash and writhing—she imagined it more than she actually remembered. Even "Mamie Lucie," who had shaped so much of Cecile's childhood. She'd become a notion in Cecile's mind, an impression more than a palpable memory. "Sundays *chez* Mamie Lucie," "Clémence's Philippe," "Joël"—the idea of them endured, yet little substance remained beyond the letters, just words without heft.

Cecile wondered if this was all that she amounted to, just a jumble of illegible feelings born of insufficient memories, of an inadequate connection to her past; she wondered if she was just a cipher, empty like the words. This possibility frightened her because, if true, it maybe explained the reason she was so drawn to Seb and his troublesome history, to Minette before him, to New Womanhood and all that. Maybe Cecile chased after others' stories, their grain and color and detail, to replenish the desert spaces in her own story, to substitute for the things she would rather forget.

And maybe this described Seb, too, all those nights in the dark, his voice telling tales with the texture of myth but that exposed horrors he seemed incapable of perceiving. Maybe just like her, he was searching for something, anything, with which to lend substance to the absence.

This shared sense of absence would explain why their lives were so easily braiding together, despite their differences: because each one needed more than just his own words, because each one needed a new story. Did Seb recognize it, too?

The cowbell on the door clanged. Seb wended his way back to their table. He leaned down, they kissed cheeks.

"Boubi says to say *bonjour*," he said.

"You were with him?"

"Just now, yes. Reviewing French history at the Danton." He unpacked his satchel, plopping workbooks and notes onto the table. "I can't keep straight Merovingian rule from Carolingian, Louis the Fat from Louis the Lion."

"There was a Louis the Lazy, too. He didn't accomplish much."

Seb was clearly nervous and crabby. She took his hand in hers.

"You don't need to worry. Things like that probably won't be on the exam."

"And if they are? This is all old hat for you, but everything is new for me."

"Hey! Stop feeling sorry for yourself. And don't take your anxieties out on me."

She mined her memory for his words. "Ganyé Hessou. You can't keep the bird from singing."

He smiled in response.

"I told you before, you will be heard," she said. "You've got a brilliant mind, Seb. Boubi, your sister, me—we're all here on your side, to help you get there."

This time, his smile looked forced.

Cecile shifted on her chair, leaning over his tightly written notes, and they got to work.

They arrived at the Rhumerie at ten, both exhausted, neither feeling particularly festive. But Minette had scolded Cecile for being unavailable, and Cecile had promised they'd stop by.

The Rhumerie was the neighborhood bar of choice for dancing. Admission was overseen by a burly bouncer—the *physionomiste*—a white Martiniquais who filled the doorway and selected who would be allowed to enter and who not, letting people in—usually the girls—only a few at a time. The last time the group had met there, he'd "randomly" excluded Seb and Boubi, making them wait on the sidewalk. Minette had made a scene, shouting "Racist!" and "Shame!" until the bouncer, while threatening to bar them forever, ushered them all in as a way to shut Minette up.

He now stood with the haggard barman at the end of the zinc counter, both of them sipping beers before the crowd turned up, usually around midnight. Cecile and Seb scanned the room. Their friends huddled at a table, sipping *cafés* and animated: Minette and Boubi, Laure, two faces Cecile recognized but whose names she couldn't recall, one white, the other African.

Minette saw them and shouted over the hubbub of the room: "*Enfin!* Our intellectual vanguard!"

The bouncer and the barman—the entire room, in fact—turned toward them. The attention appeared to embarrass Seb.

Cecile pushed in next to Boubi, who slid closer to Minette to make room. Minette resumed where she'd apparently left off. "*Alors,*" she said to the African boy, "how long then before de Gaulle puts his beak in?"

"Worker actions, unrest," he responded. "There's your Soviet aid."

Minette pointed to the neon Coca-Cola sign in the window. "And American aid, that."

Seb, who'd squeezed in beside Cecile, had once told her that Minette wore self-righteous indignation like she did mascara and that he didn't understand why Cecile felt so drawn to her. He wasn't wrong. Minette always mugged for attention. But Cecile was attached. Minette was her friend.

"So, do you feel ready?" Laure asked him.

"Ready?" Seb said. He harrumphed, staring fixedly at the dance floor though there was no music yet and no one dancing.

"What did you expect, *mec*, a Sunday stroll?" Minette shot back. "The exam to Beaux-Arts, it's not nothing!"

The band was setting up in the corner, a Dixieland group—what looked to be three black Americans and on horn a French boy, young, sixteen, maybe seventeen. They were tuning their instruments when another group of black Americans, six or seven of them, each in a zoot suit and a wide-brimmed hat, roaring reds and yellows and purples like the royal garments of lurid princes, passed the bouncer and pulled together several tables, a few tables down from where Cecile and the others sat. The bouncer looked on disapprovingly but said nothing.

De trop, thought Cecile, and *trop américain*. Yet charming all the same.

The rest of her table noticed too, then turned back to the African boy, who continued: "So, when you can't summon more than formulaic rhetoric, you resort to insults?"

Seb leaned toward Cecile. "The Yoruba boy is holding his own." She must have appeared confused because he quickly followed: "His ethnic group. Yorubas mark their children like that, on the cheek."

He helped himself to a cigarette from Boubi's pack of Gitanes then extended it toward Cecile. She took one, too. Seb smoked even less frequently than she did, but he inhaled deeply, fully.

He breathed a release of smoke. "But given the hint of Brit accent," he continued, "he's probably from Nigeria and not Dahomey."

Cecile heard in his voice a sort of pride at being able to identify the tribe to which the boy belonged. She wondered why he didn't try to connect with him, as a fellow countryman.

The lights flickered on and off, on and off, those of the surrounding buildings, too. Then all went black.

"*Mais non!*" and "*Merrrrde!*" came from various spots around the room. From the zoot-suited Americans, mocking laughter.

Cecile's group watched in silence as the thick shadow of the bouncer worked his way through the crowd and into a back room. A generator motor sputtered, loudly at first before settling, the smell of gasoline wafting throughout the Rhumerie. The lights flickered back on.

Not long after, the music began. The dance floor immediately filled. The Yoruba pulled Minette by the hand. Boubi, Laure, and the other boy rose, too.

Seb and Cecile stayed at the table of half-empty glasses, watching. She helped herself again to Boubi's Gitanes. Seb, too, inhaling deeply like he'd learned during his wartime apprenticeship in Burgundy and holding the smoke, the holding as important as the inhale.

He gawked at the spectacle of Minette, doing her own version of the jitterbug, arms waving and haunches wriggling, the Yoruba nearby but forgotten, a crowd gathering, clapping her on. The Rhumerie was crammed full, front door to bar, mostly with young people, mostly white but also with a spattering of blacks. The increasing number of blacks that Seb saw everywhere around Paris still surprised him. They had been so few before the war; it had sometimes felt like just Zansi and him. But here were Africans like this Yoruba boy, Madagascans, others from other islands . . . They were men mostly, many of whom had landed with de Gaulle at Toulon and driven the Germans out of Provence.

And now black Americans, too. The black Americans were always easy to distinguish, and not just by their manner of dress. They traveled together, rarely alone or in twos, and the raucous packs seemed to mostly care about being noticed—like these men tonight.

One of them approached their table. He wore a long purple jacket, a canary shirt without a tie and unbuttoned at the neck, and purple trousers that ballooned down his legs and cinched at the ankle. At least he had the courtesy to remove his broad-brimmed hat.

He extended a pack of Lucky Strikes. "Gitanes is fine," he said in English, to both of them but mostly toward Cecile. "But try one of mine."

Seb dismissed them with a wave, but Cecile said, "*Merci*," and fingered one free.

"Luckies the best butts they is." He dropped the pack on the table. "Keep 'em."

Then he just stood there, smiling.

"Maybe your baby would care to dance," he said finally, toward Seb.

"Maybe you ask the 'baby' for herself," said Seb, the abrupt recall of his sparse English surprising him.

The American looked surprised, too, though how else had this imbecile expected for the conversation to proceed? The man clearly didn't speak French.

"A tad later perhaps," Cecile told him, her English quite strong. "My boyfriend and I are just going to dance ourselves."

The American threw his head back and laughed.

"OK," he said, "a *tad* later then. Ima hold you to it."

He turned to go but then turned back. "There's a spot up on Montmartre." He took a Biro from his pocket and scratched out an address on the Lucky Strikes pack. "Payne's Place, a hopping joint." He dropped the pen onto the table. "You can keep this, too."

The other black Americans, who'd sat sprawled over their chairs, watching, threw out their hands for him to slap as he returned.

"Come on," Cecile said. "Don't make a liar out of me."

She pulled Seb toward the dance floor, led him alongside Minette, as close as they could get. Men surrounded her, one after another cutting in, Boubi giving way to the Yoruba who gave way to a French boy, who spun her, their legs contorting left and right. Seb danced Cecile back out to the periphery.

"Look at poor Boubi," she said, pushing into him to be heard and staying there.

Boubi was trying, without much luck, to work his way back to Minette.

As though sensing herself the topic of conversation, Minette quit her partner of the moment and began shimmying toward them. Seb wasn't in the mood for her antics. He turned his back and danced facing the musicians.

Minette inserted herself between them. "What can this *toubab* girl do for you?" she hollered directly into Seb's face over the music, playfully elbowing at Cecile, who laughed and elbowed back. "Let me show you what a real *nègre* is like."

"So, a *métisse* from Ménilmontant is going to show me how to be black?" he shot back.

"Somebody should." She flicked the lapel of his jacket and grabbed his tie, jitterbugging all the while, never missing a beat. "You're more French than the French. Hell, those Americans there are more African than you."

Seb snatched his tie free. "And this judgment, from you? Someone who has seen no more of Africa than any of them has?"

Minette smirked. "Negritude isn't geography, *mon frère*. Down here among the plain folk, it's a way of being."

Cecile hugged him to her. "Don't mind her. She's a little drunk."

But he pulled away and headed to the WC. *Une provocatrice*, he thought, working his way through the crowd, that was all Minette knew how to be. She enflamed emotion but couldn't explain a reasoned and reasonable position, much less put together a proper action—or even just act and interact properly!

He stopped at the bar on the return and drank a one-percenter, which was weak but soothing all the same. Then another. The Americans were dancing with the girls now, taking Minette by the hand, taking Laure, taking Cecile, the tails of their loud jackets inflating on the air as they spun, spinning the girls. Boubi clapped along, watching the show beside the Yoruba and the rest of the crowd.

This was what Zansi mistrusted and frankly disliked about the Young Bolsheviks. They were children in search of parties, not adults beating paths toward successes. Seb enjoyed dancing and laughing, too, the banter and the beer, the debates and the cigarettes. But he was tired, tired to his core. For months leading up to these exhausting final days, he'd been *sérieux*, working as hard as he ever had or could imagine doing. And now, with admission or failure at stake, he wanted an escape from the pressure cooker. He had no patience for the *métisse* tonight, nor for Cecile's truckling to her goading and whims.

During the third beer (which pushed him past his allotted budget for the night), Cecile appeared by his side. "Any left for me?"

He slid the glass toward her.

She finished it in one swallow. "Let's get out of here," she said.

They walked through the seventh arrondissement—Rue de l'Université, Rue de Beaune, Rue de Verneuil—the tight streets hardly wide enough for two cars to pass at once, had there been any out at that hour. On either side were white-stone buildings, each window of each floor shuttered. They turned a corner and suddenly in front of them loomed the train station at Quai d'Orsay, cast in shadows. Seb had known to expect it, but its sudden manifestation, hulking eerily at the top of the street, always startled him. He thought it an impressive block of building, massive and squat, a bit baroque but with great light—now closed, the tracks and platforms and vaulting concourses spectral and still.

They continued to the Seine then across the bridge, over the dark, rustling river. In the shadows of the quays, shadow lovers sat coiled together on the stone embankments, on the retaining walls, watching the water or looking east toward the Louvre, a darker darkness against the night sky.

A green metal clock on Place de la Concorde read 2:15. There was still considerable traffic, even at that hour, bicycle taxis and cars tooting their horns, circling the obelisk. He and Cecile strolled along the wall of the Jardin des Tuileries, where they'd sometimes meet to study beside the round pool on warm evenings, monstrous koi surfacing and descending, and raucous boys pushing toy sailboats out with thin reeds then racing around to beat them to the other side. They'd once seen a boy reach too far and fall in with the koi . . .

Well, Seb thought that the fish were koi.

Koi or goldfish? He didn't know the difference. Was there any?

At the corner stood the Jeu de Paume. Cecile said, "That's where the Fritzes warehoused the art they stole from Jews. What they couldn't sell, they burnt in great bonfires."

He faced her. They'd been here together how many times, and she'd never before broached the subject.

"My grandmother," she said, "the one they took, they also stole her art collection. I suppose it ended up here."

He wanted to know more but stayed silent. Out of respect, he thought, but was it really this? He was overwhelmed with his own burdens. Was this discretion and delicacy merely an attempt to avoid having to help her carry hers?

Up the street was the Hôtel de Crillon. Chauffeured limousines arrived and pulled away, dropping off fancy-dressed Americans and aristocratic French types, women in sleek gowns with stoles, others wearing Dior's New Look and the conical hats that reminded Seb of the ones you saw in pictures of rice farmers in Indochina.

"No rationing there," Cecile said. "Do the arrivistes in Africa also insist on looking so cartoonish?"

"I wouldn't know." Of his home he remembered so little. A block of house surrounded by earthen walls that seemed to him at the time to stretch to the sky, busy street noise just outside. His child self, in short pants and knee socks, sitting in the courtyard with a sack of marbles or twiddling dirt with a finger while, through the metal slats of the gate, boys like him but in pagne wraps or nothing at all chased each other and screamed joy at their capture.

Cecile said, "You've lived here longer—twice as long as you ever lived there. Maybe this is home now, Seb. Maybe you're as much French as Dahomeyan."

"But of course I am Dahomey!"

"Once you've become an architect," she said, "will you build sky-scrapers along the Dahomeyan coast, where there are hardly proper cities, much less modern ones?"

He didn't respond.

"The work you do will be here. You'll make Dahomey greater by showing that Dahomeyans can rank among—above!—the best French-men. But that'll be here."

"Of course I am Dahomey," he insisted. "Who else could I be?"

Koi or goldfish, Dahomeyan or French, black or white—one or the other, never the two.

"And you?" Seb asked. "After all you've been through, after all the French put your family through, is France 'home' for you?"

"It's where I am. It's all I've known. What else to call it?"

They fell silent.

Cecile pushed forward, her stride deliberate. "What are we doing, Seb—you and me? Your sister, the sneaking around. What is this?"

He slipped his arm around her waist, slowing her, pulling her close. This was as honest a response as he knew how to give, because he didn't know the answer.

He wasn't even sure he fully understood the question. Were they boyfriend and girlfriend, was this what she was asking? If so, then the answer was yes, absolutely yes. He cared deeply for her and recognized that she cared deeply for him, too.

Or was the question something else, about the future, about where they were headed as a couple? To this, he didn't know how to answer.

He found himself unexpectedly disoriented in the serpentine streets, unsure of where the river lay, of the route back to the Quartier latin. All around them was the nighttime quiet of the countryside, nothing of the city.

"I want you to take me to Le Vésinet," he said, surprising himself as much as her.

But Cecile didn't hesitate: "Let's go! Gare Saint-Lazare isn't too far."

He'd meant in the future, not right then, unannounced and out of the blue.

"Sometime when it's convenient for your parents, I mean . . ."

"For breakfast," she said. "We can wait on the platform for the first morning train out."

It was a bad idea, and not just because of the hour. "But you have work tomorrow . . ."

"I'll call in sick. I haven't been home in weeks. You'll love my mother."

It was a bad idea.

Yet, he found himself wanting to go, to sit on a sofa in a proper living room with a view on the garden, a red-posies-patterned tea service, matching cups and saucers—like in Burgundy, the order and calm of those years with the carpenter Des Launiers.

Seb also thought the trip out might offer some answers to the questions about him and Cecile, about what they were doing and could become together.

Up ahead, he recognized the Galleries Lafayette, with its broad awnings and lively window displays. Gare Saint-Lazare was just around the corner.

CHAPTER TEN

The clock atop Le Vésinet train station read 7:25. Seb followed Cecile through the just-waking town center. A barman inside the café beside the square served coffees to a crowd that was two-deep the length of the bar, a pack of schoolchildren clomp-clomp-clomping past the plate-glass window. During the war, apprenticing for Monsieur Des Launiers, Seb had watched kids in these very same uniforms—white-collared black smocks and wooden-soled shoes—every morning as he hauled damaged planks to fuel the hearth. The kids had pointed and gawked the first few times (like these did now), but soon he'd no more stood out than did the vintner's boy dropping off crates of Burgundy into doorways.

Cecile's house, once they arrived, was much as Seb had expected: a white-stone cottage with blue shutters, ivy growing from the lintel and flowers in pots in the windows. She led him up the slate walkway to the front door.

"Are you sure we should just show up like this?" he asked.

"It'll be fine. My father leaves early for town hall." She opened the door—it wasn't locked—and called inside. "Coo-coo! It's me."

Seb waited at the entrance. He heard a surprised voice—"Cecile?"—and across the living room, through the open kitchen door, he glimpsed a small woman in a worn navy-blue robe. She turned toward them, with flushed cheeks and a smile, but upon seeing Seb, her mouth slipped to a thin line. She reached one hand to the robe, the other for her hair, hanging in a long braid over one shoulder, then fled out another door he could not see.

"Maybe I should come back later," he said. "Or another time."

"Don't be ridiculous," said Cecile. "She can be a little prudish is all."

"Has she ever met an African before?"

"I'm sure she's more troubled to have a man see her dressed like that than that the man is African. Let's put on water for tea."

She went into the kitchen, but he stayed in the front room, by the door. Metal clanged, the sound of Cecile removing pots from a cupboard. "Is Papa gone?" he heard her call.

Seb couldn't hear the response, only how tentative the voice sounded.

Just then, a man appeared in the hallway, not particularly tall, in a dark suit, a bowler hat in hand, and around his waist a national sash—so rare to still see anymore. He paused and took Seb in.

"Monsieur," he said, instead of "*bonjour*," though the tone was not particularly welcoming.

In her father's defense, it was well before proper hours for visits. Others might have responded even worse.

Cecile peeked through the doorway. "*Salut*, Papa! This is my friend, Sebastien."

Her father scrutinized his daughter even more sternly than he had Seb. "How many times must I repeat myself? You should give us advance notice of your comings and goings."

"Of course, of course. I'm so sorry." Cecile's face looked in no way as cowed as her words pretended.

Her father appeared to read her "apology" much as had Seb. He placed his bowler on his head and left.

Cecile said, "We're blocking access to both doors. If he could have fled unnoticed, he would have."

Her mother reemerged, in a forest-green dress, her braid rolled into a bun. "*Jeune homme*," she said, offering her hand, formally though less cheerlessly than her husband.

"Please, it's Sebastien."

"Sebastien, then. *Enchantée*." She waved that he follow her into the kitchen. "Though I might have liked a little forewarning," she said toward

Cecile, who bounded about the room, toasting black bread on the stovetop, removing a clay marmalade jar from a cabinet.

"I'm sorry," Seb said. "We should have telephoned from the station."

"It's not your fault, it's my daughter's. I'm still trying to instill in her good manners—with little success, as you can see." She pointed toward the kitchen table. "Please, sit."

"You sound just like Papa!" Cecile mocked. Then she asked Seb: "Coffee or tea?"

"I have Earl Grey or English Breakfast," Madame Rosenbaum said, her mouth contorting in the effort to wrap itself around the foreign words, the struggle causing her to blush.

Seb looked for some resemblance between the two, mother and daughter, and couldn't find it—the mother so proper, diffident even, by comparison.

"Earl Grey, please," he said.

They sat around the small kitchen table, sipping tea from bowls, Cecile and Seb devouring the tartines, Madame Rosenbaum poking at hers with a butter knife. The orange marmalade made the bitter bread sweet-sour. Cecile and her mother exchanged pleasantries: news of neighbors; an update about the condition of an ill cousin in South America. One tidbit changed Cecile's demeanor.

"And they're sure it was Joël Goldschmidt?" she asked.

"Agnès Rantot says she crossed paths with him one day in Croissy," said Madame Rosenbaum, "that he's returned from Palestine and changed his name—"

"And he's tied to the guns?"

"Madame Rantot thought so."

Seb jumped in. "The Mallnitz train bombing? Is that what you're talking about?"

The Zionist militant group Irgun had attacked a British troop transport in Austria a few weeks before, and not long after, a substantial arms cache connected to the strike was discovered in a villa in a suburb that bordered Le Vésinet.

"He was a neighbor boy," Cecile explained. "His family was taken."

"And they say he's involved in the terrorism?" Seb asked.

"Terrorism?" said Cecile. "Really? With what the Brits are doing to the camp survivors they've 'interned' on Cyprus?"

"But this boy is involved?"

Cecile gazed into her plate. "He had a hard time during the war. A hard, hard time."

Seb wondered at the many things he didn't know about Cecile.

"Enough of this already," Madame Rosenbaum said. "My daughter says that you're preparing for the entrance exam to Beaux-Arts. Tell me, how's it going?"

Seb tried to appear confident. "Pretty well, I think."

"I'm sure it is," said Madame Rosenbaum, certain. "I know the outcome will be what you want it to be." She placed a hand over his. "But five days' worth of tests . . . What a trial!"

That seemed hardly the half of it. Her warm smile comforted him, though.

She rose and refilled the tin teapot with hot water from the stove. "So, you're from the colonies, then?"

He saw Cecile wince.

"From Dahomey," he said—adding, for clarity: "In West Africa. It's near—"

"Oh, I know precisely where it is. It used to be called the Slave Coast."

This time it was he who winced. He couldn't control the reflexive reaction, however fitting the name might once have been.

She continued: "I remember reading a wonderful article by a Catholic missionary there, on initiation ceremonies and the natives' veneration of twins. Voodoo, you know."

He dropped his eyes, embarrassed, though he knew he shouldn't be—and this made the skin on his neck prickle all the more. He wondered if, despite her best intentions, what she imagined of his people were the roly-poly types from the cartoons at the cinema, with bones poking through their noses and grass skirts.

All the world was fascinated with the mysterious so-called Dark Continent and its "exotic" ceremonies. To the *Yovo*, voodoo was obscure yet profane; at once abject and exotic; feared but coveted, too. But initiation rites weren't exotic. They weren't so unlike first holy communions, or bar mitzvahs for that matter. All three were mystical, based in a belief that something larger than the self guided one's life. Dahomeyan rites involved drums instead of chants but were not one bit stranger than a bearded man in a skullcap and shawl bobbing rhythmically and harmonizing prayers.

Still, to be polite, he said, "Yes, Madame Rosenbaum, it can be quite colorful."

"Not colorful, no." She placed her hand on his hand again—a warm reproach. "A people's faith—their religion, whatever it might be—is always important, not to be belittled. And please, it's Elodie."

She poured steaming water into his cup.

"The article also spoke of the days of the week . . ." She wrinkled her brow. "Oh, remind me, please—what's the word for Thursday?"

He was silent.

"Gozon, gonozon?" She looked to him for confirmation. "Something like that, right?"

He remained silent and dropped his eyes, embarrassed that he didn't know.

She went on: "It means the 'women's day.' The article said that business done on a Wednesday is come at carefully, but that business on Thursdays lacks rigor, 'like a woman.'"

She laughed, covering her mouth with a hand, as though embarrassed to have been caught being charming, and as she did, there it was: he found Cecile in Madame Rosenbaum's face—Cecile-Cecile, not the one who aped Minette. She and her mother shared this expression, when their eyes gently mocked the thing that their mouths were saying. It was coy but suggestive. Coquettish.

A few other names of the days of the week came to Madame Rosenbaum. As she cited them, glancing over for his endorsement, none—not a single one—was even remotely familiar to Seb.

Back at the stove, she placed more bread slices onto the wire-mesh grill pad. "Cecile tells me that your name, Danxomè, comes from Dahomey, the name of your country."

"They're one and the same," said Seb. "Just different spellings."

She gazed at him expectantly, but remembering Cecile's reaction, he told an abridged version. When he got to the evisceration, Madame Rosenbaum blurted, "Oh, what brutality!"

Cecile shot back: "Maman, please. What right do we French have to judge anyone else's supposed 'brutality'? After what we've done and seen done?"

His and Cecile's clash over his stories still stung. He liked that she defended them, and him, now.

"Brutality is brutality," Madame Rosenbaum insisted, "whoever commits it." Though she'd said it softly, her voice rang just as strongly as had her daughter's. "If these terrible years have taught us anything, it's that."

"They taught us to look first in the mirror," Cecile countered.

"Yes, fine, we've committed horrors against others." Madame Rosenbaum looked toward Seb then quickly away, adding: "And we continue to. But the lesson we must learn above all is how to forgive."

"Is that even an action? Is it actually *doing* something?"

"Ah, *ma fille*, the modern woman, filled with passion and rage . . . You don't realize just how much of an action that forgiving can be."

Cecile guffawed—"Ha!"—excused herself, and left the room.

Her mother watched her go, then said, "She makes me out to be naïve and a simpleton, doesn't she?"

"Not at all, Madame—" Seb began, but she placed a hand on his and he corrected himself: "Not at all, Elodie."

"But you see, I'm not so bad." She smiled. "We're all such mysteries."

She rose abruptly—"Just a minute"—and left the room.

A mystery indeed, Seb thought. He wanted to know more, to ask what it was that they'd suffered. It seemed too forward, though—improper, indiscreet.

He picked at the crumbs on his plate, the sound of rummaging about coming from the hallway. When Madame Rosenbaum—Elodie—returned, she held a book.

"I've been studying graphology."

"Graphology?"

"The study of one's handwriting," she explained. "A friend introduced it to me years ago, just after the German invasion, when Cecile and I were in hiding in a village in the Cantal, and I've been dabbling ever since."

She leaned toward Seb, as though confiding a secret. "Cecile's father calls it 'voodoo nonsense' and refuses to pay for lessons." Voodoo, that word again—and this time, used as a pejorative, something to be ridiculed. "But I've saved from my allowance, so he pays for the courses all the same."

Seb tended to agree with her husband's assessment, despite his crude analogy. Graphology struck him as a contrivance made to sound like science. He asked, "What is it you can see in someone's handwriting?"

"Their character, their fears, their hopes. There's an encyclopedia of insights about a person in every document that he or she writes."

"All this from just the handwriting?"

"This and much more."

She removed a letter from between the pages of the book; he recognized the handwriting as Cecile's.

"Take my daughter, for example," she said with lowered voice. "What's written is nowhere as important as the script itself. Look here." She pointed to a passage of two paragraphs. "You can see that she's willful, maybe even a little self-righteous. But dynamic, too—vigorous."

The writing was tight yet still ornate. "What in the script shows this?"

"I've not achieved competence, you understand, I'm still just learning." She giggled nervously. "But there are signs. Her dynamism and vigor are clear from the quality of the stroke, done with force and speed. And the *t*'s! Look how high she bars them." She shifted her chair closer and pointed to a few. "Consistently throughout she writes them at an acute angle, which indicates her energy and drive."

That sounded completely like the Cecile he knew. Still, he wanted to counter: But she's your daughter! It's easy to "interpret" things from her writing that you already know to be true about her character.

Elodie turned the letter upside down and scanned her finger from bottom to top. "These blank spaces that run the length of the page are called chimneys. They reveal a complex unease, a sort of emotional displacement, that she hides, maybe even from herself. One about which I worry, I might add."

This sounded like Cecile, too—an aspect of her that he recognized without ever quite understanding. He followed Elodie's finger, tracing the pattern of the script.

"And notice how the incline of the letters is inconsistent. Here, the severe back-slant. This is an attempt to conceal—even as it *exposes*—a profound, profound insecurity. It's the writing of someone who's plagued by doubt."

She cut herself off, folding the letter closed. "I've probably said too much." She replaced it in the book, appearing embarrassed. "And I'm only a student, of course, and don't know much at all yet."

"Fascinating," he said, and he meant it. He was truly sorry that she'd stopped. "Maybe I could write something out and you could tell me what you see?"

"Well . . ." She dropped her eyes, and he wished he hadn't asked.

"It should be something you've written naturally," she said, looking up just as suddenly, her eyes animated again—Cecile's, when he told the stories of his forefathers and she wanted more. "What I mean is, bring me something not written expressly to be analyzed."

He made a mental note to remember to carry a letter next time. And he found himself feeling anxious for there to be a next time, an opportunity to make another visit. He would bring one of the letters he'd received in Burgundy from Zansi; Elodie could help him uncover *her* secrets.

"You look exhausted," she said, then she called into the other room: "*Chérie!* Show Sebastien to the library so he can stretch out on the daybed for a while."

He'd only dozed on the platform at Saint-Lazare but not really slept. A quick nap sounded so appealing . . .

But Zansi.

"No, really," he said, "though thank you. I have to get back to the city."

Elodie began clearing the table. "Well, sit in the front room while I make you a basket to take with you."

He went to the sofa and sank into its plush cushions, wondering where Cecile had gotten to. The sounds of Elodie in the kitchen made him realize that he should lend a hand with cleanup, but the cushy embrace of the sofa stopped him—so, so comfortable . . .

The front room was like so many in France—formal but spare; ordered; with lots of wood, much of the furniture antique. A low table next to the sofa was topped with framed photographs of what must have been family. Among these he noted a small oil painting. Its bold colors stood out against the sepia canvas, and he recognized immediately that it was by Cecile. The brushstrokes matched Elodie's description of her handwriting—done with force and speed; characterized by dynamism and drive; perhaps a bit impulsive.

The image was of an African landscape, with a squat palace, its walls a rich earthen red, foregrounded against a shimmer of trees. There was a pointillist representation of a crowd at the palace gate, an aggregation of many-colored pagne robes. A female figure, bare-breasted and regal, stood out among them. Cecile had entitled the painting *Agontimé*, after the nineteenth-century queen Seb had told her about.

Was it art? Maybe. But distinctive? For certain—inklings of a unique voice.

What irony, he thought. He dreamt of erecting skyscrapers in a France that was not his, and she painted pastorals of an Africa she'd never seen.

The ebony frame was simple, hard to come by these days but appropriate to the content. Surely Elodie's contribution. He wondered if there was more artwork somewhere in the house, sketches and studies maybe—everything Cecile had ever shared with her, kept close to heart, just for

Elodie herself, probably in her bedroom, in a file or drawer consecrated especially to them.

The thought made Seb realize the degree to which he himself hadn't seen much of Cecile's work. Sketches in the margins of notebooks; doodling on the Tournon's white paper napkins. Their exam prep had been so all-consuming, hours and hours spent talking about what he needed to learn about art theory and history, but never anything about her own practice. He'd never asked, and she never offered.

How had this come to be?

He heard water swashing in the kitchen—Elodie, doing the dishes—and when next he heard something else, it was the silence: complete, rustic, with nature noises in the distance, birds chirping, the sound of rustling leaves. The ceiling came into focus, his head pitched onto the seatback, and a blanket lay over him. He'd been drooling.

The clock across the room read 12:20.

Merde!

Not only had he stayed out all night, but all morning as well. And he had no way to reach Zansi directly, to make an excuse, or just to notify her that he was all right so she didn't worry. There was no public phone at the rooming house; he could only leave a message with the concierge.

Merde, merde, merde!

Elodie was still in the kitchen, seated at the table, a yellow cardigan over the forest-green dress. Seb said, "May I use your—" but before he'd finished, she pointed toward the telephone, in a niche off the hallway. He rushed to it.

After he'd hung up, Elodie stopped his scrambling about, handing him a basket. "Fruit preserves and a bit of gruyere."

He thanked her—"*Merci*"—then kissed her cheek.

Then he dashed for the door.

Cecile caught up to him at the curb. "Don't fret. You'll find a good excuse to tell Jacqueline," she said, grinning pointedly rather than genuinely concerned.

Her face softened. "I fell asleep, too, and when I woke up, you looked so peaceful."

He felt uncomfortable kissing Cecile goodbye in front of her mother, who stood in the doorway, smiling. But he wanted to.

"She's quite something," he said. "She reminds me a lot of you."

"Ha!"

"She does," he insisted. "The wonder at new things and the passion. The things I love about you."

He'd not uttered the word aloud before and hadn't expected to now. It silenced her. She stared at him, her face still, something like marvel in her eyes.

"I've got to go," he said, less a reiteration of the obvious than a segue to mask the awkwardness, and he turned and started up the cobblestone street.

"Do come back," he heard Elodie call after him, "anytime you'd like."

He stopped, turned back, and took the time to properly wave goodbye. "I will," he said. "I promise."

He sincerely hoped to see her again soon.

CHAPTER ELEVEN

How was I to know that my daughter would be so enamored of blacks? Elodie began in her journal beneath the date—Friday, 22 August—and her habitual opening—Mon Cher et Très Vieil Ami, "Dear Oldest Friend." She was seated at the kitchen table and dipped the nib of her pen into the inkwell. Before continuing, she turned toward Cecile's closed bedroom door, to where her daughter, exhausted, had retired after the African boy's departure, listening for sounds of movement, for some hint that Cecile was awake and might unexpectedly reemerge. Nothing, so she carried on:

Earlier this summer, after I'd scolded her about her erratic decision-making, she accused me of despising blacks, as though I was chastising her for her choice of friends and not just for her poor choices, and it hurt me more than she could know. Her father, yes. He's always borne a provincial spirit. But me? Ah, no. I feel no contempt for black people. I just worry for her.

Is the world—this one—ready for her generation: for ma petite Cecile, for her turbulent friend Minette, for this charming but solemn boy that she brought for me to meet? Are we ready for their "modernity"?

I don't care that the boy who loves my daughter is black—not one whit! I _do_ fear that the world may not be ready to see them together. That the world is wrongheaded matters little if the result is my daughter's suffering.

She paused, glancing again at Cecile's door, wondering what her lovely yet self-involved daughter would think if she found out that her mother kept a journal. Would she want to read it, especially these passages about her? Alain, her husband, who didn't know about it—from inattentiveness more than anything else—would expect the right to scour it front to back, wanting to oversee even her very thoughts. But Cecile—would she grant Elodie this refuge, this simple private place?

Elodie wasn't certain that she would.

The cottage remained still—just the ring-ring of a bicycle bell outside on the lane, the whistling of a robin in the branches beside the kitchen window. She continued, writing directly to her daughter now, as though it were a letter to her rather than a journal for herself:

I suppose I should have foreseen it, this innate attraction. When you were five, maybe six—and *so* adorable, all dimples and plump cheeks—the Colonial Exposition came to Ile de France, and I took you. Just the two of us, mother and daughter, so that my baby might begin to know the larger world. (Your father deemed it a waste of money.) This was well before the war, people were still amicable with one another, and the Expo's main esplanade was packed with smiling strollers enjoying the costumed Siamese dancers and the Zouaves in ornate fezzes, the mock-up jungle villages and the wild animals in cages. Even the weather felt equatorial.

But you, you had no interest in the attractions I thought you ought to find interesting. Impulsive as ever, you only wanted to see the spectacle beneath a nearby poster-striped tent. As one could resist your will for only so long, I capitulated. We went there, you running ahead. The flap fell closed behind as we entered, and we were engulfed in darkness. I grabbed for your hand. Then I heard a rustling. As my sight slowly adapted, all around were eyes and teeth.

I turned and fled headlong toward the place I remembered the flap to have been, searching frantically with one hand, your resisting hand clutched in the other, and behind us, laughter. Outside in the sharp sunlight I stopped, grabbed you up in my arms, my heart racing.

From the tent emerged two African women wrapped in colorful sarongs and a swarm of children, six, maybe eight, all black as pitch, wearing rags for clothes, with almond-shaped eyes and great smiling mouths.

I flushed scarlet, I was so embarrassed.

You played with the little African children all afternoon, the rest of the Exposition no longer important. I stood with the mothers. They were stunningly black and they would smile at me then chatter between themselves in a language I could not know. I had to drag you away, literally kicking and screaming, so we would make it home in time for me to prepare supper. You made me promise to bring you again, and though I couldn't afford to, you asked day after day to return to your new friends.

As we were leaving, I remember turning to the African mothers and offering what change was left of my twenty-franc allowance—all I would have for the week. Both women laughed, deep and resonant, and shuffled away, leaving me there, my hand outstretched. You always claim to not remember the incident—and to be thankful not to!

"Oh! I needed that," she heard, and reflexively closed the ornate cloth jacket and covered it with her hands.

"Welcome back, sleepyhead," Elodie said, glancing at the wall clock. It read half past two. "I suppose your father isn't coming home for lunch. What can I make for you?"

Cecile sat opposite her. "Does he come home for dinner, even?"

"Stop that. Of course he does."

Which wasn't exactly true. But when work kept him into the night, he always phoned to let her know. Give him credit for that, at least.

Elodie placed the notebook, pen, and inkwell in the drawer beside the sink, where she kept miscellany—for the time being anyway, to prevent it from becoming the topic of conversation. At the refrigerator, she removed the remains of the previous night's dinner, raising the lid of the earthenware casserole so Cecile could see its contents.

"Barigoule? How does that sound?"

There were also eggs, if Cecile preferred an omelet.

"Perfect," Cecile said.

Elodie dumped the tangy mix of artichokes, carrots, and leeks into a pot and lit the flame, turning it low. "You might not think so," she said, "but your father loves you—in his manner, of course."

"And you?" said Cecile. "Does he love you?"

"Ha! Not as much as he loves himself."

She pushed loose clumps of vegetables with a ladle, vigorously stirring, embarrassed by her unintended outburst.

"Is he proud?" Cecile asked. "You know, to be a Jew?"

Elodie stopped then, waiting for her daughter to meet her eyes.

"With the risks he took? How can you even ask?"

Cecile dropped her gaze, fiddling with the hem of her blouse. "It's just . . . Papa doesn't, we don't really, *do* anything. Jewish, you know."

"We didn't before the war either—never synagogue, never high holidays. Only now it makes us less Jewish?"

"But your mother, she was Catholic. Is that why?"

Elodie's mother had never been part of Cecile's life, and Cecile had never been particularly curious about her before—or about Elodie's father and stepmother for that matter. A question here or there, which Elodie had always answered honestly though tersely. This interest now puzzled her.

"With time," Elodie said, avoiding a direct answer, "they would have come for us, too. We would have been plenty enough Jewish then, I promise you."

She hovered a hand above the Barigoule, to test if it was ready, then turned off the flame, divided the contents of the pot into two portions, and sat one plate before Cecile and the other at her place.

Cecile retrieved two forks from the silverware drawer. "Mamie Lucie used to have pens like the one you put away," she said.

"That pen was Lucie's," Elodie confessed, covering her mouth, as much to conceal her smile as to screen her chewing. "I lifted it one day when she'd made me angry."

Cecile smiled in return, complicitous. "Were you writing about my surprise visit?"

"How do you know I wasn't just making a list of errands to run?"

"You've kept a diary since I can remember. Did you think I didn't notice?"

Suspicion confirmed, her daughter knew.

Cecile teased: "You can't keep secrets from me."

Elodie wondered even more now if Cecile hadn't been sneaking into the notebook, reading her private thoughts.

"And you," she said, "you keep plenty of secrets."

Cecile appeared to blush. "Seb, you mean?"

"Don't pretend you're not in love with that boy."

Cecile shrugged noncommittally—or maybe just evasively.

Elodie said, "Well, it's clear that he feels strongly for you."

She noticed that Cecile wasn't eating so much as moving pieces of vegetable around, her fork scraping rhythmically against the porcelain—the scree-scree of metal tine on plate.

"Not just him, though," she said. "Your life in the city is all somewhat mysterious." She flipped a hand melodramatically up to her forehead. "*Les scènes de la vie de bohème*, I suppose?"

"Go ahead, mock me. But my life is exciting."

"*Exciting*," Elodie mimicked. Though she'd been aiming for levity, her tone was more derisive than playful.

Cecile grabbed her hand, her eyes earnest. "I love you, Maman, I do. But I'm not you. I want to be my own someone."

"You want to be everything but who you actually are!" Her outburst surprised even her, but she went on: "When I see you in those starched trousers and your imperious airs, the hardened self-assurance, I don't recognize you—you, my Cecile! Criticizing everything, dissecting everything, reviling everything. Intellectual, sure—certainly more intelligent than me—but so little feminine. You put on personalities like new clothes, but it's not *you*."

Each one met the other's eyes, anger flaring. Then both burst into laughter.

"Bravo, Monsieur Sartre," Elodie said between gasps for breath, "master of the void and of the negative." She spoke softly now but toward the wall, as though Sartre's face might magically appear there, in tortoiseshell glasses and a smile that bordered on smirk. "If this is tomorrow's woman, bravo."

It started to rain. They turned toward the sound, the patter of mice's feet against the windowpane. The steady beat calmed Cecile. She didn't know what to say to make her mother understand that she couldn't wear the old clothes anymore—absolutely could not, no.

Her mother began tracing a fingertip over Cecile's knuckles, over and back, over and back, seemingly unconsciously. "You may find this hard to believe," she said, "but at nineteen, twenty, I wasn't so unlike how you are now. I didn't want a husband. All I wanted was to learn a skill, something that would allow me to leave home—to become a nurse, a stenographer maybe."

Her mouth let loose a giggle that suggested embarrassment more than mirth.

"My stepmother refused, of course. She found your father for me to marry and instructed that I keep a nice house and be a good ear for my husband and a loving mother for my children." She looked directly at Cecile. "For my child. And that's what I've done. So tell me, would we have survived the Occupation if I'd done otherwise, if I had been some rebel and malcontent, fighting your father's decisions at every turn?"

A "rebel," a "malcontent"—Cecile thought these apt words to describe her and didn't regard either as a negative trait, as descriptions of someone she would prefer to not be. She said, "My friends, they're from the colonies, they're artists and thinkers—people striving for freedom, for justice. It was the French, you know, not Germans, who came for us."

"But not for *you*!" Elodie snapped, again uncertain of the source of this sudden pique. "Your father and I made sure of that."

She took up her fork, put a sizeable bite into her mouth, and chewed herself calm.

A booming crack—thunder. Both turned toward the window.

Maybe it was the moment—mother and daughter connecting, albeit about their differences—but a wave of memory overcame Elodie, one that didn't rise often. "Do you remember Chandesaignes," she asked, "when we fled the Germans?"

"I remember the violent thunderstorms," Cecile said.

"Every day at four," she confirmed, "as if on a timer."

June 1940, before the Occupation but after the outbreak of war, after the government had mobilized the army and recalled Alain, sending him to the front. The Germans routed them, and instead of fathers and husbands and brothers, the women and children got panicked stories of Nazi tank corps advancing on Paris in return.

Nearly the entire population deserted the capital. Elodie remembered the lines of lorries and horse-drawn wagons and automobiles weighted down with wooden crates stacked and strapped any which way, tables and chairs and rolled and twined mattresses. There were families on foot, people with cardboard suitcases and burlap sacks, whatever they could carry or fit into prams or pushcarts or shopping trolleys, crowding the roads, streaming south.

A neighbor who owned a car offered a place in his back seat. Elodie didn't consult with Lucie or with anyone. She packed a single bag for the two of them and what money she had on hand and left a letter for Alain on the mantel. Not a moment's hesitation.

It was slow going, the roads a turmoil of glinting metal and stagnant air and shrill horns, Cecile restless on her lap in the rear, nearly thirteen and too old for that perch, wedged between luggage and the side panel.

On a petrol stop in the village of Chandesaignes, in the Cantal region, Elodie inquired at the lone hotel. The innkeeper said there was one min-iscule room left, just a double bed and a dresser beneath a small window. Their neighbor tried to dissuade Elodie from staying, promising to get them as far as Pau, a short distance from the border, but Elodie said no. There was a military bivouac nearby; this gave a feeling of security. And so many others were continuing on, aiming for Spain or Portugal. She decided they should take what was available.

All this, all on her own. No Alain making decisions without consult-ing her, no Lucie criticizing her every move. Elodie took Cecile to the local school, and when the schoolmaster refused to enroll her—the academic year nearly ended, too late to accommodate new students—Elodie railed and insisted, and he relented. She did whatever needed doing, however uncharacteristic or uncomfortable, as long as things were as normal as possible for Cecile.

But nothing was normal. This was not Le Vésinet—their cottage, their street, Alain's family nearby. Down the hill, the rows of army tents made a geometry of the valley floor, frenetic with the activity of khaki-clad men hustling to and fro, here and about. Farmers with sun-leathered faces and in tartan caps towed handcarts to market in town past the scattered knots of refugee encampments pocking their fields of lavender and mustard seed. On the village square, the charred remains of La Poste, struck by lightning, listed churchward, ever threatening, never falling. And every day at four, the violent storms—thunder and cords of rain. And every day, tattered soldiers in small groups straggled into town, having been driven from the front or fleeing it, often without weapons, usually drunk, never including Alain.

The place where Elodie found reprieve was in the little church on the square, Église de Saint-François. Faith and religion had never meant much to her, ever, but day after day another crisis arose—the hotel pro-prietor threatening to let their room to a higher bidder; yet more rumors of the Germans' imminent approach—and who could know which one would prove unavoidable or insurmountable, and when that impending catastrophe finally occurred, then where would they be, she and Cecile?

But not inside the church. There, no one asked anything of her. The few people present didn't even appear to notice her. Strolling up the nave and back, into one transept then the other, she found a clarity and order that otherwise seemed increasingly impossible to sustain. She would stare at the stained glass windows until she'd decrypted the stories they told—the good Samaritan; the trials of Job; the prodigal son.

In a small chapel off the ambulatory was a statue of Saint François, life-sized, on a pedestal so low that he seemed to stand right there before her, his eyes level with hers and not a meter above her head, like the memorial to the Great War on the square. The sculptor had chiseled the figure in a plain frock and a monk's tonsure, its hands cupped, arms outstretched, and in the linked palms was carved a dove, painted white against the flinty gray of the rest. François, the patron saint of the poor and of animals. The saint of peace. Elodie wanted to crawl into his arms, like the stone bird.

Then the dove took flight—the sudden coo and the whooshing of wings!

She'd started, her heart racing. The dove, the entire place, had resonated with life.

She now asked Cecile, "Do you remember the church?"

"I used to go there sometimes after school. I tried to sketch the rose window."

"Do you remember asking to be baptized?"

It had surprised Elodie. This was before Bon Sauveur, and Cecile hadn't seemed aware of religion at all—any religion, their own, such was their negligible adherence to it, much less someone else's.

Cecile nodded yes, as she *did* remember the incident. She remembered that her mother had misunderstood the request, worried that Cecile was being teased or bullied in school, the new arrival, and a Jew, to boot. Her classmates had done neither, though, teased nor bullied. She and her friends played hide-and-seek in the surrounding fields and monkeyed in a falling-down windmill and snuck cigarettes from one boy's blind father's. They cracked wise but never spoke of anything of significance. The girls prattled on about the boys, the boys about the American film star Betty Grable. Of religion, nothing.

Cecile pushed her plate away. "I thought that if I was baptized, you might join, too, and then you might fit in better . . . I mean, if you were going to stay on there."

Elodie understood immediately: Cecile was alluding to Capitaine Garrillaud, to Fernand. She felt herself blushing. Seven years past and still as vivid a feeling for him as then.

She felt that she needed to explain herself, despite the lapse of time. "The days were so hard—so, so hard. But after I'd put you to bed, Capitaine Garrillaud and I would sit together on the sofa in the hotel parlor. He always wanted to hear about me—about my family and upbringing, about my likes and dislikes, about *me*. And he told me wonderful stories about medicine, which he claimed was more sorcery and luck than science. He was from Nice, so he talked about sailing and the sea, about tides and winds and mapping by the stars. And graphology, his latest passion! We studied his mother's letters, and it was as if I were meeting her in person, and I fell in love with her, too."

Elodie realized that she sounded as childish and impulsive as Cecile. Or as brave?

She said, "I was an idiot to think you wouldn't notice. You seemed to like him, though."

"I did," said Cecile. "He was kind. Still, I was rooting for my father."

And now it was Cecile who felt the need to elaborate, to better say what she was aiming for, because her last statement seemed insufficient. She said, "Would you have taken me with you?"

"Pardon?"

"You grew up with a father and no mother, so I mean—I could too, right?" She shifted on her seat. "Had you stayed with the army doctor, would you have kept me with you?"

Mais quelle idée! Elodie thought—viscerally—wanting to slap her daughter's face.

"You seemed so happy," Cecile explained, "and I'm such a Rosenbaum, after all. I was then, anyway. I would have only kept you tied to them."

She wanted to slap Cecile. She also had to admit to having asked herself this very thing—briefly, a fleeting thought, but one that had arisen all the same. She'd felt so much herself when with Fernand, her true self, and she'd also felt free. A new life had seemed possible—she could start over again, despite the looming war—and Cecile hadn't always appeared in those fantasy images.

Then one afternoon Alain had arrived. Elodie would never forget the sight of him: enfeebled by dysentery, eyes sunken and black, his uniform falling off him like clothes off a wire hanger. Her throat had knotted. She'd felt such profound, profound pity. And also overwhelming confusion, seeing the world she'd begun allowing herself to imagine all of a sudden come undone.

She'd slipped off to the church while Fernand and his staff attended to her husband. Saint François's benediction, inscribed in cursive script on the wall beside the statue, had revealed itself as though for the very first time: *Seigneur, faites de moi un instrument de votre paix.*

> *Where there is hatred, let me sow love.*
> *Where there is injury, pardon.*
> *Where there is despair, hope.*

> *Divine Master, grant that I may not so much seek to be loved,*
> *as to love.*
> *For it is in giving that we receive.*

The words hadn't seemed a sign—some mystical augury about what to do next—so much as confirmation of the inevitability of things.

Cecile, rising to clear the lunch dishes, brought Elodie back to Le Vésinet and the present. At the sink, she began scraping and rinsing, scraping and rinsing, the faucet running.

"You're a woman now," Elodie said to her back. "You're learning about desire and intimacy. I have, too."

Cecile wouldn't turn to face her.

So, Elodie went to her, took hold of her from behind—as much of her daughter as she could contain in her arms.

"But the only love, the real love, was for you. It was for you that I did what I did. At times it felt burdensome, sure. But more than even myself, you're the only one I've ever truly known."

Cecile's body released into hers. She turned and kissed her mother on the cheek.

Then she crossed to her room and closed the door.

CHAPTER TWELVE

Friday, 22 August (continued):

Saint François's instruction: For it is in giving that we receive.

Giving, receiving. I was reared to offer the former. Do I not deserve some of the latter, too?

I suppose that, despite the many, many things I don't understand, the one thing I _do_ know is family. It's the question I've troubled over all my life and, as a result, is the only thing that I truly trust to guide my actions.

We learn from negative examples, or at least I have—from experiences that reveal themselves as what _not_ to do. I was raised by a loving father who would have doted on me even more were it not for his weakness for women, and his debts. My _maman_, my blood mother, had been a dancer—beautiful, I'm told, an artist's model before meeting Papa. He worshiped her, but when I was just a baby, she fled Paris for her village in Brittany. She blamed the pregnancy for having undermined her career and ruining her life.

When I was of age, Papa married me into a family of means, and this met his needs: his surrender to the gaming life and the losses that had resulted; the appetites of my egocentric stepmother, who'd replaced _Maman_ with my father. I hardly knew the Rosenbaums when my father betrothed me, but he reassured me: "Do not worry, my child. They are Jews, and we are Jews. They will love you."

My new husband was handsome but did not speak—very few words, ever. He deflated like a balloon the moment he stepped inside our front door. He would sit in his reading chair, leaf through the newspaper, and wait for his supper. With others, on Sunday visits to Mamie Lucie's or out in public, he would expand and distend, become a full person again. But with me . . .

This is all old ground, much covered already in these pages, but it seems appropriate to return here today: I did not love my new husband. Not love like the motion pictures promised. I obeyed and did not complain, but how could I love? I didn't know him.

And he certainly didn't love me. Most of the time, he didn't seem to particularly like me. He bedded me, of course. The absence of anything but flesh beneath our sheets was not an obstacle for him. When I became pregnant, I rejoiced silently at this victory. Here would be love—my own.

I had no real model of motherly love. There was nothing for me to learn of this from my stepmother or Lucie. So, I thought—naïvely, it turns out—that, with the passage of years, my own maman might have something to teach me.

I sent a few letters to Brittany and tried to establish contact (this was well before the Occupation), and after a time I began receiving replies. Eventually, I posted a train ticket (I had to ask Alain for an advance on my allowance) with an invitation to spend a week with us—with me, her daughter. She arrived at Gare Saint-Lazare, I went to fetch her in a taxi. (That great distance, the exorbitant fare!) Her first breakfast, I prepared tea. She said she preferred coffee. She didn't particularly care for my child, whom she called loud and too boisterous. All that interested her the length of her stay was our financial status. She expressed surprise to find us living in so modest a house. "Are not the in-laws antiques dealers?" she quipped. On and on: the guest bedroom was so small, our set of silverware surprisingly meager . . .

We choose our friends. Family is chosen for us.

I remember the two of us facing one another across the small kitchen table. Without a hat, her hair down and before having put on her face, I was staring in a mirror.

The worst, though, was that we shared the exact same voice, one the echo of the other! I couldn't listen to her speak without hearing myself. It was impossible—so, so painful.

After three days, she told me, "You know, maybe it's best I return home." And she did, the very next morning. I took her to Saint-Lazare and put her on the train.

Motherly love, I came to understand, was there or it wasn't. All the many things that a mother needs to know can be got from examples elsewhere, or just from good sense and intuition. If I have failed, I failed while trying to do it better than was done for me.

(Ma Cecile chérie, if you're reading this, I hope it has been instructive about the real me, your mother as she truly is—the lessons learned; what not to do.)

(And I also hope that your return to the city today—that your move there in the first place—had nothing of this in it, of being confronted with an impossible mirror.)

CHAPTER THIRTEEN

Exiting the Tournon the Sunday before the exam—six hours straight of last-minute review—Cecile and Seb stepped almost directly into Jacqueline, who was walking down the street. Cecile had only seen her once before, from a distance, standing opposite Seb outside École de Médecine—just as tall as him and much darker, but Cecile had immediately known who she was. Up close now, she took note of even more: the long neck and sculpted features; her opaque gaze, that of a cat.

"*Tiens!*" Jacqueline said, offering her hand to Seb—formal, more polite than familiar. How odd a gesture, Cecile thought, between a sister and brother. "And I'd thought you were with Boubacar."

"I was," he said, "earlier," shaking her hand, suddenly stiff, also meekly deferential.

And dishonest. He hadn't been with Boubi. She and Seb had spent the night together in his room then met a few short hours later here at the Tournon, for final prep.

"What I meant was," said Jacqueline, "I thought you'd told me that you were studying for the exam today."

"We were." Seb gestured toward Cecile but didn't introduce her. "She's helping me."

Jacqueline extended her hand then and smiled, though the smile seemed forced. "Cecile Rosenbaum, isn't it? I've heard of you. You're from a family of Resistants."

She'd heard of her? It must have been from Boubi—Boubacar as she called him, so formally—because it clearly hadn't been from Seb. He just stood there, eyes dull, his bearing tense, as detached from Cecile as he seemed from his sister.

"My father, yes," Cecile replied. "They gave him a medal."

"Ah, a true patriot," Jacqueline said, beaming her forced smile.

Then to Seb: "So, you were studying." She pointed to the café. "Here?"

"It's central, more convenient than meeting at the library," said Seb, defensive, and Cecile didn't know why he should be. Everybody worked in cafés.

Jacqueline didn't say more. Her silence said everything.

Seb said nothing either, not to his sister or to Cecile, his face blank. Both just stood there, facing one another, Cecile the silent third wheel in this strained encounter.

She'd felt scrutinized by Seb before. The look he sometimes gave, uncontrolled though unintended, when she asked or said something he thought jejune or facile—when, exhausted, she might blurt just any response to a question; when she spouted Communist rhetoric. This feeling, though, standing before him and his sister, wasn't the remembered one of having inadvertently disappointed. The distance, his air of impatience, side by side with imperious Jacqueline . . .

He'd professed love in Le Vésinet; now, Cecile wanted to slap him.

Jacqueline looked toward the sky, then left and right, all around. "I love Paris at this time of year. We haven't seen an August this quiet since before the war."

When neither Seb nor Cecile said anything in reply, Jacqueline offered her hand, first to Cecile then to her brother. "Well, I don't want to keep you from your work. *Au revoir.*"

Each one in turn shook. Jacqueline continued down Rue Tournon.

Cecile spun on her heels and went the other way, up Rue de Vaugirard, toward the Jardin du Luxembourg.

Seb caught her. "Cecile, please. Cecile!" He held her by the shoulders so that she couldn't break away. "You knew my family wouldn't approve of our relationship, you knew . . . My father! You have to have known this."

"I didn't, no. I do now." She stopped fighting his hands. "Because I'm white?"

Yovo, she thought. Such an ugly word.

He followed a passing bus with his eyes rather than meet hers. "Because you're not Dahomeyan," he said, letting his hands slip from her shoulders and stepping past, grabbing the metal bars of the ornamental fence and gazing into the park. "I'm the son of the son of the king who had to be exiled far away so that a continent wouldn't rally around his name and revolt. My name is meant to incarnate his."

Gbéhanzin: the egg that the Earth desires. Cecile knew the words, they'd become hers, too—though right then they seemed flat, lifeless.

"But yes," he continued, "also because you're French. With what the French have done to my home, how could my father accept a French girl for his only son?"

She looked at him, took him all in, clutching the fence, an iron bar in each hand—a parody of a prisoner.

Him, the prisoner in this situation?

Jacqueline was wrong, Cecile thought. The quiet city didn't evoke a feeling of tranquility; it reminded her of Maisons-Laffitte after the bombings. The white-stone, six-floor walkups were hollowed vaults, their insides airless—what remained after capitulation.

She began walking. When he moved to join her, she threw out a hand. "Please! I just need you to let me be."

Cecile slept fitfully that night and found three notes from Seb downstairs the next morning. Had he camped in the lobby, waiting to ambush her as he had all those months ago?

Each one began with a similar-sounding apology:

"I'm so sorry, Cecile."

"Please meet me and let's talk."

"You know what you mean to me."

None provided the least solace. Even their sendoffs—"With all my heart"—seemed as disingenuous as his empty stare the day before, when they'd run into his sister.

Even as she tried to stop thinking about him, her mind circled back again and again to the question: What had happened? She'd begun to reveal herself, her full self. She'd even taken him to Le Vésinet. Now, Cecile feared that she might have misjudged him all along.

There was also a note from Minette:

> *Where have you been, fillette? I don't see you in weeks, you come out*
> *for a night of dancing then disappear again . . . There's an important*
> *League meeting today—important! Rendezvous at Châtelet after*
> *your shift.*

Cecile was glad for the distraction.

Minette was already at Châtelet when Cecile arrived, leaning against the railing at the entrance of the Metro, looking impatient. On the walk to the meeting, nearby at the Palais des Fêtes, she told Cecile that her father had stayed in town on a workday for the general assembly, that *syndicalistes* from all over France had come.

The auditorium, typically used as a cinema, was crammed, every seat taken and each aisle teeming with men listening to the discussion—dispute, really—that was already underway onstage, beneath the broad projection screen. (As usual, the gathering was almost exclusively men, which never seemed to trouble Minette but always stood out to Cecile.) The union leaders sat on impromptu seats—folding chairs; turned-over milk crates; a large trunk. On the far right was Monsieur Traoré, the only black person up there—the only one, in fact, in what Cecile could see of the packed room.

Scanning the crowd, she wondered if someone from the African student group was present. Maybe it would be Jacqueline, with her imperious gaze. Wouldn't that be just Cecile's luck?

The clamor and agitation all around brought her attention back to the auditorium. The debate, which was as animated in the audience as onstage, was difficult to follow, and she tried as best she could to make out the various arguments being shouted over one another.

"A parliament without full representation is not a parliament—"

"But how does this get us concessions at Boulogne-Billancourt—?"

"*Putain de* de Gaulle! He thinks the people will bring him back if he pouts long enough—"

Beyond the usual points of contention—soaring inflation, continued rationing, favoritism toward the capitalist class—a central theme emerged: the proposed expulsion of Communist Party ministers from the government. This was fueling the furor in the room.

Cecile didn't hear the comment that provoked it, but Monsieur Traoré burst from his chair—"*Mais non*, Pierre!" It stilled the chaos.

The room now quiet, Monsieur Traoré repeated calmly, almost entreatingly, toward a man standing in the first row: "*Non*, Pierre. Violence is not the way." By his sooty smock and denim trousers, the man, Pierre, appeared to be a railway worker. "Discussions first," Monsieur Traoré insisted. "Negotiations. This is what has gotten us where we are today."

"And where are we?" Pierre responded, throwing his hands in the air. "We've joined their negotiations and asked nicely, and now they threaten to have us removed from the room!"

The two squared off, letting the silence stretch.

Minette whispered close to Cecile's ear. "That's Pierre Frontin of the eastern railway workers. He and Papa are often at odds."

"You think that sabotage and Resistance tactics will get us back in it?" Monsieur Traoré said. "Against our own government?"

"Those are precisely the tactics we've used, and yes, against our own government, when they sided with the Boches."

"*Tu exagères*, Pierre!" said a man in one-piece coveralls—either a mechanic or a long-haul lorry driver. "However bad this current government, it's not Vichy."

"And how long till it becomes Vichy all over again?" Frontin retorted to general hisses and exclamations of protest. "How long!" he repeated, shouting and stomping his foot to quiet the others. "It was our neighbors, ordinary Frenchmen, who joined with the Germans." He pointed at Monsieur Traoré. "Maybe your people are loyal and docile, Souf, maybe you don't have to worry about backstabbing and betrayal. But here in the Hexagon, it's all we've known since '40, and even before. 1792! 1848!"

Hissing erupted anew around the room. Minette rose onto her toes and joined in.

"Stop that now," said Monsieur Traoré, batting the air with his hands. "Please, please, brothers. Order, please."

Minette wouldn't stop hissing, even as others around them calmed. She leaned toward Cecile, her face clenched. "Goddamned racist bastard."

When the room stilled, Monsieur Traoré continued: "I'm French like you, Pierre—every bit as much. This conversation, yours and mine, cannot advance if we resort to petty insults. And neither can our group's exchange with Ramadier"—the prime minister—"if we escalate before having exhausted negotiations."

Frontin sat, an angry gesture, plopping into his seat and disappearing from Cecile's view below the swath of faces staring, some glaring, in his direction. A man near him took up where Frontin had left off, though in a more even tone.

"At what point are the negotiations exhausted? How do we know? Pierre is not wrong. If our Communist representatives are removed, our only remaining voice may be violence."

Cecile said, "Maybe the coalition isn't large enough."

"What?" said Minette, yet focused on the debate.

Scanning the room a second time, Cecile felt certain that no one from the African student group was present—that the colonies, broadly, weren't represented, as they had been in Hyères. "Colonial subjects—they're also resisting Ramadier's government," she explained. "Like Seb and Boubi's group. If the coalition is larger, our voice will be louder, stronger."

Minette spun toward her. "Stop treating this like some episode in your sexual escapades. It's serious business." She knocked a knuckle against Cecile's forehead. "Stay focused."

Direct, as always, even to the point of callousness.

The conversation in the auditorium had shifted to logistics. Someone was saying, "It'll be a nationwide meeting, here in the capital."

"In November?"

"Yes, in two months, so locals can organize and mobilize."

"Good," said Monsieur Traoré. "Plenty of time to canvass for votes before the elections."

Minette, attention riveted on the stage, said, "I agree with Papa on most things. On the issue of violent confrontation, though, he's wrong."

As the general assembly dispersed, Monsieur Traoré embraced each girl quickly before rushing off to a follow-up meeting of the leadership. Minette and Cecile joined a stream of *syndicalistes* headed to the Café de la Poste and squeezed into a throng of men at the zinc counter there. The atmosphere remained electric, the room as loud as at the meeting. It was hard to be heard.

"Seb and I had a terrible fight," Cecile announced—flatly, just relaying information.

"Good!" said Minette. "Finally." She waved two fingers at the barman until he signaled having noted her order. "Doing all that work for him. It was demeaning."

Minette's anger always lurked just below the surface, ready to rise. Still, her outburst surprised Cecile.

"The work benefited me, too," she said, "for the Louvre exam, when I take it."

The Louvre exam was still just an aspiration, nothing she'd applied any real thought to. But Minette wouldn't know this, so it made her rationalization credible.

"All of France is in upheaval, and you trouble me with this petty crap," Minette said. "He's just a boy. Tell him what you want, and if he—"

"What I want?"

The barman placed two coffees on the countertop in front of them.

Minette drank hers in a quick swallow. "A ring on your finger, whatever. Tell him, and if he won't give it"—she pointed toward Cecile's midriff—"then you take it."

Cecile didn't want a ring, much less a baby. She hadn't considered either. What she wanted was the possibility to commiserate with her friend; she'd also hoped for input on how to make sense of the turn with Seb. Instead, she found herself defending him.

"You don't understand. The pressure he's under."

"Who isn't under pressure?" Minette indicated the men to their right and left. "Them! *They're* under pressure."

She spat on the floor.

"Ah! Ces nègres" she said, more to herself than Cecile, though Cecile stood right there beside her. "For them, white pussy is a prize."

She met Cecile's eyes. "You go and fuck somebody else, preferably another nigger. That'll get his attention."

The humming café felt suddenly still, the city outside empty. Cecile hadn't mentioned the reason for the trouble with Seb—that she was *Yovo*. Yet, it always came down to this with Minette, to shaming Cecile for being white.

"There are bigger things going on," Minette continued. "We're determining the future. France will be a Communist nation, and we have the chance to help shape it. But you, what do you concern yourself with? Chasing after boys."

Minette pushed through the crowd toward the exit. When she noted that Cecile wasn't following, she said, "Let's go. Papa will be free soon."

Cecile took in her friend, the radiant beauty that masked all the rage—not just at the world but at Cecile, too. She nodded no.

"Suit yourself," said Minette. She turned and left.

CHAPTER FOURTEEN

The entrance competition was taking place across the street, in the amphitheater at Beaux-Arts, so Cecile decided that she would rise extra early for each of its remaining four days and be gone before Seb had a chance to catch her in the hotel restaurant or in her room. She wished him well, the very best, but she wasn't ready to see him. Not yet.

At three in the morning between days one and two, unable to sleep, she took her raincoat from the hook behind the door, draped it over her nightgown, and went down and across the street to the bulletin board beneath the bust of Nicolas Poussin, which overlooked the entrance to the school. There, the results were posted for the first section of the test, general education. The list was long, but she found Seb's name near the top. He'd scored a fifteen out of twenty, a superior mark. She felt relief—and also a bit of pride, like she deserved of some of the credit, as the topic had been the one that Seb had most feared and that they'd worked hardest on together.

Later that day, it would be art history and aesthetics, the next day structural concepts and mathematics, on and on through Friday—pass and advance or fail and exit the competition. She and Seb had learned that only the fifty highest cumulative scorers would make up that year's class.

Cecile gazed into the dark beyond the bust of Poussin, imagined herself crossing the cobblestone courtyard, a satchel over her shoulder, a cardboard portfolio under an arm—a student at the most renowned art school in the world!

This was just fantasy, of course. As Minette had not so gently pointed out, Cecile herself wasn't sitting for the exam.

Cecile never did settle into a restful sleep. Later that morning, she ducked out of her hotel well before the test-takers would begin to arrive and headed in the direction opposite the one from which Seb would be coming. Tuesdays, the Louvre was closed, but she crossed the Pont des Arts as though going to work and wandered into the sprawling market of Les Halles. Called the breadbasket of the city, it was dead—not vacant, as stalls and sellers abounded, but still, with few having much on offer. She made her way to Café de la Poste, where the day before, her supposed best friend had waylaid her. Cecile stood on the very spot at the bar, ordered a coffee.

Gazing at her reflection in the backbar mirror as Minette had done, between the array of wine and liquor bottles, she tried to make sense of Minette's anger, to understand the ire she'd unleashed on Cecile. In the note she'd left at Cecile's hotel, Minette had reproached her for "disappearing"—for spending so much time with someone other than her. Was she just jealous, showing that typical girlish pettiness?

At Bon Sauveur, when Cecile would sit at lunch with Marie-Ange or Claudine, two girls who sketched beautifully, Katya would become cross and standoffish—this, even though she couldn't care less about art. But Minette wasn't Katya. She wasn't your typical girl.

She'd once told Cecile that she knew she'd end up with an African, and here it was Cecile who'd connected with one—not just fooling around, like Minette was with Boubi, occasionally and on a whim, but seriously, day in and day out. (Though it had taken a turn, of course.) So, a different sort of jealousy, then?

Cecile couldn't imagine it. For as much as Minette sought every boy's attention, she also insisted on not wanting to be bound by any single one, African or otherwise, none of them living up to the model of her father.

If not jealousy, maybe offense: Minette supposed that Cecile wanted to marry Seb—for him to "put a ring on her finger"—and from her view, white and black made "mongrels," the horrible thing she sometimes called herself. Could this have been the source of her brutal anger?

Cecile just didn't understand. One thing seemed clear, though. To Minette, she was just another white girl. How was it that she hadn't finally become Cecile?

She signaled the barman for another coffee.

Whatever the cause of Minette's outburst, maybe she wasn't entirely wrong either. "Demeaning" herself was how Minette had phrased it, and what if Cecile had indeed been blinded by Seb's qualities—by his discerning words and his imposing voice, by his seeming consideration and care—without paying sufficient attention to the rest? All those evenings at the Tournon, advancing his studies and boosting his spirits, then the nights in his room after, marveling at his stories and sneaking out before the sunrise . . . In the light of day, it suddenly felt indecent. Had she reduced herself to merely this again, to a mother and a lay? Was Seb just Joël anew?

She downed the second coffee and left. Crossed back over the Seine to the Quartier latin, to her neighborhood—hers! Up Rue Danton, past Théâtre de l'Odéon, down Rue Racine, briskly walking. The streets rustled with people, with life.

A line was forming at the cinema Le Champo, on Rue des Écoles— above the entrance, the poster for the Disney film *Fantasia*. It had won awards and praise from critics, though Minette had mocked Cecile's interest in it. "Maybe if you wish upon a star," she'd said, "you'll get to marry an American."

Cecile bought a ticket. The buoyant mouse was not Pif le Chien, hardly. Still, she found herself charmed. The imagination and gaiety; the dancing brooms, sweeping out the dusty oldness, heralding something that was new. Cecile told herself that this was what life could be: not dour and anxious and mistrustful, but full of possibility.

Though she'd reclaimed her neighborhood as her own, Cecile still preferred to not run into Seb if she could help it. So, she expanded her wanderings. After work on Wednesday, she ranged down Rue de Rivoli and into the side streets of the Marais. She had a one-percenter at a café on Rue Vieille du Temple, reading Beauvoir's recent *Le Sang des Autres*, which she found strangely, almost uncomfortably, close to her current situation. Upon her return to the quarter, she checked the list at Beaux-Arts before going to her room. Seb had done much poorer on structural concepts and mathematics than general education, slipping into the second half of the scores. Still, he'd advanced to Thursday.

After work the next evening, she stopped by the tally sheet (he'd done better, in the top quarter, though in the bottom of it) before heading north, toward Opéra. Seb had once called the building an "architectural misfire": baroque in style, sure, but with too much gilt sculpture and too many overly busy friezes. She continued on, past the simple block of church, Notre-Dame de Lorette, and up the steep Rue des Martyrs, the white-stone cupolas of the Sacré-Coeur hovering in the distance, between the buildings.

Her route wasn't random. Before leaving the hotel, she'd rummaged through her things for the Lucky Strikes pack on which the zoot-suited American from the Rhumerie had written the address of the American café. There was little chance of running into Seb there, nor into Minette for that matter. She located it halfway up Rue des Martyrs, a sign above the door announcing PAYNE'S PLACE in English, and another in the window, SOUL FOOD. Cecile translated the latter as food of the spirit and wondered what this could mean, what dishes this might consist of.

She'd changed into denims and a turtleneck at her hotel and felt terribly underdressed the moment she stepped inside. The place was more restaurant than bistro, relaxed though not informal. Men were dressed nicely, not zoot-suited but in casual jackets and ties. All were black and clearly American. A few were with black girls, clearly American, too—in dresses or skirts, a few with fashionable shawls draped over their shoulders. They all fell quiet and turned toward Cecile, standing in the doorway.

She'd planned to sit at the bar for a *demi* or a glass of wine, but there was no bar, and the ten or twelve tables were all occupied. So, she just stood there, unsure what to do.

As she turned to leave, the GI from the Rhumerie appeared across the room. "You finally came by," he said in English, approaching. He was tall, taller than she remembered, in a dark jacket but without a tie, his brilliant smile leading the way.

"I have," Cecile said. "How is it that you Yanks say . . . on a whim."

"Well, I'm glad to see you."

Conversations at the tables recommenced, no one seeming to pay her any mind anymore now that she'd been greeted by this man. The air smelled savory, of smoked pork and sauteed onions.

"You by yourself," he asked, "not with your boyfriend?"

"I am on my own," said Cecile.

"D'you stop in for dinner, then?"

"For just a drink, actually. I had assumed there would be a bar."

"Well, there'll be music in a bit, and it'll just be drinks then."

"Will it be a long time before this occurs?" Cecile asked.

"Naw, Baby." He knew his smile to be very effective. "Hang tight just a wee bit."

As at the Rhumerie, he flicked a Lucky Strike through the tear in the top of his pack and offered it to Cecile.

She took it. "*Merci.*"

He struck a match and lit it. "Name's Mack Gray."

"*Enchantée,*" she said. "Cecile Rosenbaum."

When they shook, he didn't let go.

"A few of my boys have started up a group." He let loose her hand to point at a table on the other side of the room, with three men there and, alongside them, a woman. "They play gigs here. Billy Eckstine and Dizzy—you know, like that. Sometimes some of their own numbers, too."

"Do you not have military duties to attend to?"

"Oh, we've settled things fairly well over here, I'd say." He tipped his head back and laughed. "Got plenty of free time on our hands."

A man in khaki trousers and a white T-shirt, a white apron over that, burst through the swinging door from the kitchen. He carried two plates to a couple, then, noticing Mack and Cecile, dipped back through the door and reemerged with a narrow table and squeezed it in beside the kitchen. He waved them over.

Mack led the way. "This here's Payne, Alfred Payne, proprietor and head chef."

"Cook!" Payne corrected him, his face beaming. "But a goddamn good one."

Payne took an empty chair from a neighboring table and held it for Cecile. She sat, and he patted her shoulder then returned to the kitchen.

Mack remained standing. "Wine okay?"

She nodded, and he went into the back and returned with a bottle, though just one glass.

"I'm over here with my boys," he said, "but I'll stop back by and check on you."

The band began setting up, and Mack joined them. Cecile decided to stay for a song or two. She enjoyed the levity of the American Africans, the easy way they laughed together, Payne's familiar hospitality though he had just met her. It wasn't that she didn't laugh with Minette and their friends or with Seb. She had. But this laughter filling the restaurant was winning and full of play and didn't sound spiked with bitterness.

The stage wasn't properly a stage, just the space along one wall, cleared of tables. One of Mack Gray's friends went into the kitchen and returned with a stand-up bass. Another had a horn, and the third a saxophone, which they removed from cases. They tuned up together, the woman snapping her fingers to the plucking of the bass strings, and soon, the show began—an upbeat piece. Mack had no instrument and did not even sing. He just stood there, arms crossed over his chest and tapping his foot, introducing songs or commenting on them afterward. But he was electric, conducting all the energy in the room. He roamed from table to table, chatting with this patron or that one, laughing, his head back, face tilted toward the ceiling. And from time to time, he smiled over at Cecile, his gaze fixed on her, as though in that moment they were the only two there.

She finished her glass and poured a second. Payne, still in his apron and smelling of fried grease, came from the kitchen and pulled up a chair and sat with her. He carried a water glass, and Cecile filled it with red wine.

"That's my wife Darlene," he said, tipping his head toward the singer.

"What a marvelous voice," said Cecile. "She reminds of Sarah Vaughan."

She remembered her introduction to Vaughan, at Le New York with Seb.

Payne said, "Already got one of them back home. Figured Darlene might could take her shot for it over here instead."

"Back home?"

"Mississippi," he said. It sounded like two syllables—"Miss sip"—and she took a long beat before understanding. "Me anyway. Darlene from out west, Los Angeles."

"How did you become acquainted, then?"

"The service. She had been in the Six Triple Eight."

Cecile didn't know what this meant, and it must have showed.

"A WAC," he added, though this clarified nothing. She didn't recognize the word.

They heard Mack call over a saxophone solo: "Hey now, Payne, what you doing over there with my Baby? Ain't you got something or other to look after in the kitchen?"

Laughter erupted around the room.

"Whose place this is?" Payne shot back. "Mine or yours?"

The laughter continued. Payne's wife, standing beside Mack, shook her head, smiling.

Payne leaned toward Cecile. "Old Mack, he's got it—the stuff." He pulled back far enough for eye contact, to emphasize his point. "He could become a officer."

"Oh, how wonderful," she said, unsure why this was significant. "This is wonderful for him."

"And for us all," said Payne. "The army wants more colored in command positions. That could be Mack."

"Well, I hope he will be successful." She topped his glass. "And you, do you not wish to become an officer, too?"

"I done left the service," he said, clearly proud. "Darlene, too. We run this place now—a Mississippi juke joint right here in Montmartre!"

The music picked up, the horn thundering, and she and Payne quieted. He sat with her through the rest of the set.

When the band stopped for a break, Mack lingered with some hangers-on who ringed the makeshift stage. Cecile didn't want to tie him up, thinking she needed to be taken care of. Besides, she'd already stayed much longer than she'd intended; it was a good time to slip away.

She told Payne, "This has been truly wonderful, thank you so very much." She rose, as did Payne, taking her hand.

"The pleasure's been all mine. I do hope you'll come back."

"*Avec plaisir*," she said, and by his smile, she knew that he'd understood.

She raised a hand goodbye toward Mack, who was still surrounded, mouthed "*Merci*," then turned and left.

He caught up to her just outside. "Going so soon? The evening's just starting."

"I have stayed much longer than I had expected to." It was nearly one. "I have work in the morning."

"Work! Why, I had took you and your friends for students."

"Indeed, some are. Me, I am employed by the Louvre."

He flashed his smile. "Well, in that case, okay then. But I expect to see you hereabouts again."

He stepped into the stream of bicycle taxis headed up Rue des Martyrs, likely toward the cabarets of Pigalle, and waved a proper taxi—a beat-up Citroën—toward the curb.

"Please, no . . ." Cecile said.

Who had money for taxis?

"No man would let a lady walk off into the dark night," Mack replied.

He opened the rear door, and she slid onto the seat. He extended a banknote to the driver. "That'll get you wherever you need to go." Closing the door, he said, "Goodnight, Baby," smiling as the car pulled away.

On Friday evening, Cecile sat on the pedestal of the obelisk at the center of the unlit Beaux-Arts courtyard, watching test-takers arrive, check the list, then recede, silky shadows against the wool of night. Those who'd scored well gave audible sighs yet slunk away, as though resigned to have to suffer the torture a bit longer, awaiting the final word by mail. Those who'd failed left with a resolute stride, chin thrust forward, an outward display, she imagined, to compensate for the wrecked dreams and injured pride.

She recognized Seb's silhouette. He stood there a long time then wandered into the darkness of the courtyard.

His form started when she spoke. "All that worry, and you made it through the last section."

"But did I perform well enough to be admitted?" he said, appearing to be searching for her, his voice heavy but warm. He found her and sat by her side. "We won't know that for a while still."

"How long could it take? The computing is already done."

"A certain number—who can say how many—will be admitted because their father or grandfather attended, or because their family knows this minister or that deputy."

She placed a hand on his knee, the first either had touched the other. "You gave it your best effort. It was all you could do."

They sat silently a long while. She wanted to say, I've missed you.

Instead, she said, "This time apart has been good for me. I've needed the sleep!"

She sensed the shadows of his face release, saw his broad smile.

Rotating so that they faced each other, she said, "You weren't there for me, Seb, when we saw your sister outside the Tournon. Both of you looked through me."

"I know, I know . . ."

"You treated me like a stranger"

"I'm sorry," he said. "So, so sorry."

The apology felt hollow, though—not insincere, but without substance.

It didn't address the issue that had arisen between them, much less offer a solution. Yes, she was white and he black, her of the colonizers and him the colonized, but what was each one willing to give, and to give up, in order to be together?

She wanted his love but without the accompanying feelings of furtiveness and shame. She wanted it in the light of day.

And what did he want from her? Her love, sure, but what did he mean by this? Did he even know?

Love, just another word, as foreign as *danxoménu* or *na daho*, as empty as air. For he was more afraid of his father than committed to her.

"I hoped I'd see you tonight," she said, "to congratulate you. Whatever the final result, getting this far, all the hard work you did . . ."

"And you, too! Your help got me here."

"Well, you've accomplished something," she said. "You should be celebrating."

"I'd welcome the chance to celebrate with you."

Just a word, love.

She hadn't come down to the courtyard with this particular aim in mind, but she realized now that she'd made a decision. Whatever he needed to figure out about them, about what he wanted from her and was willing to do for it, he had to do on his own, and she didn't see herself waiting around while he did it.

"Thank you but no," she told him, placing a hand over his. "I learned so much from our time together, enjoyed it so much. These have been the best months of my life, please know that. But no."

He didn't protest. He removed his hand from beneath hers and rose.

"I should go," she heard, and though she wanted to spring up and pull him into her embrace—close, close—she didn't. She watched his form move off, pass through the gateway, and disappear into the night.

CHAPTER FIFTEEN

Cecile stayed in bed the next morning, unable to will herself to get up. She'd spent most of the night reading, as sleep wouldn't come. Beauvoir's novel had offered little reprieve—none, in fact. She hated the main character Hélène, who was always acted upon, never acting, and even when that capricious, foolish girl finally fully realized the peril of the Occupation, Cecile found her commitment to the Resistance a different sort of capitulation. Completely off-putting—though better by far than the silence of her room and of her thoughts.

After such a fitful night, Cecile especially didn't want to go to work. Weekends were the busiest, and the prospect of all those people impatiently queueing for tickets all day long enervated her, the very idea of it exhausting.

She rose and dressed and went anyway.

The dwindling of the crowd in the Cour Napoleon was a clock Cecile lived by: closing time; she'd be able to go home soon. Yet, on that Saturday the mass continued to swell with the fading light, the courtyard humming with movement and chatter. It appeared to be tour groups reuniting after their museum visit and also young Parisians using the site for rendezvous before *apéros* and a night on the town. Then Cecile noted a vaguely familiar face, a head above everyone else's and smiling directly at her.

A split second of fog before abrupt recognition: Mack Gray, a brown fedora atop his head.

He strode forward. "Nice blazer," he said.

"Isn't it, though?" She posed as though on a catwalk, turning right and left in the tight space of the ticket booth. "Wearing one is obligatory."

"Well, ain't that a pity," he said. "The drab color dulls your eyes."

She wasn't falling for his obvious attempt at seduction but didn't mind it either. Especially today.

He said, "You must be off soon. It's been beautiful weather. I thought you might join me for a stroll."

"I am finished in an hour," she said, more quickly than she'd meant to. "I could meet you on the Place du Palais Royal, across the street."

They walked under the arcade along the swank Rue de Rivoli, then on to Châtelet and past the Tour Saint-Jacques, toward Le Marais. Mack asked question after question: Was she from Paris? Oh, the suburbs. Which one, and what was it like out there? What did her "pops" do? Her "mama"? Did she have brothers and sisters?

He looked to be genuinely interested but would launch the next question without seeming to fully take in the previous answer. "Papa yes, Maman no . . ." "Le Vésinet reminds of a country village . . ." "He occupies a position at *la mairie* . . . Uh, how to say? Town hall, I think." So rapid-fire were his questions that she wondered if her English was worse than she'd thought, if her replies actually articulated what she intended. Maybe he was merely being polite, moving on to the next question rather than correcting her faulty reply.

Seb would sometimes do this, too—respond quickly and by rote, as though language was an obstacle to work through, as though French was not also his mother tongue. How strange, she thought. Had they really been so different, her and him—as different as she felt she was from this one, from Mack Gray, who was, in fact, foreign and entirely a mystery to her, whose curious words evoked odd images that were often difficult to make sense of?

Passing a *salon de glace*, Mack directed her inside without asking whether she wanted an ice cream or not. She did, of course. How long since she'd had such a treat?

"Strawberry?" he said, pointing at the array of colors representing the varied flavors, and Cecile nodded, though she thought the choice somewhat random.

"Two scoops of strawberry for the lady," he said to the clerk, clearly assuming that she'd understand English. "Three scoops for me, strawberry too."

The clerk smiled. "Two scoops, then three, *oui*, Monsieur," she repeated, her accent thick. "*Un instant, s'il vous plaît.*"

She handed a cone to Cecile, then to Mack.

"*Merci*, Madame," Cecile said, turning to leave.

"*Merci*," Mack mimicked, though it sounded more like the English word "mercy."

The *glace* was delicious, the cool sweetness liquifying over her tongue. Rather than eat his own, Mack continued with the questions, licking his fingers and hand and wrist as his scoops melted onto them. He asked about how she'd ended up at the Louvre, and Cecile found herself trying to explain her connection to art.

"Lucie, my Mamie, was expert." Eating slowed her reply. "But the war, you see. She was taken. Daddie Georges, too, in a manner of saying."

"By 'Mammy' and 'Daddy,'" he said, though his words sounded nothing like the ones she'd used, "you mean your grandmama and gramps, right?"

She nodded to mask her uncertainty, though she hadn't actually grasped his question.

"You ask so many things," she said, "but I would like to ask things of you, too."

"Yeah?"

"Such as, where do you come from in the States?"

"KC, Baby!"

It sounded like a boast, but her look must have revealed her confusion. She had no idea whether he had spoken a sequence of letters or of words . . .

He clarified: "Kansas City, on the Kansas side. Home."

The lively sidewalk terrace of a café on the Place des Vosges caught Mack's attention. He flagged a garçon as they neared, and they were seated at a table. Mack ordered a bottle of champagne.

"And your father," Cecile asked, "what is his work?"

"Ain't seen him since I was six."

"No?"

"Nope. He got the Call, jumped a train to California to preach the Word, and ain't been back since."

The "Call" and the "Word" meant nothing to her, only trains and not returning.

The waiter placed two flutes on the table, then uncorked the bottle with a deliberate flourish and a loud pop! Mack appeared to enjoy the show of it. Cecile hadn't had champagne since Sundays at Croissy, when Mamie Lucie would order a "thimbleful" poured for the children, to accompany the adults having theirs with dessert. Sipping the bubbles and sharp flavor now, she said, "So, it is your mother who works, then?"

Mack seemed to revel in storytelling, though his sounded sad. "Yes, indeed—in the meatpacking plants down in West Bottoms. Ten-hour days." He finished half his flute in a single gulp. "Yours truly wasn't but fourteen when I joined along, right there beside Mama. Then lil' sis, then baby bruh followed, too. These niggers was some deboning fools!" he said, dropping his head back and laughing wide like the sky, and Cecile had no idea who "these niggers" were or why they were fools, but as with Seb, as with Minette, their evocation made her feel accountable.

"It was the service got me out of there," he said, more soberly.

"The 'service'?"

"The military, the army. Gave me some proper training. Brung me over to here so as I could meet you."

His smile was so earnest that, despite her frank misgivings about this blatant pickup routine, she dropped her eyes toward the table, to the empty flute there, her hand blanketing its base.

* * *

He insisted on accompanying her home in a taxi, and Cecile welcomed his gallantry, as she felt a little too tipsy for the Metro or a bus. In the entranceway to Hôtel des Beaux-Arts, she kept her head enough to resist the urge to invite him in.

Though why shouldn't she? She was no longer with Seb.

His face didn't give away what he was expecting. He did remove his fedora, though, the first he had all night.

She offered her hand instead, not like Jacqueline but warmly, like the American blacks at Payne's restaurant had, even the girls.

There was no sign of disappointment in his smile. "I hope to see you again soon," he said. "You have a good night."

Watching him recede down Rue Bonaparte, she rifled through her bag and found a pen and paper and scrawled the hotel phone number on it. She ran after him.

"Here is the way to reach me," she said, catching him at the corner of Rue Visconti.

She stood on her tiptoes to offer *la bise* this time. But crossing from cheek to cheek to cheek, it became something else—what the Americans called a "smooch."

After work the next day, she took the train to Le Vésinet for Sunday dinner. Her mother had invited her to come out, promising an important announcement. "PS," she'd added in the message left with the concierge. "And I want to hear all about how things are going with Seb!"

Her mother looked disappointed when Cecile told her that she and Seb were just friends now, nothing more. "Oh . . . But why, *chérie*?"

They stood in the kitchen, her mother stirring at the stove— Barigoule again, though Cecile thought she smelled something meaty baking in the oven. She tried to make light of the situation: "What, did you think I was going to marry him?"

"Such a lovely boy." Her mother faced downward, pensively stirring. "And he was kind. It's an undervalued trait in a person."

Kind? Or just afraid to say the thing that might disturb, that might wound?

Cecile considered, then decided against telling her the rest—about Seb's father, about his sister; about how he would not publicly claim her as his lover.

"I've met a GI," she said. "He's fun and quite charming."

By her mother's look, the announcement didn't appear to particularly please her.

"Oh, he's just for play, Maman. Nothing serious."

This last comment did not please her mother one bit more. She stirred and stirred, avoiding Cecile's eyes.

The invitation, it turned out, had been at her father's urging, which surprised Cecile, until she learned the reason. "Fabrice Courchène has asked him to run for city council," her mother explained as she and Cecile set the dining room table.

"Courchène, from the Rally for the French People? So, on de Gaulle's ticket?"

"Maurice Fabien had to drop from the race, you see, and Monsieur Courchène has apparently always thought your father would make a fine councilman."

Cecile stepped into the doorway to the front room, where her father sat in his armchair, *Le Petit Parisien* folded on his lap. "Papa . . . Really?"

"I'm not asking for your permission," he said, having clearly been eavesdropping. "I just need you to calm your activities for a while. Entering the race so late will make my bid challenging enough."

"My *activities*?" She set the stack of plates in her hands on the table then returned to the doorway. "What exactly do you mean by my 'activities'?"

"With that rabble you call friends? Frankly, I try not to think too much about it."

"They're students, young people finding their way in the world."

"Students?" he said. "Dressed as they dress? Behaving as they behave?"

He'd only met Minette once; he'd hardly spoken to Seb. How could he know how they "behaved"?

"Well, why don't you loosen your clutch on that money you hoard"—she was wearing denims, glad she hadn't dressed up—"and buy me nylons so that I can wear the skirts you'd rather see me in."

"You act as though I'm made of money. The war robbed us of everything, not least of which was our family."

"You're in contact with them, I suppose? With Sylvie in São Paulo, with Bernard?"

"Don't be insolent," he said. "Don't you dare."

His anger didn't cow her, as it had when she'd lived under his roof. Quite the contrary: she felt emboldened. "You don't think I know what we suffered during the war? Don't you know I suffered, too?"

"By the company you keep, I'd say not."

He slapped his hand on the coffee table, abruptly, surprising even himself, and the baubles there jumped.

"Turning up here at all hours! With inferiors and lackeys, good-for-nothings—"

"Alain!"

Cecile hadn't seen her mother enter the room. It didn't matter. She faced her father.

"Go ahead. Say what you were going to say."

He fingered the edges of the newspaper, crossed one leg atop the other, calm again.

"Do you have so little regard for yourself? What I was about to say is, if you're going to sleep around for sleeping around's sake, you'd do better to choose from a crowd who can provide you something in return—save me the expense of supporting your whims and fancies."

Cecile wasn't sure if what she felt was guilt that he knew about her intimacies with men—what he supposed were her intimacies—or shame for being the daughter of someone who thought of her friends in the way that he did. Maybe it was merely a rising fury, this visceral response after being called what he had just called her. Him, of all people.

"You primp in that pathetic sash as though the bastards who gave it to you and who you now want to join aren't the same ones who betrayed Mamie Lucie to the Nazis, then you dare to criticize me and my behavior?"

"Cecile! Alain!" she heard but continued: "And the woman you keep in Le Pecq? The meat I saw you take to her during the war, the ration cards I'm sure you still provide her? You're right, a whore is someone who's paid. Doesn't she better fit the definition than me?"

He slammed *Le Petit Parisien* to the floor. "Get out! Get out of my house right this instant!"

Another terrible night of tossing and turning, once bolting upright in a sweat. She overslept but didn't care enough to scramble to get dressed and dash to the Louvre—though she would surely need the pay, as her father was certain to cut her off.

Downstairs, she found a message from her mother: "*Mon amour*, please call as soon as you get this. Please, please!"

Mack Gray had left a message, too: "I'm on early mornings this week. Maybe you might show me around Paris some more some afternoon." There was a number.

The phone box was free. Cecile dialed, and her mother picked up almost immediately. Cecile could tell she'd been crying. Her mother insisted, as always, that her father loved her. "Please believe me, *chérie*. He truly does."

"But he doesn't respect me."

"The two of you are just too much alike to get along."

Just what Cecile wanted to hear . . .

Shut in that upright coffin of paned glass and her own stale air, she scanned the lobby as her mother went on and on, imploring Cecile to take the first step, begging for a reconciliation that seemed impossible now, if she was going to maintain some semblance of dignity.

Cecile snapped, cutting her off: "And why don't you defend yourself! Don't tell me you didn't know about the woman in Le Pecq."

The silence buzzed.

Her mother's voice returned, crisp now: "It's just the way of things between a man and a woman. It's how marriage is."

More buzzing silence.

"All right, Maman. We'll talk again soon," Cecile said before her mother could say anything more, and she hung up.

No one was queuing for the phone, so she dialed the number Mack had left. Rather than waste coins waiting to connect from the general switchboard to his barracks, she left a message. "Please convey to him that I would love to."

"Would love to what, ma'am?" the switchboard operator asked.

"He will understand," said Cecile. "Please say to him, tomorrow afternoon."

The concierge knocked at two o'clock sharp the next day—huffy and huffing, nearly out of breath. Mack had insisted she climb the four flights to let Cecile know he'd arrived, and the concierge was none too pleased with the assignment.

"This is a rooming house, Mademoiselle, not a hotel, regardless the name on the placard outside," she scolded. "I'm not here to personally deliver to you your many messages."

"I'm sorry," Cecile replied, grabbing a cardigan for the fall chill. She wore slacks and a nice blouse, comfortably casual but elegant, too.

The weather was resplendent, sunny with a light breeze. They walked toward Quai d'Orsay, then crossed the Seine. At Concorde, Mack took the lead and headed up the Champs-Élysées. "This here the most beauteous street in the whole world," he said, as though he was introducing it to her instead of vice versa.

They window-shopped the length of the avenue, past the boutiques and shops and automobile showrooms. Just how much was available for purchase surprised Cecile. She'd grown accustomed to the scarcity and want of Les Halles.

Mack said, "I'd offer to get you something, but I don't want to be too forward."

"A motorcar, really?" she teased. "I have only made your acquaintance for what, a week? Besides, I could not afford the petrol."

Mack tipped his head back, laughing toward the sky—a gesture she was beginning to feel she could predict.

"How about a nice scarf, then?" he said.

The Hermès store was just a few doors up. She didn't say no.

They went to the top of the Arc de Triomphe afterward, a new *carré* draped over her shoulders. "This here," Mack said, "be my favorite spot in all the city. Not quite the view as up on the Eiffel, but I like what the place symbolizes."

She'd lived here her entire life and never imagined going up the Tour Eiffel. In fact, she'd never before today visited this very monument they stood atop or seen the Tombe du Soldat Inconnu beneath. Too touristy.

To her own detriment, she now realized.

(In his message, he'd asked for a tour, but it was clear he'd put a lot of thought into their outing beforehand.)

The Normandie cinema nearby was playing *Cloak and Dagger*, in English, and though Mack was enthusiastic to see it, he dozed off within the first few minutes. Cecile didn't mind. She found the plot plodding and the film self-congratulatory—but the Normandie! What majesty, with its incredibly high ceiling and echoing sound. It was as though she was in a cathedral of flickering light and booming voices. She found Mack's snoring and the dribble of drool in the corner of his mouth charming, too.

Afterward, he insisted they go to the Place Vendôme. The enclosed plaza shimmered in the sunlight despite the waning of the day, the sounds of Paris dimming to nothing. They sat side by side at the base of the obelisk, bathed in warmth.

Mack said, "Ain't nothing like this in KC. Before getting posted here, I didn't know anything such as this even existed."

Minette and their group of friends shunned this area of the city as diseased—a *quartier* of profligate wealth, beyond redemption.

"It was in these apartments," Cecile said, "that German generals kept their mistresses."

"That's all done now, Baby," said Mack. "Uncle Sam got this."

The sole meunière at the Ritz cost an entire month's salary. It was as fine a meal as Cecile could remember having. When they'd finished, she told Mack that she needed to walk a bit, and he agreed. "And how?" he said. "Y'all ain't no ways afraid of over-buttering."

They were silent the length of the walk.

Back at the Hôtel des Beaux-Arts, she didn't play coy with the kiss—perhaps to spite her father, the vile things he'd said and clearly believed about her. She imagined the scene from above: Mack's mouth over hers, his long form and broad shoulders, bent over, engulfing her.

Such a cliché! Gustav Klimt, of course.

She enjoyed it all the same. Mack Gray was strikingly handsome. And also a very good kisser.

CHAPTER SIXTEEN

A week passed with no letter from Beaux-Arts, then two, then three. Seb didn't see Cecile in that time either.

He stayed in bed through the better part of several days, still exhausted from the months of prep, sleeping then rising for a snack then returning beneath the covers. Finding him there one suppertime, Zansi snapped: "Keep at the work you still need to make up or get a head start on the new lessons that are coming. But do something other than mope!"

Do what, though? He was tired of architecture and art history, of geometry and design. He dreaded the possibility of receiving a letter of admission as much as the more likely probability of a notification of failure. He was weary to the core and restless all at once. And he missed Cecile.

He took to wandering the streets of the *quartier*, killing time however he could—reading *Le Monde* at the Tournon or the Danton, or just watching people pass by. Deep down, he also recognized that he hoped to run into her—to happen upon Cecile. He found himself skulking on the Pont des Arts late one afternoon, trying to time her return from work. As night fell and still no Cecile, he hurried away, embarrassed, ashamed even, vowing to never do *that* again.

The very next morning, he inquired at École de la Sainte-Famille about odd jobs, something, anything to fill the days. As the school year was underway and positions were already filled, the nuns told him they had nothing. On his return to the rooming house, walking along the wall of Bibliotèque Sainte-Geneviève, France's national library, he noted the building as though for the first time. He'd passed it daily for years, heading out or coming home, and never paid attention—Romanesque revival in style, stately. He dipped inside.

Recalling his visit to Le Vésinet, he wondered if he could track down a copy of the magazine that Madame Rosenbaum—that Elodie—had mentioned, when she'd asked him the Fon word for "Thursday" and he hadn't known it. He should at least know something as banal as the names of the days of the week in his own mother tongue, shouldn't he—at least this? All he had were the myths passed on by Zansi.

Elodie had said that the magazine was a few years old, so the librarian he approached directed him to the lower levels, which housed archival copies. And what a discovery! Not just magazines but records of all sorts. The registries of materials contained there—volumes and volumes of them—listed a treasure of dossiers and files about Dahomey: boxes from missionary societies and from military regiments, government contracts for varied companies and the manifests of ships that traveled to and from Africa, and on and on. (He wondered if he could find the records from the *Roma*.)

The archivists were gruff men behind a wire-caged window who seemed to question with a look Seb's very reason for being there—all but one, who wore an old-style Vandyke and greeted him with a smile and "*Jeune homme*, how can I assist you?" Seb described the article as Elodie had. The archivist, who introduced himself as Monsieur Chevalier, went into the back and returned with several magazines and a pair of white cotton gloves—required before handling material, he kindly explained, as it was old and, in some cases, quite fragile.

Seb studied the tables of contents of each magazine and scanned several articles but couldn't find the piece Elodie had cited—nothing even near it in detail or scope. Monsieur Chevalier advised that, if it was information about his home he was after, he should broaden his exploration beyond a search for just that one source.

Seb's approach was haphazard. He picked boxes to leaf through based upon the enigma of their titles. LETTERS SENT—UNRECORDED, 1890–1900, ZOU DEPARTMENT (DAHOMEY)—the word "unrecorded" sounded clandestine, so he requested the records. The memoranda contained therein, though, were mostly just inventories and the like, nothing of interest. Next, RECORD BOOK, ARMY CHIEF OF STAFF, FRENCH WEST AFRICA, then ATLANTIC MUTUAL INSURANCE COMPANY, MINUTES OF PROCEEDINGS, 1894.

After a full morning of flipping through files and skimming documents, Seb came to the realization that he had little real grasp of what he was looking at. For all he could explicate the succession of Louis, from the Lazy to the Lion to the Saint, his own history was a mystery beyond the symbols of the Abomey tapestry and the random myths and legends. He needed a timeline. He needed context.

The archives housed intact copies of all sorts of newspapers, some quite common—*Le Figaro* and *L'Humanité*—and others that had become hard to find. He figured that these might give him general points of reference, dates and such. He began with *Le Petit Journal*, a daily that he'd read during his apprenticeship in Burgundy but that had been defunct since the war. It was more out of sentiment than for his research. He lost the rest of the afternoon in nostalgic revery about Des Launiers and the other carpenters, recalling the coarse jokes they'd told about the bawdy tales featured in the paper.

The next morning, Monsieur Chevalier recommended *Dans les Colonies*, an illustrated monthly that reported on France's overseas territories, and Seb struck gold. Starting with the first edition, dated 1892, he found issue after issue with Dahomey throughout. The articles were predictably one-sided, caricatural, and demeaning. Those on the Franco-Dahomeyan War belittled Gbéhanzin's "army of brutes" and celebrated how Colonel Alfred-Almédée Dodds was able to "tame" them. But Seb also occasionally stumbled upon intriguing tidbits. While the journalists covering the battles described the Dahomeyans as "savage" and "bloodthirsty" and "barbaric," they also wrote about Gbéhanzin with a kind of reverence. It seemed clear that he'd taken the fight to the French. The invading army shared this begrudging respect. After Dodds finally trapped Gbéhanzin in the forest north of Abomey, two years into the war, he didn't put the defeated king to death, though the French people called for it. Dodds exiled him in faraway Martinique, fearful that his execution might stir up the continent and that allowing him to remain was sure to.

Gbéhanzin, the shark that becomes enraged and troubles the coast—his grandfather!

Gbé We Hanzin B'ayi Djelé: the universe upholds the egg that the Earth desires.

Seb didn't tell Zansi about the hours spent in the archives and the incredible discoveries. He didn't know why. To explain his day-long absences, he made an excuse of ongoing study—about angles and planes, structure and design.

Dans les Colonies was written in French, but here and there would be words in his language, and Seb began to build a vocabulary: various numbers and the names of the seasons; *roun* was family and *dada* was king; *mindé sissi* was more difficult to translate, but from the context, he thought it was the expression for "dignity." There were also descriptions of the land—of forests and rivers and villages—and these set his blood flowing. He found an account of market day, the central event of the local economy, and it included illustrations of wooden stalls featuring pyramids of mangoes and baskets of just-caught tilapia and sardines and crabs. The reporter's prose captured the feel of the crowd and the heat and the smells.

Seb's daily reading began to conjure in him something that, given his age when he'd left Dahomey, could not possibly be memory—the suggestion of reminiscence, the tang of salt and char that remained after the last bit of beefsteak had been swallowed. Was it just his imagination, then? Was he fabricating remembrance, constructing a past that felt authentic as a way to counter the discomfort of the train ride back from Le Vésinet, the aching he'd experienced—profound, but elusive—that he now recognized to have been shame?

Elodie hadn't intended to—quite the contrary—but she'd shamed him. The kindly *Yovo* woman, the mother of the *Yovo* girl he loved, had asked him to name the days of the week, and he hadn't been able to. It was *her* who'd cited them to him! She'd known things about him—about his mother tongue, about where he was from—that he didn't know himself.

And not just Elodie but Cecile too, in her manner. She'd told him that France was his home now, that after all the years here, he was as much French as Dahomeyan.

This shame drove him to return to the archives day after day, to research and read and know his own story better than any French person could. With the exam results looming and never arriving, with his future both uncertain and fettering, the aching inside dulled with each new revelation about Dahomey, with each added layer of himself.

Leaving the Bibliotèque one afternoon, he saw his sister across Place du Panthéon, heading onto Rue Soufflot. The timing was serendipitous. A notice on the library bulletin board announced an upcoming Louis Armstrong concert at the Cirque d'Hiver, and it struck Seb as a potential opportunity: maybe their student group could establish a liaison with the famous jazzman, who'd make a great ally. Seb stepped up his pace in order to catch up and propose the idea.

At the intersection of Saint-Michel and Soufflot, where he expected Zansi to turn right toward the Faculté de Médecine, she continued on. Just then, he noted that she wasn't carrying her satchel. If she wasn't headed to a lecture or a lab, he wondered where she might be going.

He trailed fifty paces behind as she entered the wide-open space of the Jardin du Luxembourg. Even full of people, so few of them were black that every black face stood out, a gnat in a jar of yogurt. He stayed outside the spiked grating to remain unnoticed, keeping her in view as best he could. She went down the path to the gazebo where orchestras played in summer and she sat in a garden chair there, opposite a young Frenchman. The boy smiled.

Zansi's back was to Seb. Was she smiling, too?

Tousled and scruffy, the boy wore English tweed and wire-framed glasses; wrapped around his neck was a lavender scarf that looked homespun. Seb thought he recalled seeing Zansi knitting something that very color.

His sister had no real friends, not even in the ASUFC, just study partners from medical school—and him, of course. Aside from the time in Burgundy, Seb had spent nearly every day of the past sixteen years in her company. He knew her more than anyone in the world—more, he sometimes thought, than he knew himself. Yet he had no idea who this boy might be alongside whom she now strolled across the park, their shoulders brushing.

Seb let them get ahead, then followed. They exited at the gate beside the museum, turning right then disappearing from view. He hustled forward, but by the time he got to the gate, he'd lost them. He looked up and down the street, scanning the spattering of people.

Then he spotted them: through the window of the hotel across the street, at the front desk, appearing to check in.

She re-emerged alone as night was falling. Seb expected both surprise and humiliation when she saw him waiting on the sidewalk opposite the hotel but got neither. She stopped in her tracks in the doorway, but her face remained impassive.

Her stolid inscrutability as she crossed the street sparked a memory of their home—the Dahomeyan gaze: people staring, expressionless, their eyes never dropping but devoid of any hint of what was happening underneath. The insistent but cryptic looking could feel sinister, menacing even. Yet it was so common among Dahomeyans as to seem ingrained in the blood.

She spoke first. "Let's go for a coffee. The Tournon's just around the corner."

Seb recognized the choice of location to be deliberate more than merely convenient. The Tournon was where she'd caught him with Cecile.

Zansi walked along the wall of the Palais du Luxembourg, Seb following. Another memory struck him. "To live happily," their aunt Fifonsi would often say, "lead a hidden life." Her words had carried little meaning to the child Kannou but began to make sense to him now. "Secrecy is a weapon," she'd say. "You own your secrets, where your talk will enslave you."

And the word *hunxo* appeared suddenly in the dark of his mind, the Dahomeyan expression for "secrets" manifesting from some faraway place.

At the Tournon, Zansi took a table at the rear. The garçon passed, and she ordered tea.

Seb asked for a whiskey.

"That's a bit cliché, isn't it?" she said.

He wasn't angry, as she seemed to presume. He wondered if he should be. He did feel something—a profound shifting—though he couldn't define it.

"And what I saw this afternoon," he said. "What was that if not cliché?"

"Aren't you as well-placed to answer the question as me?"

He hadn't seen Cecile in nearly three weeks. It surprised him that Zansi didn't know.

"Well, you're paying for the whiskey," she said. "Too steep for my means."

The garçon brought their drinks. Zansi dropped a tea bag into the cup and poured from the small tin pot. The water browned instantly.

"I won't apologize," she said, her aspect unchanged, completely without affect.

He swirled his glass, the cubes clinking against the sides. "M'Bokolo—I could imagine you seeing that Congolese jackass. But this?"

"And you're sure that what you saw is serious enough to warrant all this glumness?"

"Come on, Zansi . . . When have you ever wasted your time on anything or with anyone frivolous?"

She laughed. It was reflexive and held no humor.

"How little you know me, brother. I'm a woman, have been since the day Father put me in charge of you before loading us onto the *Roma*. Didn't you think I had desires and needs of my own?"

"But he's French. *Yovo!*"

It was a hypocritical argument, he recognized this. But he thought he should make it all the same.

"And he's a medical student, second in our class after me." She signaled for more hot water. "He's interested in pediatrics, like me. He's well-read in anticolonial politics."

The garçon brought another tin teapot, and Seb said, "Me, too," pointing to his glass, damned the cost, because here was the crux of it, the thing he needed to know for his own case with Cecile.

"What would Father say?" he asked, tempering his tone so as not to imply that he was threatening to inform on her.

"What he would say is irrelevant," she said, her face still impassive. Then it released, suddenly, unexpectedly.

"Do you remember when we first arrived, when we were still at Father's cousin's? How, whenever we could save enough of the pittance he paid us, we'd go to the cinema?"

Seb nodded. Of course, he remembered.

"It was all you ever wanted to do," she said. "You loved any film with Charles Boyer in it and his *regard de Vénus*." The memory embarrassed Seb. "I'd catch you at the mirror trying to mimic his strange cross-eyed sneer."

"Until the day you yelled at me to stop. And good thing, too. I was giving myself headaches."

She smiled warmly, confidingly. "Well, who did you think you'd be charming, wearing his look?"

Seb shifted his eyes away.

"Father should have known," she said. "He should have foreseen this after his own confusion from being raised by the *Yovo* missionaries."

The garçon brought the new glass of whiskey. She waited for him to leave before continuing: "Remember *La Grande Illusion*? How many times did we go? All we could talk about was plotting our own escape, first from Father's cousin's and then from this infernal country. We both understood that, in order to be able to leave, to return home, we couldn't be mere servants. We had to distinguish ourselves. Success would bring freedom. But the more we succeed, the more accomplishments and prizes and opportunities, the more reason there is to stay." Zansi reached across the table, squeezed his forearm. "*N'est-ce pas?*"

She left her hand there. "I'm not asking your permission, Kannou. I'd rather you didn't even know about Claude. But you do. You're my brother, you're my family. I'm asking that you trust me."

He typically surrendered to such gestures of warmth but found himself suddenly angry. She'd led a hidden life, and now that it was exposed, this calculated tenderness was a tactic intended to return him to his place as deferential *petit frère*. But what had she revealed, actually? What had she confided? She hadn't even told him the true nature of her relationship with the *Yovo* boy, instead deflecting the focus back on him and Cecile. All the ploys and manipulation, the great effort to restore the previous order between them, the way things had been, as though he hadn't seen what he'd seen. Seb resented it.

"*You* should have trusted *me*," he said.

"And likewise you, with the Vésinet girl." She removed her hand, her expression gone cold. "Our roles aren't the same, though, are they? Mine is to make sure you rise to your appointed station. Yours, to get there."

She paused. "When you become Gbéhanzin, what will there be for me?"

Him, Seb? Not just the son of the son of the last king, but eventually Gbéhanzin himself? He'd never even considered this.

"And just so you know," Zansi added, "Father is coming."

"What?"

"In November." She removed an envelope from her purse and slid it across the table. "Escalating harassment by the colonial administration. They're threatening to strip him of French citizenship. He's appealing to higher authorities here."

Seb finished his whiskey in one swallow. "And Maman?"

She dropped her eyes. "He doesn't say."

Seb knew he should feel pleased to see his father, even if it was without their mother. He felt only dread.

Zansi appeared self-satisfied, confident that she'd regained the upper hand. So, he willed his face blank, as good a Dahomeyan gaze as he could muster. "Louis Armstrong is playing at the Cirque d'Hiver," he said and watched bafflement eclipse the condescension.

"And?" she said, unable to follow his train of thought.

The reversal was inconsequential, hardly a victory at all, but he'd take it, however minor. "The ASUFC," he said. "Forming a relationship with the American blacks, especially with one of his standing, could help our cause."

She became pensive. "Not just us. The alliance could help Father. When's the show?"

He swirled his glass, which now contained just ice. "In October."

"That's quite soon. I don't have time to organize it, what with my classes. I'd ask you to take the lead, but I wouldn't want to disturb your secretive activities."

"I've been at the library, Zansi, following your advice, continuing my studies."

Secrecy was a weapon. He was learning to wield it.

"Good," she said, dropping a banknote on the table. "Let's go, then. We both have work to do."

CHAPTER SEVENTEEN

It had been blue sky and sun all week. Mack called it an "Indian summer" and told her: "A bunch of folks is gathering for a shindig out to Bois de Boulogne before the cold blows in for good." Cecile deduced that he was describing a picnic and liked the idea.

Wearing "fatigues" (what he called his "everyday uniform"), he arrived in a Willys with the windscreen up and the canvas top removed. "It ain't a limousine," he said, faux-apologetically, parked half on the sidewalk in front of her hotel and half in the narrow street, "but it's not the Metro either." The trip across Paris was an amusement park ride, Mack accelerating to full speed, the Willys loud though not especially fast, coursing past bicycle taxis, the engine straining, the stiff breeze mussing Cecile's hair. Not being a driver, her directions were haphazard, sometimes onto pedestrian passages or one-ways in the wrong direction. Mack laughed at every miscue, wheeling the jeep around and taking off again. Once on Rue de l'Université she found her bearings, the Tour Eiffel rising above the rooftops, a polestar for Cecile, a delight for Mack.

Crossing Pont d'Iéna toward the white-stone esplanade of Trocadéro, Cecile pointed to the broad, imposing Musée de l'Homme. "We must go one day," she said. "All of the ethnographies of the world are represented inside. The Africa collection will interest you."

"Africa, sure," he replied, chuckling. "How about I drop you there instead and we meet up after at the canteen across the street?"

At Bois de Boulogne, the Americans had overrun a field near Porte d'Auteuil, beside the Roland Garros stadium. The gathering was immense, a few hundred people at least—everywhere, all around, the languorous gaits and loose-fitting clothes and easy smiles that she was growing to love about the American blacks. Folding tables and chairs filled the open space with a line of drum-barrel grills just beyond, and Mack introduced her here and there as they wended their way through all the activity. Some wore fatigues like Mack, others were in denim or khaki trousers and casual shirts. The girls, who numbered as many as the boys, were not dressed nearly so casually.

Mack said, "Give me a second, Baby," and he disappeared into the crowd.

Cecile liked that he called her this, "Baby." She liked that his manners were a little rough yet that his heart was so big, that he could be confidently brash and also quite gentle.

On the walk across the field, Cecile had noticed a few other French girls, very few. Three in particular stood out, seated on a green blanket with U.S. ARMY stenciled in white across the bottom, each in a cardigan, legs curled under her skirt, gazing about, not speaking with one another, much less to anyone else. Cecile wondered if she fit in here any more than they.

She heard: "Hey now! How you doing?"

It was Payne. He pushed a hand truck stacked with large covered pots—side dishes for the grilled meats, "slaw" and "collards" and a macaroni casserole he called "mazatti."

"Your 'soul food,'" she said. "I had never known anything like it before eating at your restaurant."

"Course you ain't," said Payne. "Colored can make heaven out of other folks' throwaways."

His smile cued her to his levity, but the meaning of his words was a puzzle.

Mack reappeared as if by magic and threw a shadow punch that Payne dodged. "Man, you still hitting on my girl?"

They shook hands vigorously and hugged. Payne said, "You best keep an eye on this one, brother. Pretty French girl like this!"

"From who, you? Nigger, please!"

It was all in fun, though Cecile found their play fairly aggressive, especially with Mack's use of the uncomfortable word. She permitted him "nigger" without comment and with only visible wincing, but once when she'd referred to Mack's friends as "American Africans," he'd corrected her. "Negroes," he'd insisted. It was confusing, especially as that word reminded her of the French *nègre*, which could be either vicious or conventional, depending on its usage, both a racist insult and the adjective used by art historians to describe work from Africa.

The English of the American blacks (of the "Negroes") was, in some ways, as perplexing as Seb's mother tongue had been, and Cecile continued to struggle to understand—and not from lack of effort. To improve her ear, she'd taken to listening more closely to the radio announcers on the AFN, and to increase her vocabulary, she'd bought an American romance novel at one of the *bouquinistes* along the Seine. The announcers were repetitive and the novel idiotic, and both seemed to be produced by and for whites. There was none of the music or joy that she heard from Mack or Payne. Yet, she carried on all the same, wanting to know more words, their sound as well as their substance, so she could better follow what was said.

Mack, serious now, told Payne: "By the way, them crates you asked after, I'm on that for you. Just give me a day or two." He turned to Cecile: "You too, Baby. What-all your folks might need, just let me know."

"What all that what?" she asked.

"Your folks, your parents," he said. "A little of this, some of that—whatever. If your folks need it, let me know."

Cecile remained confused, so he continued: "How you think Payne gets all the good things he got for folks to eat and drink?"

His dishes never skimped on ingredients or seemed to substitute one thing for another.

Mack explained: "See, Payne was a quartermaster sergeant before separating—"

"I was *Mack's* quartermaster sergeant, in fact."

"Now, it's me."

Quartermastering—the word she'd heard Mack use to describe his duties at Orly Air Base. She'd imagined it to entail supplying provisions for military units. Now, she understood that it offered broader possibilities.

She recalled her mother's frequently recurring Barigoule, her father's grousing about its meagerness. Though he might grumble, she doubted he'd refuse groceries, even though they'd come from *un nègre* by way of his libertine daughter; she'd seen how pliable her father's principles could be.

"My pay is only very little," she said, "but what I can afford would help very much."

"Ain't nobody talking pay, Baby." Mack's face—he looked hurt. "Just let me know. If I can find it, I will bring it."

Payne jumped in: "If it's good work you need, I hear they hiring local girls who speak English for clerical projects and such-like out at the military hospital at Neuilly. Part-time jobs but full-time pay, given they be paying in greenbacks."

"Greenbacks?"

"Dollars," Mack said. He asked Payne, "You hear that recent?"

"From Reiver, yeah."

Quitting the Louvre for a job that paid better and left her feeling less beholden to her father was tempting—very tempting.

Mack noticed a man across the crowd. "There's Tony Smith, hang tight one second."

Cecile and Payne watched him go.

"That Mack," said Payne, shaking his head and smiling, and he wandered off, too.

After a short parlay with Tony Smith, middlemanning some bolts of cloth that Tony had asked about, Mack looked for Cecile back at the spot where he'd left her. She wasn't there. Some brothers roughhoused, and others tossed baseballs back and forth; card games were being played on folding tables, one group slapped bones; but no Baby. He wondered where she'd got off to.

There was Darlene Payne, though. In a full-length apron over her snazzy red dress, she'd commandeered one of the drum-barrel grills, swinging a long spatula about like it was a swagger stick and she George Patton, bossing folks. Mack requisitioned a bottle of Johnnie Walker from a crate and sidled up behind her.

"Now I see where Payne gets it from."

He'd startled her, but she smiled. "So you decided to come after all?"

"Barely made it, but yeah, we here."

"We? Oh, Cecile come with you."

Darlene made a play of scanning the crowd.

"She is somewhere abouts," Mack said.

Darlene leaned close. "Carl and the boys are staying in the city tonight." She swayed her hips back and forth as if to some beat. "We talking about playing a set."

Mack watched her, mouth poutish, moving silky-like, as fine as a fifteen-cent dime.

"I got duty in the morning, early," he said. "But who knows? Might stop by."

She snatched the Johnnie Red from his hand—"Give me that"—and hit the bottle then squinted. "Blech! Go on, cowboy. Come back when you got a proper drink for a lady."

He headed after a glass and some ice chips when, what did he see? Baby, seated on one of those scratchy military blankets, nearby three other French babies but off to herself, not socializing even with them.

She didn't notice Mack walk up. "Why you by yourself?"

"I am fine, Mack."

"Cuss fine," he said. "Darlene is right over there, ain't you seen her?"

"I am enjoying the watching of people."

"Enjoying the watching?" He burst a belly laugh, then took her hand and pulled her to her feet. "Come on."

She took the Johnnie Red from his hand and hit it, squinting like Darlene had. "Oh . . . This is terrible."

Darlene had joined a cluster of three tables in a triangle. Mack recognized Wanda Simmons, Marla Jones, Donna Mae Somebody-or-other . . . Some were the wives of GIs who'd joined their husbands overseas; even more were WACs. (One night at Payne's, he'd had to explain to Cecile that WAC was the designation for women soldiers, as she'd thought he was insulting them, calling them a variation of "wacky.") He said to the group, "Youall got room for one more? This here my Baby."

Cecile felt immediately ill at ease being introduced like that, Mack claiming her as his girl. Flattered, too. This was nothing like Seb's avoidance. But she hardly knew Mack, not even a month yet, just three or four dates.

She also felt incredibly nervous being thrust upon these girls in this way. "Room for one more for what?" she whispered into Mack's ear.

"Bid whist looks like," he responded, loud enough for the others to hear.

"Bid whist? I do not know what this is."

One of the girls raised a deck for Cecile to see. "A card game. You'll pick it up easy enough."

Cecile smiled a thank you.

Mack said, "Ima be over the way," and she watched him lope off toward some boys tossing a ball back and forth in what looked like cartoonishly big, brown leather gloves.

Payne's wife Darlene pointed to a chair beside her, which Cecile took, and very quickly the ensemble of tables buzzed with howls and brass and laughter. Each of the girls looked ready for a night on the town rather than an afternoon in a grass field: puffy skirts and bobby socks, expensive-looking dresses with shawls. Each one's hair was "processed"—made with chemicals to hang straight and styled in the ways of white American girls.

Not knowing any better, Cecile had worn denims and a white cotton blouse, an olive cardigan tied over her shoulders. It was a picnic, after all. She'd pulled her hair back in what Americans called a "pigtail"—their expression more apt than the French *queue de cheval*, a horse's tail, as her bob was hardly long enough to tie.

Everyone drank sweet cocktails, filling and refilling their empty-
ing glasses from pitchers at each table. Darlene, her partner in the game,
clearly didn't like the ease with which Cecile accepted losing a hand. She
was falsely patient, reiterating over and again the rules, barely hiding her
frustration with Cecile's bumbling efforts. The other team of two, teasing and taunting, reminded Cecile of Minette—the side of Minette that
Cecile loved. She first giggled at their biting asides, covering her mouth
with a hand. Soon she laughed and laughed, too.

At the neighboring table, they were discussing recipes, and one
sounded like something Cecile had seen at Payne's. "Soul food, yes?" she
asked, leaning toward them. "And this 'lard,' it is the fat from the porks?"

The girl who'd been speaking looked at her sidelong for interrupt-
ing, but the other three laughed, and the two tables quit their games to
exchange ideas on cooking this dish or that. White beans with ham hocks
(which sounded to Cecile not so unlike cassoulet). Barbequed short ribs
(which reminded her of a dish the Chinese made). And chitterlings.

"Chitlins?" Cecile asked, unable to find the translation on the screen
of her mind.

The girl named Marla chided her. "Don't act coy, like you don't
know nothing about chitterlings. I've smelled youall's andouillettes de
Toulouse!" She pursed her lips. "The nose knows. You may wrap 'em in
sausage casings, but them's chitterlings."

Bid whist was, for all intents and purposes, over, the three folding
tables dragged closer together, lively conversation supplanting cards. The
girls spoke of their homes—cabins in the woods or entire "city blocks"
where their parents and aunts and uncles lived, each one within walking
distance of the next, and "bringing over plates" when someone was ill or
newly back in town, and in none of the stories did there ever seem to be
a single white person present.

A girl named Sammie, who was a nurse, asked another whose name
Cecile couldn't remember if her "rotation" back had been approved.

"Yes, Lord," said the other, raising a hand in the air. "Lordlordlord,
yes!"

She turned toward Cecile. "I don't mean no disrespect. I just miss my people."

"Of course," Cecile said.

"I will regret leaving," the one named Marla said, "whenever I do go."

"All you ever do is complain!" Darlene shot back. "Not enough of this, not the right kind of that. Beds too short, ranges too small. 'Not a Frigidaire in the whole dang country'—how many times have I heard that?"

"And those Turkish toilets in the cafés!" Marla said. "You right, girl. Ain't too much I will miss."

"Seriously, though," the girl who'd earlier apologized said over the laughter, "this is as nice a place as I've been. When's the last time you went to a restaurant and was served by a white man who smiled and complimented your dress?"

"That's precisely the problem," Marla said. "Intermixing with local folk is too rarified. I do more commerce with that cracker commissary sergeant than with Monsieur Le Butcher."

The others said "Mm-hm" and "Yeah," solemnly, in regret. But Cecile wanted to retort: Why separate themselves from the French as they did, then? Why not frequent the shops of Monsieur Le Boucher or Madame La Patissière? Why stay to themselves, as she'd noted among the Americans, broadly, but of the American blacks, in particular?

"These French girls put the *s* in style, though, don't they?" the nurse Sammie said.

A chorus of "Mm-hm's" agreed.

She pointed to Cecile. "Just look at you. Took me two hours to get this together, "—she waved up and down herself—" and I bet you put yourself on in less than three minutes. You put more class into a pair of dungarees than I do in a twenty-five-dollar dress."

Cecile felt her face blush, not sure the girl wasn't teasing.

"They teach you that in school?" Sammie said.

The others laughed.

"I'm serious. Do they?"

"Well, not in school really," said Cecile. "There is not so much since the war, you understand. We watch the other girls and imitate."

"Just like we do at home," another, Myrlie, said. "My cousin Ruby can make a burlap sack and twine look like the latest in fashion design."

"A real Geechee Dior, huh?"

"You better believe it."

"And your people." Sammie pointed to Cecile's chest. "Did they make out okay—you know, from all that mess?"

The rest stared.

Cecile no longer wore her Star of David as she had before, expressly to shock. It unsettled all the same. Eyes automatically went to it or nervously tried not to.

She respected when people had the courage to openly acknowledge the significance of the symbol, as these girls did. "From that mess," she said, "I suppose we did."

Their chatter picked up again. Cecile spotted Mack across the field, ignoring the lively activity around him—"his boys," as he called them, barking out laughter and slapping hands onto the tabletop, the cards and chips there bouncing. Mack was staring at her.

When he saw that she'd noticed, he smiled.

CHAPTER EIGHTEEN

Mack talked to his friend Captain Reiver, who spoke to his own superior officer, and after submitting an application, Cecile was hired in the Overhead Unit of the US military hospital system, based in Neuilly. She was assigned to a Quonset hut in a row of them, each one like the next, hers AFCENT-0317. Uniform lines of desks and file cabinets stretched from front to back, the arced interior oddly dark despite the surfeit of electric lighting. She was required to wear a dress or a skirt, and her shift began at seven, so she had to be out the door by five forty-five. The Americans were much more exacting than Monsieur Petit had been, though the job was no harder—indexing mostly, with some translation but very little typing (which pleased Cecile, as she only knew the two-finger method).

As the days passed, it shocked her how rarely she even noticed the droning regimentation of everything. Most of her coworkers were the American wives of GIs (their "dependents," they were called) or WACs. The American white girls, both wives and WACs, all wore the same hairstyle and all looked the same, blond and ruddy. They were friendly, overly so but rarely sincerely, and their nasal voices sounded like cheery whining. They no more interested Cecile than did the few other French girls, who were painfully quiet, as though it was them who were aliens in a foreign land and not vice versa.

Cecile identified more with the black girls, whose breeziness was peppered with spice, even though she feared that they looked upon her as they did the other whites. Given what she was learning about America from Mack and his friends and these girls, any wariness they might feel toward her was unsurprising—was reasonable, even. It was what she would feel toward a German, and she figured it would wane once they got to know her, once they recognized that she wasn't one of the "crackers" about whom they so often spoke.

Though everyone saw her as "Mack Gray's girl," she still had trouble seeing herself that way. She liked him plenty—very much, in fact. He was fun, and he clearly liked her. He bought her gifts, impromptu, and always made sure she had enough of whatever she might need, and her parents, too. But her experience with Seb had taught her to be cautious, to remain her own woman.

The first time she invited him upstairs to her room, he was like da Gama discovering new lands, wandering from sink to closet to window, scouring the trinkets on her dresser, scrutinizing the one picture tacked to the wall—from Chandesaignes, of her and her mother.

He didn't ask about it. He just considered it and smiled.

Moving to the easel, inspecting the sketches and rudimentary paintings stacked on it, he said, "I was afraid you might not *never* let me up here."

It was true, he'd been very patient. She joined him across the room, wondering what he thought of the work.

"You never said you was an artist. Now I get why the old job, at the Louvre," he said, fingering the pencils and brushes in the wicker basket. He picked out a cigarette butt, laughing. "You use this for an ashtray!"

What could she say? Her practice had become haphazard.

How long had it been, in fact, since she'd seriously attempted anything, since she'd even bought new paints? She'd lost all discipline.

"It is just a past-time," she said. "Maybe someday I will get better."

They perched on the windowsill in silence, Cecile leaning back into his embrace, taking the Lucky from his mouth and blowing her smoke into the night then returning it to his lips. He ran the fingers of his free hand through her hair. She wished she had a tapestry that told the story of her life. The old sketches and color studies were not it, and she wondered what he understood of her from them.

She would have liked to see the tapestry of Mack's life. For all he freely shared, he remained a bit of an enigma. He was profoundly knowing yet also strangely unformed. Unlike Seb, he wanted her nearby and in the full light of day, but he could be absent all the same. The words that best described Mack—"fun," "charming," "kind"—didn't really say anything particularly distinctive.

"What sort of name is Mack?" The question hadn't occurred to her before. Was it typically American, or specifically black American?

"Short for Macklin." His voice reverberated through her back, into her chest. "Macklin Beauregard. Growing up, I was called Beau."

How appropriate, she thought—of course, *beau. Son beau regard fait flipper les filles.*

He resumed his silence. She wanted to probe more, but it felt delicate to do so. She knew enough about slavery to know that families had been broken up and scattered, to know that many American blacks were ignorant of their antecedents. Mack sometimes mentioned his mother and siblings but never his grandparents and those who came before. Did he know them or where they'd lived before his cherished "KC"?

His torso twisted, and she turned her head to follow his gaze. Mack was peering at the Beaux-Arts courtyard across the street, clearly not recognizing it from her sketches—just another Paris monument or museum, she supposed that he supposed, a site to visit though not to know, somewhere to boast about having been to. This was what the Americans did. She found it funny. And perhaps fixable.

They spent time together as best they could, but between her early mornings and his rotating shifts, aligning their schedules wasn't easy. Increasingly, connecting took place mostly on weekends—dinner and dancing at Payne's, then back to Cecile's room.

Among the Americans, the boys did boy things, the girls did theirs. Mack and his friends typically congregated at a café across from the base, La Petite, to share a bottle and kill time before mess or hitting the sack. Lively barstool debates ensued. The frequent topic that fall was the rumor building steam of President Truman's intention to integrate the military. Captain Reiver himself, who ought to know, insisted that the order was coming down the line, that it was just a matter of time.

Mack didn't elaborate much more than this when he told Cecile about it; the entire subject seemed to confuse her. But for him and his boys, the issue raised other, harder questions. To stay or to go? Should they re-up in the service and set up over here or separate and head home? The young-bloods were of two minds about it and fell into two camps. One Wednesday afternoon at La Petite, Poota Rabbit Cole made the case for staying.

"See now, France be freedom," he said, "'cause Froggy be pragmatic about it. He can care less what your skin is, he want to know can you offer something. If he think yeah, then you as clean as gasoline."

To Mack's view, Poot and his camp were straight-up, unreconstructed Frogophiles. Mack respected the country, but those brothers woke up humming the Marseillaise.

His good friend Tony Smith was decidedly of the other camp. "Child, please," he said to Poot. "Ain't nothing free over here. Brits be cracking Italian heads, Russians cracking German heads. Just a matter a time 'fore somebody want to crack upside your head."

"German head, Italian head"—Poot pronounced "Italian" wrong on purpose: Eye-talian—"Hell, crack away! They get what they got coming, far as I'm concerned. Ain't none of that got nothing to do with me."

"And the Frogs cracking Algerian heads?" Tony Smith's voice pitched high when he was riled up. "That all right with you? Senegalese heads, too?"

"Senegalese, Congolese, Ivory-Gold-Slave Coastese," Poot shot back. "What any of that got to do with me?"

Everybody was laughing except Tony Smith. The man was *serious*—straight off the farm, not six years of schooling to his name, but Mack didn't know a soul who could make a point like Tony Smith.

Tony waited till the conversation began to still, then started in: "My people part Indian—Kiamitia Choctaw. My Granpoppa, he half and had growed up most of his youth in the Territory, around Langston."

The others quieted, Mack signaled the barkeep for a new bottle, and Tony Smith went on.

"Up around Langston back in the day was a army camp for Buffalo Soldiers. That's what Indians call the colored troopers. Well, a Buffalo Soldier would crack a Indian head just as quick as a gendarme bust up a Algerian, I shit you not, son." Tony was looking straight at Poot. "They had made that man believe the Indian deserved it. But Granpoppa, he always lament this. He say, 'Dumbest thing colored and Indians ever did was to not recognize each other as akin.' He say, 'Probably couldn't of defeated them crackers, but enough of us together would make them think twice about how they acting. Oklahoma be *real* Indian Territory then, not just a glorified reservation.'"

Poot came back at him: "Niggers ain't Indians, Nigger! How you want folk as different as night and day acting of a kind together?"

To this, Tony Smith stared for reply. Just stared.

Where most of the youngbloods were relatively new arrivals (Mack included—he'd spent most of the war in the meatpacking plants in West Bottoms, too young to enlist), Poot had been in France for the fighting. He'd spilled blood for the place. Like Mack, Poot had a French baby, and he was more proud of that girl on his arm than of the Bronze Star they'd pinned to his chest. That Bronze Star earned him the right to his views.

So, Tony Smith let the hypocrisy of his last statement slide, saying only: "Got white man boot on they neck, they got that of a kind."

Lucius Martin took up where Poot had left off. "Sheee-it, I puts mah own motherfucking boot on dey motherfucking neck, Injun, Af'can, Algee'run, whatever. Jes' don' be brangin' dat savage-ass bidness 'round me."

Of his boys, Mack liked Lucius the least. He was from Boston and had gone to college; he worked in the lab for the medical branch. Yet, he tried to act more niggerfied than regular down-home niggers and ended up sounding like a coon show act instead, his speech all blacked up.

"How you gone be like that?" Tony Smith told him. "You as bad as them crackers."

"May well be. But dis shit heah, dis wah dey had us all in, dat was 'bout freedom."

Captain Reiver was often silent during the barstool debates, but he beamed ear to ear at this last comment, and the others noted it.

Colored officers weren't allowed in the Officers' Club; that was why Reiver fraternized with Mack's group. But Reiver was an officer still and all, and would have to maintain authority. So, he rarely betrayed much feeling on what was said. That he'd smiled meant something.

Poota Rabbit, watching Reiver, piggybacked on Lucius's point. "Can't come halfway across the world, and kill as many as has been killed, and have as many of ours killed as has been, and *not* have this be about something. Can't walk the walk, on this scale, and not expect to go back and walk it in your hometown, too."

But Tony Smith wouldn't let it go. "You tell that to them Indochinese that fought the Japs and is now fighting the French, right this instant they is." And Reiver lost his smile just like that. "De Gaulle ain't a hero to them. You tell that to the Tunisians in Tunisia, to the Algerians in Algeria. If Uncle Sam call you to go over there, put your boot on they necks when all they asking for is to be free in their own damned land, would you go?"

"Back home, brother? Walk the walk back home!"

This had come from Kendrick Deen, and he'd directed it at Poot, who he was staring down, and La Petite fell quiet.

Kendrick hailed from Georgia, from a village near Moore's Ford Bridge. The recent outrage there wasn't the first time, and they all goddamn well knew it wouldn't be the last, but the crackers had killed the women, too. Cut a baby out of one. The brother they were after had fought in the Pacific, he'd just returned from a five-year stint, and it did not matter one whit. Five were lynched, all told, including the baby.

When the debates got too heavy to hold, Mack would break in. "Fuck Georgia!" he said now. "I tell you this, though: if Algerian pookie anything like Froggy pook, I'll set sail for there quicker than quick, my brother Tony."

Everybody busted up, Tony Smith and Kendrick Deen, too—even Reiver.

Lucius Martin, chuckling yet, said, "But you's gots you a gal heah."

"A piece in each port," said Mack, "that's how I do things"—all the youngbloods busting up, laughing anew.

Mack only meant to lighten the room, not to disrespect his Baby.

In his stay-or-go questioning, though, she played a role. Mack's plan had always been to return to KC after leaving the service. His middlemanning—a case of wool socks here, two crates of baked beans there, jerricans of gasoline—brought in good money on top of the army money, and he regularly put some aside, start-up for a business back home, a livery service maybe. Baby complicated the picture.

Not at first, she hadn't. At first, she'd fit right into his reveries—of buying a Cadillac show car, red with a white top and white-walled rims, and driving his pretty French Baby all over KC for everyone to see. He'd sent his mama a snapshot of them seated at a café on the Champs-Élysées; he didn't write often but he knew she needed to know about Baby. Her reply had cut him to the quick:

Macklin Beauregard—Do not bring that girl here.

Are you crazy! Across the river, you two ain't even legal.

Think of her, how she will be received. As a "nigger lover." And will you have babies? Won't their lives be hard enough? You want to curse them as "mulatto" too, on top of "colored"?

No *My Sweet Boy Bo*, no news of neighbors. Her closing had been the usual, at least: *May Jesus keep you close, Mama.*

So, if he and Baby were to be together, maybe the only plan was to stay. More than once, Reiver had told Mack that if he applied himself, put in the time for his high school equivalency, he could qualify for OCS, wear bars on his collar. "You got the whole package," he'd say. "Smart, good with figures, good with words. The others gravitate toward you. That's born, not learned." Officer rank might make a re-up more tempting.

Or Mack could follow the course Payne had set—cut loose of Uncle Sam, use his contacts to wheel and deal free of the army yoke, either here or better yet in Germany.

Or he could take his Baby back to KC, no matter what his mama said. Home.

That Cecile might have a view on these options never occurred to him.

CHAPTER NINETEEN

Seb remembered—as a boy, before being sent to France—sitting halfway up the concrete staircase in their home and watching his father through the transom above his office door. In a tie but no jacket and seated at a mahogany desk, he rat-a-tat-tatted on the imported typewriter that he prized. Other formal and grave men occasionally stopped by—activists and thinkers, Seb now understood—and they discussed colonial policy and world politics, matters that were impossibly heady to a six-year-old.

One day, a courier in short pants and a sweat-stained khaki shirt rang at the gate, with an envelope. By his father's expression, the matter was pressing. Seb was rarely allowed outside the compound and even less often allowed to accompany his father, but his mother and sister were gone with Aunt Fifonsi, the cook was at the market, and the houseboy Celestain was who knew where. His father instructed him to put on his dress shoes and get his cap.

Seb's memory of the city that was his home consisted mostly of random images and impressions. But of the day of the courier, he formed a whole picture. Cotonou: a humming, rushing, teeming downtown, with ship upon ship at rest in the port. Some looked as lengthy and broad as the busy boulevard along which he and his father walked. Lining the boulevard were tan colonial buildings with terra-cotta roofs, most two-storied, a few taller. There were more *Yovo* than he'd ever seen, in white from pith helmet to trouser cuff—though, by comparison to the masses of blacks, very few at all. Here and there among them, a woman. The *Yovo* women wore broad, drooping hats to shade their faces but which did nothing to conceal their disdain. And the noise! Lorries everywhere, motors booming up to speed or screeching to a stop, metal grinding on metal.

A black gendarme directed traffic at the hectic roundabout near the docks. More than the rest, it was this part of the memory that struck Seb now, lying alone in his bed in the dark. The police officer was in a boxy blue kepi and a dark cape, his hands in white gloves, and he was standing on a raised block marked POLICE, in the center of the traffic circle. Very officious, very formal. Sputtering lorries inched around him, alongside Dahomeyans pulling handcarts and others pedaling bicycles burdened with roped-down crates and even more still walking with impossible heaps perched atop their heads. The gendarme gesticulated and blew a whistle, its toot-toot-toot all but lost amid the honking horns and the men barking at each other and the shrieking engines. He gesticulated and blew all the same.

It was only upon Seb's arrival in Paris a year or so later, when he and his sister saw a gendarme directing the hectic traffic on Place de la Concorde, that he realized the phenomenon wasn't typically African. The chaos of circling trucks and bicycle taxis and pedestrians was familiar, the clamor and the horns, but the white face framed by the blue kepi and dark cape, atop the raised block—the face a photonegative image of the gendarme's in Cotonou—had disoriented Seb. His dismay soon became dread as all the *Yovo* faces materialized in the blur of the crowd, nothing but, their mouths hurling insults in a language that was his language, the only one he'd ever known, though clearly not his at all.

Now, sixteen years later, the black gendarme troubled Seb's sleep. Like the gendarme, his father wore *Yovo* clothes, sometimes comically formal in the equatorial damp and heat, and as with the gendarme, they were a blaring intimation of the perplexing contradictions beneath. For what sort of man put a seven- and a nine-year-old on a boat to a place he protested and reviled, a place he'd never seen himself, and ordered those children to outdo their French peers, but didn't expect, much less would he accept, that they would become a little bit French in so doing? Who was that man?

Imposing, bespectacled, and austere, he'd frightened Seb as a child. But he was, in fact, slight—narrow shouldered and probably no taller than a meter seventy. Seb's own build mirrored his grandfather's, from what he could tell from pictures in the archives. He'd inherited Gbéhanzin's physique, stocky and thick.

Gbéhanzin. Seb's father rejected the name, favoring the one used by the Catholic missionaries instead. Seb had always gotten the irony of this—an anticolonial journalist embracing a Christian name over the traditional one. The true indignity only struck him now: he didn't know his father's real name, the one bestowed at birth by a *na daho*, the one honored in the royal lineage. Seb had only ever known the other.

Seb knew his own name, at least: Kannou, short for Kannoukpô. And he knew its meaning: "The rope is not yet at its end."

He also understood that he had many names, all meaningful: Sebastien; Danxomè; and also Seb, what Cecile called him.

In the archives one morning, Seb requested a box entitled HEAD CLERIC, OUÉMÉ DEPT., DAHOMEY—1889–1919, a little bit randomly. The dates intrigued him, as they corresponded roughly with the French takeover of his home. On top of what was inside, though, was a page-long obituary dedicated to a missionary, Father Joseph Piétot. The headline read, "City Son Fallen after a Life Devoted to the Benighted." Seb recalled the name from *Dans les Colonies*; Piétot had been popular with its journalists and was often quoted or referred to.

Beyond the obituary, the box contained manila folders filled with handwritten drafts of reports and studies by the priest, as well as his collection of period magazines from France, England, and Germany. One folder, entitled ORIGINS OF THE AFRICAN CHARACTER, held several pamphlets from conferences he'd attended or spoken at, with scrawled notes about the proceedings. Piétot's observations, which seemed to aim for scientific objectivity, were hardly flattering, with mentions of "the stunted soul of the Black" and "an incipient race" and "ordinary beasts of burden."

Throughout the materials in the box, Seb saw repeated reference to the "houseboy." From the priest's running commentary, which was sometimes hard to decipher, Seb realized that Piétot wasn't casually tossing about the common (and demeaning) form of address for some African domestic nearby (whether he was, in fact, a child or not), as Seb had originally thought. Rather, Piétot had been remarking upon a specific boy, one being educated at the mission, whose actions the priest apparently followed closely. Elsewhere, Piétot also made mention of his "research subject," and as Seb read on, it occurred to him that the two, the "houseboy" and the "research subject," were one and the same person.

Piétot had cut out an editorial from *Le Temps* newspaper and made notes beside a passage, which read:

> *How many centuries, how many thousands of years has the Negro held large tribal districts in Africa undisturbed by the white man? Yet their inter-tribal struggles have not yet produced a civilization in the least comparable with the Aryan. Educate and nurture them as you will, you will not succeed in modifying the stock. The feeble races are being wiped off the earth.*

In the margin, the priest had written, "Must it be so?" Below this, he'd scrawled: "Witness the houseboy, consider his bloodlines. That one was a vicious tyrant whose currency was blood." Below this: "God has put us here to improve ourselves. He can be proof of the perfectability of the Black."

And it struck Seb: Could the houseboy have been his father?

Seb knew that his father had been raised by priests after his own father's exile, protected from rival Dahomeyan factions by a "kindly missionary," as his father had called him. Could it have been Piétot, a man celebrated for his devotion to "the benighted," using his position as head cleric to shield Seb's father when he'd been a vulnerable child? This would explain Seb's father's unlikely allegiance to the Church.

The pieces seemed to fall into place. His father hadn't been named Sebastien at birth; some priest had christened him this. Had Piétot been that priest? Before eventually doing so, Piétot might have referred to him as the "houseboy" and his "research subject," the likely roles Seb's father would have played before being embraced by the missionary.

But how to know for certain?

The next morning, Seb returned to Piétot's rambling notes and studies, combing more carefully through them. The collection of period magazines resonated differently now, with this new perspective. For a man of the cloth, Piétot had clearly been engaged with the worldly issues of his day, and from the scrawl in the margins of the pages, he appeared to hold journalists in high esteem. This might explain the respect Seb's father held for newspapers and newspapermen, and the professional course he had set upon.

A manila folder that Seb had cursorily thumbed through before caught his attention. Among many loose documents was a stiff and yellowed copy of a broadsheet, *Le Quartier Latin*, folded in half for the folder to accommodate its size. Doubting that a newspaper dubbed for romanticized Paris intellectualism would have anything to do with his downtrodden homeland, Seb had sped past it previously. This time, he paid closer attention. Contrary to what the broadsheet's name suggested, the articles were specific to French West Africa, their subject matter political in nature: inadequate medical facilities for natives in Cotonou; testimony from villagers along the Nigerian border who refused to work the nearby palm oil plantations; ongoing use of the lash in the gold mines in the north. On the paper's back page was listed its reporters and staff, and there at the top, "Sebastien Danxomè, Publisher and Editor"—his father!

"By your expression," Seb heard, "I see you've uncovered something intriguing."

It was Monsieur Chevalier, the friendly archivist.

"I've found everything," Seb told him.

It took a few hours for Chevalier to locate the entire collection—three boxes, nearly every issue from the paper's founding in 1924 until just before the war, when, according to a colonial police report on top of the first box, *Le Quartier Latin* had been shut down, its printing press destroyed. Seb plunged in.

In every issue, lengthy passages had been blacked out by censors. Seb's temper flared as he toiled through column after column and page after page, confounded by the mixture of obscure references and blocks of expunged text. One thing was clear: the articles railed against France and its colonial policies. What struck Seb even more, though—especially given the biting tone and the passion and dash—was that they were written in *French*, not in Yoruba or Fon, the prominent languages of Dahomey.

For whom was his father publishing *Le Quartier Latin*?

And though a protest paper, its title suggested something else— a sort of admiration. Who named his newspaper, the platform for his anticolonial complaint, after the prized symbol of the colonizer's intellectual heritage?

How to untangle the twist of mystery that was his father? A colonial subject and a French citizen. Of royal heritage but classically educated. The man caught between two names (one which Seb didn't even know), roiled by the inescapable stain of blood and the crushing paternalism of the priests. Gbéhanzin or Sebastien?

Seb sensed a parallel between his father's malaise and his own, two outsiders who became enmeshed with people seemingly incapable of actually seeing them. Understanding his father—why he was who he was and how this had come to be—might be the key to unpacking the contradictions within himself.

And Seb recognized that he needed to do it now, and quickly, before the man arrived, because, well . . .

Because of Cecile. She'd asked what they were doing, who they were together. How was he to answer that question without knowing the answers to his own questions—about family and obligations, about the past and his future?

If he was to win back her trust, a long, searching look in a truthful mirror was the place to start.

CHAPTER TWENTY

"I don't hear from you in over a month, and you call to announce this!" Minette's voice, though squelched through the earpiece, was hardly diminished.

"It's just a job," Cecile said, standing in the phone box outside AFCENT-0317. "It pays in ways that the Louvre did not, that our jobs *can*not."

"You've changed sides," Minette said. "You're with them now. Are you going to emigrate to the US, then?"

"*Mais, non.* Be serious," she said. "I rang you because we haven't spoken in a while, and because I miss you."

And it was true: Cecile wanted Minette in her life; she loved her. But she needed more from her, too.

Cecile's time among the American blacks was showing her how life *could* be, despite difference. The black girls at work did not speak her language, and she struggled with theirs, but they'd found a language in common. During break that morning, when the girls were reminiscing of home and deriding "the crackers" there, Cecile had dropped her eyes. But Betty Ann Stanley had chided her not to. "You ain't white," she'd said. "You French." It was a specious argument, but one Cecile happily accepted. Awkward moments arose, but unlike with Minette, she was never made to feel shame about who she was.

"I just wanted to say hi," Cecile said into the mouthpiece. "It's been a busy day. I should go."

"Already, *fillette?*" Cecile heard a softness, also familiar, but that she'd forgotten. "It's true, it's been way too long since we've caught up."

This was neither a mea culpa nor an apology, and Cecile realized that she wanted something of one—not a concession of weakness, not from Minette, but an acknowledgment that she was not the girl from the bus ride to the youth conference, that she was not just a pussy and a prize. But this was taking a step in the right direction.

Cecile said, "You'd be surprised, Minette. The American blacks, they suffer like . . ." She almost said "like we suffer" but stopped herself. "Like our colonies suffer. Like Boubi and Seb, like your father has suffered."

A buzzing silence.

"Join me with them," Cecile said, "dancing or something. You'll see, they're more like us than you think."

She stressed the "us."

"When?" she heard.

"How about next week? There's a concert that a group of us is going to."

She hadn't told her about Mack, only the new job. Minette could find out when she met him. His charm would win her over.

"We're getting tickets," Cecile said. "I'll make sure there's one for you."

Sensing Minette's hesitation over the line, she insisted: "So yes, then?"

"All right, all right—yes . . ."

"Oh, great, Minette! I'm so looking forward to it. *À bientôt.*" And she hung up.

She'd not mentioned the upcoming elections, her father's candidacy.

She'd also hoped she might get news about Seb and the results of the exam.

It could all wait, though, until they saw each other. Very soon!

Mack's brother Darnell arrived, there for the weekend en route to his posting in Germany. Mack and Cecile picked him up at the Gare Saint-Lazare in a Willys. Mack hugged him so hard that both of his brother's feet lifted off the ground.

Side by side, Darnell was Mack in miniature: half a head shorter; more slight through the shoulders; his smile as brilliant, but self-consciously so. Mack pointed to Darnell's shirt sleeve, visibly pleased. "Already!" Darnell had half as many stripes on his US Air Force uniform as Mack did on his green fatigues. "Ain't been in the service a year and here you is, bumping up on me."

Cecile was in a dress Mack had bought her at the PX, white with green and brown floral print—so very much *not* Cecile, but she wore it all the same—and she hugged Darnell too and smiled. She'd been uncommonly anxious in the days leading up to the visit. This boy was Mack's family, as much of his family as she'd yet to know. She didn't want to embarrass Mack by her appearance or conduct.

Mack insisted they give Darnell a tour of Paris. With Mack at the wheel and his brother beside, Cecile sat on the rear bench seat, her neck hunched into her collar, the Hermès square over her head. The Louvre, then the Tour Eiffel, then the Champs-Élysées, around and around L'Étoile— they never stopped. Nor did they actually visit any of the sights, zipping through traffic, the top off (though it was October and too cold for it), Mack and Darnell jabbering over the whistle of cold air, both of them howling.

"How's Mama?" Mack asked.

"She Mama, getting on like always."

"And Colleen?"

"The crazy heifer done had another baby."

"Naw!"

"She a goddamn breeding machine. Three children with three different daddies, and not nan one of them men worth two goddamn cent."

Cecile followed the conversation as best she could over the noise of the engine and despite the slang and the insider knowledge that neither Mack nor his brother attempted to translate for her. She didn't mind. Mack seemed more Mack with his brother here—more open, more vulnerable. She recognized in their ease together the familiarity of family: knowing someone's tics and habits, an embarrassing memory or the thing that could provoke a smile. She was glad to see this side of him.

"So, Rhein-Main Base?" Mack said.

"Frankfurt, yeah."

"I thought we was sending folks home."

"With Russia's monkey business in Berlin, more personnel is needed in Europe," Darnell said. "That's the feeling Stateside, anyway. If you aim to rotate back, you might ought to act sooner rather than not."

Mack glanced at Cecile in the mirror. "I ain't decided one way or the other," he said to Darnell. "Baby's people are here. I take care of them, she takes care of me."

Cecile returned his smile, but inside she felt herself clench. As was the American way, Mack said things directly. But directly said, it unsettled Cecile.

Mack drove in silence for several moments. Cecile watched the reflection of his eyes in the rearview mirror—brow furrowed, attention fixed though not on traffic as they sped past Place Blanche and down the Boulevard de Clichy, the white-stone cupolas of the Sacré-Coeur intermittently visible above or between buildings. She'd never really considered the idea of Mack leaving. She thought of him like she did Dior's New Look or Payne's restaurant, as just another addition to the city.

"If I was to re-up," he told his brother, "France is golden cause folks ain't got a pot to piss in here and need a little bit of everything."

Darnell turned in his seat and cocked his head. "What you up to, big bruh?"

Mack peered over then back at the road. "Things are happening."

"Happening?"

"I expect that, over in Germany, folks need things more than even here. Well, I got friends in the motor pool, in shipping, that sort of thing. Sometimes a crate of this or a box of that finds its way my way." He glanced at his brother. "You always been resourceful. Maybe you lay the groundwork over in Rhein-Main. I get you what you need, and you get it to who might can pay for it."

Mack focused on the road now. "There's a little risk in it. But so long as a nigger don't get too greedy, it ain't but a little."

Darnell's laugh was a cackle, a burst of insolence more than of joy. "Big bruh! Always running something."

They went to Payne's for dinner. The place was packed. Mack introduced Darnell to people around the room, then led him to the kitchen. They took a table in the corner and Payne sent out breaded pork chops and macaroni casserole and later red velvet cake, and Darnell, speaking with his mouth full, exclaimed: "This mess goddamn good as back home, son!"

Mack's friends were setting up to play, and Darlene called Mack to the stage. He shook his head no, waving himself up and down. "I ain't dressed the part tonight," he called back.

"Honey," Darlene said, "you always dressed the part."

The room burst into laughter and here-and-there applause, and Mack ambled up.

Alone with Cecile, Darnell—a bottle of beer in one hand, his half-empty cocktail on the table—smiled an oily smile but said nothing.

Cecile smiled in return. "Can I refresh up your beverage?"

"*Refresh up* my beverage?" He laughed his hyena's laugh.

In the corner, the man on stand-up bass—Cecile thought she remembered his name to be Anthony Denard—plucked strings, Darlene humming along in her liquid contralto, Mack leaning toward the other two as they synched their horns.

Darnell leered. "So, you the one?"

"Pardon?" Cecile said.

"You the one Bo hot-dogged about bringing home, use her pretty blond hair to mop up Mama's floors with." He reached across and stroked Cecile's hair, now grown long enough to drape past her shoulders. "This chocolate color will do. Chocolate's just fine."

Chestnut, actually—more auburn than brown.

She rose and went to the WC. Rather than return to the table, she stood with Payne in the kitchen as he labored over the stove, stirring a long wooden spoon in a tall stockpot. She asked nonsense questions—about dishes and recipes, anything to pass the time. When she heard the music stop and saw through the small window in the swinging door that Mack had returned to their table, she excused herself.

"Where you been at all this time?" he said, cross.

"I am not feeling well. I think I will return home."

"Not feeling well?"

"Just tired." She stepped onto her tiptoes to kiss his cheek before he had a chance to protest. "Perhaps too much of the cold breeze during our ride today."

Darnell smirked, where Mack's eyes seemed to ask pardon.

"I'm sorry, Baby. Let me get you a cab."

He walked her to the curb and hailed one, then leaned in and paid the driver. "Darnell's got a night train tomorrow," he said. "I'll check in on you in the morning, see if you can join us before he has to go."

They were blood, yes, but Mack was not Darnell. They were nothing alike.

"Please do," she said to avoid disappointing him, though she knew she'd not feel up to it. She smiled and closed the door, and the taxi pulled off up Rue des Martyrs.

CHAPTER TWENTY-ONE

Cecile walked at a clip from the Metro at Place de la République, late for her rendezvous. The choice of location for the show still confounded her. In a side street beside Boulevard du Temple, the Cirque d'Hiver—the Winter Circus, with its archly baroque façade and glass-domed ceiling—was meant for trapeze acts and clowns and lion tamers, not for men of the stature of Louis Armstrong.

The day had been wet and cold, typical for October. Minette wasn't at the agreed-upon spot, beneath the elevated bronze statues beside the entrance. No one was, the great doors already closed, a thrumming from inside causing them to vibrate. A young man in a slicker and a bellman's cap, hunched against the penetrating chill, let Cecile in.

Cecile removed her raincoat and the scarf from her head and combed her fingers through her recently cut hair. The interior, meant to replicate a diminutive Colosseum, was even more tacky than the outside, but the pulse of anticipation beat floor to ceiling. The steep-banked rows of seats were nearly full and still filling, mostly with dark faces—GIs by the look of it. Cecile was one of only a spattering of whites, those others, like her, apparently French. She scanned the room for some sign of Mack—and hopefully of Minette, too, praying that her friend hadn't changed her mind.

An usher approached. The man's face sagged, and rivulets of broken blood vessels ranged over his yellowed cheeks. "You picked the wrong night to come to the show, Mademoiselle," he said, a hand outstretched for her ticket.

"Pardon?"

"It's jungle night tonight." He smiled conspiratorially, voice raised over the din. "The Americans won't let their white and black soldiers mix. So, we get the monkeys all at once."

She snatched the ticket stub from his hand. Stupid *Yovo*! It was men like him who'd betrayed them to the Nazis.

Turning, she paused to fully take in the stage—a grand piano, a drum kit, and a double bass propped on a stand, its wooden face glistening. Above, a banner stretched from one end to the other—*BIENVENU AU ROI NÈGRE DU* JAZZ, LOUIS ARMSTRONG!—and beside the words, a round caricature of Armstrong's face, with big white eyes and bulbous red lips.

The rest of her countrymen were hardly better than this usher, even when trying to be.

The man lurked beside Cecile as she searched the crowd. "But of course," he said, casting a sidelong glance at her Star pendant and wearily moving on. "I'd forgotten the affinity your people share with theirs."

"*Sale con*," she called after him. Stupid asshole.

Most of the GIs in the crowd wore dress uniforms, trim and proper. This seemed to rebut the usher's petty bigotry and lend more grandeur to the venue. Some, though, were in long-tailed zoot suits with flared trousers and broad hats; they buzzed and cackled and stomped their feet, and this seemed fitting, too. Still, Cecile could not see Mack or his friends—Payne or Tony Smith or any of the others who she'd met and who he'd said would be with him. And no Minette.

She spotted Seb, though, at the top of the grandstand, seated beside his sister, Boubi, and some other African man. There was no mistaking them in that crowd, straight-backed and still and not interacting with each other, much less anyone else, each one facing fixedly down at the stage though nothing was happening there yet. She noted the grace in Seb's formality, his calm demeanor in the bustle all around him. He embodied the word "dignity." She'd forgotten how much she loved this about him.

If he hadn't already spotted her, he might well during or after the show. So, she headed up the stiff stairs to avoid any awkwardness.

Jacqueline greeted her first, with a handshake much like outside the Tournon. "*Tiens*," she said. "How lovely to see you again."

The kind words didn't comport with her empty smile.

Boubi rose to kiss cheeks, warm and welcoming—the opposite of Jacqueline. "How long has it been?" He answered his own question: "Too long!"

The other man had a round face and was stout, though not fit like Seb. Seb introduced him as Jean-Joseph M'Bokolo, and they kissed cheeks. Then she and Seb kissed too, cheek to cheek to cheek.

The others sat. Seb joined Cecile in the aisle, his face open, his smile tight but true. "Ah, Cecile," he said, looking pleased to see her.

"Maman still asks after you. You made quite an impression."

She was unsure why she'd begun with this.

"I very much liked her, too. I wanted to take some letters out there for her to analyze." Seb held her eyes. "But I feared it might be inappropriate now."

Cecile asked: "And Beaux-Arts? Did you make the cut?"

The abruptness of the question was no more tactful than the remark about her mother, especially if the news was bad. But she'd wondered nonstop.

"They don't seem pressed to seat the class," he said, "or to even just announce who'll be part of it."

"You haven't heard anything?"

"Not a word."

"It's been two months!"

The fall had been an endless succession of strikes and work shutdowns; postal carriers only sporadically delivered the mail, sometimes just once per week. Still, two months was an inexplicable—an inexcusable—delay.

He maintained his smile, though now it appeared mournful. "Maybe they notify those admitted first. Maybe I *have* found out by the silence, only I refuse to recognize it."

The probability that he was correct saddened Cecile, too.

He changed the subject. "We're here representing the ASUFC. We're going to try to establish a connection with Armstrong."

Boubi, who'd clearly been eavesdropping, leaned toward them and added: "For all that the French disdain us, they absolutely *adore* the black Americans. The jazzman would be a great ally to have."

Seb jumped in: "Are you here on your own? Do you want to join us?"

"I'd love to," said Cecile, glancing toward Jacqueline, who stared insistently at the stage, pretending to ignore their conversation. "But I can't. I'm with friends."

Seb scanned the crowd, then his gaze settled on a spot in the first row. Cecile, following it, saw Mack.

"Is that the—" Seb asked.

"Yes," she said. "From the Rhumerie."

Mack and his friends were in uniform and not zoot suits—formal: olive drab jackets, cinched at the waist by brown leather belts; khaki shirts and ties; braided white fourragères strung through their left epaulettes. This relieved Cecile. She realized that she cared how Seb perceived Mack, as it would reflect on how he thought of her.

She saw Seb's face close on itself and also realized that she liked seeing him jealous.

The houselights flickered off then on, off then on. The show would begin soon.

"I'd better go," she said.

"Yes, of course."

Seb leaned toward her, and they kissed cheeks—stiffly this time, coolly. Cecile said to the others, "Enjoy the evening. *Au revoir.*"

The three turned toward her, their smiles distant, even Boubi, whose gaze quickly shifted back toward the stage.

She worked her way down the steep stairs. As she neared, Mack flicked a Lucky Strike up through the tear in the top of his pack and extended it toward her. She took it—"*Merci.*" But when he leaned to kiss her, it was all she could do to not turn away, to offer a cheek, knowing that Seb would be watching.

She stretched upward to him instead, kissed him fully on the mouth. Mack fumbled his fingers through her hair. "Aw, Baby, what d'you do?"

She called "Hello!" to his friends and their dates, and most nodded or waved, though Tony Smith, Cecile's favorite, crossed to her and kissed cheeks, à la française.

"It was time for a new look," she told Mack, adding quickly: "and I am very sorry, but I think that my friend has desisted at the last minute."

"Desisted?"

"Minette," she explained. "How to say, um . . . She cannot come tonight, apparently."

"Ain't no thing," he said, unconcerned in a way she would not be, had it been her who'd wasted all that money on the extra ticket.

More than disappointment, Minette's no-show disheartened Cecile. Once Minette realized how much she had in common with the American blacks, Cecile could plan things—evenings at Payne's, outings in Mack's Willys—and she and Minette would see more of one another again and their closeness might be renewed. This, above all, had been Cecile's wish for the get-together. It also clearly was not mutually shared.

The lights dimmed, and the crowd stilled and turned toward the darkened stage. A spotlight clicked on, throwing a circle of unnatural white onto a standing microphone, just in front of the drum kit. Into the circle strode a man in black tails.

Mack bent close to Cecile's ear. "That your ex up there?" She understood that he was referring to Seb and not the man onstage. "You still see him?"

"I do not," said Cecile. "But we are not *not* friends, if that is what you're asking."

Mack faced her, and she worked hard to match his gaze, as she had nothing to hide.

Onstage, the man started in French—"*Messieurs-dames, chèrs amis*"— then shifted to a thickly accented English: "Welcome!"

The crowd surged, rising and applauding, Mack's friends stomping and hoo-ahing.

"And Payne," Cecile asked, "is he not coming?"

"Canceled," Mack said, staring away, standoffish still. "Something about Darlene."

She turned toward the emcee. "Tonight, we gather ourselves to welcome a most honored guest . . ." He Americanized the pronunciation of the first name—"*Louisse*"—and the second sounded like two words— "Arm Strong!"—the arch cadences of French misshaping his speech. She wondered if she sounded as affected when she spoke. He waited for the applause to curtail before continuing. "Africa has rarely produced such a treasure, such a tropical gem. Genius can originate from any color, beauty found in any race. To hear his boomlay-boomlay-boom is to know the bright-colored enjoyment of life!"

A strange, uneasy hush engulfed the Cirque, here and there a guffaw. Cecile liked that the emcee connected the American jazzman to his native African roots, even if clumsily. But "boomlay-boomlay-boom"? Did this man know that Armstrong played a trumpet and not some tribal drum?

She turned toward Mack, who stared back, his bemusement reflecting her own.

Glancing up the grandstand, she couldn't make out Seb in the rustling darkness to gauge his reaction.

A man shouted, "Come on! Get on with it," and booing and derisive whistling suddenly filled the space, then somebody flung the crumpled wad of a paper program at the emcee. Tony Smith began calling: "Satchmo! Satchmo!" and others followed suit, and then so too did the entire auditorium, drowning out the emcee's voice completely, even as it was amplified through the loudspeakers.

"Satchmo! Satchmo! Satchmo!"

The emcee hung his head, and Cecile noticed the rotten old usher, derisively smiling beside the exit, so obviously pleased to see confirmed his narrow beliefs about unruly and uncontrollable blacks.

"Satchmo! Satchmo! Satchmo!"

Louis Armstrong appeared beside the stage, in a white tuxedo and black bow tie, his horn in one hand. He walked unhurriedly out and placed his free arm over the drooped shoulders of the emcee. The man didn't raise his face.

"Let's just simmer down," Armstrong said into the microphone, the raw timpani of his voice booming throughout the Cirque, silencing the burst of deafening applause.

Cecile stopped clapping, too—as did Mack, looking bewitched, awed by this strange spectacle.

Armstrong led the emcee from beneath the spot as his band took their places, the stage lights coming up. The other jazzmen wore tan tuxedoes to Armstrong's black, and two of them were *Yovo*, the double bass player and another holding a clarinet. Armstrong returned to center stage and stood under the awful caricature of his own face.

"When I was a boy," he said into the mic, "in an orphanage, making chump change as best I could working in barrooms and whatnot, it was a man something like that man there what saved me."

His voice seemed more like graceful movement than sound. But what a sound! The gravel and tar, like Seb—its dignity. Cecile, the entire crowd, listened, rapt.

"His name was Karnofsky." Armstrong reached two fingers into the crease of his shirt, below the bow tie, and removed a pendant of some sort for them to see, though it was too small for Cecile to make out, even at that short distance. "A white man—Jewish, like that one."

She understood the pendant to be a Star of David and wondered how closely it matched her own.

"I wasn't but seven, but Mister Karnofsky gave me odds-and-ends jobs, hauling junk and suchlike, and he and his wife treated me like family and taught me things I needed to know that I weren't no ways learning in Storyville. Real life things."

A spattering of cheers. Here and there, clapping.

"So, let's not jump on a man for only knowing what he knows. Let's not be so petty."

The cheering crescendoed, the applause electric.

"Let's recognize rightness when we see it, even if it ain't perfect."

Mack remained fixated, leaning wide-eyed toward the stage, ingenuous in a way she rarely saw of him. And it struck Cecile: the jazzman and his troupe were like she and Mack were now, like she and Seb had been before, black with white, her a Jew. This mixed band, like her and her men, was the world as it should be—not mongrel but beautiful and new.

"Last, but not least . . ." Armstrong smiled for the first time, his mouth seemingly as broad as the one on the odious banner above, as bright as the hot spotlight. "Ladies and gents, let's have us a rollicking good roll!"

And the band began all at once—the trombone and clarinet and double bass, the drummer drumming. Only Armstrong did not play. He stood, head bowed, tapping one foot and snapping the fingers of his free hand.

GIs danced in the aisles, men in zoot suits, their whirling coattails making colorful strokes. Mack pulled Cecile to him then pushed her off, still holding on, then he twirled her. Tony Smith swung his date, Mack's other friends twisting and whirling, their arms in the air. Cecile peeped up the grandstand, though she knew she wouldn't be able to see Seb. She twirled with Mack, twirled and held on.

CHAPTER TWENTY-TWO

It had been a stomach-thumping show, the roaring and sweating jazzman spectacular. Even ceremonious Zansi's leg bounced manically to the beat. When the performance was done and the lights came up, Seb and the ASUFC delegation stayed seated. None spoke, all seemed anxious. They watched the crowd thin. Seb found himself following Cecile with his eyes as she left with the American.

Boubi, who was eyeing her too, whispered, "What are we waiting for?"

Seb pointed to an usher, an older man in an ill-fitting uniform. "He's agreed to shepherd us to Armstrong." Before the show, Zansi had convinced the man to lead them backstage afterward. "Jacqueline explained who we are and our mission."

"And that did it?"

"It cost more than the tickets," Seb admitted.

The usher climbed the grandstand toward them. Zansi grabbed the two brown-paper-wrapped parcels from under her seat, one long, the other stout, and she rose. Seb, Boubi, and M'Bokolo rose, too.

"All of you?" the usher said. "No. It's not possible."

Zansi cut him with a glare.

"*Allez, allez,*" he conceded. "This way."

He led them toward the stage, then through an exit beside it, concealed behind high drapes. They passed down a dark hallway, through a frenzy of production personnel and Frenchmen smoking cigars and New

Look women laughing uproariously. He stopped before a closed door, pointed at it, then scurried off.

Zansi stood there, frozen. Seb placed a hand on her shoulder.

She knocked then—firmly, assertively—and when the door opened, Armstrong smiled but appeared startled.

In formal schoolgirl English, Zansi began: "Good day, Monsieur Armstrong. We are the African Students' Union of Francophone Colonies—Jacqueline Danxomè, Sebastien Danxomè, Jean-Joseph M'Bokolo, and Boubacar Keita. We, the delegation of the peoples of colonial Africa, want to greet and recognize our brother in the struggle."

She unwrapped the parcels and extended toward him, in one hand, a sculpted mahogany staff and, in the other, an artisanal handbag, the smell of animal hide savage and rich. M'Bokolo's father had given him the staff upon his departure from Brazzaville; M'Bokolo offered it to the group to give to Armstrong. Their colleague Tal Amahdou's mother had brought the bag from Dakar, moving up her planned visit at her son's urgent request. With the ongoing postal strikes, Zansi had feared it would sit neglected on the docks in Le Havre if Madame Amahdou had mailed it.

The jazzman accepted the items but held each away from his body and just stood there gaping at the four of them.

"Thanks," he said finally, "thanks much," the gravelly voice uncertain, his smile an insistent stretch of broad teeth. A stylishly coiffed, light-skinned black girl appeared over his shoulder. The jazzman repeated, "Thanks," and handed the staff and handbag to her.

Zansi said, "These gifts are presented to show our great respect and are intended to formalize our new association," and she held out her hand.

He paused, her hand suspended between them, as though he wouldn't know what to do after taking it.

"Thanks much," he repeated.

The light-skinned girl—his wife?—remained silent. She held the handbag with a finger and thumb at a safe distance from her designer dress, and her eyes said what the jazzman's words would not: Who *are* these people, and what do they want with us? She glimpsed at Seb then quickly away, suspicious, unnerved even, as though in need of something more to make their appearance at her door make sense. In the very least, some explanation of what strange animal, precisely, comprised the bag. She glanced from one to another of them, then down the dark corridor, her eyes seeking someone, anyone, to implore for help.

"Thank you," Louis Armstrong's wife said decisively.

And with that, both retreated, and he closed the door.

Once back in the auditorium, the delegation made for the exit. The streets outside were quiet, with little traffic, little street life at all, most of the audience gone. The night sky shimmered with a haze of light that, in the overcast and mist, seemed to have no source. No one spoke. All looked toward Zansi.

She said, "He accepted our gifts. It was a good gesture."

But everyone understood that the encounter had been a failure.

Zansi initiated the goodbyes with firm handshakes and a forced smile, then she took off up the boulevard, not even waiting for Seb. M'Bokolo hustled after her.

A lorry passed then parked beside a nearby café. Seb and Boubi watched the driver unload wooden crates of bottles of wine.

"Let's get a nightcap," Boubi said, "a good end to an awful evening."

Seb shook his head.

"My treat," Boubi insisted. "A whiskey to wash the bad taste from our mouths."

"You go ahead." Seb started down the boulevard in the direction opposite the one Zansi had taken. "I'll catch up with you tomorrow or the day after."

He heard Boubi call after him: "Don't let running into her ruin your week. Cecile, Minette, they're just girls. There'll be others."

"That was one cut brother!" Tony Smith said after the show, and Mack shot back, "Tight!" his blood still rushing. "What that nigger got," Mack said, "he got on the legit."

Everybody talked at once, huddled in a group outside the Cirque's doors:

"They wasn't but six pieces, yet making all that noise."

"Good noise!"

"Each of them brothers took his solo and just ran with it."

"The white boys, too."

"Now *that* was true!" said Poota Rabbit Cole. "Not none of the mess y'all be trying to pass for music up to Payne's."

The others busted up, clapping backs and slapping hands.

"Nigger, please," Mack told him.

Baby, who'd been standing by, scarf over her head and bag on a shoulder, came close then. "I am very tired tonight," she said. "You have fun, but I think I will return home."

"Tired again?" She'd been "tired" the weekend before, during his baby bruh's visit. "I was hoping to have some time with you."

Her eyes weren't generous. "We will make time, either tomorrow or Sunday."

She kissed his cheek, then began walking away.

Mack reached to stop her, feeling off now too. "Hang on, hang on," he said.

His boys were silent, likewise their girls, everybody staring.

When Baby turned back, he recognized something in the look on her face. In some ways, she did not fit; sometimes among his people, she just did not *fit*. Youngbloods might be on about "Nigger, d'you see that?" or "This nigger here done such and so"—playing, of course. But his Baby wasn't ever laughing along. Her eyes would drop, and her expression . . .

It wasn't puzzlement; Baby had understood every word that was said. No, the look was pity.

On occasion, he'd catch that look when she was looking at him. He knew his Baby knew he wasn't dumb, but there was a damn sight of difference between a minstrel and a man, and he thought she sometimes acted like he was just blacked up and shuffling.

Shit. For true.

And he couldn't help but wonder: Had seeing her ex earlier, that Frenchified African nigger, played a part in this, too?

"I'll run you home," he told her. To Tony Smith, he said, "Go on ahead. I'll find you at Payne's." Then he hailed a cab, and he and Baby got in.

They were silent the entire ride.

Once outside her rooming house, she didn't get out. She faced Mack, and he found her generous eyes—soft, giving.

But what she said confirmed his earlier suspicions. "To yourselves, you are 'niggers,' it is all I ever hear—*only* from you, *never* from the whites. It sometimes makes me very tired, Mack. Very, very."

He was furious now—about-to-lose-his-mind mad. Because how was Baby going to try to tell him how to talk, what he could and should not say?

Like she had something to teach him about him.

Like she knew what it was like to be him!

He kept it together. He just said, "Oh. Okay, then." Then he reached across and pushed open the taxi door.

"Please, Mack, it was a wonderful evening. Let us not end it like this."

He stared.

She stared back.

"We'll make time," he told her. "Either tomorrow or Sunday."

"Oh," she said, mimicking back. "Okay, then."

She got out of the taxi and went inside.

Cecile paced from her bed to the window and back, wound up, thoughts racing. Some of it was guilt. She felt she owed Mack an apology. She *had* had a wonderful time at the Armstrong show—truly, truly. But his friends had annoyed her beyond belief, their lack of manners and loud talk, especially the one named for a rabbit's poo, who spoke often but never said much.

Not just his friends, though—Mack, too. He took cues from them, behaved as they did. He was not his brother Darnell, nothing like him, but sometimes not so different either.

She was also peeved with Minette for standing her up. Typical Minette but inconsiderate all the same, and Cecile had less and less patience for it.

They shared something in common, Minette and Mack, an attitude and a manner that could leave Cecile feeling unsettled. Minette either idealized black people or was ashamed of them because she was only capable of perceiving blacks, herself included, in the facile way that white people did. When she looked in a mirror, she saw the exotic coquette or the angry firebrand that she imagined all whites, including Cecile, saw when they looked at her.

With Mack, Cecile wasn't the oppressor at all. Where, for Minette, Cecile was an easy target upon whom to take out all her rage, with Mack Cecile felt seen—like at the picnic at the Bois de Boulogne, when he'd tracked her down, alone among the French girls on the green army blanket, and delivered her to the black ones and their joyous bid whist. The sympathy in his eyes when he asked about her "Granny Lucie" and what she had suffered was genuine and deeply felt.

But, though he never took out his anger on Cecile, he seemed to take it out on himself. "Nigger this" and "nigger that," all the hard drinking and empty boasting.

Seb fell somewhere in between Mack and Minette. He was proud of his heritage, even as he felt tortured by his distance from it; he was ambitious but without cutting corners. France's role in his difficult story had been a travail, but he never held it over Cecile's head.

Cecile stopped pacing and settled beside the window, gazing into the unlit Beaux-Arts courtyard below. She'd be lying to herself if she didn't admit that seeing Seb at the show had contributed to the malaise with Mack. She loved so many things about Mack, but her conversation with Seb, however brief, reminded her of all the things that she missed about him—their easy interaction, his integrity and quiet strength.

Who would have predicted it? Running into him in the streets of the quarter, sure; they shared the neighborhood and its favored haunts. But at the jazz concert, when she was with Mack? What terrible luck . . .

And, as though thinking of him could make him manifest in material form, there he was: the shifting shadow at the base of the obelisk, obscure but distinct against the darkness, stepping into the streetlight and waving up at her—it was Seb!

She grabbed her coat and dashed down the stairs.

"What are you doing here?" she asked, crossing the street.

"Why, waiting for an opportunity to ambush you, like that lunchtime so long ago."

"And what if I'd not seen you out here?"

"It would have been a long wait." He smiled.

The neighborhood was quiet, the street empty, and he sat, his back against the wall, his legs outstretched, blocking the walkway—improper, impolite even, so unlike him.

She joined him on the pavement. Their eyes met, then each looked away.

It was an uncomfortable silence.

"So, how was your meeting with Louis Armstrong, then?" Cecile asked.

"To call it a 'meeting' is to give it more credit than the encounter deserved."

She didn't follow.

Seb said, "We should have foreseen it. The black Americans are American, after all. *Yovo.* Just as narrow as the white ones."

This struck Cecile as reductive, maybe even as a bit gratuitous, as she imagined his harsh reaction to be as much due to having seen her with one of them as to his own failure with the jazzman.

"And you," he asked, "did you enjoy the show?"

"I loved it," she said. "It's been a strange evening since, though."

"With the GI?"

Yes, for certain, but she said instead: "With Minette." How to explain all that had happened between them? "It's like she sees me as the Queen Bungler. I can do nothing right."

Seb didn't respond, waiting her out with an unbroken stare, apparently wanting to hear more, Cecile imagined—which was, in fact, what he was doing, the Dahomeyan gaze, as he found her explanation too cursory to be the whole of it.

Cecile went on: "She's been very hard on me lately, unjustly so, and it's been difficult. Painful."

"She's always tough on you. And without good cause, I should add."

"You never liked her."

And he admitted: "You're right, it's true." He did not trust Minette.

Cecile said, "She's done a lot for me. I wouldn't have had the courage to leave home and move into the city if it weren't for her."

"Of course you would have!"

The exasperation in his voice surprised even him. But he didn't understand how Cecile couldn't see this herself. Then he remembered Elodie's analysis of her handwriting: *an attempt to conceal a profound insecurity . . . the script of someone plagued by doubt . . .*

He said, "You're every bit as brave as her—every bit—and twice as thoughtful."

It was Cecile's turn to pause and stare. She wanted to trust the conviction lighting his eyes, yet she questioned the sincerity of his statement.

He said, "Now you're with the Americans, and Minette resents it. She feels threatened."

She wondered if he wasn't projecting his own emotions onto Minette. If she was truthful with herself, she hoped that he was.

"Well, if that's the case, it's a misguided jealousy," she said. "The American blacks are just like us—young and suddenly free and wanting more, wanting better." She remembered the joy she felt watching *Fantasia*. "There's something winning in their levity."

She also recalled her feelings from earlier, the annoyance with Mack and his friends.

A bicycle taxi pedaled by, the cabbie ringing the bell on his handlebars, inquiring with a look if they needed a ride. Seb and Cecile shook simultaneously and watched him continue on.

Seb hadn't decided whether or not to say it, but without thinking, he did: "My father is coming to France."

"How wonderful! When, Seb?"

"Next month. Troubles with the colonial administration—"

"But the point is to see you and Jacqueline too, no?"

Seb let his awkward grin be his answer.

He said, "I found his newspaper, in the national archives. It's called *Le Quartier Latin*."

"*Le Quartier Latin*? That doesn't sound particularly dangerous or seditious."

"Would you like to see it?"

Cecile desired nothing more. "It would have to be in the afternoon. I work mornings now."

She left off that it was for the Americans and not at the Louvre.

They sat in silence—a comfortable silence, the kind shared between two people who felt they knew the other as well as they knew themselves. The night was brisk though not cold, and each one took in the traces of life all around: the murmur of voices from an apartment nearby, a woman's laughter; fingers clumsily tinkering on a piano, the treacly high keys; elsewhere, a motor racing.

Cecile sensed that, when she rose to return to her room, he would rise too—not as a gesture of politesse but to join her. She decided that she would let him. She'd maybe already decided this the moment she'd first seen him from the window.

CHAPTER TWENTY-THREE

Sharing a Lucky at the window in her room, Cecile listened as Seb recounted with dramatic flair and boyish glee a story he'd learned of in the archives, about a woman king. She was called Hangbè, and he described her as a centuries-old "Dahomeyan New Woman"—his words—who ruled for a few years before his favorite, Agaja, gained the throne. Cecile inhaled and passed him the butt, its burning tip an orange pinpoint against the shadowed backdrop of Beaux-Arts across the street, both of them facing that way during his storytelling, as though the school was just a direction to level one's gaze and not the site where his aspirations had foundered.

Mack often said, "No news be good news, right?" In this case, not so.

She only accompanied Seb to the archives once, the Monday after the Louis Armstrong show. After an hour there, they'd returned to her hotel, to her room. He showed up unannounced the next afternoon, and the midday meetings became regular—not every day, but common. The concierge, who'd never seemed particularly pleased with Mack's overnight stays, gave Cecile sour looks with Seb's comings and goings. Well, cuss the concierge (as Mack would say)! She and Seb giggled over silly jokes, legs intertwined, entangled in the sheets. He caught her up on news of their friends, what little he knew. Her anecdotes about her mother elicited calls for more.

She frequently worried that Mack might turn up unexpectedly or that, during his own visits, he might find a sock or some other article of clothing Seb had inadvertently left behind. She felt some guilt, she truly did—but at the thought of hurting Mack, only this. She didn't regret what she was doing, for what was she doing, after all? This thing with Seb was just a fling. No anguishing over disappointments and failures, no chafing about the daily grind. Was it wrong to distract oneself with a dear friend, a boy she knew as well as she knew herself, each offering the other an uncomplicated release from the rest of it?

Because the rest of it was dismal. De Gaulle's party dominated the election. In Le Vésinet, Cecile's father routed his opponent. Paris took on a nervous edge in the days after the vote. The entire country did. Newspapers featured photographs of picketers outside the window displays of the *grands magasins*, of walkouts at the coal mines around Lille, of the vacant shop floor at the Renault factory in suburban Boulogne-Billancourt. Cecile expected solidarity with the justly disgruntled workers, or at least sympathy, but saw only outrage. The kiosk keeper at the bus stop near AFCENT-0317 railed at a businessman in a Burberry and bowler hat: "Long-haul truckers blockading the roadways, the trains only running sporadically—*merde alors!* When will it end?"

The other responded, "Why, there isn't a beefsteak to be had in all of the city!"

It seemed as tin-eared as Marie Antoinette chiding the people to eat cake but was not to be discounted. The social fabric was coming undone—a dissolution, the Occupation all over again. Queuing at the bakery beside her rooming house for a baguette or just for whatever remained—a butterless croissant, a half loaf of black bread—she remarked how customers buried themselves in their layers of clothes and sustained a buffer of space with the person in front of them and the one behind. Out in the streets, she would find her eyes flitting toward the ground, up into the leafless branches of trees, off into traffic, anywhere but into someone else's face.

The listless afternoons with Seb helped pass the days. They also made the lavish weekends with Mack feel less like a betrayal.

Cecile kept after Mack about this exposition at the Musée de l'Homme, on Africa. He'd planned on taking her to a bout at the Wagram Hall, between a New York brother named Beau Jack and this African nigger,

Assane Diouf—the CHAMPION OF THE DARK CONTINENT, the marquee read, in English. But Mack conceded.

"Okay, the *musée*, then," he told her.

They walked around the exhibits, sat through a talk. All along the way, Baby went on and on about Africa's history and its beauty, like she was set on teaching him something. Mack finally had enough. "Please, girl," he said, "stop. I'm seeing what you seeing. I don't need no lessons."

He'd seen the pictures of the jungle and the heat, of colored folks wearing wraparound rags and living in mud huts, a passel of children running butt naked in the sun and grown-ass men sitting in the shade of a tree, looking straight into the lens like they didn't know what a camera was—the middle of the day and not a goddamn thing in the world to do. And Baby wanted to act like it wasn't straight up what it was: niggers in poverty.

She got hung up on one display, "Dahomey: The Latin Quarter of Africa," referred to in this way because of the number of intellectuals there. Rather than inspire admiration, though, for Mack it called to mind the Africans Baby ran around with when they first met. They wore Froggy clothes and talked proper like Froggies in an English that sounded like how the Brits talked, acting like there was something special going on with them because an African nigger hadn't ever been a slave.

Them fools not two steps from living in a tree, he thought, and they dared to look down at him?

Baby had clammed up by then, like he had spoken his thoughts aloud. "Clearly, no," she said. "You and I did not see the same exhibit."

Mack resented all the schoolmarming about heritage and ideals, like he didn't get them or didn't have them, like he was just a leaf blowing on a breeze. He knew his heritage. He knew that his mama had left northern Alabama with her own mama and little brother when just a child. Mack's grandmama had taken care of him and Mack's sister Colleen when they were wee but had died by the time baby bruh Darnell was born. Mack had even less memory of his Uncle Brother but knew the story: he'd gotten stabbed in some juke joint—owed a nigger ten dollars or was owed it himself and asked for the money. That was Mack's history, his heritage, and it was heritage enough.

For him, heritage comprised no more than the reaches of his body, what he could touch and hold, just that. And the ideal he understood was this: cultivate that green. The only nigger who wasn't a slave, to Mack's mind, was the one that had the wherewithal to get his ass up from the shade of that tree—wherever it was, the Latin Quarter of Africa or northern Alabama or KC—and cultivate some paper green, any way he could. Mack was intelligent enough to know that. Because it was green that put nylons on pale Baby's legs, that put food on her daddy's table. Mack wasn't nobody's fool: he knew the man didn't like him nary a lick, hugging up on his only daughter. A cracker was a cracker, whether he ate Piggly Wiggly yellow cheese or brie. But that one, he was Baby's daddy. So, Mack would call on his boys to send out a crate of potted meat for the man to distribute to voters, ditto paper for his campaign posters. When Baby telephoned home and Mack was nearby, her daddy would come on the line, wanting to speak to him, and later, Baby would tell Mack that he'd said he liked discussing with him—as if Mack didn't know it took that delivery to bring him around to the opinion.

Greenbacks—all the heritage and ideals Mack needed.

After they left the *musée*, back out on the street, traffic was bottled tight—cars and buses, nothing moving, everybody honking, even the bicycle taxis, dring-dringing their little handlebar bells. Baby overheard some talk—something about a demonstration against a special police force the government had raised to suppress the walkouts and protests that had been ongoing for months. She looked uneasy.

"Perhaps we should take the Metro. It will be better than a taxi."

Mack had overnight duty. "Sure," he told her. "Whatever will get us where we're going."

The Metro, it turned out, was backed up, too. They stood on the platform crowded in a pack of folks. The train pulled into the station, each car already crammed full. The doors slid open, and he and Baby and the rest pushed in as best they could, squeezing on just inside the doors.

They were headed to dinner at République, at a spot Baby had read about in the newspaper, so they had half of Paris to cross. The train car rocked side to side on the rails, Mack reading the station names at each stop—Iéna, Alma Marceau, Franklin D. Roosevelt—counting down to their own. At each one, more people pushed on, and by Saint-Augustin, he and Baby had been forced to the middle of the car.

The train sat there what seemed like days, the doors wide open, ever more folks finding a way to fit on. The buzzer finally buzzed, and the doors rolled then bounced back open, rolled and bounced open, the passengers who were blocking the closure pushing the pack even tighter together until the latch eventually caught.

It was bodies against bodies then, upright lemmings in a bucket, Mack spooning the man in front of him, another spooning him from behind. The train inched forward, barely picking up speed, and on a bend in the track, there in the dark middle passage between stations, the hum of the engine dimmed then died and then it stopped. The lights went out. Pitch black.

On every side, just bodies. A musty funk all around, and to the left, someone wheezing. Mack's right leg pressed to that man's left one; the man behind's stuff pushed up on Mack's behind. Mack hadn't been claustrophobic a day of his life, but his tie felt like an iron collar, so hard was it to breathe, everybody breathing as one—exhale and inhale, exhale and inhale, not another sound.

But who among them was going to speak up, to speak out? And to whom? To the staticky voice bursting from the PA, out of nowhere, garbled and angry, like it was them who had done wrong, speaking words Mack did not understand and just as abruptly, the voice gone?

And right then, he recalled what he and his boys had heard—about how the Krauts had carried them off to the camps in cattle cars that must have felt something like this: folks pressed up on folks, entire families, mamas and their babies. And Baby, trapped in the press of these bodies, her shoulder digging into the tender of Mack's ribcage. But in the dark and tight he couldn't see her face to see what it was she was feeling.

Dread?

Anger?

Shame?

Because it was something like shame that he felt in the pulsing dark, his stuff on that man's ass, his belly puffing into the other one's back.

The engine hummed, then the lights flickered on, and there was her face, his Baby's face, turned up at him. She found a way to free a hand and wiped a palm of sweat from his brow that he didn't even know he was sweating. Her eyes reached out—like it was him who was suffering something when Lord knew he was sure it was her who had been drowning.

The train jolted forward then rolled slow as syrup off the lip of a jug, and they arrived at Havre-Caumartin. Baby took his hand and pulled him through the bodies, and they got off.

"We can walk from here," she said, "or we will find a taxi. We will find a way."

A man's role was to care for his baby, and here it was her saving him.

Mack understood something in that moment: if they had come for her, put her on a pack train and shipped her off to the camps, she'd have been one of the ones to come back. He'd never pondered it before, but there in the Metro, looking down into her face, he saw the flipside of the same coin as him. She was white and from money but the money gone and her a kind of nigger here; yet neither of them lying down for nobody—not for nobody.

And it scared Mack. Because he also understood then a thing that Baby herself might not even have known: though she might want Mack, she didn't need him. She didn't need anyone. Baby sought out something from every single person she met, but she didn't need it. She would flower in the dunes and quiet of a desert.

This scared Mack, because it made him want her all the more.

*   *   *

Dressing to leave late one afternoon, Seb told Cecile, "My father is arriving soon. Next week, in fact." He'd been wanting to share this for days but couldn't find the right words or the right timing. "I'd love for him to meet you," he said.

She remained under the sheets, only her head emerged, and he watched her expression shift from delight to bewilderment and very quickly to anger—to fury, really.

"I mean, if your schedule permits," he added, feeling a sudden need to apologize, though he was unsure why.

"To what end, this meeting?" she said. "After announcing the Beaux-Arts flop, you think that revealing your tryst with a *Yovo* temptress is a bright move?"

He didn't understand her reaction. Returning to the bed, he asked, "Is that what this means to you now? Just casual? Play?"

She rolled onto her side, away from him. Her tone of voice eased, though not the heat of her words. "Everything is just play, Seb, to offset the burden of the rest."

He spooned her from behind, but her body didn't slacken.

"You said it yourself all that time ago in Hyères," she went on. "We're worker bees, you and I. The file girl for the Americans and the former apprentice hoping to one day be a full-fledged carpenter. We rise with the sun and help others get done what we've been told needs doing. Not dumb or dishonorable, just ordinary."

Though her words stung, she wasn't wrong. Despite the imperative to achieve, to succeed, a part of him had always remained anchored in Burgundy, in the calm of fine craftsmanship and daily routine.

"In Father's last letter," he said, "he made mention of trade schools—engine mechanics or plumbing, something of that nature. He said the country will need running water, too."

"And he would accept this for you?"

"He wasn't saying it with pride, believe me."

He thought he understood then, finally—her barbed anger, the abrupt chill. When they met at the youth conference, she'd wanted out of Le Vésinet, both the place and its spirit. But instead of something else, something new, he'd offered the sneaking in and out of his room, the hiding from Zansi—the indignity of being made to feel unworthy. Now he proposed introductions to family, and why? Because, as a failure, finally he could. How could he disappoint his father any further?

He moved onto his back, hands behind his head. "Your GI, I get it. The black Americans are forgotten children, without a past. With him, it must be easier."

She bolted upright—"*Mais putain!*"—then pushed him from the bed, pushed with both of her feet until he was completely out. "You black men will be the death of me."

Seb barked a laugh though she'd not intended humor—clearly.

Not at all.

He finished dressing—buttoned up his pants, put on his shirt. They didn't speak. He kissed her cheek then left the room.

CHAPTER TWENTY-FOUR

Cecile phoned in sick to AFCENT—for no good reason, really. The day before had been unseasonably warm, and the forecast predicted that the nice weather would last, more of Mack's Indian summer. After leaving a message for her supervisor, she called Le Vésinet and invited her mother to meet for coffee.

She caught the number 73 bus on Quai Anatole France. The Metro would have been faster, but she wanted to ride on the back platform as it wended its way through the city. They crossed the Seine then circled Place de la Concorde and climbed toward Étoile. Mack loved the Champs-Élysées but it was, as ever, just the Champs-Élysées: *surfait*; loud with automobile horns and the din of relentless motion; bright with the spectacle of dollars.

Cecile got off at George V and immediately spotted her mother, seated on the patioed terrace of a café right on the avenue, in a clay-colored dress and a navy pillbox hat Cecile had known all her life. Though they'd spoken by phone and Cecile had received weekly letters, it had been nearly two months since they'd seen each other—since the fight with her father. They hugged instead of kissing cheeks, neither wanting to let go first, then sat and for several moments just stared at one another, the width of a café table apart.

Cecile flagged a passing waiter. She and her mother each ordered hot tea, and Cecile asked, "Do you have croissants today? Or even just *tartines* of bread? I skipped breakfast."

He left without answering, aloof in the way a garçon of a *grand café* should be. (Or, at least, in the way they always seemed to Cecile.)

Though Cecile had arranged the meeting, she didn't know what to say. So, she filled the silence with the sorts of things she knew her mother liked to hear about—how the Hôtel des Beaux-Arts planned to install telephone lines in individual rooms; how she was shopping for a hot plate, as the downstairs restaurant wasn't yet open when she left in the morning and had finished serving lunch by the time she returned. She described AFCENT, the uniform rows of metal desks and metal file cabinets, the constant tat-tat-tatting of typewriters.

The waiter returned and deposited in the middle of the table a wire basket with two croissants. "It took a little effort," he said, unsmiling. "But for you, Mademoiselle, *tout est possible*."

Everything possible? Was this what her mother saw in her, too—her child all grown up, with a good job among *les américains*, making a way in life among the victors? Or did she still see a capricious girl impetuously pursuing vague dreams of *la vie de bohème dans la Ville-Lumière*, as she'd called it?

Her mother covered her mouth with a hand and giggled as the garçon walked away. "And the American women," she asked, "is it true what they say? That they're afraid of their own smell?"

"They bathe their thing with vinegar."

"The men, too?"

"The men are so proud of theirs, it's all they can talk about."

Both laughed—a *fou rire*, uncontrollable, the neighboring tables staring.

"So, the Americans are everything they think themselves to be?"

"As though emerged whole from the head of Zeus."

Their laughter trailing off, her mother reached across the table and stroked Cecile's hair. "I can't keep up. Are you letting it grow out or wearing it short?"

"Mack likes it longer," Cecile said, and her mother's face fell.

"You abide by his wishes, then?"

It was an unkind thing to say, and Cecile didn't respond to the question. Instead, she said, "You should see how he's respected among the GIs. Apparently, he has the 'stuff,' as the Americans say, to become an officer."

"Well, I'm happy for him."

"And of course, it would be great for you and Papa, too."

"He's generous," her mother said, "very generous. But please tell me this isn't why you see him, to provide for your father and me."

"*Mais non*, Maman!" It came out sharper than Cecile had intended. "He's kind, and he genuinely cares about me, so he wants to provide for you."

Both turned toward some commotion at the curb. Two bicycle taxi drivers spat insults at one another, fighting over a fare—a girl, clearly American, in a red cartwheel hat. The passersby stared. Their waiter interposed himself between the two men, gesticulating broadly and shooing them down the street.

Her mother took Cecile's hands, pulled them to her mouth, and embraced their intertwined fingers. "Ah, but where did you go, *ma fille?*" Her smile was as earnest as it was cutting, both comforting and sad. "What was it you used to say . . . You act, you do what is right for you—a new kind of woman."

Was she any less so, Cecile thought, for having chosen a good job over abstract ideas? For preferring stability over uncertainty?

"I still act, so you know," she said. "There's a big demonstration at Hôtel de Ville, for instance, and I plan to attend." She smiled mischievously. "I think I'll ask Seb to join me."

It was hard to read the look on her mother's face.

"I've seen him off and on. Helping with some research."

"With 'research,' right?"

"Maman!"

Then she noted her mother's expression—dour, disapproving even.

"I thought you liked Seb." Cecile would have bet her life that her mother did—that he was the one she'd have chosen for her.

"I do," her mother replied. "But I prefer you big, *mon amour*, regardless the man, rather than diminished."

They sat like that a while, each taking in the other across the small table, round like a waiter's platter, two empty cups in between, a half-eaten croissant on a saucer.

Cecile said, "They have a word made of letters."

"Pardon?"

"The Americans," she explained. "They say 'OK' to mean 'yes,' but also whatever you want it to, really. 'Why not?' and also 'thank you.' Anything in the affirmative."

"I've heard them say this."

"That's something worth keeping," Cecile said.

Neither wanted to leave and there was no real reason to, but Cecile flagged the garçon and paid the tab, and mother and daughter rose. They kissed cheeks then hugged again, though not like before, and parted ways, each in her own direction, her mother up toward Étoile, Cecile down to Concorde. Cecile stopped a few paces along. She turned and watched her mother—the willful stride and pert step, the decades-old pillbox and the clay-colored dress, there and then lost in the blur of US Army uniforms and garrison caps, there and then gone.

CHAPTER TWENTY-FIVE

Several thousand filled the cobbled square in front of the Hôtel de Ville, more people in one place than Cecile had ever seen. They spilled up the side streets into the Marais and back toward the Pont d'Arcole—miners, railway workers, students, a teetering carnival of humanity, a collective come together to demand equal treatment and equal rights. It thrilled Cecile, wending her way through the mass toward the front—the forgotten joy of standing up for freedom, for justice.

There was whistling and cheering and slogan-chanting. *"Allez, CGT!"* and "Down with inflated prices!" and "We want milk!" Women rang handbells, one boy beat on a snare drum. And placards everywhere, one that read: A NEW FRANCE FOR 1948!

The garbage collectors, in fouled blue coveralls, carried crates of rank refuse—clumps of rotting vegetable peels, bits of bone, the sinew of butchered beasts. They'd removed the trash sporadically for weeks, and today they launched fistfuls at the line of police serving as a barricade between the crowd and city hall, the officers helmeted and standing stiffly in long leather coats that recalled a recent time that no one wanted recollected.

Cecile had skipped work again, this time to take part in the demonstration—and cuss AFCENT! But she'd not expected such an immense turnout, she wondered where would be best to stand in order for Seb to find her. In his response to her invitation to join along, he'd written: "I can be there at about two, once I've finished at the archives." She glanced at her watch—ten past.

Ah, Seb, she thought . . . So much difficult history between them, so many disappointments. How could she have let herself slip into the morass of his demanding love again? Infuriating!

And then there was Mack. His desire for her never faltered; she carried something like glamour in his eyes, in the light of day. But too much so, and so quickly. It wasn't always clear what Mack was seeing when he looked at her.

"*Allez, CGT!*"

"*Nous voulons du lait!*"

In a break in the crowd a few meters away, there was Minette, laughing and dancing, her overcoat unbuttoned and swaying contra-tempo to her body's swaying. She saw Cecile at the same moment and dashed to her, and they hugged and twirled in the jostling mass of people.

Minette yelled close to her ear, "The revolution has arrived. It starts today," and she smiled her beautiful smile—the one from the train station in Marseille.

Brash, bold Minette!

The clamor all around wasn't a music to dance to, yet Minette pulled Cecile along, dancing her dance, everyone around dancing alongside them: a clutch of miners in soot-stained smocks, hopping from one foot to the other; a mother in a headscarf holding her child to her chest, as though in homage to a long-ago lover; a bespectacled boy with the red armband of the student unionists who couldn't take his eyes off Minette, also swaying to her rhythm.

And just beyond, Monsieur Traoré! He was chanting "We want our baguette" but noticed Cecile and smiled his broad smile and came and took her hand and joined the dancing.

"*Allez, CGT!*"

"*Nous voulons du lait!*"

Minette yelled near her ear: "And your Americans? None would join you?"

Cecile couldn't picture Mack at an event like this, even if attending were permitted by his superiors, which it wasn't. She smiled in response and rose onto her tiptoes and scanned the faces all around, searching for Seb's dark face.

The question cropped up abruptly inside Cecile: What if Mack were to propose? He often spoke as though her seeing Kansas City was an inevitability. Marriage must be on his mind.

And Seb. He wanted to introduce her to his father. What did this suggest, what could it mean? The ring that Cecile had insisted she wasn't after, also now on the way?

Mack and Seb, these maddening black men whom she loved: one American, the other African; one the descendant of slaves, the other of slavers; one light with joy, though enigmatic, the other burdened by prodigious responsibility that he was incapable of meeting. Both grounded her, each one a new home to settle into, as neither was the home she had known.

And her, Cecile—Elodie and Alain Rosenbaum's daughter, their only child, inheritor of the Tétard platter.

In the dizzying commotion and fervor on the cobblestone square, what, an instant before, had felt like an impossible dilemma revealed itself all at once to be merely heartbreaking. She loved, truly loved, only Seb.

Minette had been wrong: he wasn't just any boy, and a New Woman wasn't action without apology. Spitting on the floor of the Café de la Poste! The world must not stop at black and white, at prince and peasant, at pussy and prize. She and Seb, alongside like-minded others like the people gathered here, would make a better future, one they all wanted to live in.

Minette had been prescient in this, though: Cecile realized that she did want a ring from him. She wanted to meet his father and for the man to know her. Even if Seb was never an architect and she was only *lycée* educated, even if they were just worker bees, he an engine mechanic and she a bilingual secretary (not a hanger-on like Madame Traoré but central, relevant), neither was lesser for it, neither was smaller. They could still advance the work of freeing Africa from the bonds of colonialism. And in Dahomey, not here, because here was no more "home" for her than it was for Seb. Home would be wherever they were, together.

She scanned all around, looking for him, for the man she loved.

At the head of the mass, a Communist Party deputy was shouting to be heard over a representative from city hall, who stood on a ladder behind a row of helmeted police and spoke through a bullhorn. Words like "strength" and "solidarity" and "justice" sparked the air above the Communist deputy, while others—"order" and "banditism" and "disperse"—flashed from behind the police line. In the background, whistling cheering chanting.

The city hall man blurted, "Arras," and the crowd stilled. Their troupe of dancers, too.

A postal express train had derailed two nights before, outside that northern city. Twenty were confirmed dead, many more injured, and the government claimed that striking railway workers had sabotaged the tracks.

Another barrage of refuse was the crowd's response. Monsieur Traoré shook his fist in the air, and Minette and the rest booed, the rage as palpable as the stench of waste.

Against the din of ire and affront, Cecile didn't hear the tanks' approach. It was the sudden panic all around that cued her. Police whistles and the crowd scrambling, people pushing, stomping.

She lost Minette. They'd grabbed hands at the mechanized clank-clank-clanking of the treads of the tanks, but in the ensuing frenzy, Cecile found herself full in the tidal rush of motion away from the sound, her feet frantically shuffling so that she stayed upright, and she could no longer see Minette.

And where was Monsieur Traoré? Trampled beneath scrambling feet or the treads of the tanks, or set upon by police?

And where was Seb?

Was he out here in it too, looking for her? She sought his dark face in the mass of rushing-along faces and the panic and the commotion. There, a boy fallen and nightstick-beaten by leather-coated policemen. All over, shrieking.

She never heard the rifle's report but saw a man shot down, dropping abruptly, his blue smock burst a black dot at the chest, staining red.

The river's rush of people passed over him.

The torrent carried her onto the Pont d'Arcole. She looked for Minette, for Monsieur Traoré, keeping her legs moving so she would not fall and be trampled like the woman Cecile saw fall in front of her and who was trampled, Cecile unable even to pause, trampling her too, so strong was the current forcing her forward.

And Seb, where was Seb?

Out there looking for her, or out there trampled or shot or nightstick-beaten?

On the other side of the bridge, the tight crush loosened, the crowd dispersing into the narrow streets beside Notre-Dame. Her jacket had slipped from her shoulders and bunched at her elbows, her pink paisley blouse torn open, one shoe gone. Yet she ran with those running, past the cathedral, for the next bridge over, the Pont au Double, toward the Quartier latin—home—where she might escape the clusters of police who, no matter how fast she ran, were still everywhere. Bodies fell from the bridge, some crashing into the Seine and immediately flailing for the quay, others not resurfacing.

The thrust of bodies sent her toward the stone balustrade, and she was airborne, and she was in the water, too.

Under and grasping for the surface.

Wet, thick air, then back under.

A sudden calm there.

Silence.

When she resurfaced, she gulped for air—gulped and gulped. Treading water, she watched the scurrying across the bridge, someone airborne, and there, another again, having jumped or, like her, been forced over.

A policeman in the street above—a leather gas mask with dark discs for eyes and a hanging plastic snout—stared toward them, at those in the water. He raised a rifle. She saw smoke spit from the barrel's mouth, then heard the crack.

She turned and swam away, flailed and flailed to get underneath the bridge, out of the line of sight of the gun. She'd been here before, with collaborators and cowards, with victims and the victimized, and how did she end up here again? And where was Seb?

CHAPTER TWENTY-SIX

The meal would set Seb back a week. His plate lay empty of everything but scraps. He'd even chewed the fowl's heftier bones, grinding the thigh to a marrow paste. In the breast pocket of his overcoat, which he continued to wear in the chill of the restaurant, Au Rendez-Vous des Amis, was the letter from the Ministry of Education.

His concierge had delivered it first thing that morning. "I know you've been eagerly awaiting this," she'd said, smiling warmly. "I hope it imparts the news you wish for." Still, he'd waited a bit more before opening. Five minutes became ten became a half hour . . . He'd steeled himself for months, he'd become accustomed to the idea of rejection, of failure—that he was merely a worker bee, as Cecile had succinctly summed it up. With official confirmation finally arrived, he'd found himself incapable of facing this reality, of accepting his truth.

The letter began: *"Chèr Monsieur Danxomè, J'ai le plaisir de vous informer . . ."*

He'd refolded the paper without finishing, replaced it in the envelope, and donned his jacket. He hadn't shared the news with Zansi; he wasn't sure he would tell Cecile when he met her at the demonstration—not immediately anyway. He wanted to savor the victory for a little while, on his own. He'd worked hard—*hard*—for this moment, and finally he was achieving what his father had insisted upon, what was required of a Gbéhanzin. And just in time! His father's ship had surely landed at Le Havre; he would be in Paris any day now.

Seb had quit his hotel and walked, past the Panthéon, through the Jardin du Luxembourg, alongside the Theatre de l'Odéon, perusing the bookstalls under the white-stone arcade. He'd strolled the quiet Boulevard Saint-Germain then crossed the Seine, onto the Quai du Louvre, to this restaurant, where he'd known without acknowledging it to himself that he'd been headed all along. The meal was his reward.

Au Rendez-Vous des Amis only had five tables, all of them empty the length of Seb's lunch, the proprietor long-faced and sullen. But the meal! Cecile had claimed that the roasted chicken was the best in Paris, and it had been everything she'd said it would be.

Cecile. His wristwatch read twenty till two—already.

He decided he'd be a little late. For now, a simple dessert: tart Tatin, like Madame Des Launiers used to make on Sundays in Burgundy. The grumpy proprietor brought it over, and Seb ate slowly, lush forkful after lush forkful. He declined the *express*, though. He would have it at the Chien Qui Fume, a café in Les Halles that was said to serve the best coffee in the city and was more or less on his route.

Les Halles was always a chaos of bustle and sound, but the unchar-acteristic calm today only truly struck Seb standing at the bar at the Chien, listening to the two customers beside him who complained about the "bastard Communists" and their disregard for "civic life." The men wore suits and ties, probably businessmen of some sort, as the Bourse was nearby. The first protested: "These boycotts and strikes, they don't produce jobs, they don't raise salaries."

"Dumb bastards," spat the other.

"They cripple the economy, which cuts jobs, cuts salaries."

Seb suddenly recalled the unusual number of closed shops in the Quartier latin earlier, the few bicycle taxis and cars on Boulevard Saint-Germain. The stink of uncollected and rotting refuse that he'd barely remarked upon during his walk penetrated the Chien now, overwhelming the café smells of Arabica and Gitanes.

"They didn't suffer the Occupation in the countryside the way we did here," the second man went on. "Otherwise, they wouldn't behave this way, assaulting fellow Frenchmen."

"*Les connards!*" said the first. "I heard there were fifty dead at Arras, more even."

The barman, who until then had stood with his face down, drying glasses, nosed in: "*Les Cocos* are amassing at Hôtel de Ville, but the interior minister will have something waiting for them."

"The army?" the first asked.

The barman winked and double-clicked his tongue in affirmation. "Moch recalled a division from Germany," he said.

"From Germany?" said the first, impressed.

"Of better use here," the barman said, returning his attention to the glassware.

Seb had been in the archives, distracted by decades-old documents and yellowing newspapers, but surely Cecile had heard this news—surely.

If she had, he reasoned, she wouldn't have invited him to join her. No, she didn't know.

He dropped several coins beside his empty cup and left. He had to find her, and now. Moch, the interior minister, hated the Communists; he publicly repudiated them. If the barman was right, who could say what might happen at the demonstration?

Bahanyan. The word never appeared in *Le Quartier Latin* or *Dans les Colonies*, but Seb knew it. The Land of Disorder.

The ninth of the Abomey kings (speaking his name was forbidden) had been banished to *Bahanyan*—this, for defying the ways of the forefathers, for betraying tradition. With the decline of transatlantic slavery and fewer and fewer caravels arriving along the coast, the ninth king attempted to shift the economy away from the trade and toward the production of palm oil, which the *Yovo* needed for their factories. The ninth king killed two brothers who refused to be swayed and imprisoned scores of their followers, and still this didn't quell but only heightened the hum of rebellion. The coup was swift and brutal. Another brother, Guézo, in complicity with a Brazilian *Yovo*, dethroned the ninth king. To appease the many who still followed him, Guézo proclaimed the ninth king to have been insane, for only an insane man would upset the ways of the forefathers and rule by disorder. Guézo had the ninth king's emblem unstitched from the

Abomey tapestry, his memory discarded from history, and directed that his name never be uttered aloud again.

("Adandozan." Seb had overheard Aunt Fifonsi whisper it once, and he'd never forgotten.)

Seb asked himself now: Was this what he was risking by falling in love with a *Yovo*, against the ways of tradition and the wishes of his father—banishment and exile? Especially in this manner, rushing toward angry protestors and the soldiers sent to suppress them?

The Place des Innocents was deserted, and at the padlocked entrance to the Metro a little farther along, several rats picked at bits atop a pile of putrefying rubbish, indifferent to his presence. He hurled a clutch of *centime* coins from his pocket. One rat flinched but did not budge. The rest gnawed on.

People began to appear here and there in the upper-floor windows of buildings as he neared the Marais, leaning out, straining to hear the amplified but faint voices sifting toward them. Some had cameras. One turned it toward him. Seb kept his face down.

Rounding onto Rue de Renard, the demonstration materialized suddenly, agitated and amorphous, a mass of blur and movement filling the square outside the Hôtel de Ville and beyond. Squads of helmeted police milled in groups on the periphery, alert but composed. None seemed to notice him. And he saw no sign of the army, no troops in combat gear.

He worked his way into the throng. But how to locate Cecile among all these people? What would she be wearing? A black turtleneck and trousers—militant? He hoped not, given the turn the day could take.

Scrutinizing the crowd, Seb wondered if Minette and her father, who were surely here somewhere, might have seen Cecile. He asked this man then that woman where to find the miners' union. Each person he asked was angry, restless, and no one knew. Few even deigned to answer.

"*Allez, CGT!*" he heard.

"*Nous voulons du lait!*"

He pushed forward, veering right then left, scanning the crowd all around. Some groups carried placards identifying themselves; others wore the uniforms of their trades. Over there were the postal employees. And there, the garbage collectors. There, the railway workers: rough-faced men in soot-stained smocks who savagely beat conductors who crossed their picket lines. Here and about stood the rare individual like him, who, as a result of his loneness, seemed that much more conspicuous in the multitude.

Engulfed now, unable to see much of anything, he forced his way to a lamppost near Rue de Rivoli, where he saw people perched atop the conical base. Once there, he squeezed up between two men, one in a trench coat, the other who looked to be some sort of functionary. From this vantage point, Seb spotted a cluster of university students—bespectacled and fashionably dressed and indignant—at the head of the crowd, near the speakers. He didn't see Cecile among them. In smaller gangs nearby was a more dubious lot: younger, university students maybe but refusing to attach themselves to the organized student group. Some wore the smocks of industrial workers. (Much too large for them—belonging to their fathers?) All had red scarves or kerchiefs around their necks, and they lurked about, ignoring the goings-on of the rally, eyeing only the cordon of police that separated the mass from the Hôtel de Ville.

Behind the line of police, who were stiff-jawed but looked jittery, a man spoke through a bullhorn. Seb could hardly make out what he was saying. Then, in sailed a round missile that struck one policeman flush in the face—a rotting head of lettuce that left a greasy splotch across his cheek and knocked his helmet askew. This sparked a burst of laughter from the crowd. Seb thought he even glimpsed a smile on the face of the policeman beside the one who'd been hit. He found himself laughing, too.

He heard mechanized clank-clank-clanking, a sound that, since the war, everyone recognized—the treads of a tank. The crowd stilled. The chaotic whistling and discordant music-making went suddenly quiet. All turned toward the rear, toward the turret cannon become suddenly visible around the bend of the Rue de la Coutellerie, a hulk of blocked metal wheeling sharply toward them.

The tank braked abruptly; its engine roared. Another emerged behind it.

The mass of people shifted, pushed as one away from the roaring. The man with the bullhorn shouted something, but it was unintelligible over the din of sudden movement. Then they heard a new sort of whistling, uniform and commanding. Seb could see soldiers' helmets, a company's worth at least, crossing the Seine and pushing into the crowd, herding them toward the tanks.

Wisps of smoke rising into the air. An instant later, pop-pop, pop-popping.

Gunshots?

It all came undone. People jostled in every direction but away from the policemen who were now advancing with raised nightsticks, trampling underfoot placards and miniature flags and torn or discarded garments.

Cecile?

Seb hopped down from the lamppost and pushed into, against the fleeing protestors. He had to find her.

An older man, a postal worker, fell in front of him and was being stampeded, and Seb nearly went down over the top of him before planting his feet and grasping at arm and lapel and whatever was graspable. He was able to pull the bloody-faced man to his knees, and the man sprang up and into the rushing flight, away.

Seb continued moving against the flow, for what if that was where Cecile was? He couldn't advance, not two steps, and if he couldn't, then she wouldn't be able to either. No, she would be running away.

And it was only with this realization that he realized the folly he had just attempted, rushing toward the tanks!

He had to keep his head. He pulled himself up onto another lamppost and looked and looked. From this vantage, he admitted to himself what should have been apparent all along—that, in the chaos, he wouldn't be able to find Cecile, to spot her face. There were no faces, only shimmering motion.

He jumped down, joined a flood of people heading toward Rue du Temple, away from the tanks, which he hoped Cecile was doing too, and in this way he might find her. From behind, rifle shots—also a duller sort of popping. He felt an acrid burning in his eyes and nose, in his throat, his vision blurring, tears streaming.

On the street beside the BHV department store, a scuffle was in full swing between a group of the dodgy boys in red neckwear—worn bandit-style now, over nose and mouth—and the police, in leather coats and gas masks that made grotesques of their faces. The police worked in gangs of three or four, beating anyone they could single out, nightsticks swinging in staccato arcs. The kerchief boys were prying free paving stones and hurling them. Some had slingshots; Seb heard whizzing nearby his head. In the windows above, photographers photographed those fleeing, the kerchief boys, him.

There was a pop, and he saw a kerchief boy in oversized coveralls drop, on his back a blood dot, pooling. The boy writhed, his mouth half uncovered now and generating some sound that Seb could not hear over the roar of the rest. Ruddy cheeks and the face of a sprite—he couldn't have been older than sixteen.

Seb worked toward him, to try to help him, as did, from the other direction, two policemen: each a leather gas mask face, two indifferent discs for eyes, a hanging plastic snout. They got there first and ripped away the red kerchief and swung and swung. Seb pushed one off and dodged the blow of the surprised second. The first was on him then, wrestling him down, and Seb was on the ground, dodging and deflecting blows.

He saw the ball bearing strike the policeman's head—his helmet tilted abruptly upward—an instant before he heard the sharp ping. The metal ball dropped to the ground beside Seb, and then the policeman, on top of him.

Dead or merely unconscious?

The other policeman turned toward the shot. Seb grabbed the red kerchief from the dropped policeman's limp hand and wriggled free of his dull weight. He covered his nostrils and mouth with the wadded rag against the acrid stinging and ran toward the corner. There, kerchief boys were gathering.

It was a running battle along the Rue de Rivoli—pop-popping from the phalanx of police; the kerchief boys firing slingshots and throwing stones, and that one had a revolver. At first, Seb merely pried loose a single paving stone to hand to the kerchief boy who was manically reaching back for one, screaming some inaudible something at him. The boy reached back again. Seb clenched the kerchief he'd picked up between his teeth in order to free his hands and more easily pry loose another, then he just tied it in place. Soon he was hurling stones, too. He wasn't thinking, he was moving, moving with the kerchief boys, throwing stones then scurrying for cover, a tank enrobed in helmeted soldiers clank-clank-clanking toward them.

Remaining on Rue de Rivoli, in any open space, could only lead to disaster. The police and soldiers would overwhelm them, the tank overrun them. The kerchief boys realized it at the same moment as Seb and shifted as one off the broad street into the tiny ones beside. There was no tear gas there. Still, Seb didn't remove the kerchief.

A few would launch stones while the group fell back, then others would launch a subsequent barrage to allow those who'd not been shot or set upon to fall farther back still. Seb's aim was true, his outrage and panic faded to a hushed calm. He hurled a paving stone, saw it glance off the helmet of a soldier, remembering the roasted chicken from earlier, wishing he were headed to Au Rendezvous des Amis now for another serving—the hollow crack of the thighbone between his teeth, the smoky flavor of marrow underneath.

His crew of four dashed across Rue du Renard then up Rue Beaubourg and ducked into the entrance of the Metro at Rambuteau, throwing stones all the way, followed after by pop-popping. Seb bounded down the stairs, kicked the locked grating. Kicked, kicked, kicked. A kerchief boy followed and kicked in unison with his kicking, but another cried down: *"Mais non, vous êtes fous! Vous ne passerez pas,"* the clank-clank-clank approaching. A third joined them, and their kicking, three feet thrown forward as one, broke the lock.

They dashed into the station, the underground maze of passageways deserted, then down more stairs, into darkness. The train platform was lit enough to make out the shapes of things—benches, a trash bin—but all was still, the air heavy. And hot. And quiet. Utter silence.

Bahanyan. The Land of Disorder.

He pulled down the kerchief to better gasp for breath and, in a tick of lucidity, discarded the red rag. What was he doing? What had he just done?

He'd come for Cecile, to attempt to keep her from getting swept up in something like this, and here he was, full-on in it himself, caught up with lawless boys hiding behind cloth masks in *Bahanyan*.

Seb heard boots on the stairs. No time for agonizing, not now. He jumped down onto the tracks and, avoiding the electrified one in the middle, took off into the tunnel. The two boys followed.

In the spectral light of the platform behind, he saw policemen gathering. Several: at least eight, maybe more. Now plunging in after them.

"*Arretez! Arretez!*" Whistles whistling. White dots of light from their torches.

But Seb was pitched in darkness, starkest night—the crunch of ballast stone underfoot, the wooden crossties. The next dimly lit station lay straight ahead, three hundred, four hundred meters distant, so he knew that the tunnel continued straight too, the electrified rail to his left. He dashed on and reached it—Arts et Métiers—and dashed through, the kerchief boys still with him.

Total blackness again, and soon the tunnel bent—the wall, darker than the other dark, suddenly nearer to him. And hard to locate: the electrified rail.

Seb slowed, inched forward, the boys, too. One jumped into a niche in the wall.

"What are you doing?" Seb said.

"Move on, move on," he heard, whispered in the provincial accent that he remembered from Burgundy. "They won't see me and will run past."

"But if they do they'll beat you, maybe kill you." Seb pulled the boy out. "Come on!"

He followed the curve of the track, cautiously, the thumping of boots behind, nearing. When he got far enough to see light ahead, a few hundred meters away, he took off again—a dead sprint.

It was République station, where there were correspondences to several other lines. They ran up onto the platform. The boy from Burgundy pulled down his kerchief. The other pulled his down, too. Both bent at the waist, struggling for breath.

Seb heard boots crunching over stone in the tunnel. "We'll split up here." He pulled the Burgundian upright. "I'll go this way," he said, pointing toward the passageway that led to Line 8. "You there, and you there." Seb pushed them in the directions he'd designated. "Don't stop, keep running." And he took off.

Line 8 led to Bastille. He would double back there; the police, if they followed him, wouldn't expect that.

He ran up a flight of stairs, down a passageway, then left into another. On the platform, he listened for the sound of boots behind him. He didn't hear any but jumped onto the tracks all the same.

Hurrying, though moving deliberately, he paused before entering each station, listening for signs of the police, or of anyone who might be about, before dashing through and into the next dark stretch. Filles du Calvaire station; Chemin Vert; his namesake, Saint-Sébastien. Alone now in the black tunnel, he heard the rest: water dribbling down a stone wall; gusts from some unseen passage; the scurrying of rats over metal rails.

At Bastille, he heard talking. It was jovial, not martial, and included women's voices. He climbed onto the platform, peeked down a passageway toward the sound. It was a cleaning crew, three women in headscarves and a man, North Africans. They didn't see him.

He decided he would wait for their shift to finish, then rush past when they unlocked the folding metal grate. In the meantime, he took an inventory of himself. His clothes were filthy with soot, his hands mangled and bloody. He'd lost three fingernails in the struggle to free paving stones—a pain that, now that he finally noticed it, was both throbbing and sharp.

And Cecile, what had happened to Cecile?

He felt sure that she must be at her hotel, safe and sound, with a good story to tell. Minette courted danger, but Cecile was reasonable. And she was white, bourgeoise, likely dressed in a skirt and heels. She was not who the police targeted.

He had ventured to the very brink for her—a beating and arrest, certain deportation, maybe worse. For her, he had passed through the threshold into *Bahanyan*. Now, he must make his way back out.

When the cleaning crew moved, he moved, not far behind, listening beyond them for the sound of boots. He spat into his hands and wiped and wiped until they were something like clean, spat again and wiped his face. He brushed at the soot on his pants, on his jacket. As it wouldn't clear away, he spread it more evenly so that it was less conspicuous.

The cleaning crew stopped at the station entrance, taking yet another break. Seb noticed that the accordion grate, while pulled closed, wasn't latched. He waited until they finally gathered their buckets and mops and pushed on down the passageway. When their sound faded, he slipped out, climbing the stairs into the welcomed darkness of night.

The always-congested Place de la Bastille was nearly empty. He dipped into the maze of side streets, deciding on a circuitous route for his return to the Quartier latin. He crossed Pont de Sully, but to avoid Boulevard Saint-Germain, he took Cardinal Lemoine to Rue des Écoles, bypassing his own street and continuing toward the next, Rue des Carmes—not so much in fear of the police now as of Zansi, who might be out in the neighborhood. Climbing the steep hill, he plotted how to dodge seeing her in the hotel before he was ready to. He would undress quietly in the dark, shower four flights up instead of on their floor.

And if, by chance, they stumbled upon one another before he had properly recovered? Well, he had the letter from the Ministry of Education to deflect away any rebukes.

After cleaning up, he would call Hôtel des Beaux-Arts, as soon as was feasible.

At the summit of Rue des Carmes stood the Panthéon, lit as always against the backdrop of night. Along the white-stone lintel: *AUX GRANDS HOMMES—LA PATRIE RECONNAISSANTE.*

Who among them on this day, he wondered, had been a great man, decent and just? The soldiers in the tanks? The kerchief boys with sling-shots? Himself?

And to what allegiance?

CHAPTER TWENTY-SEVEN

Reports of unrest in the city kept the command restricted to base—everybody curious but calm, going about their business. So, when the MP raid kicked off, Mack was in the motor pool under the hood of a Willys, tinkering with a sticky carburetor slide. They came loaded for bear, wearing helmets and prodding folks with billy clubs and screaming orders Mack couldn't make out over the racket of orders being screamed all over the Quonset hut, and all of the MPs were white. One shoved him against a wall. When Mack threw a look Poot's way, another hollered: "Eyes forward!"

The MP-in-charge, a lieutenant, started rattling off names: "Carson, Carlester C." "Cole, Jeremiah H." "Denard, Anthony P." "Gray, Macklin B."

Each of those called was black, ten or twelve in all.

Mack didn't hear "Smith, Tony," and he found this a comfort.

They marched those arrested single file across the camp then lined them up in front of headquarters, hands on heads and cordoned off by the squad of MPs, at rigid attention. Officers and NCOs and civilian personnel passed by, staring curiously. Some scowled, their misgivings about colored soldiers confirmed.

The MP lieutenant barked out names again, one at a time this time. No one who went indoors came back out. When it was Mack's turn, he followed the lieutenant to an office, where he was ordered to sit in a chair beside a broad oak desk. A private was posted at the door.

Mack didn't ask the lieutenant what was going on. No need to.

The wall clock ticked forward with a dead sound. He was in the office of a MAJ D. THOMPSON, according to the nameplate on the desk—nobody he'd heard of. Next to the nameplate was a framed picture of a blond lady with two blond girls, all three in matching dresses—for Easter or some such occasion, he imagined. The faces made a triangle in the square frame, each one smiling the same toothy smile, but menacing too—reflections of a world that Mack too often anymore allowed himself to forget still existed.

He sat there twenty-seven minutes according to the clock on the wall before the door finally opened. In strode Reiver, and Mack snapped to, up out of the chair and saluting—though he'd told himself that he would not, thinking it would be a white officer.

"Sergeant Gray," Reiver said, formally, where typically he called him Mack.

He dismissed the MP and sat in the chair opposite Mack, leaning forward, his elbows on his knees. "It ain't good, brother," he said, familiar now with white private gone. "They got you dead to rights on the disappearance of materials from the commissary. The rest? Depends on you whether they put it on you, too."

The rest? There wasn't but the middlemanning.

Reiver explained that it had been a "multi-jurisdictional sting operation" stretching from ports in Normandy and Belgium all the way into Germany, that it included civilian and military personnel alike, and that was about all Mack heard. Looking over at him, listening to Reiver speak calmly and call him "brother," he understood that they would do with him whatever they wanted, as Reiver would not have his back. This was why Reiver had dismissed the MP at the door: no need of a witness to corroborate to superiors that no special arrangement was made between the coons. It was clear to Mack that he was on his own.

He wondered what was the best he could hope for. How long might he spend in the brig? And would it be here or Stateside? If it was to be Stateside, the disciplinary barracks at Fort Leavenworth weren't but a forty-five-minute drive from KC. He hoped for this, so his folks could come visit.

It only occurred to Mack just then: he was going to have to face his mama.

The thought of her face, looking disrespected as much as disappointed, shocked Mack back into Major Thompson's office—into the silence that had fallen over it. Reiver leaned back now, arms crossed over his chest, looking daggers at Mack.

"How many times did I tell you, don't bring dishonor onto yourself or onto your people? How many times!" It was the first that Reiver's voice had gone sharp, and Mack understood that the "people" he was talking about weren't their command or their country but the race. "We're under more scrutiny, I told you this. We're trying to get something good going for us and ours, and the president is even on board—the president of the United States! And here you go, messing all over us."

Mack didn't defend himself, not one bit. He stared back.

This was the same fool telling Mack to enroll in *X* program and sit for *Y* test, all so he could become an officer like him, and Mack felt like, Nigger, please! I am *not* you. I am Mack and goddamn proud to be.

Reiver: making chump change and strutting around puppy-dog happy because they put bars on his collar, and the man still couldn't get a drink at the Officers' Club!

Mack just said: "Who all knows, *sir*?" He emphasized the "sir." "Over in AFCENT, I mean. Is it common knowledge?"

"Your girl! That's what you care about right now?"

"It's what I care about most."

He didn't know how he would break the news to Baby. Obviously, he'd be leaving soon, gone for good, and what was he going to tell her?

Reiver looked disgusted. He rose, started for the door. "I put in a good word for you with Major Thompson. Until further decisions are made, you'll be assigned to the mess hall but otherwise restricted to base."

"We talking days?"

"Weeks," Reiver said, "but not many."

"And I will be sent home for sure?"

"They can't leave you here with what you been into."

Reiver stood there, hand on the knob. Mack knew he was waiting for a "thank you" for the service he believed he'd rendered.

Mack said, "I can't rightly ask for your help, but I'd like to be able to let my Baby know without her having to hear it in the Quonset scuttlebutt. We been bumping heads lately, her and me."

"Don't you think that's why she's with you in the first place," he said, "to get to the States? Come on, Mack. Knock the pearls from your eyes."

He opened the door and left.

Cecile emerged from the water cautiously—on the Left Bank, she noted, though how she'd gotten here, by swimming or the current, she didn't know. The Pont-au-Double, above her, seemed to have cleared, the shrieking and sirens elsewhere now, farther on, though still thunderous and unrelenting. Her head throbbed, and when she touched there, her hair was wet and her hand came away bloody.

She climbed the stone stairs, hunched below the balustrade, then dashed across the Quai de Montebello, into a small park. On the Petit Pont, the next bridge over, demonstrators and police still clashed, some running her way. She moved on quickly, into tiny Rue de la Bûcherie and around its bend. The sounds of commotion echoed all around, though the street itself was empty, and she remarked for the first time that her ears were ringing. In the windows above, people gazed into the distance, some down at her. She picked up her pace, limping on one shoe with a broken heel, the other missing.

Rue de la Bûcherie opened onto Rue Maître Albert. On Quai de Montebello, just twenty meters up, a tank wheeled by. Her heart raced, and she dodged as fast as she could into a nearby café—a narrow place, just the length of the bar, with three tables lining the rear wall. The barman, drying glasses—the only person present—glanced up with the clanging of the bell on the door, then stopped wiping and stared, his hostility clear.

What must she look like? A bloodied scalp and her blouse half open, several buttons gone; drenched, collar to hemline. And what had become of her jacket?

She went to the farthest table, beside a doorway that opened on a small storeroom. "*Un double, s'il vous plaît,*" she said, her voice cracking, her eyes in her lap, water from her clothes pooling beneath the chair.

She heard the clack-clack, clack-clack of the coffee grounds dispenser, the hiss and steaming of the machine. The barman walked over and placed *un double* in front of her but did not withdraw. She looked up.

His bilious face. "My regular clientele, *jeune femme*, work across the bridge at the Palais de Justice. They aren't the sort to sympathize with mischief-makers and provocateurs. You might finish quickly and push on before any of them arrive."

He returned toward the bar.

"Do you have a phone?" she asked his retreating back.

He pointed to the sign in the window—NO PUBLIC TELEPHONE— and recommended rinsing glasses and wiping them dry.

She drank the coffee in one swallow, her tongue and mouth and throat welcoming the scalding, thick liquid.

How did she get here? How had this come to pass? Running for her life, running away from home and toward the Quartier latin, toward a life, toward Seb, and somehow she had landed here—in Paris but not Paris, working for the Americans, keeping company with them, and also sleeping with one.

And where was Seb? How had they missed each other on the square?

A blaring siren—flash of police van, speeding past the front door— jolted Cecile back to now, to this café. The barman glared, rinsing a glass and wiping it, grabbing another, rinsing then wiping. She dropped her eyes.

This was Vichy all over again, Clémence's Philippe. Should she dash for the door, take her chances out on the street?

And where was Seb? Had he even come to their rendezvous?

She could go to his hotel; it was a five-minute walk away. But in her sopping clothes and with a bloodied head, would she even make it without being stopped by the police? And if he was there, what could he do for her besides explain his absence when she'd needed him most?

But what if he'd been at the demonstration and they'd missed each other and he hadn't made it out? What if he'd been overrun or rounded up, what should she do then?

The bell on the door clanged. She heard: "*Salut*, Jean-Marc!" and in reply, "*Salut, les gars.*" The double clack-clack, the hiss and steaming, the clinking of porcelain cups and espresso spoons. The newcomers—three in a tight cluster at the bar—joked roughly with the barman, with Jean-Marc. She only caught snatches of words, peeking up at the men's backs.

Regardless where Seb was, she was here. Now.

Noting the barman's feet at her table, she looked up. He dropped a green kerchief in her lap, depositing another coffee on the tabletop. "*Voila, jeune femme,*" he said cheerfully, but leaning closer, added in a whisper: "Tie this over your head."

The men at the bar were sharing some story and tittering.

"There." The barman indicated the storeroom with his eyes. "Take my sweater and cover your soiled clothes—on the shelf beside the back door. Then move along, don't tarry."

He returned to the others, big and boisterous again. "*Eh-oh, quelles conneries racontez-vous, là?*"

Cecile slipped from her seat, passed through the open doorway. Her head throbbed; she felt woozy. The tiny room was cluttered with crates and supplies. She found his sweater, a cable-knit turtleneck, enormous, and slipped it over her head.

There was a telephone on the wall. She dialed Orly Air Base, for what could Seb do for her now? Would they hide together, cowering in the dark in his room?

It took forever to be patched through.

"Mack," she said. "Oh Mack, I am in trouble."

"Where you at?" His voice urgent but soothing.

"It is near Notre-Dame," she said. She explained the location as best she could—the name of the street and cross street, the Pont-au-Double. She was crying now. "It is not a very long street." Crying and crying.

"I'll find you, Baby. Do not fret."

He hung up.

She did, too, then wiped her face and slipped back to her table.

The barman came right over, his expression even sharper than when she'd first entered his café. "I thought I made myself clear," whispering, but sternly, "to leave by the back door."

Two police vans sped past in quick succession, sirens blaring. The men at the bar glowered at her now.

"My boyfriend, he's coming." The tears spilled again. "I can't wait on the street."

He rejoined the others. They spoke in hushed tones, one or another glancing over.

She couldn't tell if minutes passed or days, hours or maybe just seconds.

She heard the gnarled engine sounds of a Willys—faintly, in the distance—then a repeated and insistent honking. She rose and ran past the men and out the front door.

On the street, four helmeted policemen ran after Mack's jeep, from Quai de Montebello. Tony Smith was beside Mack, and they stopped right in front of Cecile, brakes squealing. Mack jumped out and caught her in his arms, and she let herself release into him.

One of the policemen blew his whistle, their group closing in, encircling.

"Step the fuck back!" Mack barked, and Tony Smith descended from the Willys, a hand on his holstered pistol.

The policemen stopped, not five meters away. They fanned out more but didn't advance nearer.

Cecile trembled uncontrollably, violently. Mack helped her onto the back bench then pushed in beside, pulling her into the blanket of his embrace.

"Drive, brother," he said to Tony Smith. "Neuilly, the hospital there."

CHAPTER TWENTY-EIGHT

Elodie waited on a stiff bench in the electric-lit corridor beside the GI that Mack had sent to get her, both watching his back-and-forth with the US Army doctor in the surgical mask. A small wood-rimmed blackboard was affixed to the closed door behind them, her daughter's name scribbled in white chalk upon it, below another name.

Alain's English was stronger than hers. How she wished he were here.

"How bad she be?" she heard Mack say, which she thought she understood.

The doctor replied, "Beg pardon?"—which she did not.

Mack said, "What I mean is, will she be OK?"

Judging by the doctor's eyes, he appeared to be losing patience. "Your wife has multiple . . ." Then he stopped. "She is your wife?"

Mack nodded, which Elodie knew not to be true, for Cecile wouldn't have gotten married without telling her. Please no, she would never ever do such a thing . . .

The doctor continued, more slowly than before, as though explaining to a dimwit child. "As I said, the risk of intracranial hemorrhage is serious. Add on the laceration injuries . . ."

But it was her, Elodie, who was the dimwit. She stopped attempting to comprehend the medical jargon, muffled through the cotton mask, that she didn't think she'd be able to make sense of regardless, even in French.

Nurses entered and exited, masks over their mouths and rubber gloves stretching above their wrists. They ignored her. She overheard one say, "Some extensive," and another, "Complete the debridement before stitching."

Through the door, Elodie heard her daughter protest her pain, in English—"Please, please stop this!"—then sobbing, the meaning all too clear.

Apparently, Mack (Cecile's husband?) had the authority of consent or denial. Without consulting Elodie or even looking her way, he listened attentively and agreed to prospective courses of treatment. What did Elodie have to contribute, anyway, especially without Alain, who had enough English to challenge their conclusions and who knew French doctors who might propose alternatives? She'd left a rapidly scrawled note on the mantel; he might yet arrive to translate for her: their words, this scene, the condition of their daughter.

The doctor's next words were unmistakable. "The pregnancy seems unharmed from the incident."

"Come again?" said Mack.

All the rest stopped for Elodie, too.

"I'm sorry, Sergeant. I assumed you knew."

Mack turned toward Elodie, his eyes vacant, his face still.

The metallic corridor, the cold light.

Then he pulled her from the bench and into his arms. "You're going to be a grandmama!" He danced her in a circle, Mack's friend joining in, the two of them hopping her up and down. "We all deserve second chances. Everything happens for a reason, and we get our chance to make things right."

"Sergeant Gray, please!"

Mack and his friend paused, passersby staring. The doctor, visibly annoyed, continued explaining. Elodie only understood that they would keep Cecile overnight.

Her daughter was not clear of trouble yet.

After the doctor left, Mack recommenced the terrible dance, spinning Elodie, oblivious that she was not smiling with him, that she was only letting herself be carried along.

He abruptly stopped. "You knew, didn't you?" But he didn't await a response. "Why all the secrets? Why women always got to keep secrets?"

Had he truly wanted to know, then Elodie's expression would have revealed to him that she had no more been informed than he had.

Mack had had to claim Baby as his fiancée to get her admitted, but this last news made it worth the risk, made all the rest—countermanding Reiver, going AWOL from base; the armed confrontation with the French police—a meaningless afterthought. His Baby was pregnant!

The cracker doctor, when he first emerged from Baby's room: he'd looked past Mack, down the hallway one way then the other, only to finally realize that the nigger standing there in front of him was the man he was searching for. He hadn't even tried to disguise his disgust—refusing to lower his mask! He'd gone on and on: "Closing the lacerations . . . We can minister to the observable wounds . . ." It wasn't the medical language or the doctor's open disrespect that had undone Mack, though. It was the picture he couldn't scrub from his mind—her beautiful hair, matted maroon; the man's sweater that clearly was not hers; Baby's tortured eyes.

But now, with the coming child, the strange something that had been growing between them, between Mack and Baby, might fade. Forget that they had been fighting, forget the niggling and the nagging. Finally, she would need him. His strength. His savvy. She had called in distress and he had come and known enough what to do to get her here and minimize the mess that was this mess. And now it would be Mack and his Baby and their baby, just them—and Mack all a man, and fuck this doctor, and fuck the rest.

This doctor, impatient, had cut off Mack's celebratory dance. "Remind me, Sergeant, how was it the injuries occurred to . . . Your wife, correct?"

"We wrecked our Willys."

"But *you* came away unscathed?"

Mack didn't say diddly. He just stared.

After the doctor had gone, Tony Smith said, "You taking big risks, man, and you already way out on the end of the limb, with the MP jam-up."

"She my Baby," Mack told him. "What else Ima do?"

"And now what? You gone take her home?"

"I ain't scared."

"Brother, you ought to be. America ain't Paris. If you planning on marrying that girl, you best figure out a way to stay. Look me in the eye and tell me you know this."

Mack looked him in the eye and didn't tell him shit.

Everybody telling him what he could and could not do, what to see and what he was blind to. He saw this: she was his Baby, and she was carrying his baby, too.

Elodie remembered their meeting, the week before. She thought she understood now the reason for the impromptu rendezvous, and on the Champs-Élysées of all places. Cecile had called it a midway point, convenient for both of them, but it was neither midway nor particularly convenient. Cecile had once told her that Mack loved the area, but it was the last *quartier* in the city she imagined her *révoltée* daughter wanting to spend time.

Had she already known? Had this been the impetus for the call to meet—to announce the coming child and an impending marriage?

Elodie couldn't recall what she'd told Cecile and feared it hadn't been the right thing.

An administrator carrying a clipboard led Mack down the corridor. Nurses entered and exited Cecile's room. "*Mais, merde,*" Elodie heard, in French now, "*finissez, enfin!*"

She went to the door, wedged herself into the comings and goings of the nurses. And oh, the look on Cecile's face across the great separation of the room, haloed by rubber-gloved hands, in the cold metal and white light. What had they become, she and her daughter? The puzzle of their shared history: the pieces that, if properly fit together, might form a picture that could help them survive this. Because if Cecile went away to America, how would they find a way to see each other?

Cecile spotted Elodie in the doorway, and their eyes met. She paused her writhing and smiled—artful, complicitous.

"Ma'am, please!" A nurse forced Elodie back. "You have to let us finish our work."

And the door slowly closed, the small blackboard on it quivering as the latch latched. In white chalk:

Baldwin, Jane—WAC/419 USASC REGT

Gray, Cecile—Dependent

Elodie stood there, the water from her eyes blurring the muddle of words, and the words beneath the words, until the water blurred it all.

CHAPTER TWENTY-NINE

Seb stood at the packed bar at the Danton the night of the demonstration, still wound up, making a costly glass of whiskey last. He'd successfully avoided Zansi, but Cecile hadn't made contact and her concierge had told him on the telephone that she hadn't seen her since morning. Apprehensive of roaming the streets, he'd come to the café instead, to regroup and figure out what to do next. And who knew? Maybe she would turn up there.

He heard: "Have you seen Cecile?"

It was Minette—of course Minette, her of all people.

"Not since the demonstration," he said.

"Since the massacre, you mean."

He turned back toward his drink.

Blood-splotted plasters covered three fingertips where before had been nails. Minette didn't seem to notice. She said, "We were together briefly, she and I, but as soon as there was trouble, poof!" She made a gesture with her hand. "No more Cecile."

She forced in between him and the neighborhood *ivrogne*—a woman with spider-capillaried cheeks, in an expensive but soiled mackintosh, a glass of cheap wine on the bar top before her.

"So, are you going to offer me a drink or do you intend on drinking alone?" Minette said. But before he could respond, she signaled the barman, pointing to the bottle of house red. "I'll order my own, then."

Seb slid over as far as he could, which wasn't very far at all. The barman placed a glass before Minette and filled it nearly to the brim with the same Bordeaux as her *voisine*.

"My father and I barely made it out," Minette continued. "Her, I bet she found a taxi and fled to Le Vésinet." She took a long swallow. "You and I don't have that luxury, do we?"

Maybe she was right, maybe Cecile had gone home. It's what he would have done, had he the possibility of it.

"Or maybe she went to her American at Orly," she said.

Seb could see that she was seeking a reaction—to probe whether he knew about the American or, if he did, to rile him up about it.

He offered nothing. He sipped his whiskey.

Minette sucked her teeth. "Well, she's chosen her camp."

Seb glared at her. Such disdain: her vanity, the contemptuous smirk. Whatever the circumstances, regardless who it might injure, Minette always pushed.

Sipping what was left of her wine, she said, "Anyway, you missed quite a show."

"A show?"

"A show, yes. It always takes spectacles of bloodletting to galvanize the masses."

"And had it been your blood?"

"Then we wouldn't be having this pleasant chat, you and I, would we?" she said.

Each one sipped their drink.

He realized that Minette wasn't completely wrong, either. It took extraordinary pain to effect change. The letter from the ministry, his afternoon in *Bahanyan*—each had been a message from the forefathers, with, as lesson, the need for change. He had worked hard and was finally earning his place. Things could not go on as before.

He hadn't sought out Minette, yet here she was. So, he accepted the meaning of her arrival.

Hunxo, he thought: secrets. Vain, disdainful Minette would be incapable of keeping one.

Boubi would be angry; he would feel betrayed. But this wasn't about Boubi.

Seb nodded at the barman, pointed to his empty glass then to Minette's nearly empty one.

"So now my company seems preferable to your sullen solitude?" she said.

Her company suited his purpose, what must be done.

"It'll do," he replied.

CHAPTER THIRTY

The rapping on the door was sharp and insistent, and Seb knew right away it was Cecile. He turned on the lamp; the clock read half past two. He put on his robe before opening.

She pushed past him. "You're unhappy with me so you seduce my friend?"

He closed the door but stood beside it, his hand on the knob. "Is that what she told you? That I seduced her?"

She wore a chic *carré* as a headscarf, but underneath he could see white bandage. "Everyone knows," she said, "everyone saw you together."

"Minette threw herself at me. I should have resisted. In the moment, I did not."

She tore off the scarf and flung the balled clump at him. It struck his chest and fell at his feet.

The bandage was professionally wrapped, a gauze turban. An injury from the demonstration?

Every impulse pushed him to go to her, to pull her into his arms . . .

But he couldn't. He couldn't concern himself with this. His father would arrive in Paris tomorrow—and Cecile was all right, clearly. Seb stood rigid and proper at the door, his hand on the knob.

"You should pick your friends better," he said, though it felt terrible to say.

She removed her coat and sat on the bed. "Why, Seb? What did I do?" This girl . . .

This was the girl whose love filled him, easily, comfortably, like those late afternoons in Burgundy: elbowed at the bar in a shop-worn blue smock beside a half-finished glass of beer that the barman wouldn't let empty, enveloped in tart tobacco smoke and the leathery laughter of men whose handshakes hurt your hand when you shook and who had come to see him as nothing more or less than merely himself. This was *that* girl, seated there on his bed, eyes ringed red, head in a gauze turban, holding onto things inside him that were his only when she was there, holding on to them with him.

She was the girl who'd lain beside him all those nights, taking pieces of his stories and imagining a whole new picture. When he'd told her about the woman king Hangbè, Cecile had conjured a prettier tale, with ochered palace walls and pagne robes of azure and chartreuse, with ritual and song but nothing that hinted of brutality or betrayal. Cecile's Hangbè ended the terrible raiding and the processions of captives driven iron collar to iron collar to the coast. In her version, it was hidebound Agaja who undermined her efforts.

But Hangbè's story didn't need reinventing. She'd made Dahomey greater, not with flowery words but by war, only war. Cecile had once chided him for emphasizing the kings . . . He didn't forget the women— no! He knew to the depths of his soul that Hangbè and Na Geze and also Zansi had made him, just as much as Agaja and the rest. Him, Kannoukpô: the rope not yet at its end. Him: Gbéhanzin. Not Sebastien, much less this "Seb."

It was Cecile who didn't understand their ruthless clarity. She couldn't see that here was not home for him and never could be.

Her inability to accept the world as it was—as it must be—garbled his own view of the world. At the demonstration at Hôtel de Ville, he'd risked all the things he couldn't afford to risk in order to protect a girl that it was lunacy to try to protect, because she didn't want protecting. She wanted what she could not have: to be someone she was not.

Sending a letter would have been the right thing to do, or at least better than this. But Cecile would always be Cecile: persistent like the rustling wind through leaves and willful like the sea. This girl, *his* Cecile, would never just go away without opposition.

So, he placed the period that would finally end the sentence. "Nothing but a spoiled, little bourgeoise," he said, "that's all you are." He forced his face empty of expression, as flat as a fish's. "You think that spreading your legs for blacks makes you one."

And when that wasn't enough, when that did not hurt her enough to make her rise from his bed and leave his room, he said more.

"Your *friend* Minette"—he spat the word—"still lives with her parents in the poorest section of the city. But you, you use papa's money to quit your swank suburb for the Quartier latin."

She didn't move, so he continued.

"You dress up as a Communist and toss around rage and outrage like so much loose change then take up with your American when it gets too taxing. For you, this is a game, play."

She didn't move.

"And you of all people, a Jew. Did the war teach you nothing?"

With this last comment—words he recognized for having thought them, somewhere inside, but not ones he could actually believe—she rose. She crossed to him, slipped down the length of him, not a breath away, and picked up her scarf.

He opened the door.

She left.

CHAPTER THIRTY-ONE

Seb sat at the table in the corner, unable to return to bed, struggling with what he'd just done. Another knock, not long after Cecile's excruciating exit—assertive, though not insistent. Zansi.

In a robe, one-half of her hair pressed flat from the pillow, she said, "I'm sorry about the Vésinet girl."

Had she been eavesdropping all along, from the start?

"I know it feels impossible," she continued, "but you did the right thing."

"Spare me your sympathy. You never liked her, you always wanted me to break ties."

She paused. The Dahomeyan gaze.

"Not particularly, no. I don't like her or her circle. But that wasn't the point. You're my brother and my charge, and you faced an enormous challenge."

Her "charge"?

"One at which I've succeeded," he said, pointing to the Beaux-Arts letter, which lay atop his dresser.

"Yes, so far. And you're welcome, by the way, for my part in your success."

She crossed the room and perched on the windowsill, the movement an obvious effort to control her flaring anger.

"The challenges aren't over," she continued. "They've just begun. The Vésinet girl and that crowd, they can't help you with what lies ahead."

"She has a name, Zansi! She's called Cecile!"

He reproached himself for the outburst. He'd wanted to keep his composure.

His sister remained composed. "So does my friend, Kannou. His name is Emile. It's because of him that you've pulled away from me, isn't it? You haven't treated me the same since you saw me with him."

He didn't reply—his face flat, matching Dahomeyan gaze for Dahomeyan gaze.

"I knew you were here with her nights," she said, "with Cecile. And I was glad for you, until I saw her become a distraction. Your moodiness, the unexplained disappearances. Now that you seem to have learned balance, I'd be happy to see you with her again. You'll need something more than just your work while you complete Beaux-Arts."

Now that he had "learned balance?" Him, her "*charge*"!

"That would suit you, wouldn't it?" he said, finally seeing two moves ahead. "You and Emile, I mean."

"As I told you that day, I'm not asking your permission. But you're my family. I want our relationship, yours and mine, to become as it was before."

"You also told me about my duties to the forefathers, to our home. If I'm heir, shouldn't I begin to execute my responsibilities toward you, to give you guidance?"

"Guidance!" Her outburst was sudden and biting. "Heir? Of what? Of a Dahomey that no longer exists, that will never exist again? We're subjects, and when we no longer are, we'll have a modern nation, one that needs architects and doctors and lawyers. There won't be a king, no throne or ceremonies or rites—only a name, just that."

She paused to breathe, but her anger remained on the surface.

"Execute your duty to better our country's lot," she said, "but leave any ill-conceived notions of responsibility for my behavior out of it."

He recognized having gained the advantage. It was his turn to exude calm.

"Will you stay here, then, with your Emile? Practice here?"

He'd always known more than Zansi gave him credit for. He'd always been his own man when she could only see an obedient boy.

"And if you do," he said, "who will be your family?"

He was Gbéhanzin. Even when tradition injures, it remains tradition. The air in the room stretched.

Then Zansi smiled. "The child has become a man. When we see Father tomorrow, he'll be proud of the son he discovers."

She crossed to him, placed a hand on his shoulder and squeezed—hard—then left.

He watched her pull the door closed. *Yes, big sister, take pride in your short-sighted belief that it's you who continues to orchestrate my future.* He thought this without the least rancor, for he had something that she didn't have: *hunxo*, secrets—the lessons learned from the forefathers.

In the archives, he'd read Gbéhanzin's own words (as recounted to the Royal Chronicler, who'd transposed it for the colonial *Commandant de Cercle*, who'd recorded it in the official Log of Correspondence, Zou Department). The king told the tale of his Great War against the French:

From among the many pretenders, it was me who became Heir, who succeeded my father, the Lion Glélé. Upon his passing to the Other Place, where our dead Fathers reside, I held Grand Customs ceremonies, occasions of Sacrifice, and sent Envoys regularly—couriers to show respect and convey messages, and my conversations with my Father continued uninterrupted. After the Yovo army landed, He was full of advice and direction. At Dogba, the razor-women crept to within an elephant's tusk of the Yovo bivouac before their sentries realized my presence. The razor-women screamed out of the bush and I killed many. My razor-women killed many and sang the victory:

We were born to protect
Da-Ho-Mey!
This pot of honey
Did you not hear what happened at Dogba?
We razor-women killed a priest
Gbéhanzin killed a bearded priest.

I am told that, after this, the Yovo slept with their rifles between their legs, at the ready.

Thereafter—at Adégon, at Akpa—I was pushed back. I sent Envoys each evening, not slaves anymore but my bravest warriors, swathed in my richest cloth and bedecked in cowry. I wanted the Lion Glélé to heed my queries.

Defeat after defeat, I understood that the Envoys had not reached him.

I no longer knew upon whom to rely. Thus did I appeal to Nan Zinvoton, my dear old mother, for her country and her king, to plead with her dead husband.

"I will consent," she replied. "My only condition is this: that the ceremony take place on the banks of the sacred Couffo River and that it be you, my son, who cuts off my head and dispatches me to your father."

And it was so.

Sacrifice was all, Kannoukpô understood this. What must be done must be done. For he was Dahomey, this pot of honey.

CHAPTER THIRTY-TWO

Wednesday, 19 November:

My noble Capitaine Garrillaud—I will always remember the
look of his face when I introduced the ragamuffin poilu,
just arrived in Chandesaignes. He admitted your father to
the infirmary, assured me that he would be all right. I
returned to the hotel, but Fernand didn't come to dinner
that evening.

The following morning, I went to visit your father—a
pretext to see Fernand. After your father had dozed off,
Fernand and I walked side by side down a country lane,
past field after field of lavender and mustard seed. Neither
of us said a word. My throat was knotted, my heart rent.
When finally we spoke, it was without regard for whatever
devil or angel might have been out there to hear it. He
told me that my beauty troubled his dreams—those were
his words. And I hoped with an insane, illogical hope, that
he would say, Come, come, let's continue on, walk through
that field, over the mountain beyond and run away, start
anew. I thought of you, I did, but you weren't part of
the dream that unfolded. I allowed myself to put the idea
of you into a box, and I closed the lid so I could live one
moment more this love, the love of my life.

Just a silly girl, so young. As though my life with you could ever be a sacrifice.

The obvious joy, that day on the Champs-Élysées, when you let it be known that you'd been seeing Seb again; the pleasure of defiance, like when, as a child, you'd set your eye on some mischief and would dare me with a look to try and stop you.

And the mischievous look in your eyes at the American hospital—I understand now. You imagine the coming baby to be a tie to Sebastien, but the child could never be that. He (or she!) will be all that you are to me.

POSTSCRIPT

PARIS, 1951

CHAPTER THIRTY-THREE

Cecile chérie—here's an example (one you might find of interest) of the work I'm doing.

17 December 1950

Dear Madame Rosenbaum,

You may not recognize me by my new name—You knew me as Joël Goldschmidt. I was the neighbor boy who your family assisted during the Terror.

I am writing to you, after this long silence, to belatedly thank you. Those were trying times, and while you and your family suffered also, you, Madame, always made a point to attend to the suffering of my sister and me. Few were the heroes, but you figured among them. I am grateful.

I am in the State of Israel, an officer in our armed forces. I am posted near the border, but I am well.

Undoubtedly you have heard and read many things about our homeland. Egyptian fanatics sneak across the border and attack civilians, but we repel them by the scores. The land is ours, and it is truly the Promised Land. We have taken rocks and sand, uncultivated by the Arabs, and created a paradise.

Note the pressure when he writes—the heavy strokes. What aggression!

He has a strong hand—a sign of a heavy emotion, of a deep, lasting bitterness. And note the envelope (which I've included): an invasive personality, arrogant and selfish. (He's probably a spendthrift.)

If you turn the page over and run your fingertips over it, you will feel the tiny raised ridges made by his heavy application.

Every line is heavy in proportion to its size (it reminds me of an example of L-F Céline's handwriting that I've studied—what horror!). (And irony!!!)

Note how his t-bars
are heavier than the
vertical ones.
What will power!

One day, perhaps you will visit. My door is
always open to you and your family.
With the most sincere amity,
    Akiva Ben-Barak

The sort to assert
his personality over
others.

GRAPHOLOGICAL ANALYSIS: Oh, Martine, his poor sister!

3 January 1951

Ma Cecile chérie,

I read this recently and thought of you: "Real worth requires no interpreter: its everyday deeds form its emblem"—by Chamfort. So, you see, ma fille, here (the included letter from Joël—sorry: Akiva) is an example of someone who has always struggled with his self-worth. (Through no fault of his own, mind you; the things he suffered as a boy.) Now, he finds himself profoundly, profoundly alone.

And is Joël (Akiva!) particularly fulfilled as a result? He is in Israel, but his subalterns appear to be his only family. He accepts accountability for who he is, but is he happy with that person? His handwriting does not indicate it.

(Of course, you understand that it is <u>extremely</u> unethical for me to share Joël/Akiva's letter and my analysis of it with you. I know that you will keep it strictly between us.)

And Sebastien (who you should have forgotten by now, or be striving to), I suspect he is alone too, as what he values above all is himself and his priorities. I would be surprised to learn that he is truly happy. Don't allow nostalgia and melancholy to cloud your memory.

I'm glad to read that Mack has returned safely from this Georgia posting and is becoming more reasonable and drinking less, that you two are getting along. (Though, a "difficult" character is not a fault; never let anyone—anyone!—make you think otherwise. You are spirited, you are unwavering; these are positive attributes.)

Before I forget, I would prefer that you didn't typewrite your letters. I know you have to practice typewriting to better your skill. (It's very generous of Mack's sister to have loaned you the machine—she sounds marvelous, especially given the mother's chilliness toward you.) And yes, it's true that I never share with you what I see in your handwriting. (Nothing bad, I assure you!) But your letters are

good exercise if I am to better <u>my</u> skill enough to land more assignments and finally be able to quit at the stationery store. You've
said that you don't mind my practicing on you, but perhaps you do
(and if you do, it's perfectly fine). But if you do NOT mind, then
please write longhand so that I can improve my technique.

Enough of that. Oh, but Paris is just dead. You wouldn't recognize
it. I went to an exhibit at the Louvre, called "Art in the Town and
Country," and there were so few people about. I wandered through
all the restored galleries. I also found the art school and thought
of you.

The city is lesser without you in it. I do hope the springtime visit
you mentioned will be possible. Three years is too long a separation
between a mother and her child.

Bonne et Heureuse Année, ma chérie adorée! Kiss petit Martin, from
his grandmother.

         En espérant te lire très bientôt.

         Ta maman

CHAPTER THIRTY-FOUR

Cecile's first day back, she walked. Walked and walked: down the hill from her mother's apartment on Montmartre to Pigalle and past Payne's Place—though she kept her head bent and stayed across the street—on to Notre-Dame-de-Lorette then Haussmann's Grand Boulevards. It was exhilarating, even while jet-lagged, even though exhausted from the relentlessly exhausting trip from Kansas to New York to here, to home.

Saving money wasn't Mack's strength. It had taken several months longer than he'd promised, but they'd managed to put aside enough for a single airline ticket, with Martin riding in Cecile's lap. In the meantime, the Great Flood had closed the Kansas City airport. Cecile and Martin had taken a Greyhound to New York—forty hours and three transfers—then a shuttle to LaGuardia, to catch the flight. Martin had been patient, as patient as a three-year-old is capable of. Once settled in at the apartment, her mother had encouraged Cecile to venture off, volunteering to take care of Martin. "A restorative promenade through the city," she'd proposed—a few hours to herself to clear her head and reconnect with Paris.

Though Martin had no memory of her mother (predictably, as he'd only known her as a wee infant), he'd not resisted. From the moment they'd stepped off the TWA liner at Orly that morning, she had doted on him, offering him sweets and toys, and he wouldn't leave her side. They were as thick as thieves—what Mack often said about Cecile and the boy.

After the Grand Boulevards, Cecile crossed the Seine, and her meandering landed her where, she realized upon arrival, she'd been headed all along—to the Quartier latin, to Beaux-Arts. She passed beneath the alabaster gaze of Nicolas Poussin, crossed to the obelisk, and sat on its pedestal, her knees pulled to her chest. The courtyard shimmered with the doings of ambitious students, even in August, before classes were in session. Some carried portfolios, others sketched on easels or talked in small groups. She didn't know whether Seb was somewhere about, but she refused to let the possibility of it keep her from staying.

Sitting there, the sun dropping toward the rooftops, she admitted to herself that she was, in fact, waiting for him. No more lying to oneself about returning to the site of some longed-for artist's dream that had dimmed. What had lured her here was the hope of running into him.

Better sense blew in on the breeze. What would she say after the passage of years, after the horror of their last meeting? "Hello" and "You were a terrible shit" and "By the way, you have a son"?

Cecile followed a group of students exiting through the gate, close enough to seem to belong. Once off the grounds, she moved past them, past her old rooming house across the street, then up Rue Bonaparte. She climbed Boulevard Saint-Germain to the Danton, though she didn't stop in—all the memories there, too many. She turned onto Rue des Quatres Vents, where she dipped into a bakery for a croissant before beginning the journey back to her mother's apartment.

Her "mother's apartment." Such a strange notion, still, after nearly a year—one that Mack could not get used to at all.

"What kind of woman does that, just up and leaves her husband?" The pitch of his voice had made it clear that it wasn't an actual question. "Nearly fifty and on her own, gone from something to nothing, working the register in a stationery store because ain't a damn thing in the world she knows how to do."

Cecile had struggled to hold back her retort. She understood the tremendous courage it must have taken to leave her father—a courage Cecile had often faulted her mother for lacking but one that she'd always so obviously had. Cecile had let Mack rant. In speaking up, she risked betraying her faltering feelings about her own marriage.

Leaving the bakery, bites of croissant melting on her tongue, she wound through the alleyways to Saint-Sulpice. Inside the cathedral was heavy and dark, the air a cool musk. It reminded her of Bon Sauveur, and she welcomed the memory—the speckled sunlight through stained glass, candles flickering beneath the statue of Mary. Cecile took one from the box at the base of the altar, lit it with the flame of another, then placed it on a vacant prong—for no one in particular, in homage of the moment.

She sat in the pews. A woman in a headscarf, kneeling nearby, glanced from Cecile's Star of David to her face and smiled a tender smile, one that suggested regret, that imagined a whole history. Cecile's story was other than what this woman envisioned. She was Jewish, yes, and a survivor, but also French, like the woman herself. She'd been an artist and a Communist, too. When had she stopped seeing herself in these ways?

And in that moment in the dusking twilight of the church, she thought about Minette; she thought she finally understood why Minette had betrayed her. Minette reviled her own skin, the blackness just as much as the whiteness. Her boastful self-regard was a way to disguise the loathing. But it also made her unable to actually see anyone else—not any more than she could see herself. Minette had done what she'd done because she hated herself more than she was capable of loving another.

Cecile had also hated something of herself. Or rather, she'd hated the person she'd feared others might perceive her to be: the victimized Jew, the scheming collaborator, the colonizing *Yovo*, all the selves reflected in her face and in her history, boiled down for easy consumption. Only there was no time for such *égoisme* anymore. She had to provide food and clothes for her son, and put a roof over his head, and she had to love him with a love so big that he wouldn't harbor doubts like the ones that had fettered her.

The church bells rang, announcing six o'clock—late, late, late. She'd lost track of the hour. She took the Metro at Odéon. The train remained mostly empty the length of the ride: Chatelêt; Réaumur-Sébastopol; Saint-Denis. She was restless for sleep but anxious to see her mother, too—to spend time together and catch up on all the things they'd not been able to share in their regular exchange of letters.

They quickly established a routine. Elodie took Tuesdays and Wednesdays off from her job at the Papeterie Jehan Rictus, on the Place des Abbesses, to take care of Martin, during which time Cecile explored possibilities for temporary work—filling out applications and dropping off her resumé, even interviewing once when she'd found something promising. Her return ticket to the US had been for a month, but she'd pushed back the departure and, six weeks along, waffled about whether to go at all. One day, she would lament how plentiful and convenient things were in the States; the next, she would curse the hypocrisy and racism of the Americans. Often, though not always, Mack figured into her deliberation but in an equally Janus-faced way. He was generous and kind; he drank too much and sabotaged their future. Thus far, he hadn't protested her and Martin's delay.

Elodie encouraged Cecile to take her time, to not rush the decision, though she tried to remain silent about the marriage. She felt it wasn't her place to voice an opinion—and also, she feared she had served as a poor model.

The weekend shifts at the stationery store in exchange for taking off Tuesdays and Wednesdays was a fair trade, as far as Elodie was concerned. She wanted to make up for time lost with her grandson. It felt particularly urgent. She knew her daughter well enough to know that nothing was ever fixed, that Cecile might wake up one morning and book their return and it would all come to an abrupt end. With a pram borrowed from a neighbor, she strolled Martin through parks and to the sites of monuments. Once, she used the extra sous from freelance graphological work to take him to the zoo in the Bois de Vincennes, just outside the city, and another time, on a tour of the Seine on a Bateau Mouches. He'd been so thrilled that, at the boat ride's finish, she bought two more tickets, and they did it again.

For this Wednesday, Elodie decided on the Galleries Lafayette. The store's gilt arches and ornate columns made it like a fairy-tale castle. Martin pouted when she told him their destination, but once there, he went from plate-glass window to plate-glass window, his disappointment becoming fits of laughter. There were electric trains and teddy bears bigger than him and an entire village constructed of Meccano. Inside, he became transfixed by a long table filled with an army of toy soldiers—Napoleon's various battalions, arrayed in rows, each individual piece meticulously crafted and painted in such detail that Elodie wondered that they could truly be for children. When it was time to leave, he protested—"*Déjà?*"—in a surprisingly serviceable French, especially for a three-year-old whose vocabulary was limited in his native English.

"We need to get home and prepare dinner," she replied in French, making gestures to help him understand what he might not fully in any language.

He pointed to the toy soldiers. "*Acheter?*"

There was no spare money for whimsy like this, but she'd anticipated the request and, before heading out, pilfered a few notes from the emergency funds she kept in a jar in the kitchen. "Your birthday," she said in her difficult English, gesturing behind her, "*déjà passé*. Because I miss, a gift for you now, then."

He beamed but had difficulty choosing, settling finally on a tin soldier with white pants, a navy greatcoat with a white baldric, and a blue shako with a red plume; it aimed a musket. They queued up to pay behind a man who had the austere bearing of a school precept. Martin played as though his soldier was firing the musket, and the way the man gazed from him to Elodie first angered, then frightened her. Martin was easily confused for North African, and with the rising tensions in Algeria, in all the colonies, who knew what someone might say or do to insult or embarrass them?

"The grenadiers are the point of the spear," the man said, leaning over Martin.

Martin stilled, startled, clearly not understanding. Elodie didn't know what the man meant either.

"The grenadiers." He pointed to Martin's toy. "They were so fierce that Napoleon ordered them to wear moustaches so that they would stand out on the field." He smiled. "You will wear a moustache too one day, *jeune homme.*"

Martin smiled, too, then buried his face in Elodie's skirt.

The kitchen was the tiniest room in Elodie's flat, second only to the bathroom, which was, in reality, just a WC with a handheld showerhead attached to a miniscule sink. The apartment, ideal for her alone, was cramped with three people, even though one was just a toddler. She'd moved her rolltop desk out of the space she'd used as an office and crammed it into her bedroom. Cecile and Martin shared a cot where the desk had been.

Cecile sat at the square kitchen table that could only fit two, bouncing Martin on her lap, who remained fixated on his tin soldier. Elodie washed and peeled vegetables at the sink, an arm's reach away.

"So, you'll take the position?" Elodie asked.

The company where Cecile had interviewed the day before urgently needed a bilingual secretary and had followed up with an offer.

Cecile shrugged. "I don't know. I have to figure out what's best for him."

"Of course, you do." Finishing the carrots, Elodie started on the potatoes. "It's why I ask."

Cecile said, "How did you know the right course when I was growing up?"

"I didn't. I did the best I could under the circumstance."

"Here it's just you and me, Maman. There are no men in his life. A boy needs that."

Elodie exhaled frustration in a rush of breath. "Please, Cecile. You act as though there are none in France."

"You, of all people, should tell me this?"

"I've known good men. I just didn't marry one."

Cecile broke the heel off the baguette on the tabletop. "He needs a black man to help him become one, one day." Rather than eat it, though, she crushed pieces of crust into crumbs. "And he needs a future," she continued. "Here is only the past."

Recalling the man from the Galleries Lafayette, Elodie dropped the knife into the sink—more violently than she'd intended. "France is a different place now, Cecile."

Martin started, turning abruptly toward her, tears pooling and mouth bunching to cry.

"It's as good and as bad a place as any," Elodie said, stroking the boy's cheek, calming him.

But she didn't feel calm, not at all. She found herself feeling increasingly frustrated.

She removed her apron and went to her room, shut the door, and stretched out on the bed. Here around her was her whole life—books and photographs and letters. She wanted to imagine that her life was the entire apartment: her daughter and her grandson and the joy that she'd felt since their return. But Cecile wouldn't grant even that paltry comfort.

No, only love small. Love only the things you can hold. Here in this tiny room were the novels she read and reread, and the family portraits in their frames, and the stacks of letters, some analyzed, others remaining to be done.

When Cecile was in America, graphology had helped fill the silences between letters from her daughter. Though still a freelancer, the work remained consuming. Upon finishing training, Elodie's professor had referred her to a law office near Gare Saint-Lazare that regularly contracted out projects. She'd been sure that the firm had agreed to add her to their roster purely out of pity for the elderly divorcé. But now she received regular assignments from five different firms, some weeks more than she could analyze in a timely fashion, and she stayed up until two or three in the morning to finish. Had her ex-husband paid what the judge ordered him to, Elodie would have gladly left the *papeterie;* the graphology, though, was more than just work. It filled the silences.

She refused to ask for the monthly alimony—categorically. When she left Le Vésinet, she'd taken nothing more than the clothes she could carry in two suitcases and her photographs. She'd given up the silver service and the trifles and the rest. After all those years, she needed to be fully and finally quit of the man.

There was a light tapping at the door: Martin. He entered and came to the bedside and placed a hand on her arm.

"Mimi?"

She didn't know from where he'd come up with this pet name. "*Oui, mon amour?*"

"You mad at Mommy?"

"*Mais, non.* I only want what is best for her."

She knew he didn't understand—wouldn't, even if she could express her feelings in English. So, she pulled him up and hugged him close. "I love your mommy," she said. "And Martin, too!"

He burst into laughter.

CHAPTER THIRTY-FIVE

Cecile contacted Seb a few days later. She recognized the time to finally be right. If Martin was to know him someday—and she thought it important that Martin did know him and his family, his heritage, maybe even someday soon—then she needed to take the first steps.

Standing beneath a sharp sun at Place de l'Odéon almost fifteen minutes after the agreed-upon time, she scanned up one sidewalk and down the other, seeking out Seb's dark face on the bright swath of noontime pedestrian traffic. People everywhere, none him. He had no reason to meet her, really, and she wondered if he hadn't changed his mind. Her voice on the telephone, the request for a rendezvous—it must have startled, probably even perplexed him. Maybe his gut had tipped him off that she had a secret to reveal, and now would he even come?

The air was warm, so she removed her cardigan and draped it over an arm. Then there was Seb, striding through the crowd, smiling as he caught her attention. Elegance, therein lay his charm: the distinguished manner with which he wore his ease.

"I'm so sorry I'm late."

And the voice: full, rolling, the sea.

But she understood this in her head, dispassionately, as merely observation. Her lack of emotion was unexpected. Of all the things she thought she'd feel upon seeing him—grief and joy and probably also lingering anger—she noted only the absence of feeling, an absence so profound it became a presence.

"Ah, Cecile." He leaned over, kissed one cheek then the other, then stepped back and took her in. "It's so good to see you. I had no idea you'd returned from the States."

She didn't know he knew that she'd moved there.

"Two months now." She glanced at her wristwatch. "Unfortunately, I only have until two." A self-imposed time limit. "Do you know someplace nearby?"

"Of course, of course. Forgive me." He led her onto a side street. "You look well. Happy."

"As do you."

"I can't complain, though too often I do."

He didn't allow a silence, chattering incessantly—so unlike him. He described his final year at Beaux-Arts ("I've done better in design than I'd imagined possible"); he remarked upon the current political climate in France ("As conservative as ever, yet easier to live in, inexplicably"). He did not mention his father; he did not mention his sister.

"I'll confess," he said, "I wasn't expecting to hear from you. I was pleased, of course, but surprised."

She strode forward without responding.

They arrived at a cozy bistro in Rue Saint-André des Arts. The host seated them at a table in the window. The restaurant buzzed. All around were students and professors, businessmen and tourists. Seb's was the only dark face. She noticed that he didn't seem to notice, or maybe to care.

"It sounds like Beaux-Arts is everything you'd hoped for," Cecile said. Then she followed with the question she'd been dying to ask, though she feared he might think it none of her business. "So, you've changed your name?"

When she'd found him in the Beaux-Arts directory, he was listed as Sebastien Gbéhanzin.

"Well . . ." His smile dropped, his face a blank. "I reclaimed the one that was rightly my father's. It's a fine name, so I figured why not use it."

She knew he thought more of the name than merely this.

"Ah, Monsieur, how good to see you again." The waiter, a hollow-cheeked man with a bulbous nose, shook Seb's hand. "Mademoiselle," he said, nodding toward Cecile. "Might I make a recommendation, a dish to match your spicy sense of haute couture?" He pointed to Seb's drab gray jacket, shaking his head disapprovingly. "A splatter of the mustard sauce from the *plat du jour* would do wonders for that dull, *dull* tie."

Seb's laughter boomed over the bustling of the dining room.

Cecile ordered oysters. Seb took the waiter's suggestion, the daily special, *Lapin à la Moutarde*.

After the waiter left, she said, "You come here often."

"It's so near school, you see. François, the garçon, he's always overly familiar." He seemed embarrassed and changed the subject. "And how is Elodie?"

"*Maman*'s doing well."

She didn't mention the divorce. Perhaps he knew.

"And I heard you have a child?" He did not look away.

She held his eyes.

No, he didn't suspect about Martin. "A boy, yes," she said. "He's healthy—and so smart."

The waiter François brought their dishes, but Seb didn't begin eating. Instead, he toyed with the rabbit thigh and looked so much like Martin—his round head and the awkward tilt to his mouth, the focused attention on his fork—that she nearly admonished him as she would her son, to stop playing with the food and eat it. This made her smile.

"I was married too, maybe you heard," he said, not looking up. "A Belgian girl. We started Beaux-Arts together."

The brusqueness of the revelation jarred Cecile. "*Was* married?"

It wasn't appropriate to pry. Or maybe it was just not particularly sensitive to his obvious pain. She did anyway.

"How long have you been divorced?"

He didn't look up. "She died during pregnancy."

Cecile reflexively reached for his hand, as though this were what he needed or was asking for, and when he flinched at her touch, she realized that it was not. And there, finally, was the feeling that until then had eluded her. With the revelation of his marriage to a *Yovo* had come a rising mix of anger and envy. Now it shifted quickly, became remorse. Sorrow. Not for opportunities wasted but for the resolute inevitability of things. The way winter white stretched over the rolling Kansas fields, the great space of it.

Still, she didn't release his hand.

"It was quite sudden," he said. "To do with blood pressure, something as banal as that."

The restaurant seemed silent with his silence.

"Did you bury her here or in Belgium?"

"In Abomey," he said, and Cecile let go his hand. "My father learned he had a daughter-in-law the day he learned of her death. He insisted we bury them, the child and her, with the ancestors."

Cecile didn't know what to do with this information.

They ate largely without speaking. Now and then, a trivial question: Have you had a chance to visit New York? And Jacqueline, has she chosen a specialty? The waiter cleared the table.

"Maybe it was tactless of me to tell you," Seb said after the waiter had gone, "about my wife. Maybe I shouldn't have."

She didn't reply.

"What tempts you for dessert?" he asked, artificially chipper.

She nodded "no."

"Coffee, then?"

"Nothing, thank you." She glanced at her wristwatch. "I have to go soon."

"Yes, it's gotten quite late." He signaled the waiter.

After paying, he followed Cecile outside. Each one walked deliberately slowly.

He stopped, turned her toward him, and held her by the arms. The gesture was aggressive and intimate at once.

"You were quite special to me," he said. "We were a fine couple."

This sounded like an apology, and Cecile didn't want an apology, not like this: heartfelt but vague, for having hurt her somehow, or for disappointing, without acknowledging the precise words and very real acts that had brought them here, to this place.

History, she thought, staring back at him. A voice whose memory is all that is cherished but whose timber, heard anew, is unfamiliar. She'd once imagined a life with him; it had been the only life she could imagine for herself. Yet she hardly recognized in the person standing before her the man she'd thought she would always truly know.

Maybe sometimes there was too much history. Maybe memory was best left to that quiet place one went to Saturday mornings, sitting beside the window, with Martin napping or entertaining himself in the other room and her mother at the *papeterie*. A steaming cup of tea and a shawl were all that existed of the world. Maybe only then, as nine passed unnoticed to noon, was time ever really true.

She hooked her arm through Seb's and turned and headed toward the Metro. Soon, he'd matched his stride to hers, inadvertently or intentionally, she did not know. She glanced over and, in that moment, glimpsed the Seb that she thought she remembered from before: strong yet fragile, his face quiet but so much life behind it, thrilling like a stage curtain about to open, and as distant.

She would tell Martin about his biological father when he was older, and if he wanted to know Seb, she would encourage it. (And, of course, she would continue to try to protect Mack as best she could from ever finding out.) As for her, she couldn't know for sure that she hadn't returned to France with, deep inside, some vague hope that she and Seb might find each other again; yet, walking arm in arm, as he conveniently reimagined a past other than what it had actually been, she recognized this as a good way to quit him.

They kissed cheeks at the entrance to the Metro. "We have to do this again," he said. "Soon."

She smiled for a reply.

He didn't walk away, so she did, descending the steps into the fluorescent-lit dark of the subway station.

* * *

Elodie heard a rustling beyond her bedroom door and saw light through the crack beneath it. Midnight storm: heavy air and pattering rain against the window. The clock read three fifteen.

She'd only been asleep a few hours, her head yet foggy, but she put on a robe and padded into the hallway. She found Cecile in the kitchen, standing in a slip and brassiere at the mirror above the sink, running her fingertips over her eyebrows, her cheekbones, her nose. Cecile glanced over, then back at her reflection.

"Do you find me pretty?"

A flash of lightning through the slats of the closed window shutters and, a moment later, the crack of thunder.

"Pardon?"

"Am I pretty?" Cecile said.

An insuppressible seizing set off deep in Elodie's stomach, and she put her hand to her mouth to hold it in.

Cecile looked at her. "What?"

It wouldn't stop. Elodie pulled her robe more tightly closed, but her attempts to keep in control only caused her belly to quiver.

"What?" Cecile insisted.

Elodie pushed past and plopped down on the stool, holding her mouth with one hand, her middle with the other, but the spasms wouldn't calm. She spat out a sound, something like "Ah-ha-ha," and sensed it wouldn't stop if she did not cut it off. So, she held her mouth more tightly, pushed harder against her belly.

"Tell me, M'man," Cecile said, and she began giggling, too.

"Ah . . . Ha-ha. Ha . . ."

"Please." Cecile guffawed now. "Please." She slid down the wall and sat on the floor.

Elodie writhed, the table shaking, the porcelain salt and pepper shakers atop it rattling.

"Ah, ha-ha! Ha. Ha-ha-ha."

Her legs fell open with the effort to control her laughter, and she couldn't pull closed the slit of her robe without removing a hand from either her mouth or her belly, and to release either was to let loose the rest.

Cecile lay balled at her mother's feet, squirming.

"Ha-ha!"

"Ah, ha-ha-ha!"

"Mommy!" Martin stood in the doorway, tears glinting his cheeks. "Mommy, please!"

Both Elodie and Cecile rose on the spot. "Oh, *chéri*," Cecile said, picking him up and bouncing in place. "It's OK, it's OK."

Reaching around, Elodie pulled both into a tight embrace. "It's OK, *mes chéris*."

When she released them, Martin was still. Cecile, too.

Cecile said, "I'll put him to bed," but Elodie stopped her.

She asked, "What happened to the idealistic, willful girl I once knew?"

Cecile perched on the edge of the sink. "She was a public spectacle—impulsive, rash. Life has taught her humility." She buried her face in Martin's hair, while Martin held on around her neck. "Besides, you despised that girl."

The stark brightness of the bulb, or maybe the night air, caused Elodie's eyes to sting. "Look around you," she said. "Why, look at me. The comfort and ease I left behind, and for what? For this—nearly fifty and alone in this hovel?"

Elodie watched her daughter gently bounce her sleeping son.

"I admired that girl," Elodie said. "Every last bit of her."

"To bed," she then said, "*allez, allez*. Tomorrow is already almost here."

Cecile went to her room, and Elodie extinguished the light. She returned to bed, buried herself deep under the blankets. The darkness shifted and swelled, like everything must. Nothing, nothing was static, not even nothingness. Certainly not people.

The woman sharing Elodie's apartment was someone she felt she was only just acquainting herself with. Like learning anew the taste of tart Tatin after the baker's son has taken over for the father. The flavor is still apples and cinnamon, familiar, but somehow all its own.

CHAPTER THIRTY-SIX

13-12-1953   1205 Pershing Drive
                          Fort Carson, Colorado Springs

My petite Maman chérie,

I've been meaning to write for days but have been terribly busy and now I have neglected you. How are you? And how is your "friend" Jean Paquet??? Write and tell me all about your trip to Normandy.

Work is fine, it pays the bills. We are fine. Martin gets taller every day—I can't keep him in clothes that fit—and Lucie is <u>finally</u> sleeping through the night. You wouldn't recognize them. I discussed it with Mack and he agreed: when Martin is a little older, we'll send him to spend a month with you—Martin first, Lucie when she's old enough.

You'll love this: during Mack's visit last month to see the kids, he suggested that we take them to church. I was reluctant but we did, and afterward, I accidentally closed Martin's little hand in the car door! We had to take him to get a plaster cast. He said, "You see! It's a message. It means we shouldn't go back." (And we haven't returned since.)

I'll never get used to the hypocrisy of religion here, all the "God bless, God bless," and then they sneer behind your back. Sometimes I think I'll never get used to the US, period. The stares at my babies and me, having to know where we can and cannot go. But the Supreme Court is arguing a case that gives me hope. There is hope here.

At long last, here is the analysis of your handwriting that you've hounded me about all these years.

Your i-dots and loops have changed. What's wrong? Is Mack sending child support?

Oh, no!
(How adorable!!)

I've meant to ask what you
think of this new "art"
about which there is so much
hullabaloo? Frankly, my
dirty plates, when they've
sat unwashed in the sink
for too long, are quite
artful tableaux by these
standards.

But listen to <u>this</u>: Mack suggested that Martin should
be bar mitzvahed when he's the right age! I told him, "But
Martin has never even been to synagogue!" A Jew is a Jew;
there's no need for public validation. I have worn my Star
every day since the Germans were no longer around to
impose it on us. But it's not this that makes me a Jew. I am
one because I am. And so are Martin and Lucie. They are
all of it and none. Still, it was kind of Mack. He said he just
wants to make sure that Martin knows his roots. (Ha!)

I must sign off for now. Know that you are always in my
heart.

Cecile

(My thoughts attached seperately)

31 December 1953

GRAPHOLOGICAL ANALYSIS: What, my dear dear daughter, can I tell you that you do not already know?

THE END

Acknowledgments

Eric Simonoff has guided me through the opaque world of publishing with insight and great patience. I am hugely grateful and always will be. And Morgan Entrekin and his spectacular team at Grove Atlantic (Deb Seager, John Mark Boling, Zoe Harris, Mike Richards, and the rest) continue championing my work, and I feel incredibly lucky to have their support.

This book began as a very short story called "And in the Ruined Houses," which appeared twenty-one years ago in the literary journal, *Shenandoah*. I set upon developing it into a novel soon thereafter. Beth Ann Fennelly read the first "final" draft in 2007, and so many other patient readers have offered invaluable feedback over the years since. My heartfelt thanks to you all. I'd like to shout out a few who really helped me get over the hump: Audrey Petty, Beth Clary, Sylvie Moreau, Dina Guidubaldi, Steve Davenport, Luc Bouchard, Beth Marzoni, Lorna Owen, Rayhané Sanders—and for her great discernment and unflappable confidence, even when my own was flagging, Monica Berlin.

A number of books and articles introduced me to Dahomey's complex culture and fraught history, and my stepmother and sister, Claire and Adéwolé Faladé, helped me understand what I was reading. Thank you.

The New York Public Library's Dorothy and Lewis B. Cullman Center for Scholars and Writers was instrumental in my finishing the manuscript. Thanks to Martha Hodes and all my fellow fellows for the feedback and stimulating conversation on the red couches, and to Mary Ellen von der Heyden for the support that got me there.

Bob Markley and the English Department of the University of Illinois provided support and time to write, as did the university's Center for Advanced Study, the Dobie-Paisano Fellowship Program, the J. William Fulbright Foreign Scholarship Program, the MacDowell Colony, the Yaddo Foundation, the Blue Mountain Center, the Vermont Studio Center, and the Virginia Center for the Creative Arts. Many thanks to you all.